Amanda's BOAT

DON McGARVA

ISBN 979-8-35093-317-8

eBook ISBN 979-8-35093-318-5

CHAPTER 1

....

"What are you reading, Grandpa?"

Amanda skipped into my study as she always did, eyes wide and smiling, her face the very essence of childish curiosity.

I looked up. "A wonderful book about how to build a wood boat," I told her.

"What's it about?"

"It's about how to build a wood boat," I teased.

"No, seriously, what's the title?"

"*How to Build a Wood Boat*," I answered, grinning.

"Seriously?"

"Seriously."

She pondered for a moment. "You mean, if you read that book, you could actually build a boat?"

"Well, it's not quite as simple as that," I replied, "but someone who had experience working with wood, who had the proper tools, *and* the material, *and* some help, *and* a place to build it could, yes, theoretically, I suppose, build a boat."

"Sounds simple enough."

I chuckled. Everything sounded simple to her. "No," I told her, "there is nothing simple about it. A boat is one of the most difficult things to build out of wood."

"Why?" she asked.

Here we go, I thought. My morning reverie was over. I'd had this book and several others like it for over twenty years. Having spent my entire life building things and "messing about in boats," as a very wise man once said, I had read them all many times over. Boatbuilding represents the ultimate challenge for even the most accomplished woodworker, and I enjoyed delving into all the myriad processes, if only vicariously. It was a lovely pastime, to be sure, but strictly a fantasy. Wood boats are impractical, expensive, difficult to keep up, and virtually obsolete. They require arcane and fast-disappearing skills to build and maintain. They require unique materials that are becoming increasingly more difficult to acquire, not to mention the enormous amounts of time, space, and money needed compared to the more modern types of construction. They make absolutely no sense at all. They are also some of the most beautiful objects created by man. A well-built and cared-for wood boat can take your breath away. Its lines, its finish, its warmth draw the attention and admiration of even a non-boater. And no real yachtsman can resist the outright gorgeousness of a well-aged wood boat. I have owned several fiberglass boats and I enjoyed them all. I understand the advantages. But put a glass boat and a wood boat side by side in any marina and people will gravitate to the woodie like a moth to a flame. It possesses character and personality that are difficult to quantify, but which are somehow lacking in its glass counterpart. It's like comparing the *Mona Lisa* to a faddish movie celebrity.

All these thoughts and more were filtering through my mind and out through my mouth to Amanda as she sat at my knee looking up at me with rapt attention. It's unusual to keep her attention for any length of time, so I was enjoying myself thoroughly.

"Why are wood boats impractical?" she asked.

"Times change, honey," I said. "A cheaper material comes along, like fiberglass. More efficient processes develop whereby more boats can be produced for less money. Then more people can enjoy a great pastime for less money. It's progress. Years ago, one had to be wealthy to own a boat. They cost a lot to build and they cost a lot to maintain. Today, many more people can buy a fiberglass boat and enjoy it whenever they want without the expensive upkeep of a wood boat."

"Makes sense," she said, looking thoughtful. "But then why would anyone want a wood boat?"

"That *can* be hard to understand," I agreed. "But some people just want finer things. That's why people restore an old car instead of buying a new one that's better, safer, more comfortable, and probably cheaper in the long run. It's why people restore old houses, too. Some things just have greater appeal over a long time. They transcend being a mere object and develop a soul."

"Wow," she breathed, her expression becoming even more thoughtful.

I've got her now, I thought, feeling pretty smug. "Here, look at this," I said and showed her a picture of a beautiful old Alden ketch. The white sails were billowing and she was moving well along. Her topsides were a deep emerald green, and the varnished mahogany trim gleamed in the sunlight.

"Wow!" she said again, louder this time, and her eyes widened. "It's *byoo*-tiful!"

That was her ultimate accolade. "See," I chuckled, "I told you."

Then, after a pause, "Well, why don't you build one?"

This time I laughed out loud. "It's not so easy. As I said, you need special tools, special wood, a big place to build it, lots of time, help . . . it's just too much. Besides, I'm too old." At fifty-five, I didn't really believe that, but in practical terms it was true. I also knew, to an eleven-year-old, that sounded ancient. A good closing argument.

"Hah!" she yelped, "you can build *anything*, Grandpa. You built this house and all this furniture. And what about the dollhouse you made for me? It's *byoo*-tiful!"

Oops. I often underestimated her powers of perception. It was true I had spent virtually my whole life building and repairing things because I thoroughly enjoyed it. I had fallen in love with woodworking at a young age and knew even then it was something I would enjoy the rest of my life. I never considered *not* doing it. But building a boat, while a longtime itch, would remain unscratched. It was enough to just read about and experience vicariously the joy of all the different processes involved—planning and laying it out, cutting and shaping the wood, steam-bending the frames, fitting the joints, all things which are not that difficult when taken individually but, when added together, can overwhelm even the most enthusiastic amateur boat nut. That's why so many backyards have unfinished boats in them.

I explained all this while she sat there staring, a far-away look in her eyes.

"I could help you," she said.

I looked at her and smiled. "That sounds like a lot of fun, sweetie, but it's just not possible. Too much work, too many obstacles, not enough time . . ."

"But you said it wasn't hard."

I sighed again. It wasn't going as I had hoped. "That's not exactly what I said. I *said* each little step is not too difficult, but taken together, the whole project is fraught with problems and *very* difficult." *There,* I thought, *that should do it.*

"How long would it take?" she asked.

"Too long."

"*How* long?" she insisted.

I groaned. "I don't know, a year or so if we had everything at hand, which, of course, we don't." This was met by silence and a thoughtful expression. *Finally!* I thought. *A year is an eternity to an eleven-year-old. Back to my book.*

Jan came in just then to tell us lunch was ready. "What are you two up to?" she asked.

"We're going to build a boat!" piped Amanda excitedly.

"**What?!**" cried Jan.

"Oh, no," I moaned.

"Yeah. Grandpa says it's not too hard and it will only take a year, so we're going to build a boat."

Jan stared at me as if I had suddenly grown another head. I was off-balance and stammering, groping for words of explanation that weren't coming. "No, that's not exactly what I said . . ." I mumbled desperately.

"Well, what exactly *did* you say?" Jan persisted, arching an eyebrow.

"Didn't you say that the different jobs weren't that hard?" asked Amanda.

"Well, yeah, sort of, but . . ."

"And didn't you say it would only take a year to build?"

"Uh, yes, but . . ." I was squirming like a schoolboy.

"See, Jannie?" cried Amanda triumphantly. "We're going to build a boat. Oh boy!"

Jan was looking at me as she would a puppy who had wolfed down too much food and gotten sick. There was genuine pity, sure, but it was obvious she considered it my own fault. And it was just as obvious that she was enjoying my discomfort immensely. I was floundering; Amanda was gazing at me with pleading eyes; Jan was tapping her foot impatiently. I needed to get past this moment, buy some time to figure a way out of this mess, and retain a shred of self-respect. They became more expectant, eagerly awaiting the words of wisdom from Grandpa that would explain everything.

"So, what's for lunch?"

CHAPTER 2

All through lunch, Amanda talked about nothing but boats. I was pleased by this, of course. This was her second summer with us, and she had fallen in love with boats and sailing the previous summer. She had made friends with a little girl down the road named Sophie, whose family was also summering in Maine and who owned a small daysailer. She began spending more and more time on the water with Sophie and her dog, Chloe. They would pack their lunches and spend entire days exploring up and down the river until it was almost dark. The three of them became inseparable.

The girls were like all children who really enjoy something; they absorbed everything related to it quickly and thoroughly. We made sure the girls understood safe boating practices and insisted they go nowhere without the proper equipment. Safety became so second nature to them that we would often see them walking around town wearing their little life jackets. They began hanging around the boatyard and befriended the men who worked there, bringing them cookies and pestering them with endless questions. The men, of course, loved it and looked forward to their visits, soon dubbing them the three Moosaquiteers.

The yard itself was a beautifully quaint place, a throwback, a real old-fashioned working yard, not often found outside New England. Having been in continual service for well over a hundred years, it attracted people from all over the eastern seaboard. Most of the boats being worked on were fiberglass, to be sure, but there was the occasional wood boat, too, perhaps built right there decades earlier. Many of the men who worked there were third or fourth generation, having grown up in the yard and whose fathers and grandfathers had done the same. It was a pleasant yard in the pleasant town of Moosaquit, Maine.

I dropped by often, as I might return again and again to a museum. It was a step back in time to see the yard in full swing—boats being hauled and launched, the machine shop bustling with mechanical repairs, hearing the good-natured banter of the men as they worked, and smelling the wonderful aromas that only a boatyard can offer. When, off in a corner, the occasional wood boat would come in for repairs, the most senior of the workers would be gathered there, putting into play the accumulated skill and knowledge of generations of their forebears dating back to the time of Noah.

Also in that little corner, especially if a new wood boat was being built, would be men older still, the retired craftsmen of decades past—men who could no longer do the work but who could still impart their priceless experience to the younger men, who were merely in their fifties and sixties. These men were all slim, tanned, creased with age, and bent from the weight of their years. But their smiles were genuine and their eyes twinkled with the good humor and the sure knowledge acquired over a lifetime of doing well what they loved to do.

As the summers passed, I spent more and more time there. I became at first friendly, then comfortable, with these men, and they with me. I developed toward them a keen admiration, kinship, and respect. We talked for hours of a time long past, when a man's work was a source of pride as well as living, when skill helped define a man's character. It was a much simpler time, far less complicated and with fewer choices. To a romantic such as I, it was as close as I could ever hope to get to experiencing an earlier age.

Such thoughts were swirling gently through my mind when I was jarred back to reality.

"When can we start?"

"Hmm?" I mumbled, snatched rudely from my reverie. "Start what?"

It was Amanda. "The *boat*," she whined, clearly perplexed that I could have forgotten so quickly.

"Oh, yeah, the boat. Well, you see, Amanda, we, uh, we can't build a boat, honey. We don't have the space, or the tools, or the help, or—"

"But *I* can help!" she cried.

Jan was smiling, enjoying the show.

"Amanda," I began again, "we would need *lots* of help, like building a house. We would need special tools, special wood. We have no plans. We would need a *really* big place to build it. And have you forgotten that we all have to go back to Florida in the fall? Please understand, honey, it's just not possible. Okay?"

Amanda looked down, her face a mask of disappointment. I felt like a toad, but it was far better to be firm and end this fantasy now rather than prolong it. I finished my lunch and excused myself from the table. In a few days of sailing and playing, she would forget all about this silliness and move on to something else. It reminded me of when she wanted a puppy. She really wanted it, I know (what kid *doesn't* want a puppy?), but after a couple of weeks of playing, we never heard any more about it. I put the whole thing out of my head and went golfing.

When I got home, Jan was working in the kitchen. "Hi, honey," I called. "Anything going on?"

"Yes," she replied, a bit testily. "Amanda has been pestering me all afternoon about building a boat. She keeps asking me the same inane questions over and over, talks about nothing else. I don't know why you had to fill her head with all that nonsense."

"But I didn't," I pleaded. "We were just browsing through my boat books, when all of a sudden she sprung this on me."

"Sure," Jan said skeptically.

"It's true."

"Well, all I know is she's going to be mighty disappointed when she finally realizes you can't do it. She kept saying, 'I know Grandpa can do it; he can do *anything*.' I wouldn't want to be you." The corners of her mouth twitched upward involuntarily.

"Thanks," I grunted. "How do I get myself into these messes, anyway?"

"It's simple; you can't say 'no' to her."

"What do you mean by that?"

"I mean, you can't say 'no' to her—you never could. You get her all revved up with your cockamamie schemes, then try to smooth things over. It serves you right."

She was enjoying this *way* too much. Time to take control. "Ok," I said firmly, "I'll just have to sit her down and explain the situation in plain language. She can't go on like this and she'll have to accept it."

Jan looked dubious. "So, you're going to get tough, huh?"

"Exactly," I said, accepting the challenge. "You don't think I will?"

"I don't think you *can*. Amanda has you wrapped right around her little pinkie. It's pathetic, really."

"Pathetic, huh?"

"With a capital 'P'." She was on top of her game, grinning and taunting me.

But enough is enough. "As soon as she gets home," I vowed, "I'll have a talk with her. This has gone too far already."

"Really?" Jan said, her voice oozing sarcasm. "I can't wait."

I was getting peeved. "You just watch."

"Well, you're about to get your chance; here she comes now." Jan turned toward the kitchen. "Now, don't be too hard on her!" she teased, and left just as Amanda burst into the room.

"Amanda . . ." I began forcefully.

"It's all set, Grandpa!" she said, her face beaming.

"Amanda, we need to talk . . . uh, what's all set?"

"I talked to Sophie's parents. They know *everybody* and they told me there's a boatbuilder up Shore Road about a mile or so. His name is Angus McTigue. They said he's the *best*, Grandpa. He has everything to build a boat with and he builds them right there—only a mile away! And then I called Mommy and Daddy, and they said I could stay here the *whole winter*. I can transfer to the school up here and help you after school. They thought it was a *great* idea; at least Daddy did. They're very excited about it and said to be sure and thank you. Daddy wants you to call him."

All this poured out in one breath, it seemed. Like water through a bursting dam, it gushed forth and was over before I even had a chance to brace myself. The weight of those ten or fifteen seconds settled on me like a shroud as I sat there frozen, my jaw hanging open.

"I'm going to go tell Sophie you said yes," she cried, then tore out the door before I could recover. I hadn't said ten words.

Jan came back into the room, giggling and shaking her head.

"What just happened?" I mumbled.

She sat on the arm of my chair. "That was great, honey, I'm so proud of you." She bent down and kissed me. "I'm glad you weren't too hard on the poor thing." I was still trying to process the previous two minutes when she got up. "Come on, tiger," she said, "dinner's ready. You're going to need all your strength if you're going to build a boat."

All through dinner, Amanda went on and on about the boat. The more she talked, the more excited she got. I felt miserable but said nothing. She had told her parents, she had told her friends in Moosaquit, and she had called her friends back in Florida to tell them she was going to spend the entire year in Maine and build a boat. She was an instant hero. But as her spirits soared, mine plummeted. She was on top of the world, and I had to be the one to bring her down. *This is going to be tough*, I thought. I decided to wait until the next day before telling her. She was so happy I couldn't bear the thought of hurting her. Besides, I had no idea *how* to tell her. I needed some time to figure a way out of this quagmire.

After dinner, Amanda helped Jan clean up the kitchen without being told to and then went upstairs and straightened up her room. Then she came down to my study, walked over to my chair, and threw her arms around me and kissed me. "Thanks, Grandpa," she said.

Jan observed all this from the kitchen. She shook her head pityingly and mouthed the word "pathetic," a huge smile on her face.

Later, as Jan and I were getting ready for bed that night, I was deeply perplexed. I loved Amanda, of course, and I loathed the idea of hurting her in any way. Besides that, I was Superman in her eyes now. But this was insane. The web was getting more tangled by the minute. If I say no, she'll be crushed. But I can't say yes because it's impossible. And the longer we went on with this lunacy, the more difficult and hurtful it would be for everyone. I was in a barrel, all right.

I was desperate. "Honey," I said to Jan, "I need a little help."

"No," she corrected, "you need a *lot* of help."

Sometimes I hated her. "Very funny," I said, "but this is serious." I reiterated all the problems and snares that had so ruined my day, how every solution led to Amanda's being greatly disappointed, and my losing face with her—two very unpalatable outcomes for me. After ticking off all my reasons and rationales and fears, Jan simply said, "I have a better idea."

"You *do*?!" I blurted. *Great, a way out of this mess!* "That's terrific, honey, what is it?"

She shrugged. "Build a boat."

"**What!?**" I yelped. "You, too? Am I the only sane person left in this house?"

"Oh, shush," she said, as if brushing off a four-year-old. "You've been badgering me about building a boat for twenty years. This could be your only chance and I know you really want to do it, so why not? If you can get that guy to help you, it seems perfect. He's supposed to be good, he's close by, you'll be doing something most men can only dream of, and best of all, you'll be Amanda's hero." She ran through these points simply and logically. The last was a little jab, of course, but it was all true, nonetheless. It made so much sense, in fact, that I wondered why I hadn't thought of it myself.

"You know," I ventured, "it might not be such a bad idea, after all. I've heard the guys down at the boatyard talk about some guy named McTigue, but I didn't pay much attention because it seemed like they were talking in the past tense. I wonder if it's the same guy." I paused. "I do remember one thing, though," I continued, "if it *is* him, they all said he was the best. He seemed legendary, even among the old hands."

"Sounds like the perfect opportunity," Jan said.

"Yeah, it sure does," I agreed, lowering my guard. But I came to my senses abruptly and began enumerating all the problems, which were considerable. "We haven't wintered in Maine for over twenty years. You *hate* winter; that's why we started going south in the first place. Remember how cold it gets, how short the days are, the snow, the ice, how long it lasts? And what about our other plans—our vacations, our house in Florida? And we'll have Amanda for an entire year. Sure, we love her, but that's a lot of responsibility for people our age. Her schoolwork needs to be monitored; she'll need all new clothes for the winter . . ." I trailed off, temporarily out of steam.

Jan was smiling at me sweetly. She knew I wanted to do this, very badly, and that I was merely making up excuses for her to have an out if she wanted it. "I remember," she said, "but no matter how bad the weather is, it's only one winter. You'll be so excited about building a boat, you won't even notice. And our vacations can wait a year. Big deal. As far as Amanda is concerned, any extra responsibility will be more than offset by having her with us for the whole year, her first winter up north. She's getting older, you know. Pretty soon she may not want to spend time with us old folks. And what little girl doesn't want to buy new clothes?" She paused. "I think I know how much this means to you. And it's something Amanda will treasure for the rest of her life. I really don't see any downside."

I absorbed all this gratefully. She was right; it was a rare opportunity and one that almost certainly would never again come my way. I knew she could sense my eagerness. "It *would* be great," I agreed. "But are you certain? Once we start, there'll be no turning back."

"Absolutely," she said without a moment's hesitation.

Problem solved! I gave her her a big hug and a kiss. "Thanks, honey. I'll go see him first thing in the morning."

CHAPTER 3

·····································

I was up early the next morning, eager to meet this fellow, McTigue. After recalling the snippets of conversation from the boatyard, I had come up with many more questions and no answers. As I remembered, the men had shown a reverence bordering on awe when speaking of him and his skills. He seemed to be on a different plane from everyone else. But if that were the case, I thought, why hadn't I ever heard of him? Why didn't he work at the yard? Maybe he was just too old. Maybe it was a different McTigue. Whatever the answers, my curiosity was whetted to a keen edge as I left the house to begin my quest.

It had rained during the night and the air was still heavy with moisture as I meandered the mile or so up Shore Road that separated our summer home from the McTigue homestead. When I arrived, I had to peek around some hedges to make sure I had the right place. I had driven by many times, but the property was so well hidden from the road that it couldn't be seen closer on. As I skirted the hedge, I came upon a curving pathway that led me onto the property. Once inside, I could see that it was a huge area, with only a small corner of the property fronting Shore Road. I was feeling intrusive, but my reservations were overcome by the simple beauty of the place. The main house was a large three-story Colonial in perfect proportion. Its clapboards were well-maintained and gleamed with a shiny coat of white paint. Dark green trim and a real slate roof were a perfect complement. Down a lane was another building that needed paint and cleaning up but, all in all, seemed sound and utilitarian. I presumed that was the boathouse, as there was a railway leading from the building down to the river. In the back were many acres of assorted gardens, several outbuildings, livestock, and woods. And it all nestled right up against the Moosaquit River. Norman Rockwell couldn't have painted a more perfect New England homestead. As I approached, I couldn't help smiling—it was just that nice.

Ducks, chickens, and geese scattered as I walked up the lane, the geese giving me a threatening hiss as they ran away. I teased them as they scurried off and was chuckling at their impotence when from somewhere in the back came a deep "**WOOF!**" that stopped me in my tracks. In a heartbeat an enormous black dog bounded around the corner and aimed right at me, covering the distance between us with huge strides. I had only enough time to throw my arms up defensively in front of me before I was stunned by the force of his body slamming me to the ground. In a split second I was trapped under the weight of the huge animal, making escape impossible. I was terrified, thrashing about and yelling for help, when I suddenly realized that I wasn't being mauled at all. The dog, instead of attacking me, had me pinned by the shoulders with his paws and was slurping my face like it was an ice-cream cone. The more I struggled, the more he licked and wrestled. He was clearly enjoying himself. And once it dawned on me that I wasn't going to be eaten alive, I began having fun too, wrestling back. We were thus rolling around in the dirt and the mud when a man came out the door, took one look, and said, "DUNCAN, NO—SIT!"

The dog obeyed immediately, but with obvious regret, and sat down beside me, still wagging his tail furiously.

"You okay?" he asked.

"Sure, I'm fine," I said, feeling sheepish. I stood up and brushed myself off as well as I could.

"That wasn't very smart," he said, "coming in here like that, unannounced."

I had to admit he was right about that and apologized profusely.

The man appeared to be in his eighties, a little over six feet tall, with a lanky build and longish arms with large, strong-looking hands. He had a full head of almost pure white hair that looked impossible to tame with comb or brush. He was ruggedly handsome, but had a dour, sad expression which my intrusion had done nothing to assuage.

Feeling extremely awkward, I introduced myself. "My name is Jim Cairns," I said, extending my hand.

He merely nodded.

"Are you Angus McTigue?" I asked.

"Yes," he replied. "What do you want?"

His manner and the situation put me a little off-balance. "I came to ask for help," I said.

"What kind of help?"

"It's about a boat."

"I don't work on boats."

So far there wasn't the first hint of civility, compassion, or curiosity in his manner. He was not hostile, either, just brusque. I couldn't read him very well, but it absolutely was not going well. I was groping awkwardly for something more to say when he asked, "What's that?" pointing to my left side.

I looked down and saw I was bleeding rather freely from a cut suffered either from my fall or from my wrestling match with Duncan.

"Oh, that's nothing," I replied, "I'll put a bandage on it when I get home."

"No, you'd better come in. My wife will take care of it for you." He glared at Duncan. "BAD BOY!" he scolded, and the poor dog hung his huge head in dismay. As I followed Angus inside, he called up the stairs, "Hilda!" and motioned me to a chair.

Presently, a small, pretty, silver-haired lady came down into the parlor. "What was all the commotion, Angus?" she said, then stopped short when she saw me, a look of horror on her face. I caught a glimpse of myself in the hall mirror. I was a complete mess, covered with mud, my clothes torn and askew, and on top of that, I was dripping blood on their hundred-year-old pine floor.

"Duncan!" she hissed. "Angus, you simply *must* do something about that dog before he kills somebody!"

Angus began to protest but was cut short.

"Look at this poor man," she said. "He's a mess and he's hurt."

"Oh, I'm fine," I attempted.

"No, you're not!" she said. "We need to look at that hand. It could get infected."

"No, really, it's okay. I didn't mean to cause any trouble." Feeling foolish and intrusive, I began edging toward the door. "I was just leaving."

"He was just leaving," echoed Angus bravely.

"You're not going anywhere until we get you cleaned up. There's a bathroom in the hall. Wash up, then we'll put something on that gash in your hand."

The "gash" was little more than a scratch, and I tried again to protest, but to no avail. She brought us to a small table. "The two of you wait right here. I'll make some tea and then we'll fix you up as good as new." She bustled away, muttering under her breath.

I apologized again and went to the bathroom to clean up. When I emerged, I looked almost presentable. I had tucked in my torn shirt, cleaned off most of the mud, and put a tissue on the "gash," which had practically disappeared with washing. But while I was cleaning up, I had hatched an idea. I dislike tea and knew I was intruding, but I was hoping that, maybe with a little guilt, Hilda could become an ally in my quest. I felt a twinge of remorse, but things were looking pretty bleak; I was willing to try almost anything.

I sat at the table across from Angus. We had endured an uncomfortable several minutes of silence when Hilda returned, carrying a beautiful silver tray with teapot, creamer, sugar bowl, and three Delft teacups and saucers. I openly admired it and complimented her.

"Thank you," she said. "My great grandparents got this for a wedding present when Victoria was on the throne. It was passed down to my grandmother and then to my mother. My parents gave it to me when they sent me to America just before the war. It was almost all they had of any real value. They were both killed during the war. It's my greatest treasure and I love to use it whenever I can."

I was touched. "I can understand your pride," I said. "My wife would love it."

"Oh, is she English?" asked Hilda, brightening.

I grinned. "No, she's Italian."

"Oh. Well, I'm sure she's very nice," she said graciously. "Now, what brings you here?"

I took a deep breath and told them of my desire to build a boat and how Angus had been so highly recommended. There was a quick glance between them and several awkward moments passed.

"You know," Angus said, "maybe I was a little abrupt outside, but you caught me off guard. It's true I used to build boats. Right here. Did it for years. But I don't build any more. I retired recently."

"I assumed that," I said, "but I was hoping you might help more in the way of instruction, as a guide and teacher. I'd like to do as much of the work as possible, but I'll need help—tools, wood, a place to build it, and, most of all, some guidance. I want the experience, but I can't do it myself."

He was looking at me keenly. "You ever build a boat?" he asked.

"No," I answered honestly, "but I've worked with wood all my life and I've owned a couple of wood boats that I have worked on. And I've done a lot of reading."

Angus wrinkled his nose. "You mean you've *read* about building a boat?"

He made it sound as hopeless as it no doubt was. I felt it slipping away "Angus," I began, "I've worked my whole life. I *like* to work. I've built some nice things and I take pride in my work. If I knew how to build a boat, I wouldn't need you. But I *do* need you. I want to do this very much and I need your help. This has been a lifelong dream, and at my age, I probably won't get another chance. I'll do it any way you want, on whatever terms. I know it's a big project that requires a big commitment in time and effort. I'm very willing to make that commitment, but I can't do it alone. You can keep the boat after it's done and sell it if you want. I'll pay you for your time and the use of your tools and boat shed. Please just tell me you'll consider it."

Angus was looking me square in the eye. For the first time I thought I discerned a glimmer of encouragement in his features. My hopes rose.

But then he looked away. "Son," he said, "I'm sorry. I just can't do it. You seem sincere and I'd like to help you, but I can't."

It seemed pretty final, but I persisted. "Angus, I don't want to insult you, but if it's about money—"

He looked up and his manner softened. "No," he said, "it's not that. Not that at all." He hesitated. "But I can't do it and that's that. It's out of the question." He got up, indicating our meeting was over. I looked over at Hilda for support, but she lowered her eyes. They seemed to be sparkling, as if she were about to cry.

I knew I was imposing and began to feel terrible. I rose quickly and, apologizing sincerely for my intrusion, I headed for the door. When I looked back to say goodbye, Hilda was still seated at the table and Angus was facing away. For whatever reason, they would not or could not get involved. I left quietly. As I walked down the path, I approached Duncan, still sitting where he was told to. Seeing me, his eyes brightened and his tail began wagging back and forth again, sweeping leaves in a small whirlwind. His large head split in a joyful grin and he began where he had left off earlier, licking and romping like an oversized puppy. I knelt down and mussed his head while I talked with him for a while. Then I turned and left, my mission unfulfilled.

CHAPTER 4

....

When I got home, Jan was working at the sink with her back to me. When she turned around to greet me, she burst out laughing. "How did it go?" she teased.

"Great," I groused. "I got attacked by a huge black dog, got knocked down in the mud, tore open my hand, ripped my clothes, and got turned down. Aside from that, perfect."

"Oh, I'm sorry, honey," she said with genuine sympathy, even though she was still laughing. "Why did he turn you down?"

"I don't know for sure. He didn't elaborate. They were nice enough, but quite firm in their decision."

"They?"

"Yes. I met his wife, too. What a sweet lady. She patched me up after the attack." Jan started laughing again. I must have looked ridiculous. "She's

English, and as different from Angus as she can be—cheerful and outgoing. Loves to entertain. She made me tea while I was healing."

"You hate tea."

"Yeah, but I was hoping it might help win her over. It didn't."

"They sound nice."

"Oh, they are, but they seem to live up there pretty much by themselves. It's a beautiful place, by the way. You can't really see it from the road, but once you get on the property, it's stunning. You'd love it. The house is a beautiful old Colonial, the grounds are well-kept, everything in its place. And, it's right on the water. It's perfect. They even have animals."

"Sounds beautiful. I'd love to see it."

"I don't think so. They're *very* private."

Jan sighed. "Well, what now?" she asked.

"It's dead, honey," I said. "I just don't see any other way to do it. Too many obstacles."

"Yes, I suppose so. And you're too old, too," she added, hoping to lighten the moment.

"Thanks. Maybe you could tell Amanda?" I ventured, already knowing the answer.

"Not a chance," Jan parried. "This is *your* party. But don't worry. She'll be disappointed, sure, but she'll get over it. She's eleven; she has a different fantasy every day."

"I hope so, but this seems different. I can see her desire and her enthusiasm and her commitment when she talks about it. I know, because I feel it, too."

Jan smiled and kissed me.

When Amanda came home from playing, I sat her down and told her what had happened, and she *was* disappointed. I felt awful. In her little mind, it was practically a finished product and now it was gone for good, yanked away in a heartbeat. We chatted for a while until it was time to eat, then, to help make her (and me) feel better, I offered to take her to Littlefield's the next day for ice cream. "Oh boy!" she cried, apparently forgetting all about her disappointment. I had averted a potential crisis with a masterful stroke and felt pretty darn clever.

During dinner, the conversation was mundane—what Amanda did all day, how was Sophie, vague plans for the rest of the summer, etc. The usual small talk. But my mind was off on a different tack. I couldn't stop thinking about Angus and Hilda, kept going back over our meeting. They seemed so nice, but lonely somehow, even sad. Perhaps it was my imagination, but I sensed an undercurrent of melancholy in their lives. I kept searching for clues but couldn't come up with anything. I finally decided to dismiss the whole affair. *I'm sure it will pass*, I thought, trying to convince myself.

We awoke the next morning to a beautiful late-spring day. The sun was shining brightly in a cloudless sky, birds were singing, and the air was a delicious mixture of balsam pine and seaside smells. It was the Maine of my childhood and it tugged strongly at my emotions. Amanda was up at six, eager to go to Littlefield's, the town pharmacy, as I had promised. I reminded her that they didn't open until nine. She had to have breakfast, clean up the kitchen, straighten her room, and do a few more little chores first. She tore through these impediments like a dervish and was done by seven-thirty.

"Ready, Grandpa?" she asked.

I sighed. It was still an hour and a half before they opened. I had an idea, though, something that would wind her down a little, and be fun for both of us. "Honey," I began, "it's much too early. Let's take a walk in the woods. It's a beautiful day and not too hot, yet. We haven't done that in a long time."

She eyed me suspiciously. "When will we be back?"

I grinned. "Don't worry, honey. I won't forget."

She beamed me a smile and said, "Okay, Grandpa, let's go!"

So off we went, across town to the edge of the woods where the footpath of the nature preserve started. It was cool in the shade of the woods and the scents of the forest were strong and sweet. We covered ground quickly. I pointed out different types of trees and flowers for her, and her eyes brightened with wonder as she got caught up in the magic of the woods. Tiny chipmunks darted out of our way as we continued along the narrow trail. Over the next half hour, we saw birds, squirrels, a raccoon, a porcupine, and some ducks in a small pond with their new chicks, fuzzy-headed little squawkers that made Amanda laugh. The forest was alive with activity after the long, cold stillness of winter.

This land had been given to the town to be used in just this way—to preserve a small patch of natural woodland so it could be enjoyed like this by anyone, anytime. I visited often, savoring the solitude, as if returning to a time and place of my youth that was fast disappearing. The outside world was becoming ever more hectic, but in the forest nature's timeless cycle remained unchanged, season after season, year after year. It was like a cathedral, calming and inspiring at the same time.

We wandered along the path for a while, then rounded a slight bend. As we came to a small clearing, we stopped short. I had always admonished Amanda to be as quiet as possible in the woods so as not to scare the animals away, and now it paid off. On the other side of the clearing, not fifty yards away, stood a doe and her fawn, nibbling on the tender shoots of grass. We both saw them at the same time.

"Awww," breathed Amanda softly. She was visibly moved by the scene of the mother caring for and protecting her baby, which couldn't have been more than a few days old, judging by the gangly legs.

As quiet as we were, the doe had already sensed danger. She looked right at us, her ears and tail standing at attention, as still as a statue. The fawn, oblivious, continued eating. We froze, remaining totally silent, hoping she would realize we were no threat. After a few long minutes, the doe relaxed somewhat and began eating again, but now a little closer to her baby. We watched for a while, then backed up slowly, continuing on a different path as it wound around a couple of small hills, then to another clearing. We found ourselves on the edge of a high bluff overlooking a magnificent view of the river. Amanda was awestruck.

"Wow!" she whispered breathlessly. "You can see forever!"

It was enthralling. Looking one way, we could see all the way down the river to where it emptied into the ocean, three or four miles away. In the other direction, our gaze followed the winding of the river up into the mountains and the forest as far as we could see.

"How far does it go?" she asked.

"I don't know, honey, but it's a long way. Maybe a hundred miles or so. It goes way up into the mountains."

"Someday, I'd like to go all the way to the end and see what's there."

I smiled. "Maybe someday, but right now we have a date at Littlefield's."

"Yay!" she cried.

When we turned to go back, my eye was caught by the McTigue place, about a half mile distant. It looked even more majestic from afar, like a perfect jewel set into the side of the riverbank. We lingered for a moment, drinking in the beauty, then retraced our steps back to town.

CHAPTER 5

....

Littlefield's was a real old-fashioned drug store, the kind every town and city had years ago but which was now found only in out-of-the-way places which had been bypassed by modern "progress." It was a pharmacy, of course, but much, much more. It was a meeting place for everyone to catch up on local gossip; it was where you went for small grocery and toiletry items; it was a warm retreat in the winter, where folks gathered around the giant wood stove in the middle of the old plank floor; it was a post office, too, a very important function when towns were more inaccessible than they are today. And, most important for us today, it was a soda fountain. But it was not a fast-food-emporium-type soda fountain like we see so often today (the whole town was not a *fast* anything). The fountain had its own section of the pharmacy, taking up perhaps a fourth of the entire store. A gleaming U-shaped mahogany counter extended almost twenty feet with old-style wrought-iron stools along the entire length. Small tables and booths were set away from the counter for youngsters who desired a little privacy. Behind the counter were the original fountains that spewed forth their wonderful concoctions—locally made root beer, ginger ale made with real ginger, and Moxie, that impossible-to-define bittersweet soda (or "pop," as they say in New England). There were national brands, too, of course, but the offbeat stuff was what really set the place apart. The fountain was always staffed by local kids, and you would be hard-pressed to find anyone living in or around Moosaquit, no matter their age, who hadn't worked there at one time or another during their youth.

I loved taking Amanda there and it was a rare week that passed without our dropping in at least once for a special treat. They still made shakes, frappes, sundaes, and ice-cream sodas like they did when I was a child, forty-odd years ago. And they still used locally produced milk and cream. The flavors varied, depending on the time of season. Blueberries, strawberries, raspberries (red and black), peaches, and maple syrup were just some of the choices. Some of the flavors weren't common elsewhere, like orange-pineapple, blueberry-raspberry, a cherry vanilla to die for, and my all-time favorite, frozen pudding. And they still served them in the thick old-fashioned glasses and dishes, just like their grandparents did. The portions were not just a choice of one or two scoops, either. They were works of art, each kid piling it on, trying to outshine the others. It was a great place for a kid's first job, and they all loved working there.

The first time I took Amanda there, her eyes were like pie plates. She had never seen anything like it. Having grown up in New England, I took Littlefield's for granted as an inalienable right, but to her, growing up in Florida, it was as foreign as outer space. She adapted quickly, though, and pretty soon she was such a regular she was accepted as almost a "native."

When we walked in, Bobby, the kid behind the counter, greeted us. "Hi, Mister Cairns. Hi, Amanda."

We returned the greetings and sat down. Amanda ordered her favorite, an old-fashioned root beer float, but Bobby was already working on it. He liked Amanda and took special care of her.

"The usual, Mister Cairns?" said Bobby.

"Yup, frozen pudding, straight up." Bobby chuckled politely, as he always did at my corny jokes, but Amanda's order came first, of course. She always grinned when the giant glass full of bubbling root beer appeared, overfilled with gobs of vanilla ice cream so that it ran down the outside of the glass. The glass was frozen, so the root beer stuck to it before it reached the counter. She waited until my ice cream came, then we both dove in. We passed several minutes in relative silence while we devoured our ice cream, only occasionally nodding and grunting our approval. We had shared this ritual many times over.

We were almost finished when I heard a voice behind us. "Excuse me."

I turned around and found myself face to face with Angus McTigue. "Well, hello," I said, completely off guard. "How are you?" He was perhaps the last person I expected to run into.

"I'm fine," he replied without embellishment.

"Can you join us?" I offered.

"Actually, I have to be going home soon," he said.

"Please. You have time for a Moxie, surely."

He seemed unsettled, but surprisingly, he relented. We made room and he sat down. "Is Moxie okay?" I asked.

"That's fine, thank you."

"How about a Moxie for Mister McTigue, Bobby?"

"Sure thing, Mister Cairns, coming right up." He smiled at Angus. "Good morning, Mister McTigue."

Angus returned the smile and the greeting. His Moxie came and he took a sip. He seemed slightly uncomfortable. After a moment or two of awkward silence, he said, "I saw you sitting here and I just had to came over to apologize. I was feeling out of sorts yesterday and wasn't very hospitable."

I waved it off. "Oh, it's nothing."

"No," he said, "you came to me for help and I got angry with you. I'm sorry."

"Well, I showed up at your house unannounced, upset your wife, got your dog in trouble, and asked for a favor which I had no right to expect. Let's call it even and start over." I stuck out my hand. He nodded and engulfed it. It felt like a vise.

Looking across me, he asked, "And who's this?"

"I'm Amanda," she answered.

For the briefest instant, Angus seemed startled, his expression flashing briefly but profoundly to what appeared to be a look of mild surprise, then back to his normal placid expression. It was so stark that it took me by surprise, but then was over so quickly, I thought I might have imagined it. Amanda missed it entirely, but I was sure something had shaken him, if only for a moment. He hesitated briefly, then said, "Hello, Amanda. I'm Angus McTigue."

Amanda's eyes widened with a big smile. "Mister McTigue!" she cried. "You're the boatbuilder, right? Grandpa told me all about your dog!"

Angus smiled again, with a genuinely kind expression. He had recovered, but I still felt he had been affected by something. *Must be my imagination*, I thought.

"Yes, Amanda, I used to build boats, but I don't anymore," he replied, with no further explanation.

"Amanda is the reason I came to see you yesterday," I said. "She and I were looking through some of my boat books and she got the crazy idea to build a boat. She wouldn't quit. Since it's something I also have always wanted to do, I'm afraid I let my emotions get the better of me and I acquiesced. I never should have let it get that far. Anyway, it's over now and we'll do something else this summer. Right, Amanda?"

She lowered her eyes and mumbled, "Yes, sir, I guess so."

Angus was looking at her with a kindly expression. "You know, Amanda, building a boat is hard work."

"Grandpa says it's easy."

Angus looked at me with a comical frown that made me chuckle, but I felt compelled to admonish her. "Amanda, we've been over this and that is not what I said."

"It kinda was," she whined.

"That's enough, Amanda," I said, as gently as I could.

"Yes, sir," she said softly, but it was clear the idea was not completely put to rest.

"I'm sorry, Angus," I said. "It's just that she really was so excited about it. I explained to her why we couldn't do it and I thought it was over. In fact, that's why we're here now. There's nothing like one of Littlefield's sodas to make you forget your troubles."

Angus softened and looked at Amanda for a long moment. She was fiddling with her empty soda glass and sucking air up through the straw. Then he smiled and got up, offering me his hand again and looking me straight in my eye. "This was nice," he said, "thank you."

I felt uncomfortable. I had done nothing that he should thank me for, but I automatically replied, "You're welcome."

Amanda and I walked home in uncharacteristic silence, her head bowed while she kicked stones down the road. It was apparent the wound of her disappointment had been reopened by the chance meeting with Angus. I understood what a childish fantasy it was (for her *and* for me), because I was also disappointed; I just couldn't let her see it. I sensed we'd be eating a lot of ice cream that summer.

CHAPTER 6

···························

The next day was Thursday, and that could only mean one thing—GOLF! The day was sacrosanct. My foursome had met every Thursday for the past four seasons and nothing short of an act of God or a dire emergency could interfere with our routine. We didn't even call one another anymore; we just met at the course and played, same time every Thursday. It was the highlight of my week.

I was up early, had breakfasted, showered, and done my morning stretches before seven o'clock. I already had on my golf shoes, and my pockets contained all I would need for the next few hours—a couple of golf balls, some tees, and a ball marker. Inside my golf bag were a sweater, a windbreaker, some snacks, and more balls, just in case. I even had on my lucky shirt; nothing was left to chance. In forty-five minutes, we would meet on the first tee and embark on another four hours of insults, lies, and laughter. *God's in His heaven . . ..*

DING-DONG.

It was the front doorbell. *Probably one of Amanda's pals wanting to play*, I mused. *But at seven-thirty?* I would have to talk to her about this. "Amanda," I called up the stairs, "someone's here."

"I can't come down right now, Grandpa," she shouted back.

"Great," I muttered, "now I'm her butler."

I walked to the front door and drew it open, expecting to see one of Amanda's friends, and found myself staring directly at Angus McTigue's knees.

"Angus!" I cried, totally surprised. "Please come in. What brings you here?"

But he just stood there. "Still want to build that boat?" he said, without any introduction or emotion.

"Uh, what?" I replied, stunned.

"The boat; do you still want to build it?" He appeared to think I was a little slow.

"Oh, yeah, the boat," I repeated, completely flabbergasted. "Gosh, Angus, the thing is, you caught me off guard a little." *A little?!* Again, I offered, "Please come in and sit down." I was feeling a little foggy.

He entered and I led him to the dining room, my mind racing to figure out what was going on. Was he serious? Yes—Angus seemed always to be serious. Did I really want to do this? I wasn't sure, now. A lot of emotions had been dredged up in the last couple of days. And what about Amanda? These thoughts were colliding around my mind as I led him to the table.

Until I knew what was going on, I had to keep everyone in the dark. There wasn't enough ice cream in the whole town to go through that disappointment again. We sat down. "Let's talk out here," I said. "I don't want Amanda to hear anything."

"Okay," he replied.

I didn't know exactly where to start, so to buy some time, I asked, "Are you serious, Angus?"

As expected, he merely said, "Yes," without further discussion.

"But, why now? What changed your mind?" I was struggling, and I'm sure he sensed my discomfiture.

"Look," he said, "if you really want to do this, I have a set of plans that have been kicking around for a while. She's a small sloop, about twenty-five feet long, and as pretty as a picture. She's rigged for single-handing and she's not terribly complicated to build. I think it would be perfect for you." While he was talking about the boat, his whole demeanor changed from the stern, taciturn man I had met earlier. His manner, if not exactly bubbling, was expressing genuine enthusiasm for something he obviously loved to do.

My head was spinning. I was excited, of course—what an opportunity!—but what if he changed his mind again? What if Amanda wasn't really that serious and it turned out to be a passing fancy? What would Jan say? I looked into his eyes and saw total honesty. Weighing all the pros and cons I could think of in about two seconds, I made a decision. I got the very strong impression that this was a last chance, a shot at the gold ring. If I backed out now, I was sure he would never approach me again.

"Wait here," I said.

I raced up the stairs. Jan was still in bed, reading.

"Honey, you've got to do something for me," I whispered excitedly.

"Why are you whispering?" she bellowed.

"Shhhh! I don't want Amanda to hear."

"Hear *what*?" she said, again louder than necessary.

"Never mind. Just call the guys and tell them I won't be golfing today."

"WHAT?" she said, this time very loud. "You *never* miss your golf date. What's going on?"

"Please," I begged, "just do it and I'll explain later. Okay?"

"Well, all right, I guess." Then, "When do I find out?"

Her curiosity was thoroughly aroused now. "When I get back, promise. Thanks, honey. See ya."

I went back downstairs, grinning.

Angus looked up at me. "Well, what do you say?"

"Let's go look at those plans," I said, feeling like a kid on his first date.

We left the house and walked up the road to his house. Very little was said along the way because that's how Angus liked it. But that was okay. I tend to be introspective also, so I understood. Besides, I was mulling over dozens of questions I had, without coming up with many answers. I was so excited by the prospect of finally being able to build a boat, and with an expert with me every step of the way, that I was afraid I would lose my perspective. I felt completely off-balance, but I knew for certain I wanted to do this and was hoping feverishly we could make it happen.

Shortly, we arrived at his place. As we walked up the lane, Duncan saw us. He exploded in a frenzy of barking and tail-wagging as he raced toward us. I braced for another onslaught, but Angus just said two words, "NO" and "SIT." The huge dog slid to a halt and sat down obediently, if not enthusiastically. He was clearly disappointed and looked to me for support.

"He's a good dog," said Angus, "but a little rambunctious. Hilda keeps telling me to tie him up, but I can't do it. He wouldn't intentionally hurt a fly and he never leaves the property. And anyone who comes here unannounced usually doesn't do it twice."

"Amen to that," I said, grinning. I had to admire the beast. He was huge but playful as a puppy and didn't appear to have an aggressive bone in his massive body. "What is he?"

"A Newfoundland–Saint Bernard mix," he replied, reaching out to ruffle his head and ears. "Good boy." Duncan looked adoringly at his master, cherishing the attention.

The dog truly was enormous. "How much does he weigh?" I asked.

"About a hundred and ninety," he replied. "He still thinks he's a puppy, though; kind of awkward when he tries to climb up in my lap." Angus chuckled as he talked about the dog. It was the first time I saw him laugh. "Come on, boy," he said to Duncan as he led me down a narrow path to the boathouse. The path was somewhat unused and overgrown—not up to the standards of the rest of the place. When we got to the boathouse, Angus opened the door and motioned me inside. It was a large open building with a fairly high ceiling. There was a loft along the entire length of the building, about fifteen feet or so deep. The main floor was littered with all manner of detritus—lawn furniture, animal feed, junk appliances, a car, even an old sleigh. I was somewhat surprised by this. Angus noticed and apologized, saying he'd had no reason to come out there recently. He said it needed a good cleanup, but I looked right through the mess. To me, it was Heaven on Earth.

He brought me to a massive wooden workbench that had a couple of vises attached. On this bench he had cleared a space and laid out the plans for the boat. They were obviously not new plans. The paper was faded in some places, and most of the edges were frayed with age. But the boat was indeed a beauty. She was exactly as Angus had described, pretty as can be and just the right size. As I scanned the plans, I could almost see her finished up and sailing. I don't think I could have imagined it more perfectly. She was not overly large, but definitely a real boat, a small yacht. Everything seemed to be falling into place, but while we were looking around, I'd had a little time to formulate some questions.

"Angus," I began, "she *is* pretty, but, really, can we do this?"

He just grunted derisively. I waited for further enlightenment, but none was forthcoming. I took it as a yes.

"What about material?" I asked. "Where will we get the wood?"

He led me to a large overhead door that opened to a separate part of the building and pressed a button on the wall. When the door went up, my jaw dropped. All I could do was stare. There, piled up neatly, was wood as I had only dared to dream of. Not only was the room full of lumber but the boards were all sorted according to species and size specifically for boatbuilding. There were planks of mahogany, teak, spruce, white pine, white oak, cedar, ash, and fir. Off to the side was the big stuff, from four to six inches thick, by a foot or two wide, mostly white oak but also black locust and some hackmatack for specialty applications that required great strength or rot-resistance. I inhaled deeply. It smelled wonderful.

"Angus, I'm speechless. Where did you get all of this beautiful wood? It must have cost a fortune!"

"Most of it I cut myself, right on this property. I've accumulated it over fifty years, so it's well-aged." He said this with obvious pride. "Only the mahogany and the teak came from somewhere else. I could get along without it, but the stuff is just so beautiful, I can't resist it. Besides, when I bought this, it cost a tenth of what it does today."

His eyes gazed upon the wood with such simple and honest affection that I was touched. I understood completely.

"But that boat needs an iron ballast keel," I said. "Where do we begin to build *that*?"

Again, Angus said nothing, just motioned me out the back door. It led to a fairly large open field. We began walking, with no words spoken, of course. I was by now accustomed to his reticence and comfortably at ease with it. In fact, I liked it. Presently, he stopped and pointed. There on the ground lay a large object covered by a tall, dense growth of hay. I stepped closer for a better look and banged my shin on something very hard. I parted some hay and there was a large rusty lump. It was about fifteen feet long by three feet wide by a couple of feet high. The rust told me it was iron.

"Is this what we'll have the keel made from?" I asked.

"That *is* the keel," he said.

"But . . . you mean . . . this is already made for that boat?"

"Yup." Again, no elaboration.

"How long has it been out here?" I asked.

"About forty years."

This was like pulling teeth. "Why?" I asked.

"Just never got to it," he replied.

"In forty years?" I said, incredulous.

"Nope," he said, with a tone that shut down any further inquiry.

Okay, I thought. "But that's a big thing already done, right?"

"Yup."

We went back inside the boathouse. I wandered back to the plans on the bench, studying them more closely. I noticed the cover page was missing, which would normally have the designer's name, a rendered drawing of the finished boat, and the boat's name on it. I suppose after forty years, it's not unusual to have misplaced a few things, but everything we needed to build her was there, and that's all I cared about. As my eyes traced over the graceful lines, I began to get very excited. We were really going to do it! "When do we start?" I asked, eager to begin cutting wood.

"Not so fast," he said. "First, we have to clean this place up. We couldn't build a canoe in here the way it is now. We'll need plenty of room—setting up the keel, laying down the lines, it all takes a lot of space. And we have to sort out the wood that we need and bring it in here so it'll be at hand."

I looked around and had to admit it *was* a bit of a mess. He followed my eyes and apologized yet again. "It's just been a while since I've worked out here. I'm ashamed the place got so disheveled." But his apology fell on deaf ears. By then, nothing could have dampened my spirits.

"No problem," I said, excited at the thought of getting on with it. "Shall we start after lunch?"

"No, we'll start tomorrow," he said. "I've got some things to take care of and you probably do, too. I know this is sudden, but that's how it is." He hesitated, groping for the right words. "A few things need to be said," he began. "It's not terribly hard work, but there's a lot of it and it tends to go very slowly because of the kind of work it is." He glanced at the golf shoes I was still wearing. "Once we do start, there won't be time for much else or we'll never get her finished. We'll work pretty much every day except Sundays until we see how it goes. It's a big commitment on your part, so I'll only say this once: if you ever feel like quitting, for any reason, just tell me. There'll be no hard feelings. Fair enough?"

I grinned. "Fair enough, Angus, but it won't happen. I've been fantasizing about this for years." I drew in a big breath. "I was certain that it would remain a dream, but all of a sudden, I can see it happening. Thank you."

"Don't thank me yet," he said with the briefest trace of a smile.

"Tomorrow, then?"

"I'll be here."

"Great," I said, grinning, and turned to leave. "What time?" I called over my shoulder.

"Seven."

I stopped. "Seven? *Here* at seven?"

"Is that a problem?" he inquired.

"A problem? No, no. Not at all. Just seems kind of early to actually start working, that's all. I mean, you're right, we should start early. Get more done that way." I sounded a little goofy, even to myself.

"Seven is not early, not this time of year," he said, his eyes boring a hole in me. "I was going to say six. The sun is already up almost two hours by seven and I hate to burn daylight."

"Yeah, me, too," I said, not very convincingly.

"Wear heavy shoes and thick pants. Also, a long-sleeve shirt will protect your arms from the rough wood. It'll be warm, but you'll be glad you're covered. And wear work gloves."

"Anything else?"

"Yes. Eat a big breakfast."

"Okay," I said. "See you at seven." I turned to go, then caught myself. "Uh, Angus, there is one more thing . . ."

"What's that?" he asked cautiously.

"I don't know how you feel about this, but, uh, you see, this whole project is kind of for Amanda as well as for me. Heck, if not for her, I never would have come to see you."

I was beginning to feel I was on thin ice, that perhaps this might be asking too much, when his face actually broke into a big smile. "You want to bring Amanda?"

"Only if it's all right."

"Of course, it's all right," he said sincerely. "I assumed you would bring her along. I've told Hilda all about her and she can't wait to meet her. By all means, bring her, anytime you want."

I left, feeling as excited as I'd been in years.

When I walked in the house, Jan and Amanda were there waiting for me. I let them know by my expression that something big was up. Jan tried to be cool, but she clearly was agitated.

"I want to know what was so important that you cancelled your golf game," she said.

"Yeah, what's up, Grandpa?" echoed Amanda.

"Oh, nothing," I replied airily. I wandered into the kitchen. "Anything to eat?"

"Grandpa!" yelped Amanda.

"Okay, okay, I'll tell you . . ." I began. They both leaned forward in their seats, dying to hear the big news.

"Well . . ." I said, then paused. "You know, I could sure use a soda."

"GRANDPA!" Amanda squealed again, louder. But she jumped up and ran to the refrigerator, retrieving a can of soda, then sitting back down on the very edge of her chair, her eyes eager with anticipation.

"Well?" she said.

I looked at my drink. "You know I can't drink soda without ice in it." This time Jan raced to the kitchen. She brought back a big glass of ice, set it down in front of me, and shot me a look that said joke time was over.

"Okay, here's the deal . . ." I said, drawing it out. Amanda was squirming. I looked right at her and said, "We're going to build a boat!"

She leaped out of her chair. "YIPPEE!"

Jan was elated, too. "That's great, honey." she cried, "but what happened? What changed his mind? Why didn't you tell me?"

"I couldn't," I said. "Angus showed up here at seven-thirty and dropped it in my lap. That was the doorbell you heard. I was stunned, of course, but I made a quick decision to go for it. I felt it was a last chance. I think if I had hesitated, he would have given it up for good. I still had some questions, so I didn't want to tell you until I felt comfortable with everything. And, obviously, if I wasn't sure, I couldn't tell you, Amanda, because I didn't want to disappoint you again." She ran over and threw her arms around me and kissed me. I felt like a king.

"So, anyway, that's where I went, over to his place. We went through the boatyard, looked at the plans—"

"Plans? He already has plans?" said Jan.

"Yep. Says he's had them for forty years."

"FORTY YEARS?!" Jan cried.

"Yeah, that was my reaction, too. He told me he never got around to it. In forty years! I guess things move a little slower in these *heah pahts*," I said, emphasizing the Maine accent at the end.

Amanda laughed and said, "When can we start, Grandpa?"

"Tomorrow morning, honey. Seven o'clock."

"*Seven o'clock?*" Amanda repeated, her enthusiasm suddenly diminished. "Isn't that a little early?"

"That was also my reaction," I said. "Then he kind of implied he'd really rather start at six, so I said seven was perfect. Says he doesn't like to 'burn daylight.' He's a bit of a character, but a tough old bird and as honest as they come." I got up. "Come on, Amanda, let's go over my books. If we can find something similar, I'll show you what she looks like."

That afternoon, Amanda and I pored over my boat books, looking for similarities to the boat we would be building. It was a big day for both of us. There was a lot to talk about, and talk she did. She chattered nonstop about the boat, how it would sail, what her first Maine winter would be like, the fall and spring, the new friends she would be making at her new school, anything and everything that popped into her hyperactive little mind. Her excitement was infectious. I remembered back years ago when I was her age and first wintered in Maine. I knew exactly what she was feeling. Later, when she's grown, she might have a different take on Maine winters. But for now, it was all a new and exhilarating experience. And, on top of it all, we were going to build a boat! She was bubbling.

"Grandpa," she asked, "what happens to the boat when we're done building it?"

Hmm . . . I thought, *good question.* I hadn't thought that far ahead. I was so anxious to build the thing, I hadn't considered anything else. "I don't know, honey. We never discussed that. I guess he'll probably sell it."

"Why?"

"Well, he has to make money, for his time, for his material. It's what he does for a living."

A thoughtful look. "Can we buy it?" she asked.

"No, I don't think so, honey. It would cost a small fortune. Remember, that's why these kinds of boats are so rare. We'll just have a lot of fun building her. Okay?"

"Okie dokie, artichokie," she giggled, her face beaming.

I laughed. "Let's see if we can find a boat that looks like ours." From that moment on, it became "our boat." Everything we saw, we compared to our boat. It was great fun and almost like actually owning it.

The entire rest of the day was like Christmas Eve for both of us. Everything we did or talked about revolved around our boat. We discussed what color it would be, how big it would be, what name we would call it, how it would sail—a dozen different things. Amanda had turned into a good little sailor the previous summer and she knew a lot about the smaller boats, like the Sunfish and the Sailfish, but she could see this was a "real" boat. She felt she was moving up in class.

Late in the afternoon, Jan came into the study smiling and shaking her head. "You two have been in here all afternoon! What's going on?"

"We're brushing up, Jannie," Amanda said.

"Brushing up on what?" asked Jan.

"You know, brushing up," Amanda replied, as if that explained everything.

Jan and I exchanged smiles. We were thrilled to have Amanda for the summer, and now she would be with us for the whole year. Any reservations we'd had were wiped out completely by Amanda's excitement. And already, Jan had changed her view about wintering over. Like me, she was seeing new experiences through a child's eyes. Amanda was eleven and would soon be doing other things—things that wouldn't include us. We understood that and were treasuring these times with her. They move on so quickly. I wondered if she would feel the same if she were even one year older. We could see a huge difference in her from just last summer and knew she was growing up fast. Building this boat was a godsend in so many ways, it seemed almost preordained.

CHAPTER 7

....

After dinner, Jan and I were discussing the coming adventure. She mentioned, "You know, this has all happened very quickly. Is there anything you need to do, anything you need to buy, before you start?"

Typical Jan, always trying to think practically. "No, not really," I said. "Angus mentioned a couple of things, but—"

"Like what?" she interrupted.

"Oh, nothing, really. He just mentioned the usual stuff, very general things—wear some heavy shoes, long pants and shirt, gloves, things like that. And get this, eat a big breakfast!" With this last, I couldn't resist a derisive snort. "Like I'm a kid on my first job."

"Well?" said Jan, with her usual skepticism.

"Oh, come on, honey. I'm not a rookie. I've worked my whole life. I think I know how to dress and what to eat. I hate boots and I hate gloves; they're so bulky they get in the way. I'll wear shorts and a tee shirt like I always do in the summer; that boathouse is like a sauna. He's just being overly cautious because he doesn't know me, that's all. He'd say the same thing to a high school kid he just hired. Besides, he's a lot older than I and probably needs to keep warm."

"I don't know . . ." Jan mused, "it seems Angus would know a lot more about how to build a boat than you do." She was always twisting things around like that.

"What I wear has nothing to do with how to build a boat," I retorted. "I'll decide what I wear, and what I eat, okay? This whole discussion is silly. What could there be about building a boat that's different from any other work?" I snorted. "Eat a big breakfast! Heck, the guy has to be eighty years old. I think I can keep up with him." I couldn't help slipping in a little sarcasm. "I'm a big boy and *I'll* decide what to wear and what to eat. End of story."

She didn't look convinced.

The next morning at five-thirty, I went in to awaken Amanda, but she was already up, bathed, dressed, and had made her bed. I was pleasantly surprised—she was not known for her neatness. Things were working out even better than I had hoped.

We went downstairs and Jan asked us what we wanted for breakfast. Amanda wanted pancakes (she always wanted pancakes). I said my usual—two eggs and some fruit and coffee.

"Do you want some toast?" she asked.

"No, thanks."

"How about some pancakes?"

"No, just the eggs and fruit, thanks."

"Oatmeal?"

I stared at her. "Oatmeal? I *never* eat oatmeal. What's going on?"

"Well, Angus said to eat a big breakfast. I'm just trying to help. It's a long time until lunch. You'll be working hard and you're going to get hungry."

I sighed. "Honey, I appreciate your concern, but please, just fix my eggs. I'll be fine."

"You know best," she said in a tone that indicated quite clearly she didn't believe it for a second.

After breakfast, Amanda and I hopped in the car and drove up Shore Road to Angus's place. It was only a mile, but I was eager to get started. And, I thought, we'll get there early to show him I'm serious. I'd have another cup of coffee while we waited for the old guy to get ready.

When we arrived, we walked up the path to the house and knocked on the door. It was about six-thirty and I was feeling a little smug. *Hope we don't wake you.*

Hilda answered the door and greeted us warmly. "This must be Amanda," Hilda said, looking down at her with sweet affection. "How do you do, dear?"

Amanda, being a very polite young lady, smiled and answered, "Good morning, ma'am. I'm fine, thank you."

"That's good," Hilda said. Then, looking at me, she asked, "Would you like to come in?"

"No, thanks, Hilda, I brought a coffee with me. I'll just drink it out here while we wait for Angus to get ready."

"Oh, Angus is down at the boathouse. He couldn't wait any longer."

He couldn't wait any longer? I thought. *We were a half hour early!* I led Amanda down the path to the boathouse, chuckling to myself. I had to admire the guy.

Angus was inside the boathouse hovering over the plans. He looked up as we entered and his face lit up when he saw Amanda. Then he gave me a quick glance, taking in my shorts, the tee shirt, and the sneakers. A brief hint of a frown appeared on his face, then dissolved into an "oh, well" look and a shrug.

Amanda smiled and said, "Good morning, Mister McTigue."

"Good morning, Amanda," Angus returned. "I'm glad you could come; we're going to need all the help we can get." He looked at her fondly. "How old are you, Amanda?"

She drew herself up to her full four feet, two inches. "I'm almost twelve, sir."

"She turned eleven last month," I added helpfully. She shot me a glare that could have etched granite.

Angus smiled. "You know, Amanda, most of the work we'll be doing is pretty hard, but there are plenty of ways you can help us. There'll be lots of fetching and cleaning to be done. If you could help us with that, we can concentrate on the building and get the boat done sooner. And Hilda can always use help. She has to feed all the animals, pick the vegetables in the garden, go shopping . . . and she's always doing something in the kitchen. Can you do that?"

Amanda would have promised him anything at that point. "Yes, *sir!*" she answered enthusiastically, bringing another smile to his face.

"Do you have a camera?" he asked.

"Yes, sir."

"Good. You can be our official photographer, keep track of our progress."

"Oh, boy!"

"It would also help if you took care of Duncan."

Amanda didn't know the dog's name and a quizzical expression crossed her face. Angus pointed out to the river where Duncan was bliss-fully swimming around, chasing ducks and barking. She lit up when she saw him. "Oh boy!" she cried. "So that's the dog that attacked Grandpa. You bet I'll take care of him. That'll be fun!" Then, perhaps recalling my story, she asked, "He's kind of big, isn't he?"

Angus opened the door and called, "Duncan, **come!**" Immediately, the dog swam to shore, shook once, then bounded to the shed, his face sporting an enormous grin. He charged into the boathouse, dripping wet, and went right to Amanda. His tail was wagging furiously, but his manners were impeccable. He sat next to her, gazing into Amanda's face with unbounded love while she patted his head and made a big fuss over him.

Quite a change from the other day, I thought. *What a great dog!* "Duncan!" I called and held out my arms to him. In a flash, he spun around, leaped, and knocked me flat on my back. Immediately, he flopped down on top of me and began noisily licking my face, his sopping body drenching me with ice-cold river water. Amanda was laughing hard, but Angus just looked at me and shook his head, apparently thinking I didn't learn very quickly.

"Duncan, **NO!**" he said, and the dog stopped immediately. He went back to Amanda and sat right next to her, again gazing into her face as if she were the rising sun. It was to become a common theme. Duncan bonded with Amanda immediately, as dogs often do with children. He would do anything and everything Amanda wanted him to do. I never once saw him jump up on her, or even jostle against her. I, on the other hand, apparently was fair game. I had to be constantly on the alert or the beast would ambush me and take me down. It was great sport for him, and the more I resisted, the more he seemed to enjoy it. I quickly learned to keep a sharp weather eye on Mister Duncan.

"Well, are you ready?" asked Angus. "Time's a wastin."

It wasn't even seven o'clock yet. I admired his spirit but made a mental note not to be early anymore. He gave Amanda a push broom that was bigger than she was and told her to start cleaning out a large area over in one corner. That was where we would be stacking the wood once we got the rest of the bigger stuff moved out. Amanda and Duncan cheerfully fell

---

to and were soon hard at it, Amanda struggling with the enormous broom and Duncan chewing happily on a large pine stick.

Now it was time for us to get started. At last! I could see that a lot had to be done before we could even begin to think about the boat, but I was thrilled that we were actually on our way. And even though I was anxious to get as much done as quickly as possible, I was keenly aware of the age difference between us. I judged Angus to be at least twenty-five years older than I and, besides, he had been retired for a while. I didn't want to push him too hard, so I reluctantly held back so he could set the pace. But, as we got into it, I realized he was in better shape than I had thought. He never hurried, but he never slowed down, either; he just moved along at a steady, comfortable pace. I adjusted quickly to his easy rhythm.

We worked in this manner for some time, moving stuff off to one side, or outside, or into a growing pile that would eventually be taken to the dump. Angus was relaxed and efficient. He seemed greatly pleased to be cleaning up the boathouse. At one point, he expressed just that sentiment, apologizing a third time for the mess. He was clearly a very meticulous man, and it chafed at him to have his workplace in such a state. I waved him off cheerfully, knowing that what we were doing was a necessary preliminary that would allow us to soon be working on the boat. I was euphoric. After a couple of hours, the place began to look presentable. As we removed the stuff, Amanda would come behind and sweep up after us. Things were moving right along.

As we finished removing the last of the big stuff, I went to the water cooler for a drink. I was comfortably warmed up now and breathing freely. Angus joined me.

"Looking much better already," he said, obviously pleased that his shop was once again fit for proper work. I started to make small talk, but he was already headed back to work. I shook my head. It was the shortest break I'd ever had.

We got back to work, moving at the same steady pace. It was good to be getting things done, of course, but it had been a while since I had actually done any real physical work. I was starting to feel that perhaps a more substantial break might be in order. I also was starting to feel a familiar rumble in my stomach. We had been working for more than two hours, nonstop, and it wasn't even nine o'clock yet. Well, I thought, if Angus can do it, so can I. We forged on, our pace as methodical as a metronome.

After what seemed like several more hours, I was downright hungry. Angus kept moving along with no apparent feelings, but I was starving. Surely, it must be close to lunchtime. I stole a glance at my watch—not quite ten o'clock! I looked again to make sure it was working. The second hand swept along, nice and steady . . . tick, tick, tick. Two more hours until lunch! This was not good. Angus looked comfortable, showing no signs of slowing down, but something had to give, and soon.

At ten, sharp, Hilda came out to the boathouse. She was carrying her tray with a plate full of fresh-baked cookies and three glasses on it. It was like a mirage. *Oh, thank God*, I thought. She approached me with a big smile on her face. I could smell something delicious. Then, unbelievably, she walked right past me!

"Amanda," she said, "I brought some cookies and milk for you, dear. I hope you like them. They're chocolate chip." Chocolate chip! I *love* chocolate chip! Amanda thrilled at the plate full of homemade cookies and stopped what she was doing immediately. I inhaled deeply, the sweet aroma teasing my nostrils. She and Duncan sat down with Hilda. They chatted away while Amanda dug into the pile of cookies.

My tongue must have been hanging out, because all of a sudden, Hilda said, "Oh, my goodness, James, what am I thinking? Here, I brought this for you." She handed me a glass of iced tea, then brought the third glass to Angus. Iced tea! I looked longingly at the pile of cookies, which was steadily shrinking before my eyes. Amanda was laughing with Hilda as she devoured the feast, pausing only to tell Hilda how delicious they were. She broke one in half and gave it to the dog, giggling as she watched Duncan wolf it down. He so obviously enjoyed it, she gave him the other half, too. I couldn't take it any longer.

"They sure look good," I said, not at all subtly.

"They're wonderful, Grandpa. They're the best cookies I've ever eaten!"

There were two left. I was desperate. "Do they taste as good as they smell?" I asked shamelessly.

"They sure do, Grandpa. Do you want one?"

In fact, I wanted both of them, but as I reached, Duncan thrust his nose in and upset the plate, knocking the cookies to the floor. I gaped in horror as they disappeared instantly into his huge maw. He broke into a blissful smile as he licked the last of the crumbs off his chin. I was stunned into silence.

"Oh, that's too bad," said Hilda. "You're a bad boy, Duncan!" she cooed, sounding more like praise than a scolding. She and Amanda laughed as the dog thumped his tail.

I was still trying to absorb this disaster when Angus admonished, "Finish up your tea, son, we're burning daylight."

Somehow, I got through the rest of the morning. My stomach was growling, my mind was spinning, and I felt weak, but true to the male code, I said nothing. Angus and I worked on, removing the last of the impediments and sweeping up. Hilda had asked Amanda if she wanted to help feed the animals. She jumped at the chance and off they went. Duncan curled up in a huge ball, contentedly sleeping off his mid-morning snack. His face was a mask of sheer bliss as he no doubt dreamt of future cookie bonanzas. Except for an occasional twitch, he lay completely still.

Just before noontime, Angus announced that maybe we should knock off early for lunch. The place was all cleaned up except for a couple of stray objects that were well away from where we would be working. "Early" is, of course, a relative term. It was ten minutes to twelve. In any case, I jumped at the idea with such alacrity that Angus seemed a little startled.

"Great idea, Angus!" I said, before he could change his mind. "I'll call Jan and have her make lunch."

I picked up the phone and dialed. When Jan answered, I told her we would be home soon and to please have lunch ready. I tried to keep the desperation out of my voice.

"Sure," she said. "Would you like a sandwich?"

"Uh, maybe two sandwiches, honey," I said. "And if we have any salad, that would be great, too."

"How about some fruit?"

"Yeah, fruit. That sounds good."

"We have some leftover macaroni and cheese. Would you like that, too?"

My mouth was watering. "Oh, I forgot about that," I said. "Yeah, that would be great."

"Anything else?" she said. I could have sworn I heard just the slightest bit of "I told you so" in her voice, but it could have been my imagination.

"Do we have any soup?" I asked.

"Sure," she said. I could almost hear the smirk.

I hung up. "Okay, that's done. I'll fetch Amanda and drive home. We'll be back about one."

Angus looked at me. "You *drove* up?" he asked. "It's only a mile."

"Uh, yeah, I know. I just wanted to get here nice and early, that's all. And, you know, that's a long way for Amanda." It sounded weak, even to me.

"I suppose," he said. He looked doubtful.

When we got home, lunch was laid out on the table. It was the best lunch I had ever seen. I washed up very quickly and dove in. Jan and

Amanda chatted brightly as they picked at their salads. Amanda told Jan all about Duncan and how he knocked me down again (Jan shot me a look very much like the one Angus had given me); she described Hilda's cookies in exquisite detail; she went on and on about how hard she had worked and how important Angus had made her feel. Jan listened, intrigued, and asked just the right questions.

After a while, Jan said to me, "You're being awfully quiet." So I was. I hadn't said two words since sitting down, just shoveled in the food. First the salad, then the soup, the two sandwiches, the macaroni, the fruit, and two glasses of soda. Jan had a knowing smile on her face.

"It's just that I'm thinking about the boat," I attempted. She wasn't buying it.

"Sure," she said. "Feel better, now?"

"I do, thanks. Do we have any ice cream?"

Jan laughed. "Don't overdo it, now. You know how you are."

"What does *that* mean?"

"It's just that you tend to overcompensate. You didn't eat enough breakfast, so now you're eating two lunches."

I groaned. "Can I please just have some ice cream?"

"Okay," she said, impending doom evident in her voice.

After a couple bowls of ice cream, I felt rejuvenated, my morning ordeal but a distant memory. I just needed to eat a little more for breakfast, that's all. And maybe take a snack for the midmorning break. Tomorrow would be different.

When it was time to go back, I called for Amanda. When there was no answer, I looked around for her and found her curled up on the couch, fast asleep. We couldn't help smiling. She'd had a big morning and she was pooped. Jan got a blanket and covered her up, tucking her in lovingly. "I guess I'm flying solo this afternoon," I said.

After a hug and a kiss, I was out the door. I had decided to walk back instead of drive. Angus's comment, though innocent enough, had stung a little. Besides, it was only one mile and a beautiful day, so off I went.

When I got back, Angus was waiting, of course.

"I think we should get the wood out next. We'll bring as much as we can out here and sort it so it will be at hand. We could lay down the lines first, but I'd rather do that tomorrow. After we get the wood out, we can paint the floor so it will be dry in the morning. We should be able to lay down the lines in one day."

"You're the boss," I said. I was itching to get started. I really wanted to begin with the lines, but I understood his point.

We went to the wood storage room. The overhead door was already up. Angus explained which wood we would be using for each different phase. Then, he worked backward so that the beginning stages would have the necessary material close by. He said all this clearly, simply, matter-of-factly. When he was done, he looked at me.

"Any questions?" he asked.

"Nope. Let's do it." I had, in fact, followed what he said pretty easily. Most of it was simple enough, with some adjustment for the uniqueness of building a boat instead of building, say, a house.

We fell into the same pace we had used earlier. I think you could set a watch by his movements—they were so well-planned and deliberate. The work was easy and pleasant; we simply each took an end of a plank and carried it to where we would need it. Very little was said while we walked through our monotonous routine. Every once in a while, I had to stop and admire a particularly fine piece of wood. It was so beautiful I couldn't help running my hands over some of the planks. When I did, Angus smiled like a proud parent. It was obvious they had been harvested, cut, dried, selected, and stored with almost a mother's love. As often as not, Angus would tell me where it had come from and when he had cut it. They were almost like children to him, whose names and birthdays he never forgot.

Around two o'clock, I began to feel logy. My body was getting tired and my mind started wandering. The enormous lunch sat in my stomach like a sack of cement. We had brought out most of the lighter wood and had moved on to the heavier stuff, mostly white oak, three and four inches thick, some of it up to twenty feet long. We carried what we could handle, but some of it was simply too heavy and would have to be moved with a forklift or a dolly. As the wood got heavier, I got logier. My muscles were protesting. My mind was drifting. I was sleepy. Angus, of course, showed no signs of hunger, fatigue, thirst, or any other emotion found in normal humans.

Around three o'clock, Angus asked if I would like to take a short break.

"No," I grumbled, "I'd like to take a *long* break." I was getting cranky.

He looked a little surprised. "No problem," he said, "I'll go see if Hilda can bring us some iced tea."

Oh, boy, I thought, sarcastically, but kept it to myself. "Thanks, Angus. That would be great."

"There are a bunch of thin slats over behind those teak planks," he said. "We'll need them for laying down the lines. Why don't you get those out while I'm gone?"

"Okay," I said, only half listening. *I sure could use a nap,* I thought.

"Be careful moving that stuff," he called over his shoulder as he left.

"Yeah, yeah," I muttered. *He treats me like I'm an idiot.* I went back inside the storage room and located the slats behind the teak. I began shifting the pile of planks to gain better access. It was a mundane task that required absolutely no concentration, perfect for my present state of mind. As I was shifting the stack, though, the planks began to wobble, then tilt ominously. I grabbed at them, but too late. The top board came loose, teetered, then came sliding down the pile, right on top of my sneaker-clad right foot.

"YEEOW!" I howled, grabbing it while hopping around on my other foot. While doing so, I stepped on another piece of wood, lost my balance, and fell right into a stack of rough-cut fir. It might as well have been a nest of porcupines. I yelped again as the long needle-like splinters dug deeply into my exposed arms and legs. I slowly and carefully extricated myself from the now-jumbled pile of wood and was limping painfully over to a chair to sit down when Angus rushed back in. He took one look at me and shook his head.

"You okay?" he asked.

"Yeah, I'm fine," I answered, disgusted with myself. He had left me alone two minutes and I had almost killed myself. I got the distinct feeling he was thinking the same thing.

He helped me to the chair. I sat down and assessed the damage. I was sore all over, but it appeared nothing was life-threatening. The biggest casualty was my pride—I felt like a fool.

Angus said, "Maybe that's enough for today."

I wanted nothing more than to go home, take a hot shower, dress my wounds, and go to bed. But his pity was obvious and it stung. "No way," I said. "This is nothing. Just get me some tweezers and some Band-Aids. I'll be fine."

Angus looked skeptical. "You sure?" he asked.

"Of course. This looks worse than it really is. I want to finish up before we knock off. Remember, we're laying down the lines tomorrow." I hoped I sounded braver than I felt.

"If you say so," he said doubtfully, and off he went.

As soon as he left the building, I let out a moan. I was in agony. I didn't *think* anything was serious, but everything throbbed. The splinters felt like hot coals on my skin. I began pulling out the larger ones while I waited for Angus to return. I was pleasantly employed thus when I heard a commotion outside, followed immediately by the sight of Hilda rushing through the doorway, carrying what looked like a small suitcase and with a frantic look of near-panic on her face.

"Oh, you poor man!" she cried. "Here, let me take a look."

Angus had followed her in at a safe distance. I threw him an accusing glance. *Why is Hilda here?* He shrugged his shoulders helplessly. He seemed sympathetic, but I could see that I was on my own. "Should we call a doctor?" she asked.

"No, of course not, Hilda, It's nothing, really. Just a scratch." I was bleeding profusely.

She opened the case. Inside were several bottles of liquid, pills, bandages, adhesive tape, a tourniquet, a splint, tweezers, scissors, a blood pressure monitor, and a snake-bite kit. I had to laugh in spite of my situation.

"Now, you just sit right here," she admonished, "and let me have a look at you." She looked at me critically. "Let me see your foot."

"Really, Hilda, it's all right."

She took my foot in her hands. Before I could protest, she asked, "Does this hurt?" and twisted it forty-five degrees.

"OOOWW." I spasmed backward, almost falling off the chair. "No, that's not too bad," I said, pulling my foot free.

She eyed me. "Are you sure?"

"I probably just need to walk around a little and loosen it up. I'm sure it's fine." I moved my foot out of her range.

"You know," she said, "you really should wear work boots out here. Didn't Angus tell you?" She turned around and gave poor Angus a scolding glance.

Turning back to my foot, she said, "We have to get those splinters out, but first, we'll put some iodine on."

IODINE?! OH NO! "Uh, actually, Hilda, it's just a few splinters, nothing at all, really. Once I get them out—"

"No, you need to put something on those cuts. You don't know what you could catch out here."

I remembered back when I was a kid, my mother put iodine on *everything*. It had been at least forty years, but the memory was vivid. "No, please, Hilda—"

"Oh, don't be silly," she said. She had already poured a liberal amount on a bandage and, before I could stop her, she plastered it against my open flesh. It felt like boiling acid. I howled like a coyote, closing my eyes tight and grimacing, just like I had forty years ago. It was excruciating, but after a few moments, the worst of the pain was over and I carefully opened my eyes.

"Now," Hilda said, "I'd better get those splinters out."

"Oh, no!" I said in a voice that left no room for interpretation. "I'll take the splinters out myself."

Hilda snorted. "Men are such babies," she said as she handed me the tweezers. "I'll go get you some nice tea."

I set to work removing the splinters. It was tedious, but not as bad as I had feared. By the time Hilda returned with my "nice tea," I was done. I taped a couple of large gauze bandages over the scrapes, forced down my tea, and was as good as new. Almost.

We finished moving the wood without further incident. The floor where we were to lay down the lines still needed to be painted white, but Angus offered to do that after I left. I protested briefly, then acquiesced. It was a minor job, but I was beat, and secretly glad for his offer. It was five o'clock. In the last ten hours, I had gone from almost starving to being as bloated as a boa constrictor; had almost broken my foot; had impaled myself on a cactus patch of rough wood; had been tortured with iodine; and had worked my muscles to exhaustion. I was done.

As I left the building, all I could focus on was getting into the car, driving home, and . . . uh oh. It dawned on me. I had left the car home and walked. *Oh, no!* My heart sank as I looked down Shore Road. Our house may as well have been in the next town. I had two choices: hobble home on one foot and make a complete fool of myself, or go back inside like a man, swallow my pride, and ask Angus to drive me home.

Thirty minutes later, I staggered through the front door. Jan was waiting for me with a tall cold drink in her hand (it was *not* iced tea!). Hilda had called and told her all about my ordeal and Jan very correctly assumed I would need a bracer or two. She smiled knowingly with a mixture of love, pity, and feminine chiding. I took the glass gratefully and limped to my chair, easing myself down carefully. Amanda bounded in and threw herself at me, hugging me tightly around my neck. I winced in agony, but her sweetness made me forget all about my pain.

"Did you finish, Grandpa?" she asked, fully expecting, I suppose, to go sailing the next day.

"Not quite, sweetheart," I said with a smile, "but we did make a good start. Tomorrow, we begin the actual work on the boat. Remember, it's going to take a long time. You'll be a year older by the time we finish her."

"That's okay, Grandpa, I understand."

I hugged her back, then asked Jan, "Is dinner ready?"

CHAPTER 8

....

The next morning dawned bright and clear. And early. When I awoke, it was not quite five o'clock. My aching body wanted to go back to sleep, but I knew it was useless to try; it was already like noontime outside. I dragged myself out of bed as quietly as possible, so as to not awaken Jan. Every muscle screamed in protest; my foot throbbed with each pulse; the abrasions on my arms and legs felt like a bad sunburn. I was, in short, a wreck. I limped to the shower, turned it on as hot as I could stand, and let it pound down on me. It was heavenly. It felt so good, in fact, that I stayed in the shower until all the hot water was gone. After, I spent a half hour or so stretching gently. Slowly, reluctantly, I was coming back to life.

Jan was up by then. She asked me how I felt.

"Not too bad," I lied.

She smiled. "Good. You didn't seem too chipper last night when you went to bed at eight-thirty. I was worried about you. Maybe you should take a day off, rest your old bones."

I snorted. "I can't take a day off. I've only *worked* a day! Anyway, today should be a lot easier. We're laying down the lines—no physical work involved, thank God."

"Laying down the lines? What does that mean?"

"In a nutshell, we make a full-size plan of the boat on the floor of the shop."

"I thought you already had plans."

"We do, but we also need the full-size plan so we can transfer the measurements directly to all the pieces as we build them. We'll take the dimensions from the architect's scale plans, blow them up to full-size, and transfer them, or lay them down, onto the floor. That's why it's called 'laying down the lines.' It's also called 'lofting' because years ago it was normally done up in the loft, out of the way of the actual building of the boats."

"Is that why you paint the floor white?"

"Yep. You want to be very sure of your measurements, so you need a clean surface to work on. I've never done it, of course, but the theory is pretty straightforward. I'm really looking forward to it."

Jan smiled. "Good. What do you want for breakfast?"

I grinned. "Oh, the usual—a dozen eggs, two stacks of pancakes, oatmeal, fruit, juice, toast, and coffee."

She laughed. "No, seriously."

"Eggs and pancakes would be great, honey, and some fruit."

"Okay," she said. "It'll be ready in twenty minutes. Go get dressed and wake up Amanda. I left you something on the bed."

I went back in our bedroom to get dressed. There on the bed were a pair of cotton work trousers and a long-sleeved plaid shirt. On the floor was a pair of brand-new work boots. *Good old Jannie,* I thought, smiling. I donned the trousers and shirt and slipped on the boots. Everything fit perfectly. I glanced at the mirror and posed. At least I *looked* like a boatbuilder!

I went to get Amanda, but again she was already up and about.

"Morning, sweetie," I said cheerfully. Amanda always made me feel better.

"Hi, Grandpa," she replied. "Are we laying down on the lines, today?"

"Something like that, honey," I said, chuckling. "Better hurry; breakfast will be ready soon."

"Okie dokie, karaoke."

As we ate, Jan noticed I was wincing quite a bit. She mentioned again she thought I should take the day off.

"I'll be fine," I said. "My real concern is Angus. He's a lot older than I am. If I feel like this, he must be in agony. Maybe that's why he wanted to lay down the lines today. Smart move. Anyway, I'll take it easy on him."

Jan looked at me askance. "You'd better take it easy on yourself. You're not as young as you used to be."

"Thanks."

After breakfast, Amanda and I got into the car and drove up. I didn't care what Angus thought; the way my foot felt, I didn't even consider walking. Upon arriving, we got out and walked up the path to the house. As we approached, I was thinking, *There really is no reason to start this early. We have an easy day ahead of us and I know Angus has to be at least as sore as I am. But he said seven, so seven it is.* Hilda greeted us again, radiating warmth when she looked at Amanda. She clearly was captivated by the child's charms. "Good morning, darling," Hilda said.

"Good morning, Missus McTigue," Amanda replied politely.

Hilda pretended to look disappointed. "Why don't you call me Hilda, dear?" she said. "We're old friends now."

But Amanda glanced at me. She knew the rules.

I smiled at Hilda. "It's just that her parents insist upon her showing respect for her elders."

Amanda seemed mildly disappointed, but then brightened almost immediately. "I know, can I call you Aunt Hilda?"

Hilda beamed. "Why, of course you can, darling." They both looked to me for approval.

I shrugged, smiling. "If that's okay with Hilda, it's fine with me." Then, cautiously, I asked, "How's Angus?"

"Oh, he's fine. He's down at the boathouse. Waiting."

Waiting? I choked back a snort. "Guess we better get going, then. Thanks, Hilda," I said. "Let's go, Amanda, we're burning daylight!"

"Oh, Amanda, dear," Hilda said, "I'm going berrying this morning before I feed the animals. Would you like to go?"

She wrinkled her nose. "What's that?"

"We go into the woods and pick berries," Hilda explained.

"For *free*?!"

That made Hilda laugh. "Of course."

"Oh, boy, I'd love to go. Can I help feed the animals, too?"

"Amanda . . ." I began to admonish, but Hilda just smiled.

"It's all right, James," she said. Then, to Amanda, "Of course you can, sweetheart, anytime."

"Yay!" Amanda cried, then caught herself. She turned to me. "Can you get along without me this morning?"

"We'll try," I said.

"Goodie," she bubbled, and off they went to pick berries, grinning and chatting like old friends.

So, I continued down to the boathouse alone. I was anxious to get going but still concerned about Angus. I hoped he was all right. When I walked in, he was standing at the bench, studying the plans. When he looked up, I couldn't believe my eyes—he looked ten years younger!

"Good morning, Angus."

"Morning."

"How do you feel?" I probed tentatively.

He looked puzzled. "Fine, why?"

"Oh, nothing, nothing at all. It's just that I was a little sore this morning. I didn't know how you might feel."

He just snuffled. I waited in vain for elaboration.

Over in the corner was a freshly painted section of the floor. Nearby, there was a small stack of long, flexible slats we would use to make the curved lines, a couple of straightedges of different lengths for the straight lines, a chalk line, and a tape measure. In the middle of the floor lay the iron ballast keel, on its side. I wondered how he had got all this accomplished.

"Did you work all night?" I asked in jest.

"No, it wasn't too hard. I painted the floor right after you left—it was still early—then I got the forklift and brought the keel over. The layout tools were all together in the storage closet. Nothing to it." He glanced at my feet. "Nice boots," he said, with the faintest trace of a smile.

I grinned. "Thanks. Jan got them for me yesterday. Steel toes." I couldn't always tell when Angus was serious and when he was jabbing me, but I was starting to feel more comfortable around him. I liked him.

"How's the foot?"

"It'll be sore for a while, but I'll survive."

"Good. Well, let's get to it. This really is easy work, but there's a lot to it. Don't want to burn any more daylight."

"Great," I said. I was ready.

"Where's Amanda?"

"She deserted me. Apparently, she thought it would be more fun to feed the animals and pick berries than to hang out with a couple of old guys like us."

Angus chuckled, then turned more serious. "She's a bright little girl. You're very lucky." I was sure I detected the merest hint of sadness in his voice.

We walked over to the old bench and he began to tell me more about the plans. He explained, in plain language, how we would transfer this pretty picture into something full-size on the floor that would allow us to measure, cut, shape, and verify virtually every piece of the basic hull. I had tried to do this in my mind many times, but having the benefit of his knowledge and experience brought many of my questions into sharper focus. Slowly and meticulously, he described each step until he was sure I understood. Because of his natural reticence, I was expecting difficulty understanding him. Instead, his explanations were simple and precise. He clearly was in his element. In a half hour, he had covered everything.

"Got it?" he asked.

My head was spinning with all the new knowledge. "I think so," I said.

"Don't worry," he said with a grin, "it's a lot easier to do it than it is to explain. So, let's do it."

I agreed. We began snapping lines, and drawing parallel lines, and erecting perpendicular lines, and measuring diagonal lines, until the floor looked as if a group of kindergartners had been let loose on a giant sketch pad. We labeled everything clearly as we went along so as not to get confused by all the lines and intersections. It was easy to see how the untrained eye could take one look at this gibberish and retreat to a simpler endeavor like, say, calculus. But, as we proceeded, the future boat became more and more real. I was mesmerized.

In no time at all, Hilda and Amanda appeared at the door with something that grabbed the attention of my senses. I looked up, surprised.

"Hi," I said. "What's up?"

"We brought you a treat," Amanda said.

"But it's only . . ." I looked at my watch. Amazingly, it was ten o'clock. We had worked for three hours! Not at all like yesterday, I thought. Hilda had baked a fresh blackberry pie that filled the boathouse with its delicious aroma. All of a sudden, I was ravenous. We dropped everything and fell to. In a matter of minutes, the pie was history and Duncan was noisily cleaning the plates. We chatted for a while as we basked in the afterglow of the wonderful treat.

"Hilda," I said, "I have to tell you, that was delicious."

"Why, thank you," she replied, "but I never could have done it without Amanda. She picked and cleaned the berries, and helped me with the crust. She's a good little cook." Amanda smiled proudly. She was enjoying her new adventures and seemed drawn to Hilda. She asked a few questions about the boat, looked around to see what was happening, then was off with Hilda to feed the animals. Angus and I returned to what we were doing, working pleasantly through the rest of the morning.

The plan was taking shape, now. We had all the parallel horizontal lines marked down and the vertical station lines laid out perpendicular to them. From these intersecting points, we could refer to the set of plans and measure the offsets which would, if done correctly, show us how to construct each piece. Angus was very deliberate while we were doing this. He kept emphasizing that any mistake made now would transfer to the finished boat. It was a lot easier and cheaper, he said, to erase a line on the floor than to recut a twenty-foot board. No argument there.

When we reached a convenient stopping point, we broke for lunch. I went to find Amanda and had to drag her away from feeding the turkeys. On the short drive home, we chatted excitedly about our respective mornings. I had called Jan before we left, so lunch was all ready for us when we got there. Amanda and I tore through it like a tornado. Jan kept asking about our morning, but we were so eager to get back that not much was said. The plan was occupying my mind totally, now; it was difficult trying to think of anything else. In ten minutes, we were done with lunch and hurrying to get back to our respective tasks. Jan gave us an indulgent smile as we raced out the door with a hasty "thanks" and "see you later."

Angus was already in the boathouse (did he ever leave it?) when I returned.

"We're ready to draw the construction profile," he said.

"Great." I was looking forward to this part the most. The construction profile is an exact outline of the shape of the hull. It's the first thing that actually looks like the future boat; it kind of gives one encouragement after all the preliminary stuff.

We performed this task with little fanfare. While the construction profile looked impressive, most of the really exacting work was already done. Still, it was taking longer than I thought it should. I knew Angus was going slower, giving me the opportunity to absorb all we were doing. With my usual impatience, I kept trying to move things along; with his usual deliberation, Angus kept holding me back. It was a perfect match.

By late afternoon, the profile was completed. I stared at it, giddy with excitement.

"Wait here!" I said to Angus and flew out the door. I ran over to the house to fetch Amanda. She was in the kitchen with Hilda.

"Amanda," I cried, "do you want to see what our boat looks like?"

"Oh, boy, Grandpa, I sure do! C'mon, Aunt Hilda!"

We raced back over to the boathouse. Angus was standing by the bench, looking impatient. But when Amanda ran in, all excited, his entire demeanor changed. His face softened as he smiled tenderly at the bubbling child. Amanda stood before the huge drawing, transfixed, her eyes wide with wonder.

"It's *byoo*-tiful, Grandpa," she gushed, "and so big! How long before it's finished?"

CHAPTER 9

·····································

The boat now began to take shape, slowly but deliberately. Angus was right, of course. The work was exacting in the extreme and could not be rushed. The more I watched him, the more I appreciated the immense knowledge, skill, and patience he possessed. We might spend a half-day working on one piece, but when we put it in place, it seemed to have grown there naturally. He was a master. The pieces were never forced but fitted together, tight, before fastening. And when they were finally fastened, the feeling of strength was palpable. I would often hit a finished joint with my palm to test its integrity. It always responded with a gratifying "thunk" that brought a smile to my face.

Piece by painstaking piece, our boat grew before our eyes. It actually *looked* like a boat. The shape was unmistakable, the lovely curves of the hull arched gracefully fore and aft. We were really doing it!

Amanda was also having the time of her life. The boat was still paramount, but she was experiencing so many new things, especially with Hilda, that she needed even more hours in her lengthy summer days. Hilda had practically adopted her, and her feelings toward the older woman bordered on reverence. And when Hilda met Jan, they also discovered a mutual affinity that quickly blossomed into a deep friendship. The three of them became "the girls," continually performing "chores" like berry picking or baking or animal feeding, or they would go shopping for the different clothes we would all need soon enough as fall, and then winter, loomed.

But for now, the days were sunny and long and full of new adventures. The work progressed steadily as I settled into an easy routine, seeking to emulate Angus's methodical pace. And my physical condition changed— my wounds were now a distant memory, I had lost a little weight, my muscles felt stronger, my hands had gotten calloused, and, at the end of a well-spent day, I was pleasantly tired. I slept like a new baby.

Toward the end of summer, we had been working on our boat for almost two months. We had laid down her lines, allowing us to measure every piece full-size before cutting and fitting; we had leveled the iron ballast keel and fastened the wooden keel to it, upon which everything else would rest; we had built and installed the molds which would define the exact shape of the inside of the hull; we had installed the ribbands the entire length of the boat over the molds, against which the finished frames would lay; and we had bent and installed the frames inside the ribbands, against which the planking would fasten. The molds and the ribbands were strictly for laying out and sizing. Despite the considerable work involved in their construction and installation, they would eventually be removed and discarded. They could be used over and over to build more boats identical to this one, but ours was a one-off, so all that work and material got put aside.

So, toward the end of summer, there she sat, ready for the planking, which would define her essence more than any other stage of her building. I was thrilled at the prospect and was certain I detected a trace of anticipation in Angus. Planking is an almost mystical process. It's when the skeleton begins to look like a real boat. With each piece, the boat looks more and more finished. It's an illusion, of course. Even after the planking is fully installed, the boat is nowhere near completion. But it's a very sweet illusion that comes from a uniquely enjoyable task.

Long planks of amenable wood are cut to shape, put in a steam bath for a half hour or so if necessary to make them limber, then removed, and, while still hot, bent around the frames to the shape of the hull. After they are bent and clamped to the frames, they are fastened, tight. As the plank cools and dries, it takes a "set" to the shape of the hull and will stay there indefinitely without further stress. If all goes well, Angus said, we should do a plank around per day, meaning a starboard plank, a port plank, and a stern plank of the same width. Of course, all did *not* go well at first. Because of my lack of experience, various problems arose, mistakes were made, and it took a while to find our rhythm. But when we did, it went like clock-work. Each day began the same way. The process for cutting and fitting a plank is the same for each plank, so that became routine. Pretty soon, we could foresee the entire process—how long it would take to cut the plank, shape it, steam it, bend and clamp it, and fasten it. This is a huge oversim-plification, but the sequence became very familiar and we actually started getting the three planks done early, leaving part of the afternoon free. It was the most fun I'd had up until then. And there was an added bonus: during this stage, a third pair of hands can save a lot of time and running around. Amanda pitched right in and did herself proud, fetching tools, nails, clamps, anything we needed but didn't have right at hand. She had a stake in it now. It really was "our" boat.

Many afternoons when we finished early, I would steal back out to the shed, ease myself into the "crying chair," and spend long moments admir-ing the boat. I was proud to be building something of such lasting beauty. Sometimes, I would study the plans again, seeing and understanding even more with my newfound experience. It was a deeply gratifying time for me.

On one of those days when we had finished early, Angus asked me if I would like to take a walk around the property. All during the building of the boat, I had badgered him with endless questions about the home- stead—its history, his family, the different buildings, the animals. It was just such a lovely spot that I couldn't help myself. Most of his answers were terse or downright evasive, so I was pleasantly surprised at the invitation and jumped at it immediately. Amanda was off with Duncan, so the two of us set out.

As we walked along, he began filling me in. He told me the property was about three hundred acres. It used to be much larger, but the years had taken their toll. The original plot was settled by his great-great-grandfather well before the Civil War. Thomas McTigue was also a boatbuilder, who had emigrated from Scotland. The spot he chose to settle was perfect—there was an endless supply of wood, plenty of competent labor close by, and the river led down to the Gulf of Maine. The McTigues were hard workers. Between the farm and building boats, they had a good life and prospered. When the Civil War came along, the economy took off. The Union Navy badly needed boats, and Thomas got a huge government contract. For five years, the yard worked double shifts, turning out a steady stream of boats of all sizes. He made a fortune. After the war, Moosaquit returned to being what it remained to this day—a rustic, sleepy little village.

But Thomas had been a canny businessman. By investing wisely, he had founded a family dynasty. Children and grandchildren came along. They all learned a trade and they all got an education. Only after that did they choose their life's course. The descendants became successful busi- nessmen, cabinet makers, teachers, army officers, lawyers, one even going to the Maine senate. Through it all, there was always at least one son who continued the family boatbuilding business. The McTigue name gained renown, and tycoons would come from all over, eager to have their yachts built at the prestigious McTigue Boatyard.

Walking on, Angus continued his narrative. He was proud of his heritage and he would point out this barn, or that outbuilding, and give a brief history in response to my questions. I was fascinated by the whole story, but I could sense in his manner that he knew the time-honored way of building boats, his way, was dying. He talked me down through the generations until he got to his own young manhood, then kind of trailed off. I knew better than to try to pry, so we continued in silence for a while.

Then he said, "I want to show you something." He led me toward a path that wound off into a thicket. We walked for a short distance, the thicket ended, and we were standing on a bluff overlooking the river. Just below us lay a small graveyard. It was a serenely beautiful setting. He motioned me toward a bench where I sat down reverently.

"Your family?" I asked.

"Yes," he replied. "My forbears all the way back to old Tom are buried here. He laid it out in 1853. Hilda and I come out here often, especially in the fall. It's a great spot for contemplation."

"Do you and Hilda have any children?"

"No," he said, looking out over the little graveyard, perhaps anticipating my next question.

"What's going to become of all this?"

"I don't know," he answered quietly. "There's no one left in the family to take it over. It seems a shame, after all these years, to sell it off, but that's probably what we'll have to do. It's the way these things happen, I guess. The property was originally over a thousand acres, but it kept getting cut up. Children would inherit a piece, then sell it, or their kids would sell it. That's why my father donated the property for the nature preserve. He wanted at least some of the land to be protected for future generations."

"I didn't know the preserve came from this property," I said. "It's a treasure. I go there often."

We talked on for quite some time. Angus seemed comfortable relating his story. This was a first, so I just sat back and listened, feeling privileged to be taken into his confidence. Over the brief time we knew each other, I had developed a great deal of respect for him. He exuded enormous inner strength, confidence, and humility—a rare combination of traits in any man. Conversely, he seemed to be getting more comfortable with me, more familiar. He even loosened up with an occasional joke, something I would have dismissed as a virtual impossibility until recently. In short, we were becoming good friends.

He continued as the sun lowered behind us. He told me about that Sunday long ago, when the news of Pearl Harbor flashed over the radio, changing everything forever. He tried to enlist, but because of his background, he was sent to Miami to oversee the construction of PT boats on the Miami River. He was twenty-four years old. While there, he met a pretty eighteen-year-old English girl who had been sent by her family to America before the war broke out. It was love at first sight. His face lit up with a remembering smile as he related the story all these years later. Those were uncertain times and things moved along quickly. Within three months, they were married. When the war ended, they moved back to Maine and settled into the pleasant routine of married life on the farm. His mother had died earlier and his father had retired, leaving everything to him. The farm provided a good living, but his passion was building boats. He elevated the McTigue name to a new level of respect as the post-war boom fed the demand for more recreation. He prospered for many years, until the advent of fiberglass began to eat away at, then collapse, the market for wooden boats. He cut back his help until he was working almost totally by himself. But he was a determined man. He continued doing what he loved, turning out an occasional boat, but mostly doing repairs and renovations. There was no rancor or remorse in his tone, just an honest relating of events. He had a strong spirit and seemed to deal with everything that was thrown at him without complaint.

Angus was winding down now. He seemed relieved, like he had gotten something off his chest. He looked at me a little sheepishly. "I guess I've rambled on for quite a while," he said.

"Not at all," I countered. "I've enjoyed it. Ever since the first day I came here, I've admired this property and wondered about it. Thanks for filling me in. I think you're a lucky man."

Angus eyed me and his manner changed slightly, I'm not even sure how. But he gave me a strange smile and assumed a far-off expression, as if he were contemplating something of weight. Then, "We'd better get home," he said. "Thanks for the company."

"My pleasure. I'd like to do it again." I meant it.

When we got back to the house, Hilda, Jan, and Amanda were waiting. They surprised us with a sumptuous dinner, complete with English bone china, linen napkins, and sterling silverware. We ate, drank, and laughed well into the evening—a perfect end to a perfect day.

CHAPTER 10

....

As the planking progressed, I noticed the days beginning to shorten. It was subtle at first, the sun inching lower just a tad each day as we walked home in the afternoon. Labor Day was approaching, and with it a sea change in our comfortable little routine. Summer would be unofficially over; even though the calendar told us we had three more weeks, we knew better in this corner of the world. The mornings would arrive a little later every day, with a definite crispness in the air greeting us when we arose. The evenings would come sooner, too, almost imperceptibly at first, then with startling swiftness. And, of course, Amanda would begin school, setting off another exciting chapter in her life. Her excitement was at a fever pitch and it warmed us all.

For my part, I looked forward to autumn with an almost childlike glee. It had been many years since Jan and I had stayed in Maine any later than Labor Day. Memories of this fabled season were rushing back to me—the cool days, the frosty evenings, pumpkins, apple season, the smell of burning leaves, the ethereal beauty of the woods as they changed from a deep green to a riot of color that almost defied belief. Summer in Maine is wonderful, but autumn is my favorite. It defines the essence of New England. As the days shorten, the pace slows down. The "summer people" wisely head south to continue their warm-weather pursuits. The kids are back in school. The whole town takes on an entirely different personality, one more settled, more relaxed. People still scurry around, but with much less urgency. The pressure is off, so to speak.

And so, the little village eased comfortably back to what it had been for most of its three-hundred-year history—a quaint, quiet community whose residents lived more in concert with Mother Nature. The firewood was cut, split, and stacked; the basements were sealed off and insulated; the excess fruits and vegetables were canned; the winter clothes were either purchased new or brought out of storage for another year. All this and much more was done in anticipation of what everyone knew was coming—a long, hard Maine winter. Through it all, there is no fanfare, no frantic sense of urgency. It is simply the way of life in these parts. Angus and I moved steadily along with the planking until, one day in mid-October, only one plank on each side remained—the "shutter" plank.

This boat was planked in two distinct operations: from the top, or "sheer" plank, down to the maximum curve of the bilge, and from the bottom, or "garboard" plank, up to the same place. This is because the natural curves of the boat's sides and bottom make it almost impossible to do a neat and tight job otherwise. When the planking from these two directions comes together (if all goes well), one plank is left to seal, or shutter, the hull. The shutter is one long, fairly uniform plank that ties the entire planking job together. It is a truly beautiful thing to see. It is also a seemingly impossible thing to actually build. In our case, the plank needed to be just over twenty-five feet long, twist one way and then the other, match the curve of the hull, fit perfectly tight on the inside of the hull against both the plank above it and the plank below it, have a concave curve on its inside surface to lay tight against the bent frames, have a slight bevel on both outside edges so as to take the caulking that makes the joints waterproof, and angle perfectly into the stem forward and into the transom aft, without being even one-eighth of an inch too long or too short. That's all.

Angus eyed me mischievously. "Tomorrow's a big day," he said. "Are you up to it?"

I hoped I had misunderstood him. "Up to what, exactly?"

He grinned. "You've come far, Jim. Why don't you make the shutter by yourself?"

"Uh, Angus," I stammered, "I—I really don't think I—"

"You wanted to do this, remember? Look, it's the same as any of the other fifty or so planks we've already made." He grinned. "Sort of. Just take your time with the measurements, check them twice, and then cut them out r-e-e-al careful. Nothing to it. Let's see what you've got." The gauntlet was thrown.

I laughed out loud. "And where will you be?" I asked.

"I've got a doctor's appointment," he said. "I should be back before noon. But I'm telling you, you can do this. And, if you can do this, you can do everything else required for this boat."

It was meant to be a comforting little speech, but I wasn't so sure. I glanced over at the gaping hole that ran the entire length of the hull. It was fraught with peril—the angles, the curves. Fit one plank to fill the entire void, tight, so as to repel tons of raging sea for the next forty years. It wasn't possible.

"Okay," I said. "See you at seven."

On our way home that afternoon, Amanda asked, "Why are we walking so fast, Grandpa?"

"Hmm? Are we? I'm sorry, honey, I didn't realize," I answered. But I did realize. I was in a hurry to get home, to study up on shutters. Angus was generous with his praise, but I knew that fitting a shutter was not at all like fitting the other planks. I was hoping maybe with my newly gained experience and some serious cramming tonight, I could get through the next day without too much embarrassment.

As we came through the front door, Jan was there with a tall, cold drink. "Not tonight, honey, thanks." I went straight to my study and began opening my books. Feverishly, I read again for the umpteenth time the steps involved in making the shutter. I had read about them so many times already that I knew what was written before I got to it. But still I forged on, looking for any new clue, any scrap of information I might have missed the previous twenty times.

Presently, Jan came in. "So, what are you up to?" she asked.

"Oh, just checking a couple of things," I said casually. I had seven books open in front of me.

Jan smiled. "Do you think you'll have time for dinner?"

"Already?" I looked at my watch. It was getting late and I had read nothing I didn't already know. I was doomed. I hadn't felt like this since the night before finals in high school. I let out a groan.

"What's the problem?" Jan asked.

"Angus wants me to make the shutter plank tomorrow. By myself."

"So?"

"So, I've never done it before and it's very involved."

"You've been making planks for an entire month," she reasoned.

I sighed and began to explain the unique vagaries of that particular piece.

She interrupted. "Big deal. You take a little more time, you take a little more care. What's the problem?"

"Yeah, that's what Angus said, too. Didn't make me feel any better, though."

Jan sat down beside me. "You're being silly," she said. "You've worked with wood your whole life. This is just another thing made of wood. Besides, Angus has confidence in you; that must mean something."

She had me there. Maybe I *was* being silly. It's just a piece of wood, after all. You cut it, you shape it, you bend it, and it fits. Yeah, what was I thinking?

"You know, Jannie," I exclaimed, "you're right! This is no more than a logical progression for me. It's the same as anything else that I haven't done before." I gave her a sheepish smile. "I must be getting old. Thanks, hon. Let's eat."

Next morning, I strutted into the boathouse with barely concealed confidence. I had exorcised my initial fears and now realized how baseless were my earlier reservations. Angus was there, as usual. He had picked out a suitable plank and laid it out on four sawhorses. It was a flawless piece of mahogany, well over the twenty-five feet we needed, a good eight inches wide, and an inch and a quarter thick. It must have cost a fortune. A lesser man would have quailed at the thought of cutting into that pristine piece of timber; one slip-up and it's off to the trash pile. I stifled a momentary tug of doubt and got right to it. Angus was watching me, a boyish grin tugging at the corners of his mouth. He was having fun, I could tell.

I gathered the tools I would need, took a deep breath, and began transferring measurements. The process is necessarily tedious—everything must be done to the thickness of a pencil line—so I was being extremely cautious. As I worked on the plank, I was again struck by its beauty.

"Angus," I said, "this is a gorgeous piece of wood. Where did it come from?"

"I picked that up in Miami when I was down there during the war. It's Cuban mahogany. The log came to the boatyard just before the war ended and I sort of requisitioned it. The government was closing down the facility and simply discarding everything. I couldn't bear it, so I asked the chief and he told me to take anything I wanted. Cost me a bundle to get it home."

"So, this board is more than fifty years old?"

"Yup."

"What would it cost now?"

"Well," he drawled, "*if* you could find a piece that size, and *if* you could buy it, which you can't because of the embargo, that single board would probably cost as much as a small car."

I got a chill. I've owned special pieces of wood for years, waiting for just the right time to use them, but never on a scale like this. I glanced again down the length of it. It seemed to be even longer now, more precious than before. My mouth was strangely dry. I kept thinking about this lovely piece of wood—how it had traveled from the forests of Cuba, to a boatyard in Miami to help construct the mightiest navy the world has ever seen, to the woods of Maine, to sit for over fifty years, waiting for this moment in time to fulfill its destiny under my hand. It was a cool October morning, but I could feel beads of sweat on my forehead.

"See you later," Angus said.

"Wait!"

Angus looked back, startled. "What's the problem?"

I realized I had reacted a little too strongly. "Just want to know when you'll be back, that's all."

Angus smiled. "I told you, later on this morning. You okay?"

"Yeah, sure. So, you want me to lay this out by myself?"

"Yes, and cut it, too, if I'm not back."

"Are you sure?" My recently acquired confidence was fading fast.

"You'll be fine," Angus said, trying to allay my fears. "It's just a piece of wood."

"Yeah, that's worth more than a car."

"A *small* car," Angus corrected. "Be careful, and remember, check and recheck *before* you cut anything. We'll install it after lunch." Off he went, whistling. He seemed awfully chipper to be going to the doctor.

I went back to work, but with considerably less cockiness. I tried to bury my negative thoughts, but they seemed to be bubbling just below the surface, eager to attack the slightest weakness in my will. *Just another board,* I told myself, *just another board.* "That's right," I answered myself, "just another board that's absolutely irreplaceable." It wasn't starting out well.

I gathered myself and set to work. After transferring measurements for what seemed like hours, I looked at my watch—nine-thirty. I went over the layout to make sure everything was in order. Everything was. So, I rechecked it. Still good. *When is Angus coming back?* At this moment, thankfully, Amanda came in with my morning snack.

"How's it going, Grandpa?" she said.

"Couldn't be better," I replied with all the aplomb I could muster.

"I brought you some ice cream we just made. It's peach."

"You made this? It looks delicious."

"It is. I licked the beaters and the bowl, then Duncan finished the job." She was enjoying herself immensely and it showed in everything she did. Her schoolwork was topnotch, her room was always neat, and she was showing a real flair in the kitchen under the guidance of Jan and Hilda. I couldn't have been prouder of her.

I sat down gratefully and devoured the ice cream. It *was* good. "Almost as good as Littlefield's," I chided. She gave me her mock scowl and we laughed. Duncan waited with uncharacteristic patience for his turn and then break time was over.

"Time to go back to work, Grandpa," Amanda teased as she picked up the dish and returned to the house.

And, so it was. I reluctantly returned to the board and checked again the lines I had just checked fifteen minutes earlier. Perfect. Nothing left now but to cut it out. I gazed again at that perfect plank, lying there at my mercy. *Just another board*, I reminded myself and fetched the saw. After one more quick check of the layout, I began cutting. Beginning at the stern end, I proceeded along the upper line, as carefully as I have ever cut anything in my life. It was very slow work. The wood was hard, the line was curved, and the angle of the cut changed continually. But the saw was sharp and my concentration keen. The cutting proceeded uneventfully down the length of the plank, splitting the pencil line perfectly. My reservations began to subside as the plank changed shape. Presently, the top edge was finished. *Almost half-way*, I thought.

I then began cutting back the other way, from the forward end, along the lower line. After a half hour or so, that was done. I was immersed in my cutting, feeling better as I went along. Only the ends remained. They were angled and beveled, presenting a minor challenge, but with patient diligence, they also succumbed to my skills. I carefully went along the entire length of both sides, cleaning up any minor imperfections with a wood plane. After the ends were touched up with a small block plane, the piece was finished.

Then, having worked up close on the plank for the better part of two hours, I stepped back to admire my efforts. My heart sank as I took in the entire length. The once-beautiful piece of wood was transformed. It swooped one way, then took a devious turn the opposite way. It was straight for a short distance, then made a small "S", as if it couldn't make up its mind which way it wanted to go. The bevels likewise twisted to and fro, in a screw-like fashion. I was horrified. I looked at the hull. There was no apparent relationship between the plank and the space it was supposed to fill. *What have I done?* I thought. I must have been out of my mind to even attempt such a thing! This revered piece of fifty-year-old mahogany was ruined, to be used now only for scrap or patches. I was alone with my thoughts in my private little hell. *What will Angus say? This is how I justify his trust?*

"How's it going?"

I jumped as if stuck with a cattle prod. "Angus!" I cried. "You're back!"

"As I said I would be," he replied. "Are you okay? You look a little pale."

"No, no, I'm fine, just fine," I said, trying to think of a way to break the news.

He walked over to the plank. "So, you got it done."

"Angus, I'm so—"

"Looks pretty good, too."

"Huh?"

"The plank. It looks good."

"But . . ."

"How long did it take?"

"Uh, actually, I just finished."

"Really?" He glanced at his watch. "I suppose it's better not to rush it." In my fragile emotional state, I couldn't tell if he was toying with me or not.

"After lunch, we'll steam 'er up and fasten 'er in. See you in about an hour." And he left.

A reprieve! I raced out to find Amanda. She was out in the pasture playing with the ducks. "Come on, honey, time for lunch."

"Coming, Grandpa."

On the way home and all through lunch, I could think of nothing but my imminent shame. When Jan asked me how my morning went, I shifted my eyes evasively. "Okay," I said without conviction.

Jan sighed. "What happened?"

"Why do you say that?"

"Because of the way you're acting. What did you do?"

"How am I acting?"

"What did you do?"

"I'm not a child."

"What did you *do*?"

I groaned. "I ruined a priceless piece of mahogany. Angus went to the doctor and left me to cut the shutter plank and I ruined it. It's a mess."

"Oh, honey, I'm sorry," she said, this time with genuine pity. "What did Angus say?"

"He didn't say anything; just looked at it and tried to act as if nothing happened. Maybe he can fix it, but I doubt it."

"You mean Angus saw it was ruined and didn't say anything?"

"Not exactly. He said, 'it looks good.' That's what he said."

Jan looked puzzled. "But if he said it looks good, how can it be ruined?"

"You don't understand. He was just being nice, that's all. You know how he is. Right now, he's probably trying figure out how he can salvage some of that wood. It came from Cuba fifty years ago, and now I've ruined it."

"Fifty years!" Jan exclaimed. "Wow!"

"Now do you see why I'm so upset? I wanted to wait for him to get back from the doctor, but he said I could handle it. I feel terrible."

"What are you going to do?"

"What else can I do? I'll go back and face the music. I hope he understands."

Jan gave me an encouraging smile. "Angus thinks the world of you, honey. I'm sure he'll get over this."

"I hope so."

Amanda and I walked back after lunch. "Why are you walking so slow, Grandpa?" she asked.

"Am I, honey? I didn't realize." Amanda shook her little head, apparently unable to figure out how fast or slow we should be walking.

When we entered the boathouse, the steam box was already set up and cranking out heat. Angus was puttering around, setting out what we would need for the job. It took me a moment to grasp the significance—we really *were* going to try to install the thing! I sauntered over to the plank to see what he had done to fix it. It lay where I had left it, undisturbed. As casually as I could, I walked around it, inspecting every inch of both sides of its twenty-five-foot length. It hadn't been touched. Strange.

"Hi, Angus," I said.

"Afternoon."

"What are you doing?"

"Getting the steam box ready so we can put in the shutter." He was a fountain of information.

"I can see that. But how do you know it'll fit?"

"We'll see pretty soon."

"Did you check the measurements?"

"No. Didn't you?"

"Well, yeah, several times."

"So?"

This was killing me. "Angus, I'm sorry. I tried my best, but I guess I just wasn't up to it. I've ruined your beautiful plank."

He didn't even slow down. "What are you talking about?"

"The plank," I reiterated, "I'm afraid I've ruined it."

"Were you careful marking the lines?"

"Of course."

"And you checked them?"

"Yes, several times, but—"

"Then how could you have ruined it? It looks fine to me."

"It does?" I looked at it again. It seemed even more tortured than before. "Look at it," I said. I was exasperated and embarrassed. "It's all bent, and curved, and twisted. There's no way it can go into that perfectly straight opening."

Angus stopped what he was doing. He put a kindly hand on my shoulder, led me to the chair, and motioned me to sit down. He began talking to me in a tone he might use to explain something to Duncan.

"Look," he said, "I guess you've never done this before, so you don't understand how it works. That board starts out nice and straight, right?

"Uh-huh."

"But the boat is curved, in at least two directions, right?"

I nodded sheepishly. "Yes." I felt like I was in first grade.

"I've seen them look much worse than that. It's amazing how they come around after they've been in the steam for a while. You'll see. By this afternoon, you'll be getting out the plank for the other side. Why, once we get that thing started, she'll drop in that hole like a baby in its mother's arms." He grinned maliciously. "And if it doesn't, I know some tricks that'll *make* that stubborn stick go where she doesn't want to go. Have faith."

And he was right, again. Once the plank was properly persuaded by the steam, she bent around just as sweet as you please. We began at the stern and swept it around the curve of the hull, the odd-looking plank fairly snuggling into the opening. It went like clockwork. When we got to the bow, the end of the plank nestled into its permanent home with nary a whimper. I knew at that moment exactly how a new father felt. We spent the next hour fastening this all-important plank while it was still limber from its steam bath. The starboard side was planked. Not finished, mind you, but planked. I allowed myself to slide down onto the chair, emotionally drained. Angus said, "I'll be right back," and went over to the house.

While he was gone, I simply sat and viewed the hull with wonder. What I felt at that moment was far beyond my ability to express. I knew there was much work yet to be done, but if we had quit right then, I would have been satisfied. To have had the opportunity to work with such a master and to have become good friends with him in the bargain was more than I could have hoped for. I just wanted to savor the moment.

Angus came back from wherever he went. "It's a great day," he said. "Feel like a hike?"

It *was* a great day. I had been inside all day, too preoccupied with my job to notice the autumn spectacle going on outside. "Sure," I said, pleased. I motioned toward his hand. "What's in the bag?"

"You'll see. Come on."

CHAPTER 11

....

Angus and I left the boathouse and walked along a familiar path. We had spent considerable time together recently on these little jaunts and I was learning my way around the property pretty well. Sometimes we talked, sometimes we simply ambled along in silence, absorbing the quiet beauty of the place. These walks had become almost therapeutic for both of us; he seemed to draw inspiration from the land that he loved so much, while I looked forward to his discourses on the homestead, the history of the area, and his encyclopedic knowledge of boatbuilding. Our friendship was growing stronger, more comfortable as the months rolled on. On this particular trip, however, he said very little. In short order, I could see that we were headed for the little cemetery, one of my favorite spots.

We arrived and sat down on a bench. The sun was shining brilliantly in a clear blue sky behind us, bathing the entire valley below in a golden glow. The trees were at their peak of color, their vibrant beauty shimmering in a soft, cool breeze. We sat in silence for a while, content to simply drink in the magnificent autumn afternoon.

Presently, he turned to me. "I want to tell you something," he said.

I nodded, waiting for him to continue.

"I've been building boats for over fifty years," he began. "Now, I don't want you to get a swelled head, but that shutter plank you made was as pretty as any I've ever seen. It went in better than you or I or anyone would have any right to expect. You've done yourself proud."

My mouth surely hung open. I hoped I wasn't blushing. As friends, we were constantly exchanging kidding insults and jabs, but such honest praise caught me off guard.

"Gosh, Angus, thank you" was all I could muster.

He smiled. "You're welcome. You know, it's customary at certain stages of one's education to celebrate. So, I propose a toast."

He reached into his bag and pulled out a bottle half full of amber liquid and two crystal tumblers. There was no label on the bottle. It looked old.

"My father gave me this when Hilda and I got married," he said. "It's a single-malt scotch, pot distilled. Comes from a small distillery near my ancestral home, just north of Dundee. I've never seen it over here—too small an amount to export, I guess. I was never much of a drinker, but my father wanted me to have something of our Scottish ancestry. Told me I might want to mark special occasions with it. With your permission, I'll consider this one of those occasions."

Hearing such praise from someone I so respected took my breath away. The Nobel Prize wouldn't have meant nearly as much. He set the two glasses down on the bench and poured a couple of ounces in each one. He handed me one, we clinked glasses, and he said, "To a job well done."

WOW! I took a small sip, swished it around, and felt the potency as I swallowed. It had a definite smoky, peaty taste unlike anything else I had ever drunk, but it was not at all harsh. It rolled smoothly over my palate before descending down my throat, radiating its warmth all the way. I could almost hear the bagpipes!

We sat silent for several minutes, sniffing, sipping, swishing, and swallowing. I couldn't have been more content.

"Angus," I said presently, "can I ask you something?"

"Shoot."

I hesitated briefly, hoping I wouldn't break the spell of such a perfect moment. "I've wondered for quite some time, what made you change your mind about building the boat?"

He looked at me in his frank, unsettling way, then turned and gazed off into the distance at the river and the woods below. He remained silent for several long moments then took another deliberate sip. "A couple of things," he said finally. "When you came to me for help, I saw something in your eye. I've loved boats and boatbuilding all my life, so I understand. But even though I was touched by your enthusiasm, I couldn't do it, for various reasons. After you left, I realized I had been brusque, and I felt bad about it. Then, when I saw you at Littlefield's, I merely wanted to apologize. But you were so gracious, and Amanda was so sweet, that I began to waver. After getting home, talking with Hilda, and doing a lot of thinking, I decided to do one more boat if you still wanted to. I already had the plans and the keel; it seemed like a natural. Besides, Amanda was so disappointed, I felt terrible.

I teased him a little. "So, it wasn't me but Amanda who changed your mind?"

Angus chuckled. "In a sense, I guess so. She's a beautiful little girl who wants to build something with her grandfather. Who wouldn't be touched by that?"

I let a smug grin cross my face.

Sensing something was up, he asked, "What's so funny?"

"You're right," I said, "she *is* a beautiful little girl, but she's not my granddaughter."

He stopped in mid-sip and gave me a questioning look.

I explained. "Both of Amanda's grandfathers died before she was born. When Jan and I met her parents, she was still quite young, about three years old. We became very close friends immediately and, of course, fell in love with Amanda. All the other little girls had grandfathers. I guess she felt left out, so she started calling me Grandpa. It stuck."

Angus liked the story. "But she doesn't call Jan Grandma."

I laughed. "Yeah, that's because she called her Granny Janny once. Jan decided she wasn't quite ready for that yet, so she talked to Amanda's parents and got the rule waived. Besides, she already has two grandmas."

"Makes perfect sense," he said with a grin, then stood up. "We'd better go; the girls will be looking for us soon."

We walked back in silence, absorbing the peaceful surroundings. I asked him how the doctor's visit went.

"Okay," he said.

Guess talk time is over, I concluded.

Approaching the house, we could smell dinner cooking. Angus and I exchanged glances and smiled knowingly. During the week, we all had our own schedules—Angus and I worked on the boat, Jan and Hilda went shopping and worked in the kitchen or with their sewing, and Amanda had very full days with her school activities, tending the animals, helping us with the boat, and spending as much time as she could with Jan and Hilda. We ate together often, but Fridays had become a pleasant ritual. We quit working a little early, relaxed with the girls while they got dinner ready, then spent the evening talking, laughing, and dining. It was a wonderful time, giving us a chance to get caught up with each other's plans and activities. I was especially pleased to see Amanda enjoy our time together. She was bubbly and outgoing, eager to share with us her exploits at school. And she appeared to genuinely delight in our company. Not many eleven-year-old girls would be too enthusiastic about spending time with the old folks, but it was clear she enjoyed herself thoroughly.

When we approached the house, Amanda burst out of the door and ran toward me. "Great job, Grandpa!" she cried, leaping up at me and hugging my neck.

Jan followed close behind, a huge smile on her face. "We heard the news, honey! Congratulations!" She gave me a big kiss. "Angus told Hilda that he'd never seen a better job. I'm so proud of you; and you thought you'd ruined it!"

I tried to look modest. "Aw, shucks," I drawled, kicking up some dirt. "I knew all along it would fit."

"Yeah, sure!" she giggled, and squeezed my arm.

Hilda came out to add her two cents' worth. "It's not often that Angus says things like that, James. You can be sure he means it." She was beaming. "Now, come in and sit down; we fixed an extra-special dinner tonight in your honor."

For one of the few times in my life, I was truly embarrassed by all the hoopla. Luckily, it didn't interfere with my appetite.

We have long twilights in Maine, even at that time of year, and after our wonderful dinner, we decided to enjoy dessert out on the porch. It was a perfect evening; there was a glow in the west and not a breath of wind. Occasionally, we could hear a whip-poor-will off in the distance, but all else was quiet. Angus and I sipped our coffee contentedly while the women enjoyed their tea. Amanda nursed a hot chocolate with a peppermint stick in it. Duncan was curled up in a huge ball at her feet, snoring lightly.

We were talking of various things—the boat, the end of fall, the coming winter—when I impulsively blurted out, "Why don't you folks have Thanksgiving dinner with us?"

It seemed an innocent, natural offer, but for some reason, Hilda seemed flustered and immediately said, "Oh, I don't think so, James, we couldn't possibly—"

But then Angus immediately jumped in. "Of course, we will. That sounds like a capital idea. Just capital!"

I had to laugh. It was very unlike Angus to be so ebullient. We'd had wine with dinner and were enjoying a brandy with our coffee. That, combined with the celebratory toast of scotch earlier, had apparently put him in an expansive mood. He was leaning back in his chair, smiling, brimming with benevolence for all mankind. "We'll even supply the turkey," he said.

"WHAT?!"

The shriek startled us all. Angus bolted upright and Duncan began barking; we all looked at Amanda. Her eyes were huge; a tragic expression of disbelief was on her face.

"What's the matter, honey?" I asked, concerned.

She was staring at Angus, near tears. "Do you mean, supply the turkey to *eat*?"

Poor Angus. "Well, yes, honey, that's why we raise them, to—"

"But you can't! You can't just kill them and eat them!"

It became immediately clear, now, what the problem was. Of course. Amanda had fed the animals almost every day for months. They ran to her every morning and followed her around while she fed them by hand. She had even named most of them. Angus may just as well have suggested we barbecue Duncan.

He wasn't smiling now. "Well, actually, Amanda, no, of course not. You see, what I meant was, uh . . . I didn't mean one of *our* turkeys. No, no, not at all. Why, they're like children to me. What I meant was . . . uh, what I mean is . . ."

Angus's predicament was becoming increasingly painful to watch. Without thinking, I jumped in with the first thing that popped into my head. "Amanda," I said, "what Angus meant was, he has a cousin over in Aroostook. He raises turkeys. We've already talked to him and Angus wants to order a turkey from him, just before Thanksgiving. That way, we'll get it fresh, not frozen. We wanted to surprise you. Right, Angus?"

"Uh, yeah, Jim, that's right. Sure is." He was squirming.

"Honest, Uncle Angus?" Amanda said. She was eyeing him closely.

"Honest Injun, Amanda," Angus replied. Some of the color had returned to his face. "You don't have to worry, honey, I wouldn't let anyone hurt one of *our* animals, you know that."

"Thanks, Uncle Angus," she piped. "I knew you wouldn't." She ran over and threw her arms around him. "I'm sorry I yelled at you."

"That's okay, honey," he said, patting her hand. "These things happen."

There was a brief moment while everyone exhaled, then Jan said to Angus and me, "Why don't you two boys go into the library while we clean up. Come on, Amanda, I'll wash and you dry."

"Okay, Jannie!" she piped, the crisis over.

Angus and I excused ourselves and went into the library.

"Thanks, Jim," he said, "I was floundering a little."

"A little?" I laughed. "You were going down for the third time."

"Well," he grinned, "I guess that's it, I'm officially out of the poultry business!" He lowered himself shakily into a chair. "I didn't even know I had a cousin in Aroostook. That was a great idea, Jim."

"Yeah," I deadpanned. "Capital."

CHAPTER 12

The next day, I strode purposefully to the boathouse. I had crossed a threshold the previous day and was eager to get on with it. As I walked along, I noticed the leaves were falling with a vengeance. In a week or so, the trees would be bare, announcing that winter was close on. I involuntarily pulled my collar tighter around my neck.

As I neared the boathouse, I could smell the smoke from the wood stove inside. It was a comforting aroma, one that evoked pleasant memories of decades past. I entered, greeted Angus, and surveyed my domain. He had already got out the second shutter plank and laid it across the four sawhorses, awaiting my bidding. Having done this before, perfectly, my confidence was at a high pitch. Here was simply one more inanimate piece of wood to be measured, cut, shaped, and fastened as I saw fit. I gathered the necessary tools and fell to.

As I worked, I chatted with Angus. He was puttering around, sharpening tools, checking the joinery plan, trying to look busy. But I knew he was just keeping an eye on me, ready to assist if I needed help. He was like a mother hen, watching, scolding, making sure the chicks didn't do something stupid. I chuckled inwardly and kept up the banter. He meant well.

"Pay attention to what you're doing," he said, more than once. "Are you sure of those measurements?" "Slow down, there's no rush."

But I wasn't rushing, just moving confidently along, one sure step at a time. With my newfound confidence, I finished marking this plank in a third the time the other one took. There it lay, the lines transferred, ready to be cut. I went to get the saw.

"Did you check those measurements?" Angus said.

"They're good," I assured him. "I checked them as I went along." I was surprised he even brought it up.

"Maybe you should check them again?" he offered.

"Okay," I sighed and made a perfunctory pass over the measurements again, just to make him happy. Everything was in order. I proceeded with the cutting, just like the day before—up one side, then down the other side. I trimmed the ends, cleaned up a couple of rough spots with a plane, and pronounced it ready to install. The steam box was fired up and ready to go. The girls came in with a fresh-baked apple pie just as we put the plank in the steam box. Perfect. By the time we finished our break, the plank would be ready. By lunchtime, we would have it in and temporarily fastened. A nice short day lay ahead.

The pie looked magnificent. Amanda beamed with pride when she told us she had made it all by herself from apples they had picked the day before. It was stuffed high and the crust was a perfect golden brown. The aroma from the butter and the apples and the cinnamon made our mouths water. We were in high spirits as we sat down to attack the offering. The plank needed about an hour, so we would have ample time to do justice to Amanda's effort. We wolfed down the first piece in seconds, along with a steaming mug of coffee. We gave Duncan the scraps, then caved in and had another piece, this time at a more leisurely pace. We chatted for a while, letting the pie settle. Amanda glowed as we all showered her with attention and praise. She had done a remarkable job and was visibly proud.

After another cup of coffee, there was still plenty of time. The remainder of the pie lay there, mocking me, but not for long. I cut another, smaller piece and downed it while Angus watched in humorous awe. I poured a third cup of coffee and sat back, resting the cup in my lap.

"I hope you'll still be awake when that plank is ready!" he chided.

I grinned. "I'm fine," I assured him, stifling a yawn. It was one of those gorgeous fall days—nippy and breezy outside, warm and snug inside. We made small talk and relaxed. Plenty of time, yet. Amanda began scooping up the empty plates and what was left of the pie. Duncan, knowing break time was over, ambled over to his bed beside the wood stove. He pawed it a few times, circled twice, then collapsed with a happy grunt. Before long, we could hear his low, rhythmic snoring. He looked so contented, I had to chuckle. After half a pie and three cups of coffee, I felt like curling up beside him. The heat from the stove warmed my face, making my eyes heavy. The only sounds were Duncan's steady snoring and the gentle crackle from the wood stove. So peaceful. I couldn't help letting my eyes slip closed for just a moment. I was *so* relaxed.

Then, suddenly, it was time to install the plank. Angus was far away, over on the other side of the boathouse, calling to me. I could barely hear him. "Did you check the dimensions?" "Slow down." "Don't get careless." But I just laughed at him. I didn't need him anymore. I decided to do this plank all by myself; that would show him. I went to the steam box and grabbed the twenty-five-foot plank. In his far-off voice, Angus called, "Be careful, it's hot!" But it was too late. The steam box, which had somehow grown to the size of a small car, tilted, then tipped over completely. Horrified, I watched as the torrent of scalding water flew up into the air, then, in slow motion, came down toward me. I was unable to move. Closer it came, growing larger. I tried to run, but I was anchored to the floor. It kept pouring closer . . . closer . . . getting bigger . . . I was helpless.

"YEEOOWW!"

I bolted upright, scaring everyone. Angus, Jan, Hilda, Amanda, and Duncan were all staring at me, wide-eyed with genuine concern. But their concern dissolved immediately into helpless hysteria as they, and I, realized what had happened. I had fallen asleep with the cup of coffee in my lap, with predictable results. I leaped up and danced around, flailing away at my pants in a vain attempt to cool my burning flesh. The more I danced, the more they all laughed. And, if that weren't embarrassing enough, more was to come. Duncan saw his chance and, in a final humiliation, he pounced. Down I went under him as he licked for all he was worth, my frantic gyrations merely adding to his fun.

Angus groped his way to a chair, tears streaming down his face. "I guess you're awake now!" he croaked when he was finally able to speak.

"More coffee, honey?" Jan offered.

"Very funny," I snarled. Duncan let me up and I brushed myself off, feeling ridiculous. The coffee had cooled somewhat and, after a quick inspection, there didn't seem to be any serious damage, except to my pride. I was anxious to get back to work and put this ridiculous episode behind me.

"Come on Angus," I said, "we're burning daylight."

"That's not all you're burning!" he shot back, exposing me to another round of ridicule.

But by then, I was laughing, too. How could I help it? Even Duncan seemed to be enjoying the show, his tail wagging and a huge grin splitting his face. It was all great fun, but finally, mercifully, it was time to get back to work.

We got everything ready and pulled the final plank from the steam box. Soon, the hull would be complete (except for fastening, fairing, smoothing, caulking, and painting!). We began at the stern as before but, as we laid it in, something was not quite right. Angus got a block plane and adjusted the angle of the plank end. Much better. Then, a foot or so farther up the plank, it was a hair too wide. It wasn't much, but after trying to force it, we realized it would have to come out and be trimmed slightly, just a skosh. So, we took out the plank, planed the edge, and reinstalled it. There. We proceeded up the port side, but little things continued to crop up. Unlike the previous day, every inch was a battle. We would fit a section, then have to remove it to make another adjustment a foot or two away. Then it wouldn't lay tight against the frame and it would have to be removed again to shape the back of the plank to the curve of the frame. It was grueling work. After two hours, we weren't even half-way done. We lifted off the plank to trim yet another wide spot and, when we put it back, the section next to it was too loose. Now, being too tight is one thing—you can always take more wood off a plank—but being too loose is fatal. The joint can never be sound and tight. Angus stepped back and mopped his brow.

"Let's take a short break," he said. "We're getting punchy."

Throughout the ordeal, Angus had taken everything in stride. There were no snide comments regarding my skills, no oblique references to my heritage, not even a reproachful look. He just kept plugging away as if things were going exactly as he expected. I was being *very* quiet.

The girls came in with lunch, but Angus waved them off. We needed to get the plank in before it cooled, and we weren't even half-way yet. After a brief timeout, we were back at it. Angus got out a saw and cut off the offending piece. I felt like crying, but he simply took the front half of the plank and motioned me forward. Now I understood what he was doing—brilliant! We began at the bow with the cut-off piece and worked sternward, fitting and fastening as we went. After another hour and a half, we were almost back to where he had cut the plank. There were many whacks with the sledge, near-continuous trimming, supplications to the Almighty, and some colorful language, but no more narrow spots. Angus cut about two feet off the end of the plank that was too narrow, then made a piece to fill the gap while I made two butt blocks to fasten the filler piece securely to the rest of the plank. It was getting dark out, but at last we were done. Stepping back, we checked the job. In spite of all the tears and woe, it looked fine. The filler piece fit so well, it was barely discernible. The shutter lay fairly against the frames and the seam for the caulking was a thin, uniform line the entire length of the hull. It looked exactly like the plank that went in so well the day before.

I was limp. "Angus," I moaned, "that was a nightmare. How could that one be so different from the first one?"

He gave me a kindly smile. "Attitude, Jim" he said. "You got cocky. Truth is, this one was much closer to the norm than the first one—why do you think I was so impressed yesterday?" He draped his arm over my shoulder. "Jim, there's no rhyming or reasoning with a shutter. It does what it wants to do. It has the soul of the devil. You have to do whatever coaxing, praying, begging, swearing, threatening, and sledging is necessary to convince it to stay put long enough to stick a nail in it. When you think about it, it's a wonder any of them ever fit."

I looked askance at him. "What happened to 'it's just another piece of wood'?"

Angus threw back his head and laughed. "If I had told you the truth, you would have been paralyzed with doubt. Remember, a little fear keeps you honest; too much fear and nothing gets done. But if you get cocky, the gods will gladly step in and slap you silly. Building a boat is a very humbling experience."

"Amen," I agreed. It was reassuring to hear this from someone whom I so respected. I stuck out my hand. "Thanks again, Angus."

CHAPTER 13

....

The few weeks leading up to Thanksgiving passed in a pleasant rush. Amanda was thrilled over her first New England autumn, experiencing things she had only read of up until then. She went apple-picking several times with Hilda and Jan. Then, after baking a couple of pies, she helped Hilda preserve the rest of the apples for later. They also made cider and apple butter. In late October, the three of them spent an entire day searching out the perfect pumpkin to carve for Halloween. Of course, they also picked up several lesser specimens for baking and canning. She carried firewood, collected autumn leaves, and bought all new fall clothes.

And Hilda was delighted to have her around. She greatly enjoyed Amanda's company, of course, but in a more practical way, Amanda was proving to be a big help around the farm. The amount of work that had to be done on a daily basis was considerable, especially in the fall. Whatever mundane task needed to be done—weeding the garden, preparing meals, cleaning the house—Amanda would pitch in gladly. Now, some tasks were more enjoyable than others, naturally, but she never complained or whined.

And her zeal for the boat had only gotten greater as the construction moved forward. She could see now that there really *was* going to be a boat someday. Whenever a task arose that she could manage, especially when Angus explained how important it was, she threw herself into it, body and soul. She sanded, scraped, swept, tended the fire in the wood stove, all with good humor and enthusiasm. And not a day went by that she didn't want to be brought up to date on our progress.

But above all were her beloved animals. From the beginning, it was apparent she had developed a warm kinship with them all, the geese, the turkeys, the chickens, and the ducks. And Duncan was, for all practical purposes, her dog now. He followed her worshipfully wherever she went, happy just to be in her presence. She fed and watered all the animals almost every day. Afterward, she would play with them and talk to them for hours. When both Angus and Hilda suggested that she might be working too much, she would have none of it.

"But they need me," she said, and that was the end of it. Nothing could dissuade her from her responsibilities. She was up early, rain or shine, and walked the mile or so that separated our house from the McTigues'. We told her she didn't have to go when it rained, but that suggestion, too, went by the board. We bought her a little yellow slicker for those cold, wet mornings and she would trudge up Shore Road, looking like a tiny fisherman on a steady course to her appointed rounds.

After school, she would get off the bus at the McTigues' instead of going home. "Saves time," she explained. Once there, she would come to the boathouse first to see what Angus and I had done that day and try to help us. There was plenty to do during that time and we were always happy to have her around anyway. The hull, though it looked finished from a distance, had much left to be done on it. The planks were only partially fastened, enough to keep them in place. Each plank needed two fasteners at each frame and at the stem and stern ends. All told, we would have to drill, counterbore, set, and plug over a thousand bolts, rivets, and screws. We then had to plane off the hard edges of the planks, level the plugs, sand and scrape the entire hull until it was fair, caulk and pay the seams, then finish-sand everything in preparation for painting. As daunting as that sounds, it usually goes easily enough and is quite pleasant work, albeit time consuming. It is also the kind of work that is perfectly suited to a little girl eager to help in the building of our boat. Once I showed her how to plug the fastener holes, she could do it as well as Angus. I bought her a little mallet, mixed up some glue, and turned her loose. She would carefully dab some glue into the counterbored hole, put some on a wooden plug, then lightly tap it home. Sometimes she would work for a couple hours, sometimes her mind would wander and she would go off to help Hilda or play with the animals. But there were lots of holes to fill and when she returned, she would get right back to it.

Angus and I spent hours planing and scraping the hull. It was mindless, easy work that allowed us to talk and laugh as we moved from section to section. After a short while, I began to develop a sense for removing just the right amount of wood in just the right places. I was pleasantly surprised how quickly it became second nature. Angus told me I was "starting to get the hang of it." That was good enough for me.

By mid-November, we were done smoothing the hull. All that remained was to caulk the seams before she was ready for paint. I had read about the caulking process for decades without ever having actually done any of it. Slightly embarrassed, I confessed this to Angus.

He just chuckled and said, "Watch this." He draped a length of cotton caulking over his left hand, twining it in his fingers. Beginning at the stem, he began pushing the thin strand of cotton into the top seam with a small wheel. He moved along swiftly, with no apparent difficulty, for about three feet. He then went back over it and hammered the cotton down tight with a caulking iron and a mallet. He continued thus until he reached the stern end of the seam. The whole operation couldn't have taken more than fifteen minutes.

"There," he said. "How's that?"

"That's it?"

"Yup. The only real trick is to get the right amount of cotton in the seam. Here, you try it."

I picked up the caulking and the wheel and fell to. In short order, I began to get the feel for it and soon enough, the second seam was caulked.

"Not bad," Angus said and pointed out a couple of places where the cotton was a little too full or too sparse.

I nodded. "I always thought this was a mystical art."

"Yeah," Angus chuckled. "Caulkers would have you believe that. But, in fact, there's a lot of leeway, especially with today's sealants. Remember, too little is better than too much, within reason. When you put the sealant over the cotton, it will hide a multitude of sins. Don't get cocky, but this really is pretty straightforward."

"I don't think I'll ever get cocky again," I told him, "at least not while building a boat. You taught me well."

He grinned. "Good. Here, you take the port and I'll do the starboard. We'll be done in no time."

For the next few hours, the boathouse rang with the rhythmic sound of the caulking irons—a lovely melody that, only a few months earlier, I had never expected to hear. It was sweet music to my ears.

By the time Amanda arrived with our afternoon snack, we were done. We sat down to enjoy a piece of fresh pumpkin pie.

Angus nodded toward the boat. "What do you think, Amanda?" he asked.

"It's *byoo*-tiful, Uncle Angus. What's next?"

Angus smiled. "We're going to paint her," he said.

"REALLY?!" Amanda cried. "WHEN? WHAT COLOR?"

Her excitement made us laugh. "Calm down," Angus said. "This will just be the prime coat. It'll be a dull white color and not very pretty. But we're doing it now for a couple of reasons. The cotton caulking needs the paint, it'll protect the wood, and, when the paint dries, it will show imperfections in the hull we missed the first time. Then we'll smooth them out and it'll be perfect. Besides, the boat will look more finished with paint on her, even if we still have a long way to go. Be sure and take pictures."

"I will, Uncle Angus," Amanda said, looking at the boat wistfully. "She sure is pretty. When will it be finished?"

CHAPTER 14

....

The Saturday before Thanksgiving was a beautiful clear day, but cold. The leaves were all off the trees now, which only added to the brilliance of the sunshine. A stiff, gusty breeze was blowing them in constant motion, making it seem even colder than it was. And though the calendar said one more month of autumn, folks hereabouts knew better. Winter had arrived early.

But in the boathouse, all was cozy and comfortable. The wood stove was doing almost constant duty now, as it would for months to come. Angus and I were absorbed in the joinery plan, with him explaining to me how the ceilings, the deck, the deckhouse, the bulkheads, and the interior cabinetry would all come together.

I had thought I had a decent grasp on all this, but my mind was sagging under the emotional weight. "Angus," I said, "I'm starting to think it's a miracle any boat ever gets finished."

He just smiled his patient smile. "Jim, it's important to understand how all the processes interact, but it's just as important, once you begin work, to concentrate on one stage at a time to completion. If your mind gets too active, or too far ahead of your hands, you can get overwhelmed by the sheer volume of work that's involved. Remember the planking and how you were always trying to make it go quicker? It seemed intimidating, but we just kept doing two or three planks a day, and pretty soon it was done. Same with the fairing. That's a small boat, but she looks like a battleship when you start planing and sanding the entire hull. But do one section at a time, correctly, and before you know it, you're done. Remember what Captain Bligh told his men in that lifeboat: Always look back at how far you've come, not ahead to the miles remaining. That's a good philosophy in most things, but especially so if you're crazy enough to want to build boats."

I nodded but had to admit it was easier said than done.

He patted my shoulder. "Don't worry, son," he said, "in twenty or thirty years, you'll begin to catch on."

"Thanks."

As we were thus occupied, Amanda came in with a nice morning snack of oatmeal cookies, still warm and soft from the oven.

"Hi, Grandpa; hi, Uncle Angus. Look what I made for you."

The aroma was heavenly. Duncan was curled up in his bed beside the wood stove, but as soon as Amanda came in, he sprang like a terrier to get his share of the action. It was amazing how a dog of his bulk could move so quickly when sufficiently motivated. We poured a cup of coffee and sat down to the cookies.

"How is the boat coming?" Amanda inquired.

"Fine," Angus replied. "We have a little work to do inside, then, after Thanksgiving, we'll begin to deck her over. Maybe by Christmas, the deck will be finished."

"Oh boy," she said and clapped her little hands together. Surprisingly, Amanda was still very much into the project. I expected that, like most kids, she would lose interest, especially since the boat wasn't even going to be ours. But if anything, she was even more involved now than when we started. She was constantly badgering me about the progress, what color it would be, what I think it should be named, etc. As much as the boat meant to me, it was even more special and fun because of her excitement. She was having the time of her life and was ever eager to help whenever and however she could. She made us all proud.

"What are you doing today?" I asked her.

She beamed. "Jannie and Aunt Hilda and I are making the menu for Thanksgiving dinner. I can't wait 'til you see it! We're going shopping later on to make sure we can get all the stuff. It's going to be a real feast!" She looked over at Angus. "Shouldn't you call your cousin in Aroostook, Uncle Angus?"

But Angus wasn't listening. He was absorbed in a cookie—nibbling, chewing, savoring.

"Hmm?" he mumbled distractedly. "What? I don't have—"

Almost too late, I jumped in. "Angus doesn't have to call him, honey, because he already called him last week and it's all set. We'll have the bird by Wednesday. Right, Angus?"

Angus looked like he had choked on his cookie, but he made a heroic attempt to recover. "That's right," he said, stammering nervously. "All set. Yup. Heh, heh. I—wouldn't forget that—no siree. Why, just this past week, I called—uh, I called—"

"Your cousin," I offered.

"That's right! My cousin. Yup. Jebediah. Heh, heh. Had a nice chat with him, too. Everything's fine. Yup."

Amanda was looking at Angus with a jaundiced eye as he chattered on like a magpie. I caught his attention and made a cutting motion with my finger across my throat, but he couldn't help himself.

"Mmmm . . . great cookies," he said. "The best I've ever had. Yup."

I observed his performance with unbelieving eyes. This icon of physical and emotional strength—my idol—was reduced to a blathering boob by an innocent question from an eleven-year-old little girl. He appeared on the verge of an emotional collapse.

"How's everything going out here?" By the grace of God, Jan walked in just in time.

Angus pounced. "Great, Jan, great. Just great. Heh, heh. Couldn't be better. Yup. Just finishing up our break and then, right back at it. Yup. Bird'll be here Wednesday. Heh, heh."

Jan, alarmed, took a step backward. She gawked at Angus, then at me for explanation.

"Amanda tells us you're going shopping for Thanksgiving dinner," I said. "Better hurry before the stores close." It was not quite ten o'clock. I made a subtle nod toward Amanda and then toward the door, praying Jan would pick up the hint.

And, bless her, she did. She gathered up the leftover cookies, tossed one to Duncan, and said to Amanda, "Let's go, sweetie, Aunt Hilda's all ready."

"Okay, Jannie," said Amanda. She followed Jan to the door, eyeing Angus the whole time. As they left, Jan glanced back at me with a look that clearly said "you owe me one!"

Once they were safely gone, Angus slumped in his chair and exhaled deeply. He looked drained. I walked over to him and bent over. I waited until he noticed and looked up at me. Then I bent lower still, until our eyes were even. I held his gaze for a few seconds. Then, I said, "JEBEDIAH?"

I was glad he didn't have a mouthful of coffee. He threw back his head and roared with laughter. That got me going, and pretty soon we were helpless, he from emotional release and I from the complete absurdity of the situation. We simply couldn't stop.

"I couldn't think of anything to say," Angus croaked.

"Gee, no kidding. But, really, Angus . . . Jebediah?"

That set us off again. We were laughing so hard we could barely speak. I had to sit down.

"I couldn't help it," Angus wheezed. "I was caught in the headlights and I knew it. Thank goodness Jan came in. Oh, brother!"

We were still cackling and wiping our eyes when Jan stuck her head back in the door to see if we needed anything while she was out. Her expression was priceless.

"Honestly," she said, shaking her head, "I don't know how anything ever gets done out here!"

CHAPTER 15

....

I had been looking forward to Thanksgiving for weeks. Aside from the feast I knew was in store, Angus and I had, some time back, decided to take the day off. The thought of an entire day with no pressing obligations had been germinating and growing more appealing by the day. I had planned accordingly. What I planned to do was, basically, nothing. I can be as lazy as the next man when I put my mind to it, and this promised to be a good test. I decided I would sleep in (something I almost never do), have an unhurried breakfast of all the things I don't normally eat, take a long, hot shower, settle in with a good book or a crossword puzzle, and maybe take a short nap before lunch. After lunch, perhaps a stroll through the nature preserve if I wasn't too exhausted from my morning routine, then another, longer nap to relax me for dinner, which, I was informed, would be at three o'clock, sharp (and don't be late!). After an hour or two of extremely pleasant dining and conversation, I might watch a little television. But only if I felt up to it.

When I awoke that morning at six, as I always do, I yawned, snuggled in, turned my back to the window, and fell back into a blissful slumber. I dreamt of long summer days, of sailing, of golf, of sunning on the beach like a turtle. I'm sure I was smiling as I slept. When I re-awoke, it was almost eight and I felt thoroughly refreshed. I sat up and stretched like a cat, then slipped into my bathrobe and slippers to head downstairs, spurred on by visions of bacon and eggs, French toast, and fresh coffee.

But when I pushed open the kitchen door, I beheld a scene of total chaos. Scattered everywhere were pots, pans, roasters, bottles, groceries, mixing bowls, pie tins, dozens of strange-looking utensils, and a giant fresh turkey (its label from the local market discreetly removed) perched right on the stove where I had planned to scramble my eggs. Charging about this war zone were three possessed females, their eyes glazed over with singleness of purpose, all conversing at once in a strange tongue, to no apparent end.

Bravely, foolishly, I took a deep breath and waded in. I determined to cook my breakfast as quickly as humanly possible, then retire to the sanctity of my office to enjoy it at my leisure. I hoisted the bird to make room on the stove.

"Grandpa, stop!" Amanda said. "You can't move the turkey."

"I can't? Why not?" She had a look on her face I hadn't seen before.

"I'm stuffing it," she said.

"But I need to use the stove," I explained.

"You can't right now," she said.

"I can't use my own stove?"

"No."

I looked around for support, but the other two were looking at me with the same expression as Amanda. They appeared shocked I would even consider venturing into their kitchen.

"But my breakfast—" I began feebly.

"You should have gotten up earlier," Jan retorted. "There's no room for you now."

"But I'm hungry," I pleaded pathetically, appealing to their gentler natures.

Amanda ordered, "Have some cereal, Grandpa; it's better for you anyway."

"Cereal?" I whined, making a face. "I don't like cereal. Couldn't I just—"

"No," Jan said tersely, "I'm sorry."

She didn't look sorry.

My own home and I can't even have breakfast! But it's a wise man who knows when he's licked, and I was licked. I turned and slunk from the kitchen, a beaten man.

As I wandered back into the living room, my spirits low, the phone rang. It was Angus. "Jim, have you had breakfast yet?"

"What do *you* think?" I responded.

"Yeah, that's what I thought. Me neither. Listen, why don't we go to the diner? We haven't been there in a while and they have great breakfasts. And, it's peaceful." His eagerness was palpable.

"Angus," I said, "you're a genius. Can you pick me up in a half hour?"

"Sure, see you then. Just come outside when you see the car."

"Why, you scared to come in?"

"Yup."

I laughed. "Just checking."

I ran upstairs, rejuvenated. Why didn't I think of this in the first place? The food is great, the girls make a big fuss over us, I can eat whatever I want, and I don't have to cook. Pretty darn slick!

After my shower, I was a new man. Returning downstairs, I congratulated myself on how well I had handled what could have been a sticky situation for a lesser man. I sidled discreetly over to the window to watch for Angus.

I heard Jan say something, but I couldn't understand what it was. I looked from behind the curtain. "Hmm?"

"I said, did you wipe down the shower?"

Wipe down the shower? I never wipe down the shower. "No, honey," I answered honestly, "why would I wipe down the shower?" I couldn't even grasp the reason for the question.

Jan wailed, "I just cleaned the bathroom! Now it's got water in the shower!" She was actually trembling, seemingly on the verge of tears.

My world was coming apart. I didn't even know what we were talking about. Trying to calm her down and inject some rationality into the situation (and praying Angus would show up real soon), I asked gently, "Jannie, honey, how can I take a shower without water?"

She snapped. "I get up early so I can clean the house before company comes over. Then, I have to prepare all this food, and bake the pies, and set the table, and clean up the dishes, and make sure everything gets done all at the same time, while you lie in bed half the day doing nothing and all I'm asking is for you to wipe down the shower!"

Her voice, shrill to begin with, had elevated to the pitch of an air raid siren. It would have unnerved any man. I took a prudent step backward.

"Now, now, calm down, honey," I pleaded, using my most soothing tone. "Of course, I'll wipe down the shower. No problem at all. I should have known better. My fault entirely. So sorry."

"That's okay, sweetie," she sniffled and went back to what she was doing as if nothing had happened.

I flew up the stairs, wiped down the shower in thirty seconds, and decided to wait by the *upstairs* window until I saw Angus pull up. When he came into view, I raced back downstairs, bolted to the front door, threw a hasty "see ya later" over my shoulder, and left before I could get into any more trouble. Angus was pulling up to the house as I leaped into the passenger side. I don't think the wheels had even stopped turning.

"Well, good morning!" he cracked. "You must really be hungry!"

I ignored his banter. "You won't believe this; I try to make a little breakfast and they treat me like a common criminal, in my own house!"

But Angus wasn't properly appreciative. In fact, he laughed. "So, you actually thought you would be able to just go into *your* kitchen and use it at the same time *they* were using it? How old are you?"

He had a way of expressing complex issues in very simple terms. I grinned sheepishly. "Yeah," I had to admit. "Just because it's my house, and my kitchen, and my breakfast! What was I thinking?"

When we arrived at the diner, we were met with LaVerne's usual banter, along with waves and greetings from all the other patrons, who I noticed were all men. Apparently, we were not the only ones who couldn't eat breakfast in their own homes on Thanksgiving.

Once settled in, and with no pressing need to rush back, we spent a relaxing hour or so at breakfast. I had a huge omelet with ham, cheese, and mushrooms, two orders of bacon, blueberry pancakes with maple syrup, Indian pudding, and coffee. That late-morning nap was becoming more appealing by the minute. We chatted for a while about nothing in particular and had another cup of coffee. It was a thoroughly enjoyable morning, and during our third cup of coffee, the conversation eventually drifted around to the boat.

"What do you think you'll do with it?" I asked him.

He looked vague for a moment, then said, "Oh, I don't know. I haven't really thought about it much. It's going to be a beauty, but the market for wood boats is pretty poor. I'd have to find the right person, someone who really wanted it, could afford it, could maintain it, and would appreciate it. Most folks have moved on to fiberglass. It would have to be someone special."

"Yeah. It's a shame. All that skill and work and knowledge that it takes to create something so beautiful, and nobody seems to want to make the effort to enjoy it."

"Oh, I don't think that's necessarily the case, Jim. There's always someone who appreciates finer things. Look at yourself, you're spending an entire year and a lot of effort working on a boat that's not even yours, just for fun."

"True enough, but it's something I've wanted to do my whole life. I look at it as an education. I've learned more working with you than I ever learned in college. It's cheaper and a lot more fun, too." I felt an awkward pause, then, "Angus, I know I've said this before, but it bears repeating; I really can't express how grateful I am to you for doing this. It's been a thrill of a lifetime for me, for all of us, really. You and Hilda have become like family to all three of us. Thanks again."

As always, he was looking me right in the eye. With utmost sincerity, he smiled and said, "Not at all, Jim. I feel that I'm in your debt."

Every once in a while, he caught me flat-footed, and this was one of those times. It was such a gracious thing for him to say that a response would have been superfluous. I simply nodded.

"Well, anyway, I hope you find someone for the boat," I mumbled.

"I'm sure I will," he said. Then, after a short pause, he looked at me knowingly and said, "Want to go back and look her over?"

I lit up. "Let's go!"

Our day off had lasted almost exactly two hours.

When we got to the boathouse, Duncan stirred from his fireside bed long enough to glance at us through sleepy eyes, then fell back asleep with a thud.

"Great watchdog," I joked. We walked to the bench where the plans were laid out. Again, I was struck by their age. They *looked* old, as if they should be in a museum. The printing process was old, the lettering and numbering were old-style, all the pages were curled and cracked and, in some places, brown. But they were beautifully done, obviously by hand and obviously by someone who, long ago, had put a great deal of effort and integrity into the creation of something so sublime. I felt proud and grateful to be involved in its culmination after all these many years.

We spent the rest of the morning checking details, going over the plans, weighing which woods we might use for the deck and the cabin top—basically just goofing off. But it was good for me because I always had questions and Angus always had ready answers, brief and to the point. It was a nice change of pace to be able to mull over things without the immediate need to put them into practice; it definitely promoted perspective.

Around eleven-thirty, I mentioned I was starting to get hungry.

"Back to the diner?" Angus suggested.

"No, let's go to my place. The girls have been cooking all morning. We'll grab something quick, then come back here."

Angus looked skeptical. "You sure?"

"Why not? There's more food than we can eat in a week. Come on." Angus followed, but with little enthusiasm.

When we got to the house, we were overwhelmed by the mixed aromas of turkey, sweet potatoes, squash, pumpkin, mincemeat, stuffing, apple pie, cake, oyster stew, fresh bread, and gravy. Things were obviously moving along better now than in the morning.

"Hi, honey," I yelled.

"Hi, sweetie," Jan replied. "Did you have a good breakfast?"

"Sure did," I said. I looked around. There was food everywhere—pies were cooling, the tureen of oyster stew was sitting over a warming candle, several large dishes of vegetables were prepared, Hilda was frosting a coconut cake, Amanda was overseeing the ice-cream maker, and that wonderful Aroostook turkey was visible through the oven window, turning a golden brown. Through all this, Jan was moving about like a field general, directing her troops, checking progress, making sure everything was on schedule. I had to smile. It was heaven.

"Say, what can we throw together for a quick lunch?" I inquired.

Jan stopped and looked at me as if I were simple.

"What are you talking about?" she exclaimed. "There's nothing here—you can see that."

"There's nothing *here*? To *eat*?" I was astounded. All I could *see* was food.

"This is for dinner. You can't have it now."

"Why not?" I ventured, not too wisely. I noticed Angus quietly backing out the door.

"Because it's for *dinner*," Jan repeated, this time with an edge to her voice. "If you eat it now, you can't have it for *dinner*. Besides, you'll ruin your appetite."

Her logic was unassailable, but it was difficult to see how any six people could have put a dent in that quantity of food. And my appetite has never been ruined.

"Not even a little snack? Some biscuits, a slice of pie?" I knew I was groveling, but I was hungry. This time she didn't even answer me, just gave me a stare that cut off any further discussion.

"Ice cream?" I whimpered, looking over at Amanda.

But she, my favorite little girl in all the world, was unmoved. "Sorry, Grandpa, you'll have to wait for dinner."

For the second time in four hours, I had to retreat from my own kitchen. Angus was in the living room, gloating.

"How'd it go?" he jabbed.

I just frowned and said, "Diner?"

"Yup."

We re-entered the diner to a chorus of good-natured catcalls.

Laverne sidled over to our table. "Don't you boys have a home?" she chided.

I gave her an exaggerated scowl. "I don't want to talk about it."

"Your wives threw you out, didn't they?" she mocked.

I sighed melodramatically. "Laverne, please, all we want is a nice, quiet meal. We've had a tough morning."

"It's about to get tougher. We closed two minutes ago."

Angus and I both sat up as if we were stuck by a hatpin. "WHAT?!" "NO!" "Oh, please, Laverne, please, we'll eat fast, honest. Just get us a bite of something, anything. *Please.*"

"Oh, stop whining," she giggled. "I was only teasing you."

We heaved a collective sigh. "You're an evil woman, Laverne," I said.

"So I've been told. What'll you have?"

We both ordered double bacon burgers, fries, and the best banana pudding on the planet. And coffee.

"Just something light, huh?" she joked.

"Yeah," I said, glancing at Angus, "don't want to ruin our appetites."

After our ordeal, and by the time the food arrived, we were both famished. Without further repartee, we dove in. In a matter of minutes, we were wiping our chins and sitting back comfortably.

"That was delicious," Angus said. "I haven't had a hamburger in months. And that pudding—oh, my!"

"Best place in town," I agreed. "Shall we go back? We can get a few little things done before dinner, then enjoy the rest of the day."

"Capital idea," he said, and we both laughed.

Laverne brought the check. We gave her a nice tip and wished her a Happy Thanksgiving on our way out.

"See you for dinner, boys," she crowed.

"Very funny," we replied in unison.

We puttered in the boathouse for the next couple of hours. We didn't want to start anything major, but there are always little tidy-up things that need to be done, things that get overlooked or pushed aside when concentrating on the big picture. We brought everything up to date just in time to get cleaned up for dinner. I had a jacket with me and Angus surprised me by coming down dressed in a nice three-piece suit. We put Duncan in the back of the car and headed over.

CHAPTER 16

······································

We drove over to the house with mixed emotions. The dinner promised to be extraordinary, of course, but the morning's experience had put us a little on edge. We didn't know *what* to expect. After we pulled in and stopped the car, I hesitated briefly, waiting for Angus to get out first, then realized he was doing the same thing. Sporting a couple of timid grins, we got out of the car and approached the door. As we did, we were overwhelmed by the aromas emanating from the kitchen. Suddenly, I felt like I hadn't eaten all day. We pushed open the door and ventured inside.

"We're home," I called.

The three of them swept into the living room, all smiles and pretty dresses and perfume. They looked absolutely perfect.

"Hi, honey," Jan said as she gave me a kiss. Then, pulling back, she smiled and said, "You smell like pine. You went back to the boathouse, didn't you?"

"Yeah," I answered, "we had a nice, unhurried day."

"What happened to taking the day off?" she teased. "I knew you couldn't stay away from that boat for long."

Amanda ran to us excitedly and gave us both a big hug. "What did you get done, Grandpa?" she asked.

"Not a great deal, physically, honey," I said. "But sometimes you have to take time and plan things, work out problems, bring things up to date; that's what we did today. It was almost like a day off."

Hilda was eyeing Angus tenderly. "Did you have a nice day, Angus?" she asked.

"Sure did," he said. "We had a nice breakfast and lunch at the diner, saw some old friends, fiddled around on the boat—couldn't have been better."

"You look great, Uncle Angus," piped Amanda, beaming, "but why did you wear a suit?"

Angus smiled at her tenderly. "Well," he said, "if you girls can go to all this trouble, I figured the least I could do was dress up for the occasion." He paused, then asked, "Do you really think I look good?"

He was shamelessly fishing for another compliment, and it worked.

"You sure do, Uncle Angus," she said. "You look like a movie star!"

He grinned broadly and gave her another hug.

"I hope you didn't eat too much for lunch," Hilda teased. "I know how those girls like to spoil you two."

"No," he deadpanned, "not at all. Just a snack, really."

"That's good, because we've prepared a magnificent Thanksgiving dinner for you."

"Yeah," Amanda cried excitedly. "Wait 'til you see what we fixed!"

As they turned and led us toward the dining room, Angus and I exchanged glances—*Are these the same girls we saw this morning?*

With exaggerated fanfare, they threw open the door and stood aside so we could see.

My first reaction was utter astonishment. The sheer amount of food was more than I could take in at one glance. The turkey, the stuffing, the gravy, potatoes, sweet potatoes, squash, beans, corn, oyster stew, biscuits, salad . . . it seemed endless. And it wasn't just the quantity; everything was in a beautiful china dish, or on a silver tray, or in a covered wicker basket. The utensils were sterling, the glassware was Waterford, the dishes, English China; all complemented perfectly with fine linen napkins and a hand-embroidered tablecloth. Two wine coolers stood like sentinels beside the table, one icing down champagne, the other with sparkling apple cider for Amanda.

Flickering brightly in the middle of this largesse were two large tapered candles in their antique brass holders. The girls had outdone themselves. I stole a glance into the kitchen. What had looked like a battlefield just hours earlier now appeared unused. How could this be?

I turned to Angus to comment and could see that he was even more affected than I was. With an almost dazed expression on his face, he turned to Hilda. After a moment's hesitation, he swallowed slightly. "Gosh, Hilda," he said wistfully, "I haven't seen these things in years."

She seemed slightly unsettled, as if wary of his disapproval. "It's all right, isn't it, Angus?" she said.

But he broke into a wide smile. "Of course, it's all right. In fact, it's more than all right; it's perfect. You just caught me off guard, that's all. It's been such a long time." He went to Hilda and embraced her, holding her for several moments. It was a touching moment, but also somewhat puzzling. I threw a questioning glance at Jan, but she was clueless, also.

To avoid any further discomfiture, Jan began issuing orders. "Angus, you and Jim sit at the heads of the table; Hilda, you sit over there next to Angus; Amanda and I will sit on this side so we can fetch to and from the kitchen."

That broke the ice. We proceeded to our appointed chairs and sat, everyone talking joyfully at once. But even as we did so, I noticed Angus, ever so discreetly, wipe a finger across his eyes.

When we were all settled in and the drinks were poured, Angus spoke up. He seemed quite moved. "I'd like to propose a toast," he said. "Many thanks to our dear friends who honor us with their affections, and to the three lovely ladies who went to all this trouble. To friends, family, and wonderful memories." The three girls were beaming and blushing with pride. We all reached forward, clinked glasses, then dug in.

For almost an hour, we ate like there was no tomorrow. Everything was so good and so plentiful that self-control was difficult. As one course finished, another took its place, endlessly it seemed, as if we could have eaten for a week. Through it all, the banter, the compliments, and the laughter continued nonstop.

Eventually though, the pace slackened and we had to face reality; the finish line hove into sight. Jan and Amanda cleared the dishes, then brought in all five desserts at once to howls of laughter, feigned protest, then surrender. They had made an apple pie, a mincemeat pie, a coconut cake, Indian pudding, and ice cream. It was almost more than our senses could absorb, but we gathered ourselves bravely and pushed on, determined to do justice to their magnificent effort. Hilda declared herself stuffed and settled on a very small slice of mincemeat pie. Jan had the cake and a little bit of ice cream. Angus enjoyed a manly slice of apple pie topped with a scoop of ice cream to match. Amanda had never tasted mincemeat pie or Indian pudding, so she had both, the pudding right on top of the pie. It looked disgusting, but she devoured it eagerly and pronounced it "wicked good." I wasn't up to making any difficult decisions, so I had a small helping of each.

Afterward, it was a very subdued group indeed who greeted the coffee and tea that were brought out on the same silver tray that Hilda had used the day I met her and Angus. That had been only six months earlier, but it seemed a lifetime ago. Upon seeing seeing it, I couldn't help reflecting back over the momentous changes that had occurred in our lives in that brief speck of time. We had become as close as a family. We shared our houses, our meals, intimate conversations, experiences. And it all seemed so natural, as if we had known one another for decades. Amanda thought of Angus and Hilda as much more than good friends; they were like a real aunt and uncle to her. Except for sleeping, she spent more time at their home than ours. Between the boat, the animals, and the cooking, she had gained experiences from them both that she would treasure for a lifetime. Jan and Hilda had become like sisters, doing everything together. I think they found a closeness that both were lacking previous to their meeting. They spent long hours together, shopping, cooking, and talking about everything.

Angus and I had become close in the way men do—we worked, we joked, and we laughed together while building a strong bond of mutual trust and respect. After only six months, I didn't have a closer friend in the world.

But above all, Amanda held sway. I don't believe Angus and Hilda could have loved her more if she were their own. They were smitten from their first meeting and in a very short time had developed a deep and profound love for this ebullient little girl who had brought so much joy into their lives. She was perhaps the child they never had and, coming so late in their lives, it may have been all the sweeter.

These happy thoughts were drifting contentedly through my mind while I observed the idyllic setting. Everyone was happy, laughing, contented, secure. In this vein, everyone talked at once about everything. Jan had begun working with Doc Thompson at the animal shelter, finding homes for lost and injured animals. Amanda was doing wonderfully in school (better than she ever had, in fact) and had landed the lead in the upcoming school Christmas play.

And Hilda, God bless her, was more excited than I had ever seen her. She was positively giddy as she told us excitedly, "Guess what! I have some wonderful news; Angus and I are going to the Boston Opera House next month to see Dame Olivia Hamilton! She's only going to be there for one night and I got tickets as soon as I heard. She sells out everywhere, but I called right away and got two of the best seats in the house. I'm so excited. Isn't it just the best news ever, Angus?"

Angus tried manfully to look pleased, but it didn't seem to me like it was the best news *he* had ever heard. "That *is* great, Hilda," he offered chivalrously, "can't wait."

I smiled inwardly. I didn't know much about Dame Hamilton, just that she was a brilliant soprano, perhaps one of the greatest ever, and that she possessed a fearsome reputation as a difficult perfectionist. The press joked about her as "that Hamilton woman" because of her mercurial tirades, but her talent was unassailable. She sang for, and was personal friends with, royalty, heads of state, and captains of industry worldwide. Less well-known were her charitable functions for causes mostly relating to children's welfare. She was a giant in the music world, and she was English. That was enough for Hilda. I made a passing remark about Dame Olivia's reputation and Hilda's English spine stiffened.

"Dame Hamilton is *not* difficult," she retorted, "she's a genius. One has to make allowances for such a brilliant talent. Those savages in the English press have no sense of propriety or taste."

Properly chastised, I offered a hasty "Sorry."

"Why do you call her a dame?" asked Amanda. "Isn't that kind of rude?"

As she always did, Hilda smiled sweetly at Amanda. "No, darling, this has a completely different meaning. You see, in Britain, 'Dame' is not a slang word but a title, bestowed by the Queen herself upon commoners who have excelled in their fields and brought honor to the British Empire. It is the female equivalent of 'Sir,' which signifies knighthood, and is a great honor." She cast me a caustic eye. "It can sometimes cause jealousy among lesser minds." I made a mental note not to make any more cracks, however innocent, about anything even remotely English.

Amanda was impressed, her eyes wide. "Wow!" she breathed. "She must be great."

"She *is* great," said Hilda, with finality. "We're so looking forward to it, aren't we, Angus?"

Perversely, I was enjoying Angus's plight. I couldn't imagine him sitting at the opera among the swells of Boston, but I'll give him credit; he responded as if it were the answer to a prayer. "Oh, yes indeed, Hilly," he said, the ghastly effort of a smile on his face.

Hilda started, then smiled girlishly. "Why, Angus," she said, "you haven't called me 'Hilly' in ages. How sweet." She walked over and kissed him on the cheek.

Amanda giggled. "Uncle Angus," she cried, "you're blushing!"

It was true. All eyes were on him and he was shuffling like a school-boy, trying mightily to change the subject.

"Aw, stop it," he protested. "I'm not blushing; it's just warm in here, that's all." It was perhaps sixty-five degrees, tops.

Amanda ran over to Angus and jumped in his lap. She threw her arms around him and made a big fuss, kissing him on both cheeks. Now his face was really on fire and Jan, seeing her chance, also got in on the action. Pretty soon, the three of them were kissing and tickling and teasing poor Angus until he was a helpless, happy puddle of mush. I had to laugh. Outside the boathouse, I'd never seen him so at ease, so animated. Despite his protests, it was plain he was reveling in the attention of these three girls who meant so much to him.

We lingered over our coffee and tea, savoring the moment and just enjoying each other's company. I think we all felt that this was one of those perfect times we would cherish forever. The evening deepened amidst the conversation, the laughter, and the comfortable security of being among close and loving friends.

But eventually even the best of times must come to an end, and we began winding down. Hilda insisted on helping Amanda clean up the dishes, while Jan made sure all the food got put away. She made a huge batch of leftovers for Angus and Hilda to take home and there was still more than she could fit in the refrigerator. Everything else went into the freezer. In short order, they had cleaned up everything while Angus and I pretty much just stayed out of the way. We had retired to my study and chatted amiably about the boat, and what we'd be doing next, how she was coming along—just small talk, really. But while we did so, he seemed pensive, as if there was more on his mind.

The girls, all finished up, came into the room. "Thanks for the help, guys," Jan cracked. I smiled and gave her a kiss. The three of them had done an amazing job. They had worked virtually nonstop all day, beginning before I even got out of bed. They had cleaned the house, prepared and cooked an unforgettable meal, set a magnificent table, served the meal, drinks, dessert, and coffee, and now looked as fresh as a spring bouquet. Remembering the events of the morning, I had to marvel how it had all come off so smoothly. I glanced at Jan and gave her a "well done" nod and a wink. She beamed me a tired, happy smile.

"Ready, Angus?" Hilda asked, her arms full of bags and bundles of food.

"Yes, I suppose so," Angus replied, rising. But still he hesitated, seemingly unsure about something. He shuffled a bit, then said, "Folks, I can't begin to tell you how much this evening has meant to us." He looked over at Hilda. She was smiling at him lovingly. "We kind of stopped celebrating holidays a while back, and you folks have given us the best Thanksgiving we've had in a long, long time." His voice caught just a little and I noticed Hilda had lowered her eyes. "We just want to thank you so much for a wonderful day." It was a lot for Angus to say at one time.

Jan went over and kissed Angus, then Hilda. I threw my arm around him and hugged him while we shook hands. By then we were all getting a little misty-eyed. Amanda hugged them both hard, her cheeks wet, then hugged Jan and me also.

But then Angus continued. "You folks have become like family to us, really the only family we have left." He glanced nervously at Hilda, fumbled for a moment, then said, "We'd love for you to celebrate Christmas with us."

"Why, we'd love to, Angus," I answered at once. "We'll probably still have plenty of food left by then." My flippant answer was merely intended to lighten the moment for Angus, who was looking more uncomfortable by the second. But I noticed that upon hearing Angus's invitation, Hilda had looked up quickly, obviously surprised. Her tears were flowing freely now, and there was a look almost of adoration on her face. *What is going on?* I wondered. She went to Angus and embraced him warmly. Again, I looked to Jan, again with no clarification.

We saw them out the door, shaking hands and hugging again, and watched as they walked to their car, holding hands like a couple of teenagers. Jan was touched. "They're so sweet," she said, sniffling.

I smiled and put my arm around her, pulling her close. "They sure are," I agreed, "but what's up? All the secret glances, the surprised looks, the sudden emotional outbursts—do you know what's going on? And where did all the fancy dinnerware come from?"

"I noticed that, too, but I have no idea. Maybe they're just lonely and sentimental, I don't know. Maybe the day was just too long. I know it was for Amanda." She motioned into the living room where Amanda had crash-landed on the sofa, dead to the world, Duncan curled up beside her on the floor. I had to smile.

"The dinner stuff was all Hilda's," Jan continued. "She was excited about the dinner and wanted to use it, so a couple of days ago we began bringing it over. It was all boxed up, like it was in storage. She has an amazing amount of truly beautiful things, said they never use them anymore.

She was so proud and happy to be showing it to Amanda and me and to be using it again. But I had no idea she hadn't told Angus. That was kind of awkward for a moment, wasn't it? Anyway, it all worked out well." She gave a happy sigh. "What a great evening! I can't remember having such a wonderful time in years. It was such fun to plan a big project like that and have all those fancy things to play with. And Amanda loved every minute of it!"

We looked over at her. "I guess she's done for the night," I said. "Might as well just leave her right there. She's getting too big to carry up the stairs, anyway."

Jan smiled. "I'll get a blanket and pillow. She'll be fine. Duncan will keep her company." At the sound of his name, Duncan popped up his head and broke into a big grin, apparently understanding every word. He lay his huge head back down and by the time Jan got back with the blanket and pillow, he was again fast asleep. After all the work and excitement and food and emotions, we were glad to be heading upstairs. Finally, gratefully, it was time to say goodnight. What a day!

CHAPTER 17

....

After we all had a long, relaxing Thanksgiving weekend, it was time for Angus and me to plan the next phase of the building—the interior joinery work. This meant a pleasant change of pace for us. We would be working inside the boat now, building cabinets, lockers, bunks, the galley, the head, bookshelves, all the details that determine how comfortable a boat will be. At twenty-five feet, our boat was smallish but not a daysailer. Seaworthy is what she would be, a real blue-water boat capable of extended journeys. And if people would be spending that much time on her, they'd better be comfortable or there would be a mutiny for sure.

I was enjoying all phases of the boat's building, naturally, but this particular part promised to be the most pleasant for me for a couple of reasons. First, Angus had asked me my opinion on which wood we should use for the interior, and I had immediately said, "White pine."

He grinned knowingly. "Good choice."

I loved everything about this wonderful wood. It worked beautifully; sawing, cutting, and shaping easily; it was gorgeous to look at and only got more gorgeous as it aged; there was an endless supply of it; and, as much as anything, it smelled wonderful. Every day, upon arriving at the boat, that sweet pine fragrance would take me back to when I was a young boy helping my grandfather build his little cottage on the lake. That was over forty years ago. The cottage is still there and still in the family. And every spring, when it's opened up for the season, the smell of pine is still there, almost as strong now as it was so long ago.

The other reason, somewhat vain, that added to my pleasure was that, in this stage of building alone did I feel comfortable working alongside Angus. With a lifetime of furniture-building behind me, I felt for the first time that I was almost on equal footing with him. After an admittedly awkward beginning several months back, Angus had kept his patience and helped me along immeasurably. As we proceeded, he gave me more and more responsibilities, bolstering my confidence. My progress was not without its setbacks, but Angus stuck by me while I found my sea legs. I couldn't have hoped for a better teacher or a more trusted friend. Now, when we worked side by side, he treated me as an equal. In my heart, I knew better, but it still felt good.

As we continued working on the boat, the girls were in a constant dither of excitement. Christmas was coming, Jan had new responsibilities at the animal shelter, Amanda was immersed in her upcoming play, and Hilda was on pins and needles because of the approaching opera with Dame Olivia Hamilton. The happy result of all this activity was that Angus and I were left pretty much uninterrupted for days at a time. We worked and kidded and laughed all day long. It was wonderful. The unhappy result was that the morning and afternoon snacks that we had come to so eagerly anticipate were no longer forthcoming. I dropped a subtle hint about this to Jan and was told, rather snippishly I thought, that their time was "too important" right now and that I needed to be "more responsible." I inquired as to the importance of *my* time, but that didn't go well. So now, Angus and

I had to stop work twice a day and walk the fifty-or-so yards to the house to get the snacks the girls had made the night before—a major inconvenience. We mitigated this dilemma somewhat by dragging an old refrigerator and a microwave over to the boathouse and congratulated ourselves on our ingenuity and independence.

These days went by quite pleasantly for me, but as the date of the opera approached, Angus became increasingly edgy. He began complaining, mildly at first, then with growing desperation as what had seemed so distant a few weeks earlier became a looming nightmare.

Two days before the opera, out of the blue, he spouted, "Now, Hilda doesn't want to come back the same night—says it's too far. So, we're getting a hotel room. In *Boston*! Do you know how much a hotel room costs in *Boston*? Now I've got to take two days off, dress up in that monkey suit (Hilda had rented a tuxedo for him), drive to *Boston* (he kept expectorating the word as if he were trying to dislodge something vile in his mouth), and sit through God-knows-how-many hours of *opera* (he made another sour face)." The ordeal was throwing him off his game, no question.

I sympathized, but I couldn't help myself. The absurdity of poor Angus driving to Boston in a tuxedo just to suffer through a couple hours of classical music made me chuckle.

"It isn't funny," he snarled.

"Oh, but it is," I corrected, deciding to poke him a little. "What possessed you to agree to go in the first place? No normal man would have done that. She could have gone with Jan instead and everyone would have been happy."

He sagged down onto the bench. "I know," he pouted, "but she was just so excited about it and it seemed so far off . . . I guess I had a weak moment."

I laughed again. "Oh, don't be such an old poop," I said. "You can use a break, and the culture will do you good. Heck, you might even meet someone who's not a lobsterman."

He glowered at me. "I don't *want* a break and I *enjoy* the company of lobstermen."

I was getting to him, so I continued. "Well, anyway, you're in it now. But I really think you're making too much of it. Sounds like a good time to me. In fact, I kinda wish I could go."

He just shook his head. "Let's talk about something else."

"Two more days," I intoned ominously.

"I need some pie."

The next day, Friday, dawned cold and dreary. It was thirty-four degrees, raining, and a thick, damp fog enshrouded the boathouse. We couldn't even see the river fifty yards away. It didn't get light until eight-thirty, and by four o'clock it would be dark again—a typical late-fall day in coastal Maine.

Uncharacteristically, Angus came into the boathouse late. He was, if possible, even more depressing than the weather—scowling, muttering, generally making his life, and everyone's around him, miserable.

"Good morning, sunshine," I greeted him sarcastically.

"Hmmph," he growled. It was his only response.

This was serious. Aside from the day I had met him, I had never seen Angus so grumpy. I stopped what I was doing and tried to cheer him up. "You look like crap," I offered. "Are you okay?"

"Ahh, it's just that stupid opera tomorrow," he said, looking as if he'd just eaten a lemon. "It's all I can think about. And, on top of that, Hilda woke up this morning with a sniffle and I had to cook her breakfast, boil her tea, make her toast and jam and . . .."

I grinned. "So, you had to do one day for Hilda what she does all year long for you?"

He made a face that made me laugh. "I didn't know you were such a sensitive man. Maybe you really would like to go to the opera instead of me?"

"No chance, buddy. Since the boat's going so well, I'm taking the weekend off. There's a good game on TV, I've got a new book and a couple of magazines to read, and I'm sleeping in. And, since you'll be in Boston, I won't be tempted to come over and work on the boat." A final dig.

"I'm happy for you," he growled.

"Look," I said seriously, "this is ruining your life. Why not just tell Hilda you'd rather be shot than go to Boston?"

He looked abashed. "No, I couldn't do that," he said morosely. "She's so excited; she thinks I'm excited, too. I couldn't let on now how I really feel. Plus, she doesn't get out much, so I suppose it's not too much to ask of me. There are other reasons, too . . .." He trailed off.

"Like what?" I asked.

"Oh, nothing," he said. "Don't mind me, I'm just thinking out loud. Let's get to work."

And we did. Angus seemed more contrite after his pity session and pretty soon he was his old self, immersed in the work, moving at his sure, steady pace. We were at the finishing-up part of the cabinetry, leaving little construction to do on the interior. It was turning out beautifully. The layout was simple, and Angus's experience and attention to detail made it all flow together. The proportions were perfect, all the joints were tight, there were no sharp edges; everything just looked the way it was supposed to look.

Quite often while we worked, Amanda would leave her other chores to come aboard and play make-believe. She would pretend to be sailing, or putter in the galley, all the while peppering Angus with questions. Three of us in the cabin of a twenty-five-foot boat could make things a bit cramped, but Angus took it in stride, patiently smiling and answering her questions in his plain, clear manner. Occasionally, to make her feel more important, he would ask her about the layout—where she thought the stove should go, or the sink, or the bookshelf. She would wrinkle her brow in a serious manner, considering all options carefully, then tell him her thoughts. He always took her advice, puffing up her little ego. Once she inquired as to where a little girl would keep her dolls. We both chuckled, but the next morning there was a little built-in box that slid neatly under the bunk. I just looked at Angus and shook my head, but he grinned happily when Amanda saw it and made a big to-do about it.

At some point, Jan poked her head in to tell us lunch was ready. She had come over to make lunch so Hilda wouldn't have to. We washed up and went inside.

Hilda looked terrible. She was bundled up in her housecoat and a couple of blankets, her eyes were red and watery, and she had some kind of homemade English poultice tied around her head vertically, like you see in cartoons. I tried not to laugh, but she looked ridiculous. "Poor Hilda," I said, walking toward her to give her a hug. "I hope you feel better than you look."

"Don't come near me," she croaked. "I'm a walking epidemic."

Poor thing. I blew her a kiss and sat down to eat.

"How's it going?" Jan asked.

"Couldn't be better," I said. "The interior is almost done. After that, the biggest part of the actual construction is over. Angus says we've come a long way in only six months and we're way ahead of schedule. Since he's going to Boston, I'll probably take the weekend off and watch some football."

"That's great, honey," she said. "You can both use a break."

"You know, that's exactly what I told Angus." I looked over at him with an exaggerated grin and a big thumbs-up, but got no reaction. I guess one can only poke a bear so many times.

"Come on, we're burning daylight" was all he said, and we left to go back out to the boathouse.

As we were walking over, I said to Angus, "Hilda looks awful. Are you sure she's all right?"

"Sure, she's fine," he said. "She gets these little colds periodically. She'll take some aspirin, put some whiskey and honey in her tea, and be as good as new tomorrow. Works every time."

We puttered through the early afternoon, tying up loose ends, making a list of supplies for the plumbing and electric work, cleaning up messes here and there—pleasant, easy work. Come Monday, we'd plan the next phase.

About midafternoon, I was finishing up one of the bunks when Angus said, "We're out of pie here. I'm going over to see what there might be over there for us. Be right back."

"I'll be here," I said.

I continued diddling for several minutes, just passing time until Angus got back. But when he did return, he had a worried look on his face and there was no coffee or pie. I was immediately concerned.

"What's up?" I asked.

A bit shakily, Angus replied, "I'm taking Hilda to the doctor. She's feeling a lot worse and says she's having trouble breathing. I called and he said to come over right away."

I was stunned. "Can I do anything to help?"

"No, thanks. I've got her in the car already. I just wanted to let you know before I left. I'll call if I need anything."

I looked in his eyes and saw deep concern. "Good luck, old friend. We'll be here waiting. And remember, we'll do anything we can."

"I know you will. Thanks." He hugged me and left.

I called Jan and told her what had happened.

"Oh, the poor dear," Jan cried. "I hope she's all right. Is there anything we can do?"

"I asked Angus the same thing. He said he would call if he needed anything. Look, why don't you throw together a quick dinner and bring it over. I told Angus we'd be here when they got back. We can get caught up while we eat."

"Okay. I'll come over as soon as Amanda gets home from school."

"Okay, honey, see you then."

I went back to work, but my heart wasn't in it. I couldn't help thinking of Angus and Hilda. They were such sweet people, yet it didn't seem they had anyone else in the world close to them except us. How terribly frightening it must be to grow old like that, just the two of them. It brought home to me fully how much they meant to each other, how much they depended on each other. After all they had done for us, I was glad to be there if we were needed. And I prayed for them.

It was already dark when Jan and Amanda arrived around four o'clock. The weather had worsened, adding to our anxiety. The fog was gone, but it was flurrying, the wind gusted strongly, and the temperature was plummeting. We were in for a hard freeze by morning.

After another half hour of nail-biting, headlights appeared in the drive. We all ran out to greet them, crowding around, trying to help, Duncan barking happily. I opened Hilda's door.

"Are you all right?" was the first thing out of my mouth.

"Of course, I'm all right," she retorted. "Don't make such a fuss."

I noticed her speech was slurred. "Here, let me help you," I said.

"Oh, pooh, I don't need any help," she said, then leaned heavily on my arm until we got inside.

I grinned, relieved. She was cranky as a coot—a good sign.

"How do you feel, Hilda?" Jan asked.

"Hungry" was her terse reply. "I had no lunch, then had to sit through the whole afternoon while that young doctor did God-knows-what to me. You'd think they'd have a little something for you to eat if they're going to keep you all day."

She was scowling as only an Englishman can scowl. I had to chuckle in spite of myself. Jan had taken Hilda's unsubtle hint and began serving the food.

"Well, what's the verdict?" I asked as I dug into my dinner. I also had missed my afternoon snack.

"Oh, that young quack thinks I have pneumonia," she said, "but I don't believe it. I told him so, too. Making a big deal out of a little cold. Hmph." She was eating like a lumberjack.

We all looked at one another and at Angus.

"Pneumonia?"

"Yeah," Angus said. "He suspected it right away, then did a couple of tests to confirm it. But he said she's in good shape, generally, and as tough as a boiled owl." He looked over at Hilda and smiled lovingly. She was weaving slightly and her eyes were wandering. "He loaded her up with antibiotics. That's why she's talking the way she is."

"That's right," Hilda said indistinctly, "gave me a bunch of expensive shots and some pills to take later. I told him all I needed was some good strong English tea with a little whiskey and honey, but he said I couldn't have any alcohol while I'm taking these pills, if you can imagine. What that young man needs is less schooling and more practical experience."

She was her old self again, albeit a *lot* more ornery. I had finished my dinner and was so relieved that I dug into my dessert—a nice slab of chocolate pecan pie.

"What's the prognosis?" Jan asked.

Hilda scowled anew. "Says I can't do anything for three days. Just stay in bed, get plenty of rest, take my pills, drink lots of liquids . . . he'll check my progress Monday, but he thinks it will take as much as a week to get over it completely."

"Oh, no, Hilda," Jan cried. "What about the opera tomorrow night?"

I stopped eating and perked up. *Omigosh!* In all the excitement, I had completely forgotten about that. She had been looking forward to that opera every day for a month. What a letdown! I felt so terrible for her, I could barely finish my pie.

Hilda sighed, a little deflated after her rant against modern medicine. "I know," she said. "And I feel terrible, but not just for me. I know how much poor Angus was looking forward to it."

I snorted into the glass of milk I was drinking, barely avoiding a major incident. I looked at Angus. He was patting her arm solicitously.

"It's all right, Hilly," he said with perfect sincerity. "There'll be other times."

She gazed mistily at him through one of her roving eyes. "Oh, Angus," she trembled, "you're so understanding."

He tried to look bashful and humble, but I could see his smug satisfaction. He avoided my eyes.

Then Hilda brightened somewhat. "I have a great idea," she slurred. "Jan, why don't you take Amanda to the opera? She'd love it, and everything is all paid for."

Amanda leaped out of her chair. "Oh, boy!" she cried. "I'd *love* to go. Can we, Jannie? Please?"

"Oh, honey, I'm so sorry," she said, "but I can't. I have to work all weekend at the shelter. I'd love to take you, but I'm filling in for someone who is sick. If I don't go, they won't have anybody." What a shame, I thought between bites. It was obvious she really wanted to go. And poor Amanda was crushed.

Then Jan said, "Angus, why don't you take Amanda? You both want to go so bad, it seems a perfect idea."

"Bravo, Jan," said Hilda.

"Yay!" cried Amanda.

"Great idea," I threw in.

Angus's face turned a greenish gray. He didn't look so smug anymore. I leaned back, grinning. *Hah!* I thought. *They've got him now!* But my old friend was made of sterner stuff. He stammered only once, then recovered heroically. With a most tender expression, he looked Hilda square in her eyes and said, "Hilly, you know how much I want to go to that opera, and I'd *love* to take Amanda, but I could never leave you alone, not now. I want to be here if you need me."

Jan's shoulders sagged. "Oh, Angus," she sniffed, "that's the sweetest thing I've ever heard." A tiny tear made its way down her cheek.

Amanda went over to him, also sniffling, and threw her arms around him. "That's all right, Uncle Angus, I understand. You're so sweet to look after Aunt Hilda."

Angus put his arm around her. "Thank you, honey, I appreciate that."

Oh, brother! This was just too much. The three girls were fawning all over him as if he were Sir Galahad. I cut another piece of pie.

I was enjoying my second helping when I noticed it had gotten awfully quiet. I looked up in mid-bite to see the four of them staring at me—Hilda as sternly as her condition would allow, Jan with her left eyebrow a good inch above her right, Amanda round-eyed and innocent, and Angus with the most diabolical smirk I'd ever seen on a human being.

What's going on?

"Well?" Jan said.

"Well, what?" I said, completely in the dark.

"Are you going to take Amanda to the opera?"

"WHAT?" I blurted through my pie. "What are you talking about?"

"Well," Jan went on, "we're all busy. You're the only one left who can take her. I asked you once, but you were too busy stuffing pie in your face. What do you say?"

An icy hand gripped my bowels. *This is all wrong; it can't be happening.* My mind raced, grasping for an escape. "Honey," I began uncertainly,

"I'd love to go, of course, you know that, but I've got a ton of things to do on the boat this weekend. I just don't see how I can get away."

But she was on to me. With an unblinking eye, she replied evenly, "Nonsense. At lunch today, you said you were practically done inside and you were going to take the weekend off and watch a *football game.*" These last two words were spit out between clenched teeth.

Angus chimed in helpfully, "And don't worry about the boat, Jim. I can finish the little bit we have left in an hour or two by myself, no problem."

Thanks, Angus.

Jan was still looking at me, her left eyebrow now even higher. "Well?" she said.

I was in serious trouble. As a last resort, I threw out the only thing my muddled mind could come up with. "Honey, Amanda, that opera is a very formal affair. I don't even have a suit up here. I'd look awfully silly showing up in my L. L. Bean sweatshirt. And besides, Amanda, you don't have any dressy things, either." I tried to look contrite. "I'm sorry, I'm afraid it just won't—"

Again, Angus was right there for me. "Oh, don't worry about that either, Jim," he said. "You can wear my tux. We're about the same size."

Amanda piped up excitedly, "And I've got the dress I'm wearing in the school play. It's got sequins and feathers and bows; it's *byoo*-tiful!"

I looked around desperately, first at Jan, who was still in arched-eyebrow mode; then Hilda—no compromise there; at Angus, with his fiendish grin; then Amanda, who just looked up at me with her big, round blue eyes and mouthed a single word, "Please."

That did it, of course. I was cooked like a Christmas goose and I knew it. I pulled her to me, gave her a big hug, and said, "Of course, we'll go to the opera, sweetheart. Wouldn't miss it for the world. Just had to iron out a few wrinkles, that's all."

She was ecstatic. She wrapped her arms around my neck and hugged me tight. "You're the best, Grandpa."

In spite of the situation, I felt great. In seconds, I had gone from pie-stuffing bozo to hero. Jan kissed me on the cheek. Hilda, wheezing like an old bellows, blew a kiss in my general direction. And Angus, the happiest of all, slapped me on the back. "Enjoy the show, Jim. Sure wish I could go."

CHAPTER 18

· ·

We said our goodbyes and left to go home to pack for the big weekend. On the way, Amanda was bubbling over. It was like when she found out we were going to build the boat—giggling, jabbering, making no sense whatsoever. She was so excited I almost didn't mind the way I got snookered into it. And, I had hatched an idea that might take some of the sting out of going to the opera (out of desperation, comes inspiration).

"Instead of going to Boston tomorrow afternoon," I offered, "how about getting an early start and seeing some sights? We could walk the Freedom Trail and see a lot of the stuff you've only read about in History class. The weather is supposed to be perfect, and the Trail is only about two miles long—an easy walk. We can have a nice lunch at Faneuil Hall and people-watch. How about it?"

She was thrilled, of course. What eleven-year-old wouldn't be excited about a fancy weekend in the Big City? The level of her chatter became even greater and more incoherent. I congratulated myself, hoping it wouldn't be so bad, after all.

As soon as we got into the house, she flew off to pack and to try on her dress. Jan was grinning and shaking her head. "You're certainly handling this well. I know how you feel about opera. Are you sure you're okay?"

I laughed. "Look how excited she is. This will be a lot of fun for both of us, and she'll learn something, too."

Jan was smiling affectionately. "She *is* excited. At first, it didn't seem like you wanted to go, but I'm glad you're taking her."

"Well, I'm looking forward to it, too," I said. Then, after a pause, "Especially the opera."

She laughed and gave me a kiss. "You'd enjoy anything as long as you're with Amanda. I'm jealous." I smiled and gave her a hug.

"Ta-da!"

We turned around to behold the spectacle of Amanda in her school play dress—a full-length lavender skirt with tiered white ruffles all the way to the floor, a pink and white bodice bedecked with purple ribbons, large puffy sleeves with yellow bows, and multicolored sequins sparkling all over like a Christmas tree. Capping off this vision was an enormous blue bow on her head that was flopping under its own weight like the ears of a depressed beagle. I gaped, speechless.

She pirouetted for us. "Do you like it, Grandpa? I told you it was *byoo*-tiful!"

The thing was hideous. I looked to Jan for help, but she was glaring at me like she always did when she thought I'd say something stupid.

"Well, gosh—honey," I stammered, "I—I don't know *what* to say."

Her little face fell. "Don't you like it, Grandpa?"

"Oh, yes, yes, of course I do, honey. Sure, I like it. I *love* it. It's, uh . . . stunning. You just caught me off guard, that's all. It's so . . . *ornate.* You don't think it's *too* nice, do you? I mean, it's only an opera." I was babbling.

"Jannie," she whined, "Grandpa doesn't like my dress!"

"Now, honey," Jan soothed, "don't be upset. Grandpa just doesn't have any fashion sense, that's all. Your dress is lovely. You'll be the belle of the ball, I promise."

Amanda brightened immediately, gave me a "so there" look, and flounced off to change.

I glared at Jan. "Thanks for the help," I deadpanned. "No fashion sense? Are you kidding me? The thing's a monstrosity! I can't take her to the Boston Opera House in that outfit. I'll be laughed out of town."

Jan stared a hole in me. "Don't you dare say a word to her about that dress. Remember, she's only eleven years old and she thinks it's 'byoo-tiful.'" She grinned. "She's a fairy princess in the play and that's her outfit; just be glad she isn't bringing her magic wand."

"The bow," I pleaded, "can we at least get rid of the bow? She looks like she has two heads. It flops around like a broken wing."

Jan sighed. "I'll put some spray starch on it. That might help."

"Maybe you should varnish it."

Amanda came back into the room all aglow. "I'm so excited, Grandpa," she gushed. "It's going to be so much fun, I can't wait. Thank you so much for taking me." She gave me yet another big hug and a kiss while Jan looked on, grinning as usual.

"You're welcome, sweetheart," I said as she snuggled in my lap. "I'm sure we're going to have a lot of fun. And I really do like your dress, honest. I'm sorry if you got the wrong impression." After a pause, I tried another tack. "But, you know, Amanda, as pretty as it is, we might be able to make it even better."

Amanda leaned back, immediately suspicious. Jan was behind her, glowering at me again.

"Well," I began, "I was just thinking, instead of the bow—which is great, don't get me wrong—but maybe a pretty little hat might go better overall, you know, more *operatic*. What do you think?"

"No, Grandpa," she said with finality. "The bow is part of the ensemble."

"The what?"

"The en-sem-ble," she repeated, as if to a child.

Jan had stopped glaring and was almost laughing out loud. I sighed again. "You're right, honey, the outfit just wouldn't be the same without it."

"Thanks, Grandpa," she said and jumped off my lap to go pack.

Jan sat on the edge of my chair and put her arm around me. "You're learning, dear," she said. "A little slow, but you're learning."

CHAPTER 19

KNOCK KNOCK

I was jolted awake. "Huh . . . what?" Trying to find my bearings, I rolled over and groped for the alarm clock—6:10. It was black as pitch. *What's going on?* I wondered. Groggily, I called out, "Amanda?"

"Yes, Grandpa?"

"What are you doing?"

"I'm all ready to go," she called through the door. "You said we should get an early start and I didn't want you to oversleep."

In the dark, I could hear Jan giggling. "She's right, honey. I heard you say it."

Fully awake now and with no chance of falling back asleep, I eased myself out of that soft, warm bed. Yikes! The thermostat hadn't even kicked on yet and the floor was like ice.

"Thanks, Amanda," I called, "I'm up now. Go downstairs and start the coffee, okay? Jannie'll be down soon to start breakfast." At that, Jan began an exaggerated snoring sound. "Very funny," I said.

She yawned. "I didn't say anything about an early start. That was entirely your brainstorm." She pulled the down comforter up around her head. "Mmmm . . . this bed feels sooo good."

I know when I'm being blackmailed. "Okay," I said, "what'll it cost me?"

She popped up. "Take Amanda and me Christmas shopping in Freeport next week?"

"Shopping?"

"Uh huh."

"In Freeport?"

"Uh huh."

"Can it be something else?" I pleaded. "I'd rather shovel snow than go shopping."

"Suit yourself," she pouted. "Amanda and I will just have to skip Christmas this year. That's okay, though; I'll just tell her you didn't want to take us shopping. I'm sure she'll understand." She made an exaggerated yawn. "Boy, this comforter's so cozy, I could stay here all day." She snuggled down even deeper into the fluffy cloud, a blissful smile on her face.

"All right, all right," I said, eager to get down to breakfast. "I know when I'm licked."

She popped up again, amazingly rejuvenated. "Great. If Hilda is feeling better, maybe they'd like to go with us?"

Seeing a chance to get somewhat even with Angus, I smiled inwardly. "I'm sure they would."

"Oh, boy!"

As always, I felt revitalized after a long, hot shower. As I skipped down to breakfast, I could smell things coming together—sizzling bacon, percolating coffee, warm pancakes, frying eggs. The table was set and fresh orange juice was at each plate. I never understood how Jan did all this in such a short time. Everything seemed to just materialize out of nowhere. But after twenty-five years, I stopped wondering and simply accepted my lot gratefully.

Amanda chattered throughout the entire meal. She had done a school project recently on Boston and was bubbling over with things she wanted to see—the *Constitution*, Paul Revere's burial site, The Old North Church, Faneuil Hall . . . she couldn't stop. I let her ramble on, grateful she took such an interest in something a lot of kids her age find boring. This might be fun, after all.

When breakfast was over, Amanda jumped up to help Jan with the dishes, but Jan shooed her away. "Run along and get ready, sweetheart," she said. "I'll take care of this."

"Okay, Jannie, thanks," she said and rushed off in a whirl.

With a chuckle, Jan said, "Does she ever do anything at normal speed?"

I gave Jan a hug. "Thanks for breakfast, honey. It was great, as usual."

It was getting light as I went out to warm up the car. The weather was cold, but clear—a beautiful day for a drive to one of my favorite cities. Amanda emerged from the house with her little suitcase and overnight kit, then went back and got her dress, which was on a hanger.

"All set, sweetie?" I asked.

"Almost, Grandpa," she answered, and went back inside the house. When she returned, she was carrying a cardboard box large enough to ship a microwave in.

Curious, I asked, "What's that?"

"My bow," she answered, tucking it gently inside the back of the car.

I smiled. "Oh, yeah, I almost forgot—the rest of the ensemble."

She got in the car, strapped herself in, and I closed the door for her. As we backed out the driveway, the sun was just peeking over the horizon. Right on time.

The drive down to Boston was pleasant and uneventful. It's normally a little over two hours, but we took a few side roads so I could show her some of the places I had known when I summered there as a boy. In all honesty, I did this more for myself than for Amanda, but she was sweet and only yawned a few times. I tried to keep her interest by talking about the things we would see and do. With all the detours, I figured we would get to Boston around ten o'clock, giving us plenty of time to visit the *Constitution* before having a nice lunch at Faneuil Hall. After that, we might tour The Old North Church before checking into the Copley Plaza to get settled in and have a nap. Amanda snorted at the idea of taking a nap while on vacation, but I knew better. After getting up so early, traveling, sightseeing out in the cold, and having a nice lunch, she would be more than ready for a snooze. And frankly, so would I. As excruciating as the opera promised to be, I didn't want her, or especially me, falling asleep during the big night.

We arrived in Boston shortly before ten. It was still chilly, but compared to home, it was practically springtime. The sun was brilliant and there was no wind—a perfect day for sightseeing. We bundled up, got our tourist guides, and headed for the *Constitution*.

Amanda had read up on the legendary ship and riddled me with questions, but she still was stunned when the grand old lady hove into view.

"Wow!" she breathed. "It's *huge*." She stood there, trying to absorb the sheer size of it. "How long would it take to build something like that?" she asked, no doubt likening it to the building of our little boat.

"Not as long as you might think, sweetie," I said. "They had huge crews of men working on these ships, every day. That's all they did, dawn to dusk. The big timbers would have already been roughly dimensioned before they got here, almost ready to put in place. Different trades would perform the same tasks over and over, just like an assembly line. And, they wouldn't build just one ship; they would build sister ships all the same, reducing the time required for each one. Remember, we were a young country and spread out over a large area. We needed a strong defense."

"Wow," she repeated. It was all she could say.

We bought our tickets and got in line for the next tour, which began almost immediately. I had always been fascinated by this direct link to our early history and had visited many times, but I was most pleasantly surprised by Amanda's eagerness. Our Coast Guard guide began by rattling off dozens of details about the ship—its size, its weight, how many trees were required to build it, how many guns it carried, how many men served on her, etc. Amanda drank it all in, visibly impressed. But when she heard it took three years to build, she looked at me oddly.

"Only three years to build this huge ship?" she queried me, clearly impressed.

"Yup."

"And they built another ship just like it at the same time?"

"Yup," I answered, proud of my little prodigy.

"How come it's taking you and Uncle Angus a whole year to build our little boat?"

Her frankness took a little wind out of my sails. I tried to explain, going over my previous arguments: the large gangs of men, the differences in methods, specialized crews for different tasks, etc.

She interrupted. "And they only had hand tools, no power saws, no drills, no forklifts?"

This wasn't going well. "Uh, that's true, yes, but—"

"And they worked outside all winter; no boathouse?"

"Well, all that is true, honey, but you have to remember that times were just different then. Half the town may have been involved in just the building of these ships, with no other distractions. And, you know, sometimes it's easier to build large things than little things—more room for error." I wasn't even convincing myself.

She looked dubious. "I suppose so . . .," she mumbled, and trailed off, obviously unconvinced. I sensed some of my luster tarnishing.

We continued our tour through the three decks. Our guide, a young lieutenant, was most impressive. He knew his subject well and took pride in his duty. When questions arose, he handled each one with knowledge and clarity. He went into detail when describing the battles, life aboard ship, what the men ate and drank, how the ship came to be known as "Old Ironsides." Amanda was riveted by it all. Sometimes, however, the narration might have been a little too descriptive. When she found out why the ship's surgery (hospital) was painted red, her expression changed and she became slightly pale.

"Are you all right?" I asked.

"I think so," she answered unsteadily. "It must have been horrible to live like that."

"Things always look different from another time, honey. It *was* very hard, but all wars are hard. There just wasn't any other way. They did what they had to do to protect our young country. That's why we have holidays and museums like this, to make sure our forefathers' sacrifices aren't forgotten. I hope you won't forget."

Her little face got very serious. "I won't ever forget, Grandpa, I promise."

I hugged her close. "That's my girl."

The tour lasted a very pleasant hour, then she wanted to visit the museum gift shop and buy some souvenirs. Another forty-five minutes. I mentioned lunch, but she insisted we see the Bunker Hill Monument first. She was on a mission. "We can eat lunch anytime, Grandpa," she chided.

"Okay, sweetie. Whatever you say." I was enjoying it as much as she was.

Boston proper occupies quite a small area for such a major city, and so much of our history is concentrated there that it's a wonderful city for walking, especially on such a perfect day as this. So off we went, covering the short distance to the Bunker Hill Monument quickly, Amanda chattering the whole time. She was taking in every detail, the excitement obvious on her beaming face. But when we arrived at the monument, she began looking around, trying to picture what went on here so long ago. There were houses, gas stations, apartment buildings, all types of distractions.

She was perplexed. "How could they fight here, Grandpa?" she asked.

"Remember, sweetie," I said, "that was a long time ago, over two hundred years ago. None of this was here, just a couple of hills and a few houses. Even the landscape has changed. The important thing is that, on this site, many years ago, we fought the first major battle with the British to gain our independence. It was a historic moment, the birth of our country. Pretty big stuff, don't you think?"

She shook her head in awe and muttered, "Sure is."

When we left the monument, it was getting on toward one o'clock. By then, we were in complete agreement as to our next stop—lunch. We got in the car, drove the short distance across the bridge to the vicinity of Faneuil Hall, then walked the rest of the way. It had warmed up considerably (by New England standards) and people were milling about, enjoying this gift of a gorgeous winter day. Market Square was bathed in a golden glow that took some of the bite out of the cool temperature. We decided to eat outside so we could enjoy the fresh air and the bustling activity. After lunch, Amanda lodged another complaint against a nap, but I overruled her and in a matter of minutes, we were pulling up to the front of the hotel.

"Is this a nice motel where we're staying?" she asked.

I smiled. "I think you'll like it."

When we got to the entrance, two men in uniform approached us.

"Good afternoon, sir," said one of them. "Do you have a reservation?"

I said yes and gave him Hilda's name.

"Very good, sir. I believe your room is ready." He got our luggage while the valet took my keys so he could park the car.

"Please follow me, sir and miss," said the doorman formally as he led us toward the entrance. Amanda was grinning broadly, reveling in all the attention. As we passed into the lobby, I heard her suck in her breath. I knew the Copley by reputation, but even I was unprepared for the luxury that greeted us.

"Wow," Amanda said softly.

I leaned down and whispered, "Do you think it'll do?"

Her face lit up into a huge smile. "It's *byoo*-tiful, Grandpa!"

After checking in, the porter led us to the elevators, then up to the eighth floor to our room. Amanda was giggling from all the attention and could only gawk at everything without saying a word until after we were in our room.

She looked around. "Golly, Grandpa, this is the nicest motel I've ever seen. I can't wait to tell Mommy and Daddy."

I grinned at her. "I'm sure they'll be thrilled, honey, but remember, this is a *ho*tel, not a *mo*tel. Big difference."

We unpacked, the dress going on a hanger and the box on the floor of the closet, since it wouldn't fit on the shelf. I hung up the tux, made sure everything was in order, and prepared for a nap. Amanda was at the window, looking out over the Boston skyline, trying to be inconspicuous.

"Nap time, sweetie," I said.

"Aw, Grandpa, I'm not tired at all. Really. I just want to look out the window for a while, okay? Please?"

"Tell you what, lie down for a few minutes and read the rest of your brochures so you can tell me what we'll see tomorrow. When you're finished, you can get up and do whatever you want."

She jumped at it. "Okay, Grandpa!" she cried, apparently not believing I could be so easy. She slid under her covers and snuggled in. "What a soft bed. And these pillows are huge!" Her little head almost disappeared as she lay back and sighed.

"Here's your reading stuff, honey. Be quiet now, because I'll be asleep," I said, sliding under my covers.

"Okay, Grandpa," she said, and started reading.

In less than two minutes, I could hear her deep, even breathing. I congratulated myself, rolled over, and was soon also fast asleep.

CHAPTER 20

....

"C'mon, sweetie, time to get up."

"Huh . . . what?" Amanda awoke from her deep slumber slowly, looking around, trying to place herself. When it gradually dawned on her where she was, she bolted upright. "What time is it, Grandpa?" she blurted.

"Relax, it's only five-thirty."

"I slept for *three hours*?"

"Uh, huh." I had to laugh. She was completely disoriented, looking around, trying to focus. "Relax," I soothed her, "the show doesn't start until eight. We have plenty of time. Let's have dinner here at the hotel, then come back to the room to change. Then we can walk to the opera house; it's only a couple of blocks." No sense being seen with that dress any more than absolutely necessary.

The mention of food aroused her somewhat and she groped her way out of bed. I told her, "Go take a nice hot shower. It'll help wake you up."

"Okay, Grandpa," she mumbled through a yawn.

After her shower, she was functioning almost normally. She got dressed in her nicest school clothes and we headed down to have dinner.

The maitre d' greeted us immediately as we entered the dining room. He smiled, bowed from the waist, and said, "Good evening, sir. Good evening, miss." He had a deep voice with a formal British accent. Amanda stared, not knowing what to say or do.

"This way, please," he said, and led us to our table. He made a show of pulling out Amanda's chair for her, causing Amanda to giggle self-consciously. She was out of her element, but was clearly enjoying the attention. She sat down, almost lost in the huge armchair, and looked around, but remained silent. I cleared my throat as a reminder.

"Oh," she remembered, "thank you very much, sir."

"You're quite welcome, miss." He turned to me. "If there is anything I can do for you, please ask. Henri will be with you forthwith," he intoned, and retreated.

Henri materialized immediately and gave us our menus, while another server arrived with a pitcher of ice water. In a strong French accent, Henri ran through the list of the day's specials—duck l'orange, osso buco, chateaubriand, vichyssoise . . .. To Amanda, he may as well have been speaking Chinese.

I ordered a Tom Collins. Henri bowed and said, "I'll be right back with your drink, sir, and to take your order."

When he left, Amanda looked at me and said in a low voice, "Wow, Grandpa, I couldn't understand a word he said."

I smiled. "Just forget about the specials and look at the menu. The descriptions are under the names of the entrees. Find something that sounds good to you and try it. I'm sure there's something you'll like."

She looked back at the menu again and I could see she was looking to the right of the page, at the prices. "Kind of expensive, isn't it?" she asked, somewhat taken aback.

"Don't worry, sweetheart," I said, smiling, "this is our big night out. We don't do this very often, so enjoy it and get anything you want."

"Anything?"

"Yup, anything."

"Okay. Thanks, Grandpa."

Henri returned with my drink, which was perfect. He turned to Amanda. "Have you decided, young lady?" he asked.

"Yes sir," she replied.

"Good. What can I get for you?"

Amanda sat up straight and said, "I would like a hot dog and a root beer float, please, with French fries and lots of ketchup."

I put my hand to my forehead. The corners of Henri's mouth rose slightly, but he never betrayed his professional manner. "Excellent choice, miss," he said. "And how would you like your, uh, hot dog prepared?"

She replied, "At Littlefield's, they steam the hot dogs and grill the bun in butter. Can you do that?"

Henri said, "I'll ask the chef, miss." He made the necessary notes, then turned to me with a puckish grin. "And you, sir?"

I decided on a Greek lamb dish. He thanked me and left to put in the order. I would have given a hundred dollars to see the chef's expression when he got Amanda's request.

We made small talk while we waited for our food. She was bursting with excitement about the opera and couldn't stop asking me questions about it: "What are we seeing?" (I didn't know); "What's it about?" (I didn't know); "How long will it last?" (not long, I hope); etc. The fact I knew nothing at all about the evening didn't dim her enthusiasm one bit. She worshipped Hilda, and if Hilda said it was good, that was the end of it. For my part, I planned to be properly fortified by another Tom Collins and a nice glass of wine with my dinner. I hoped that would get me through the evening.

Our meals were delicious. Amanda told Henri the hot dog was "almost as good as Littlefield's," and we tarried over dessert. Being in no mad rush to get to the opera, I had a glass of sweet wine with dessert. All in all, it had been a lovely evening, but now, having put it off as long as possible, it was time to don my tux and do my manly duty.

We went back to our room to get ready, Amanda using the dressing room while I changed into the tuxedo. After only five or six attempts, I got the bow tie right (I think I had tied my last bow tie at my wedding). I slipped into the jacket, checked myself in the mirror for any last-minute adjustments, and I was ready.

I turned from the mirror and there was Amanda, in full regalia and smiling proudly. I staggered. The dress was the same atrocity as before—I had steeled myself for that—but the bow had somehow doubled in size! Could it be my imagination? No, it was definitely bigger. I couldn't take my eyes off it.

"How do I look, Grandpa?" she asked coyly.

I was glad I'd had the second glass of wine. I swallowed hard and said, "You look beautiful, sweetheart. Jannie was right, you'll be the belle of the ball." My eyes were riveted on the bow. "Uh, honey, is that the same bow? It looks . . . different."

"Sure, Grandpa," she replied. "Jannie just sprayed it with starch, that's all. It doesn't flop anymore."

So, that was it! She was right, it certainly didn't flop anymore. The two sides of the bow stood a good three inches taller and came to a point, like a startled cartoon rabbit. But as proud as she was, I didn't have the heart to say any more. I just stuck out my elbow and said, "Shall we?" She giggled, hooked her arm in mine, and we were off to the opera.

CHAPTER 21

....

As we walked, we could see the opera house from blocks away. It was lit up like a launch pad and abuzz with activity. Limousines came and went, unloading their gentrified cargo of Boston's upper crust. Amanda and I could only gape at the lavish spectacle—beautiful designer gowns for the women, tailed formal wear and top hats for the men, gloves, furs, more jewelry than a museum. Newspaper photographers were everywhere, continually snapping pictures for the next day's society page. Suddenly, I felt like a janitor. The tuxedo, which I had thought so spiffy in our hotel room, now felt like overalls by comparison. I wanted to fade into the shadows, but Amanda had other ideas. Not sharing my insecurities, she waded right into the throng, apparently feeling on equal footing in her fairy princess outfit. I followed warily, at a safe distance. She mingled easily in the crowd, taking the measure of the women's outfits in comparison to her own. As she was so engaged, a noted dowager of Boston society (a Mrs. Cottsworth, whom I recognized from the society pages) seemed to catch sight of her. She approached Amanda.

"Hello, dahling, how are you?" she asked in her Beacon Hill accent.

Amanda replied, "I'm fine, ma'am, thank you."

"That's a beautiful dress you're wearing."

Bless you!

"Thank you, ma'am; your dress is nice, too."

I choked. The woman's dress was almost certainly a designer original and probably cost as much as our house. But the lady just smiled graciously and said, "Thank you, dahling."

Presently, several other leading ladies of Boston society had joined Mrs. Cottsworth and gathered around Amanda, chatting it up as if they were classmates.

"Where are your parents, dahling?" one of them asked.

"My grandpa's over there," she said, and pointed me out.

I froze.

Mrs. Cottsworth called to me, "Sir, do come over and say hello."

I began jabbering. "Well, actually, ma'am, I, uh . . . we have to, uh—"

She cut me off. "Nonsense," she said. "Come here, please." The "please" was gratuitous; it was clear she was not accustomed to being refused.

Feeling like an obedient child, I sidled over and introduced myself. The ladies were as nice as they could be and were enchanted by Amanda. It seemed she was the only child there and the ladies doted on her like grand-mothers. Amanda, of course, gloried in all the attention.

Mrs. Cottsworth leaned down to Amanda and asked, "Would you like your picture taken for the newspaper, dahling?"

Oh, no! I thought, but Amanda was thrilled.

"Oh, *yes*, ma'am," beamed Amanda, "that would be so cool!"

Mrs. Cottsworth looked around, saying to no one in particular, "Now, where's Herbert?" Then, spotting small mousy a man in his mid-fifties with a camera, she called out, "Herbert, come here, please."

The man scurried over like a well-trained puppy, gushing solicitously.

"Yes, madam?" he begged.

"Herbert, I would like you to photograph young Amanda here and her grandfather."

It was obvious that Herbert was accustomed to agreeing with Mrs. Cottsworth and agreed instantly. "Why, of course, Missus Cottsworth, anything you say, Missus Cottsworth." But upon actually catching sight of Amanda in her fairy princess garb, he hesitated momentarily. "*This* little girl, Missus Cottsworth?"

Mrs. Cottsworth replied with just one word. "Yes."

"Certainly, Missus Cottsworth, certainly." Poor Herbert He circled Amanda and me like a cat, searching in vain for the most advantageous angle, but his frustration was evident.

"And, Herbert . . .," Mrs. Cottsworth said.

"Yes, madam?"

"Please make certain the picture goes in tomorrow's paper."

Herbert blanched noticeably. "But, madam," he wheedled, "I can't promise you—"

Mrs. Cottsworth leveled a glare at him that cut off any possibility of negotiation.

Herbert sagged. "Yes, madam, of course, madam." He quickly snapped a picture of all of us, then fled back to the entrance for more suitable quarry.

Sensing an opportunity to escape, I pounced. "Come along, Amanda," I said, "it's time to take our seats."

"Okay, Grandpa. Bye, ladies."

They all responded at once, smiling merrily.

"Ta-ta, Amanda"

"Enjoy the show."

"Love your dress."

We could hear the orchestra tuning up as we walked back to the entrance and gave our tickets to the lady at the booth. Weaving our way through the lobby, we passed under a portal into the opera house proper. Upon entering, we were stopped short by the sheer magnificence of the place. All I could think of for comparison was pictures I had seen of royal palaces. Its size was breathtaking. The seating area seemed to go on forever. Adding to the feeling of spaciousness was the total lack of supporting columns to impede one's view. Everything was on a grand scale—the draperies, the seats, the stage, even the orchestra pit. Throw in the throng of Boston swells, and I felt even more like a bumpkin. Amanda's mouth was hanging open. All she could say was "This is *byoo*-tiful!"

We were approached by an usher (who was dressed far better than I). He only raised his eyebrows slightly upon seeing Amanda's outfit, showed us to our seats, and gave us the program for the evening. Hilda was right, these *were* some of the best seats in the house. We were three rows behind the orchestra pit and almost dead center. The orchestra, the stage, the wings, all seemed almost within our reach. So far, at least, I was overwhelmed and humbled by the grandeur of the place.

My next, and even more pleasant, surprise occurred when I looked at the program. In my ignorance, I had assumed that all shows at the Opera House were operas. And being a cultural barbarian, I hadn't even bothered to find out what we were going to see. I discovered, to my utter delight, that the concert was a Christmas program. Dame Olivia was the centerpiece, to be sure, but there were two other features also—a choir and a dance troupe. *Hmmm*, I thought, *maybe this won't be so bad*. I nudged Amanda and pointed at the program, "A Classical Christmas." She beamed and clapped her hands, enthralled with the entire experience.

The lights dimmed and the orchestra ceased warming up. In a moment, all the crowd's bustle and conversation stopped. It was quiet as a tomb. Presently, we heard the "tap-tap" of the conductor's baton, then the stage lights snapped on. The orchestra and chorus opened with a brief, lively version of "We Wish You a Merry Christmas," immediately followed by an off-stage voice intoning, "Ladies and gentlemen, Dame Olivia Hamilton."

Sweeping onstage like a queen, she acknowledged the thunderous applause with a gracious bow. She was dressed beautifully in a gown of classic simplicity; every detail of her person and manner was flawless. Her very presence demanded one's full attention. After a couple more bows, she held up her hands to quiet the audience. In a crystalline voice, she thanked the crowd warmly, reminding them that a generous portion of the evening's proceeds was slated for donation to a local children's hospital. She introduced the orchestra, then the group behind her, which turned out to be a children's choir from a local church. The kids all mugged cutely at the applause, no doubt aware of their good fortune and eager to show their stuff.

Dame Olivia then began the program proper, opening with a beautiful rendition of "Adeste Fidelis." I had, of course, heard this beautiful carol countless times, but never the way Dame Olivia sang it. I knew her reputation and was expecting something special, but I was, very simply, stunned by her talent. She imbued a sensitivity and a warmth that mesmerized me; it seemed she was singing to me alone. In short, I was hooked immediately and felt sure everyone else in the audience felt the same way.

As she sang, I observed her more closely. She was a woman of classic beauty, every detail of her appearance attended to perfectly. She easily could have been a *real* fairy princess! But what struck me most forcefully, I think, was her size. She appeared to be a tiny woman, not much taller than Amanda. Where that magnificent voice came from, I couldn't imagine. There were no microphones anywhere that I could see, and the place was huge. But every note, every inflection, came through perfectly clearly;

nothing was lost at either end of the scale or from being drowned out. Even when she, and the choir, and the orchestra, rose to a crescendo, everything was clearly audible without being overwhelming. It gave me tingles. When I glanced at Amanda, she appeared to be in a trance; she was still as stone, her mouth hanging open. I presumed that she liked it!

When the song ended, the audience erupted in applause. Again, Dame Olivia bowed imperially and held up her hands to quiet the crowd. I understood the need to move on to the other songs, but it was truly difficult not to get swept up in the appreciation of her talent.

Several numbers followed in the same manner: "Joy to the World," "Hark! The Herald Angels Sing," "O, Little Town of Bethlehem"—timeless standards that seemed somehow elevated by the magic of Dame Olivia's presence and talent.

We were so immersed in the show that the time flew by. Before we realized it, the program told us it was almost time for intermission. Dame Olivia introduced the final number of the first half of the show, Handel's "Hallelujah Chorus," and exited the stage as the choir gave a lovely rendition of that masterful work. At its conclusion, the audience erupted again, the curtains closed, and the lights came up.

Amanda turned to me. "Golly, Grandpa," she said, "I didn't think it would be *this* good!"

"Me, neither," I had to admit. "Come on, let's get a snack before intermission is over."

"Oh, boy. Do you think they have root beer floats?"

I laughed. "I doubt it, honey, but let's go see what they do have."

We got a couple of sodas and some candy to tide us over and went back to our seats. It was plain that Amanda was deeply impressed with the entire production, especially Dame Olivia.

"Boy, Grandpa, Aunt Hilda sure was right. Dame Olivia *is* great." She sighed dreamily. "And so beautiful!"

I agreed wholeheartedly. My feelings about our little trip had changed dramatically. The day had been perfect and I was enjoying the evening as much as Amanda was. I couldn't wait for the second half to begin, and we still had a full day planned for Sunday!

At the first sound of the offstage announcer, the crowd quieted completely, then exploded as Dame Olivia walked on. After calming the audience, she smiled beatifically and said, "Ladies and gentlemen, we are pleased to present a special treat for you tonight. If you are like me, Christmas just doesn't seem like Christmas without 'The Nutcracker.' We have with us tonight a troupe of young people from The Children's Ballet. They are going to perform three movements for you from that perennial Christmas classic. Please give a warm welcome to . . . The Children's Ballet."

After polite applause, the orchestra began with "The Dance of the Sugar Plum Fairies." The children entered from both sides of the stage, romping through their roles with enthusiasm, if not precision. There were occasional miscues, as one might expect from children but, overall, they managed to be very serious and very cute at the same time. I watched Amanda during the performance. She was delighted, giggling and moving with the music through it all. I think it was her first time seeing "The Nutcracker," and it must have added to her enjoyment to watch children who were about her age performing so well. Being a bit of a ham, she may have felt that was something she could do also.

The whole performance of the three movements lasted perhaps twenty minutes. When it was over, the applause was far louder than it had been when they began. Amanda jumped up out of her seat and was clapping excitedly, a big smile on her face. The children bowed sweetly, obviously thrilled by the reaction of the crowd, then bounded off the stage. Dame Olivia came out, clapping, and called them back for another bow. The applause grew even louder as the children happily bowed and curtsied again. They had worked hard and won the hearts of their audience—the ultimate reward for performers at every level.

As the children exited and the crowd settled down, Dame Olivia once again commanded the spotlight. I was struck anew by her magnetic presence. I simply could not get over how she held the attention of the entire audience, so easily it seemed, in the palm of her hand. I wondered if that was an acquired talent, like juggling, or if some people were simply born with it. She made it seem so natural that I instinctively leaned toward the latter.

She sang continuously for the better part of an hour, performing several lovely standards as well as some classical works which I remembered hearing every Christmas, but whose names I never learned. It was a stunning performance; one I shall never forget. She finished with an "Ave Maria" solo, with the merest hint of accompaniment from the orchestra. Her clear, sweet voice was all that was needed. It carried effortlessly to the farthest reaches, to every seat in the house. At the conclusion, after a moment of absolute silence, the audience exploded. These august society folks were clapping and whistling and stomping like adolescents at a rock concert. Everyone was standing, shouting, trying to do justice to the miracle they had just witnessed. The roar was deafening. Dame Olivia smiled even wider and thanked the crowd with numerous curtsies, but the bedlam continued. Someone came on stage and handed her an enormous bouquet of red roses, which she cradled in her arms as she continued acknowledging the audience's appreciation. After what seemed like ages, she left the stage, but the noise, if anything, got even louder. The crowd began the chant, "Encore!" "Encore!" which intensified until it seemed the building wouldn't stand it. Dame Olivia came back, smiled sweetly, and spoke briefly to the conductor. She then took center stage, gathered herself, and began a lovely rendition of "Silent Night." As she finished the first verse, she paused briefly, asking the audience to stand and join her in the second verse. And we did, Amanda and I belting it out with all our heart. As we finished and were applauding, I glanced over at Amanda. She was so moved by the performance that tears were running down her cheeks.

That's so sweet, I thought. *She probably doesn't even know she's crying!* But then she looked at me, and *her* face lit up with surprise.

"Grandpa," she exclaimed, "you're crying!"

"I *am*?" I said. Awkwardly running my fingers across my cheeks, I realized it was true. We had both been affected in the same way by the matchless performance. I pulled her close and gave her a big hug.

She was smiling hugely and still clapping, but a problem had become apparent. "I didn't bring a purse, Grandpa," she sniffled. "I don't have a hankie."

"That's okay, honey. Here." My tuxedo had a beautiful silk handkerchief in the breast pocket, so I offered it to her first. She took it, fluffed it open, carefully wiped her cheeks, then blew her nose lustily into it. "Thanks, Grandpa," she said, handing it back to me.

"Uh, sure," I replied. I retrieved it cautiously, folded it a few times to find a relatively dry portion, then patted down my own cheeks.

The entire audience was now up and exiting through all the aisles. Rather than stand in line, we decided to remain seated until the crowd dispersed. We relaxed and talked about the show and how much we had enjoyed it. Amanda went on and on about Dame Olivia—her lovely voice, her gown, how beautiful she was. It was clear that she had acquired a new heroine.

Presently, it was time to leave, so we got up and followed the last of the patrons out. As we entered the lobby, we noticed there was a crowd gathered at the far end.

"Grandpa," Amanda asked, "what's going on?"

I looked over. There was a line of patrons and a poster that read, "Get an Autographed Poster of Dame Olivia Hamilton and Support Our Local Youth Group — Only $100.00."

A hundred bucks for a poster! I thought. "Oh, nothing," I replied, picking up the pace. "Come on, honey, it's getting late."

"Okay, Gran . . . WAIT!—There she is! Look, Grandpa, Dame Olivia is signing posters!"

Being so small, Dame Olivia was hidden from my view initially, but sure enough, there she was, signing posters and shaking hands as the line passed in front of her. Amanda was hopping up and down, she was so excited.

"Can we get a poster, Grandpa, please?"

"Amanda, honey, that's a lot of money and it's a long line. We'd better get back to the hotel. We've got a big day tomorrow and—"

"But, Grandpa," she wailed, "I'll get to meet her and shake her hand and—and it's *only* a hundred dollars! And it's for a good cause, and—"

Out of desperation, she began wailing like a banshee, attracting the attention of an elderly couple who were passing by behind us. The woman stopped and gave me a withering stare, no doubt wondering how I could be so crass. Her husband stayed behind her, taking it all in. He was clearly amused by my predicament and sported a good-natured grin. *Buddy*, he seemed to be thinking, *you don't have a chance!*

But a hundred bucks!

Amanda looked up at me and said softly, "Please." She had perfected this little con over the last few years, primarily because it never failed. She knew that, unless it was something completely absurd, or outright illegal, I had no defense. "Sure, honey," I groaned, "you're right, it's only a hundred bucks."

We purchased our poster and got in line. I was conscious of people gazing at Amanda's outfit, but she was oblivious. Her entire attention was focused on her new heroine, who was drawing ever nearer. While we proceeded in line, I took the opportunity to observe Dame Olivia more closely. She was, if possible, even more beautiful than she had appeared on stage. Her persona was that of a complete professional, without seeming at all condescending. Her smile was radiant and she looked everyone directly in the eye, as if they were the only ones in the room. She would sign the posters quickly with a flourish, then shake hands warmly and thank the people for their support of the children. A couple of young men who were standing to her right and slightly behind her would then direct the people along, discreetly but firmly.

The line moved along well, and soon we were next. Amanda was fidgeting, her stare unblinking. As we moved into place before Dame Olivia, she appeared mildly surprised as she took in Amanda's bizarre getup, then smiled even brighter, more genuinely.

"Finally," she said, looking sweetly at Amanda, "someone my size!" The people in line chuckled, but Amanda said nothing. She was hypnotized. "Did you enjoy the show, dahling?"

That broke the spell. "Oh, *yes,* ma'am!" Amanda gushed. "It was the best show *ever.* I wouldn't have missed it for *anything.*" And on and on. Once Amanda began talking, the floodgates were open. She could talk to anyone.

Dame Olivia listened patiently, seemingly charmed, then broke in, "Do you live in Boston?"

"No, ma'am. I live in Florida, but I'm staying in Maine this winter, in Moosaquit, up the coast. My grandpa and Uncle Angus and I are building a boat there. I've never seen snow before. It took us three hours to get here, but it was worth it."

When Amanda paused for breath, Dame Olivia broke in again (it was the only way to slow down Amanda once she got going). "My goodness," she said, "all that sounds so exciting. I envy you. And thank you for coming such a long way." She looked fondly at Amanda, then said, "I see you have a poster; would you like me to sign it?"

Amanda couldn't contain herself. "*Would* you? Oh, yes, ma'am. *Thank* you, ma'am." She was bouncing from one foot to the other.

Dame Olivia was giggling now, clearly enjoying herself, but I noticed a change in the demeanor of the people behind us. The indulgent smiles had turned to impatient shuffling of feet. Preparing to write, Dame Olivia asked, "What's your name, dear?"

"Amanda, ma'am."

Dame Olivia smiled. "That's a very pretty name for a very pretty little girl."

Starstruck, Amanda blurted out, "You're the most beautiful woman in the whole world!"

At that, Dame Olivia tossed back her head and laughed out loud. She sounded like a crystal bell. "My," she said, glancing sideways at me, "what a perceptive child." Still chuckling, she signed the poster in a large, flowing hand and gave it back to Amanda, who cradled it like a newborn child.

At this point, one of the young men to Dame Olivia's right, thinking correctly that Amanda had taken far more time than anyone else had, moved forward.

"Come along, Miss," he said, "this way plea—"

That was as far as he got. Dame Olivia turned to him immediately. With no outward sign of emotion, she froze him with a single stare. The unfortunate young man turned a mild shade of avocado and cowered backward, obviously terrified. The other usher seemed amused by his companion's pickle, but he also moved discreetly back a step. In that brief moment, I saw how Dame Olivia had got her reputation. *Better tread lightly here*, I thought. "We really should be going," I said politely, anxious to get off this stage. "Come on, Amanda."

"Please wait," Dame Olivia said. She hesitated very briefly, seemingly mulling over something, then said, "Amanda, how would you like to have dessert with me after the signing?"

I was flabbergasted. "Gosh, Dame Olivia," I began, "that's a lovely offer, but we couldn't possibly impose on—"

She waved me off. "It's no imposition at all, really. How about it, Amanda?"

Without even looking at me, Amanda blurted out, "We'd *love* to! Oh, boy! That'd be great, wouldn't it, Grandpa?"

I didn't know what to say. It seemed so surrealistic, I wasn't even sure it was happening. I felt extremely uncomfortable, but her offer seemed genuine, and I certainly couldn't insult a person of her stature by refusing. I mean, how many people get an invitation like this? Amanda was focused on me expectantly, hanging on my decision. "Why, of course, Dame Olivia," I finally said, "we'd love to."

Amanda clapped her hands excitedly. "Oh, goodie! What's for dessert?"

Dame Olivia turned to the recently chastened young man and instructed him to escort us to her dressing room. Eager to return to her good graces, he guided us politely away as Dame Olivia turned back to her line of guests, gracious as ever.

The usher let us into the dressing room and told us to make ourselves comfortable, explaining how to ring for him if there was anything we needed. He said Dame Olivia would be along shortly, then left. Amanda wandered around the small room, looking at pictures, admiring the gowns, primping at the makeup mirror. I was very unsettled, my only thought being, *What are we doing here?* I found a chair, sat down, and tried to relax.

After what seemed an eternity, the door opened and in walked Dame Olivia. She smiled warmly as she greeted us. I introduced myself, a bit self-consciously, but she immediately put me at ease with her natural charm and grace. She appeared much more relaxed now, more human. I even thought I detected a note of relief in her manner, as if the strain of performing at her level had taken a toll. We exchanged small talk as she removed her makeup. When she was done, she pushed an intercom button and said, "We'll have our dessert now, James."

"Yes, ma'am" came the reply.

Dame Olivia settled into an overstuffed chair with a contented sigh. She then turned to Amanda and said, "Now, tell me all about this boat you're building."

Well, that's all it took. She told Dame Olivia everything—how big it was, what kind of sail it carried, all the work she did on it, when it would be finished, and on and on. Dame Olivia listened intently as Amanda went on about Angus and Hilda. She laughed when Amanda told her about Duncan and how he would attack me when I wasn't looking. And she smiled warmly, almost wistfully, when Amanda told her about all the animals and how she took care of them. Amanda's enthusiasm was infectious. Dame Olivia seemed genuinely delighted to hear it all. The dessert came, cherries jubilee, but Amanda just rambled on, encouraged by the participation of her new friend.

"Hilda is from England, too," Amanda said. "She thinks you're the *best*."

Dame Olivia was in a playful mood. "From England *and* she likes me? She sounds brilliant!"

"Oh, she is. She makes the best apple pie in the world! She's teaching me all about cooking—her and Aunt Jannie."

"Aunt Jannie?" inquired the diva.

"That's Grandpa's wife," explained Amanda.

Dame Olivia glanced at me sidelong, then back at Amanda. "Your grandpa is married to your aunt?" she asked.

"Yup," replied Amanda, apparently seeing no need for further elaboration.

"Long story," I said with a grin.

"Anyway," continued Amanda, "Hilda bought the tickets for your show and was really excited about seeing you, but she got pneumonia yesterday and—"

"Pneumonia?" Dame Olivia looked startled. She turned to me. "My goodness. That can be serious. Is she all right?"

"She's going to be fine," I assured her. "Angus took her to the doctor right away and it was diagnosed immediately. She just can't go anywhere for several days. It's a shame, because I can't tell you how much she admires you and how much she was looking forward to seeing you perform. So, she insisted I bring Amanda instead. She'll be thrilled to hear we got to meet you."

Dame Olivia's expression softened. "How sweet. She sounds lovely."

The two of them carried on in this manner, like old friends who hadn't seen each other for some time and were getting caught up. For my part, I stayed out of the way, enjoying my cherries jubilee. Except for my explanation of Hilda's condition, I might as well have been the doorknob, for all I contributed to the conversation.

We must have been there close to an hour when the door cracked open. It was James. "The limo is here, ma'am," he whispered gently through the opening.

Dame Olivia sighed. "All right, James, tell them I'll be along shortly."

"Yes, ma'am," he said, retreating.

"And, James . . ."

"Yes, ma'am?"

"Bring another poster, please."

"Yes, ma'am."

Dame Olivia turned to us apologetically. "This has been such fun," she said, "but I'm afraid I really must get to the airport. Amanda, did you bring a camera?"

"Yes, ma'am," Amanda replied.

"Good. When James comes back, he can take a picture of us. Would you like that?"

"Oh, yes, ma'am! That'll be great. We can show Hilda!"

James returned with another poster and dutifully took a couple of pictures of the three of us. Dame Olivia unrolled the poster and with her large pen, wrote:

DEAR HILDA,
KEEP A STIFF UPPER LIP AND GET WELL SOON
I'M SORRY I MISSED YOU
YOUR FRIEND AND COMPATRIOT,
OLIVIA HAMILTON

She rolled the poster back up, inserted it into its tube, and handed it back to me.

"That was a beautiful gesture," I said warmly. "It will positively make her day. Thank you so much."

She smiled. "Angus and Hilda sound like such wonderful people. I wish I had met them, too." She turned to Amanda. "Well, sweetheart, I suppose it's time to go. Do you have your poster and your camera?"

"Yes, ma'am."

Dame Olivia went to her dressing table. When she came back, she handed Amanda a business card. "Here, darling. If you would like to write to me, we can be pen pals. All right?"

"Oh, yes, Dame Olivia, that would be super!"

"And," the Dame continued, "now that we're pen pals, why don't you call me what my friends call me—Livvy?"

Amanda was ecstatic, but then she caught herself and looked to me for approval.

I shrugged my shoulders and smiled. "After everything else that's happened tonight, how can I say no! We'll call this a special exception—of course it's all right."

"Thanks, Grandpa," she cried and rushed over to give "Livvy" a big hug.

"Come on, honey," I said, "we don't want to wear out our welcome."

"Okay, Grandpa," she replied and turned to Dame Olivia. "Livvy," she said, "can I please use the bathroom?"

Olivia smiled and said, "Certainly, dahling. It's over there down the hall."

"Thanks, Livvy."

I was shaking my head as Amanda left.

"What a lovely child," said the Dame. "You're very lucky."

"Yes, I am," I agreed.

As we passed a moment or two in a slightly awkward silence, I took the opportunity to express my appreciation. "Dame Olivia," I began, assuming the pen-pal privilege did not extend to me, "I have to say something. This has been a magical evening, one Amanda will remember for the rest of her life. I don't know why you singled her out, but I'm so glad you did." I took her hand in both of mine. "Thank you so very much," I said with all the warmth I could summon.

She nodded graciously and said, "That's very sweet, Jim, but in all honesty, I believe I enjoyed the evening at least as much as she did. You see, I've always loved children. That's why I do so much charity work for them. When I saw Amanda in that outlandish outfit, I couldn't help myself—she stole my heart."

"Well," I said, "for whatever reason, I'm so glad we had this time together." I paused. "Do you have any children?"

"No. I pursued a different course. I was blessed with a rare talent which was discovered at a very young age. I realized my good fortune and did all I could to develop my gift." She grew pensive. "I've been all over the world, Jim. I've met kings, queens, and presidents. Enormous opportunities were open to me because of my voice. It's been a wonderful, fulfilling career and I truly would not have traded it for anything. But no one gets blessed with everything in this life." She paused. "I didn't get . . . that," and she nodded in the direction of Amanda, who was coming back up the hallway.

"All set, Grandpa," she said. Then, "Livvy, where are you flying to?"

"India."

"Wow! That's so exciting!"

"I suppose," replied Dame Olivia with just a trace of melancholy, "but I think I'd really rather be going to Maine."

Amanda laughed. "If you do," she said, "please come visit us. I'll make you a blueberry pie!"

Dame Olivia smiled. "It's a deal," she said, and gave Amanda a long hug.

"Thank you again, Dame Olivia," I said, and held out my hand. To my utter astonishment, she got up on her tip toes and kissed me on the cheek.

"No," she said, "thank *you.*"

We walked back to the hotel on a cloud. Amanda jabbered on about the entire evening while I kept going over it in my mind. It was all so extraordinary that I could scarcely believe it had actually happened. What a story we'd be telling Hilda!

CHAPTER 22

....

After walking back so late to the hotel, we slept in the next morning. When I finally did awaken, it was already past eight o'clock. I looked over at Amanda. She was snuggled down in her bed, still fast asleep, with the rolled-up poster lying next to her. I got up, took my shower, and got dressed while she dozed on. The big night must have drained her; she looked like she could sleep all day. I roused her gently, reminding her of all the things we had to do. She awoke, grudgingly at first, and then, after finding her bearings, greeted me with a big sleepy smile and a "Good morning, Grandpa."

"Hi, sweetie," I replied. "Time to get up. I'm going downstairs to get some coffee. When you're ready, come down and we'll have breakfast, okay?"

"Okay, Grandpa," she said through a yawn.

"Don't go back to sleep, now," I admonished as I was leaving.

She laughed. "I won't, Grandpa, I promise."

Exiting the elevator in the lobby, I saw a stack of newspapers piled on a sideboard. I picked one up, went to the dining room, and chose a table with plenty of light so I could read. The waiter came over to ask what I would like to drink. I told him coffee and orange juice for now, that there would be another person joining me soon. The breakfast buffet was laid out invitingly, but I wanted to wait for Amanda. He brought my coffee and juice as I began sorting the paper—first the sports section, then the front page, then, because it was Sunday, all the other sections that were not in the everyday editions. It was a Sunday morning ritual I had savored for decades.

I was pleasantly leafing through the thick stack, sorting out what I wanted to read and setting aside what held no interest for me—the classifieds, local news, the society page—when my attention was instantly drawn to the photo on the very first page of the society section. There we were, in a picture that took up half the page, Amanda and me, surrounded by the social elite of Boston. Amanda was in the middle of the picture, standing tall and smiling proudly in her fairy princess dress. The local dowagers surrounded her and were all smiling down at her maternally. I, fortunately, was off to the side, stiff as a poker and with a silly smile stuck on my face. I gawked at the picture and burst out laughing. *Wait 'til Angus sees this!*

I was still chuckling when Amanda came to join me, wide awake now and bubbly. "What's so funny, Grandpa?" she asked.

I pushed the paper in front of her and watched as her expression turned to astonishment. She squealed with delight, attracting the looks of everyone around us, as she read the caption over the photo:

'YOUNG PRINCESS ATTENDS CHRISTMAS GALA'

The story rambled on, relating how Amanda had traveled so far to attend the event, mentioning her role in the upcoming school play in Moosaquit, and dropping other assorted personal trivia. Apparently, she had jabbered on to the society ladies about her entire life's history and they pieced together the caption for the photo. It could only have happened to Amanda.

I shook my head, pleased to see her so tickled by the bizarre turn of events. We got a few more newspapers so we could tear out the photo and story from each and send them to her parents and friends. She was like a queen bee, aflutter with all the attention.

The waiter came back to our table and took Amanda's drink order (root beer), then we launched an all-out attack on the lavish buffet. After a hearty breakfast, we were on our way. It was another picture-perfect day in Boston, but the forecast for central Maine was calling for more severe weather—high winds and the possibility of a snowstorm. Amanda was excited about the forecast, as it hadn't snowed yet and she, like all kids, thought snow was great fun. I knew better. We would cut our day short and go home early. Since we had only half a day, we decided to begin walking the Freedom Trail at Faneuil Hall, visit the Old North Church and as much else as we could comfortably see, then head back home. We could eat lunch on the road to save time.

Visiting the venerable old landmark was a first for Amanda and she was deeply impressed by seeing the actual church and steeple from the legendary story of our birth as a nation. Her eyes were wide with wonder as she listened to the enactor telling the story of the lanterns and the heroic rides of Paul Revere, William Dawes, and Dr. Prescott to warn of the coming British assault. I have to say, it gave me tingles as my imagination took me back to that fragile time so long ago and how different it all could have turned out.

After, we visited the North Bennet Street School, which is right across the street from the church and is dedicated to preserving crafts and skills from our colonial past. It's a wonderful school and I stop in there whenever I'm in the area. The students there produce beautiful work and it's encouraging to know that there are still young people who care about our esthetic heritage.

Because of the late start, we were running out of time, so we headed back toward Faneuil Hall, passing by Paul Revere's home and several other attractions Amanda wanted to see. But she started to get whiny. "Grandpa," she sniveled, "why do we have to go home now? We're missing a lot of good stuff. And the weather's *byoo*-tiful. It's not going to snow. It's *never* going to snow!" She was pouting.

I didn't know whether to scold her or be pleased she was so interested in our history. "That's enough, Amanda," I said. "We can always come back another time. These things will still be here. And, remember, winter hasn't even officially begun yet. Believe me, you'll see plenty of snow before it's over."

"Okay," she moped, setting me up. After a pause, she ventured, "Maybe we can stop and get some fried clams for lunch?"

I had to laugh. She played me like a fiddle. "Okay," I said. "We'll go back part of the way on Route 1. I'm sure we'll find something that will satisfy you."

That lit her up. "Thanks, Grandpa!"

We went back to the hotel, checked out, and within an hour, we had found a nice take-out. We stocked up on fried clams, French fries, root beer, and a couple slices of homemade pie before getting back on the interstate and driving north. As simple as it was, the bags of food suited us perfectly. We drove on, enjoying our feast and revisiting yet again the amazing weekend. Amanda kept going over her brochures, looking at the society page photo, and unrolling, then re-rolling, her precious poster. She was itching to get home and tell everyone about her adventures of the weekend and her new friendship with "Livvy." It made me grin every time she said the name, imagining how Hilda would react.

When we pulled up our driveway, it was almost five o'clock and totally dark. The wind was howling and a spattering of snow was beginning to fall, but the real nasty weather seemed to be staying north of us. Amanda was disappointed, but I breathed a sigh of relief, feeling we had dodged a bullet.

Jan came out to meet us and Amanda flew into her arms, talking a blue streak, making no sense whatsoever.

"Whoa, slow down," Jan laughed as they hugged. But Amanda couldn't stop. She kept babbling on, trying to tell Jan everything at once, tripping over her tongue, getting confused, starting over.

Trying to calm her down, I said, "Amanda, let's get our luggage into the house before it gets worse. Then we'll call Angus and Hilda. If Hilda is up to it, we'll drive over and you can tell everyone about our trip all at once. Okay?"

She was somewhat chastened, but since large, cold raindrops and snowflakes were beginning to splatter down on us, she agreed. In no time at all, we had stowed everything and were safely inside the house.

I phoned Angus and Hilda and got a nice surprise when Hilda answered the phone.

"Hi, Hilda," I said, "how are you feeling?"

"Good as new," she replied in a firm voice. "I told you that young doctor didn't know what he was talking about. Pneumonia, indeed. Hmmph."

I chuckled. "Well, I'm glad you're feeling better, Hilda; you scared us all. Do you feel like having some company?"

She fairly leaped through the phone. "I certainly do," she blurted immediately. "I want to hear all about Dame Olivia. I baked a pumpkin pie today and Angus is putting on the coffee as we speak. I can't wait."

Her excitement made me chuckle. "Okay, Hilda, we'll be over shortly."

I hung up, smiling. "She sounds great," I told Jan and Amanda. "She even baked a pie for us and said to come over right away; she's dying to hear all about Dame Olivia." I chuckled. "Boy, is she going to be surprised!"

Jan looked at me. "Why is she going to be surprised?" she asked.

Amanda and I exchanged cryptic glances. "You'll see," she said.

"Oh, no," she groaned comically, "what have you two done now?"

I tried to sound mysterious. "Come on; you'll find out soon enough. Do you have Hilda's present, Amanda?"

"Sure do, Grandpa."

"Good, let's go."

We got in the car and drove the short distance up Shore Road. As we pulled in, we could see Duncan running up the drive. He knew the sound of the car that brought Amanda and he was dancing around, barking happily. Amanda got out and gave him a cupcake that she had brought for him. It disappeared down his maw in an instant. She then made a big fuss over him, as she always did. He kept circling her, grinning wetly. He felt so good that he glanced at me, perhaps considering taking me down, but I wasn't in the mood. I cut short his fun with a firm "NO!" He got a comically disappointed expression on his face, as if he were amazed that I could have discerned his intentions. Disappointed but undaunted, he followed us into the house.

Inside, we all greeted one another with hugs and kisses, as if Amanda and I had been gone for a month instead of two days. Hilda was indeed looking much better, moving around well and with her old spirit.

"You look great, Hilda," I commented and hugged her warmly.

"Thank you. I'm feeling much better. I don't know why I have to stay indoors, but Angus insists. I think the sooner I get off these pills and back to my regular routine, the better off I'll be. I'm going crazy, just sitting around here all day."

Amanda piped up, "I have a special surprise for you, Aunt Hilda."

Hilda smiled sweetly at her. "Thank you, dear, but I have something special for you, too. I baked a fresh pumpkin pie today and I made some hot cocoa, too. Would you like that?"

Silly question. "Oh, boy, that sounds great!"

"Good. Now you just sit right there while I fix everything, and then I want you to tell me all about Dame Olivia. And don't leave out a thing, all right?"

Amanda laughed. "Okay, Aunt Hilda."

Hilda went into the kitchen. Presently, we could hear plates rattling and silverware tinkling. I said to Angus, "Boy, she looks great."

He smiled. "Yes, she's made a remarkable recovery. Attributes it all to her English tea and scones. Said she'd be all better except for those pills she's taking." He shook his head comically, but his relief was obvious.

I happened to glance over at the sideboard and saw the Boston paper there. "Did you read the paper, yet?" I asked casually.

"No," he answered, "I usually read it later in the evening, after all the chores are done. Why?"

Amanda couldn't hold it in any longer. She hopped over and got the paper, then brought it to Angus with a big smile on her face. He was perplexed, obviously wondering what could possibly be in the Boston paper that would be of such interest to her. She opened it to the society section and handed it to him. He looked at the "Society Page" headline first, without interest, then let his glance fall to the picture. His eyes popped out and he whooped a colossal roar, causing Duncan to leap up and Hilda to come running in from the kitchen. Jan, having no clue, hurried over to see the big news. Angus was now laughing hard, trying to catch his breath as he read the story aloud. Jan and Hilda were amazed and giggling at the same time. "How in the world . . .?" Jan wondered.

Hilda gaped at the picture. "Why, look at you two," she said. "One day in Boston and you're on the front page!" She looked at Amanda. "No wonder you said you had a big surprise for me. That's wonderful, darling."

"Actually, Aunt Hilda, that's not the big surprise," said Amanda.

"You mean, there's *more*?" said Hilda, intrigued.

"Yup," said Amanda, fairly bursting with her secret knowledge.

But Hilda wouldn't let Amanda tell just yet. She had her own way of doing things and had planned this evening carefully. The picture was a huge stumbling block, but she would not be deterred. "You just hold the news until I get back. I won't be a minute."

Hilda scurried back into the kitchen and now the rattling and tinkling took on a more frenzied pace. In a trice, she was back with her tray full of goodies—pie all around, coffee for Angus and me, tea for her and Jan, and cocoa for Amanda. She set down the tray, doled out our snacks, then sat on the edge of her chair across from Amanda.

"There," she said. "Now, tell me all about the show, and don't leave out *anything*!"

It was cute how excited she was.

"Well—" began Amanda.

"What did she look like?" Hilda interrupted.

"Oh, she's *byoo*-tiful, Aunt Hilda, even prettier than her pictures. And—"

"How was she dressed?" Hilda interrupted again.

"She wore a lovely white gown, not fancy, but *very* pretty. And—"

"How were the seats? Could you see her well? Could you hear all right? I know that's a pretty big place and I was hoping you'd be able to see her—"

Angus interjected, chuckling, "Hilda, calm down," he implored gently. "Amanda is trying to tell you, but you keep interrupting her."

"I do?" she asked, genuinely surprised. We were all tickled by her enthusiasm. Hilda possessed such strict decorum that it made us laugh to see her so animated. "I'm sorry, dear," she said. She was blushing slightly but urged Amanda, "Please go on."

And Amanda did, telling Hilda all about the opulence of the opera house, our perfect seats, the songs Dame Olivia sang, the children's ballet troupe, the church choir, the orchestra and the pit, the thunderous applause and encore, and our joining in the singing of "Silent Night" at the end.

Hilda was enraptured. Except for an occasional "Oh, my" or "How lovely," or sometimes just a soft sigh, she was finally silenced by her eager attention to Amanda's narrative. When Amanda reached the end of the program, Hilda seemed almost drained of emotion.

"That was just wonderful, dear," she said, leaning back in her chair. "Thank you. I'm thrilled that you had such a lovely time."

"That's not all, Aunt Hilda," said Amanda, grinning.

Hilda leaned forward again in anticipation. "There's *more?*"

"Yes. As we were leaving, we saw her signing posters and shaking hands. The posters were only a hundred dollars, so Grandpa bought one and she signed it for me." At the mention of a hundred dollars, Angus chuckled and shot me a sly wink. I just shrugged and grinned sheepishly.

Hilda gasped. "You *shook hands* with Dame Olivia?" It must have seemed beyond belief.

"Yup," replied Amanda, "and afterward we went to her dressing room and had dessert with her—ice cream and cherries. It was yummy."

Hilda was now beyond gasping; she was speechless. Her eyes were round with awe, her face a perfect picture of amazement. Recovering only slightly, she began babbling. "Dessert? With Dame Olivia? In her dressing room? But, how . . .?"

Amanda continued, "It's like this, Aunt Hilda; Grandpa says Livvy didn't—"

Hilda interrupted again, looking to me for clarification. "What's a 'livvy'?" she asked.

Before I could respond, Amanda jumped back in. "*Livvy*, Aunt Hilda, that's Dame Olivia. We're pen pals now so that's what I call her. It's easier. So, anyway—"

Hilda appeared on the verge of a relapse, sagging back in her chair, making strange noises in her throat. If the other revelations were shocks, this one was the knock-out blow. She shook her head dazedly, as if seeking a return to sanity. "You call . . . Dame . . . Olivia . . . Hamilton . . . 'Livvy'?"

"Sure, that's what all her friends call her. Anyway," Amanda continued, "I told Livvy all about you and Uncle Angus and the boat and how you got sick and all, and she sent you this. *This* is the big surprise!"

She gave Hilda the tube with the poster inside. With a confused expression Hilda opened up the tube, removed the poster, and unrolled it in front of her, holding it there for several moments. When she lowered it, there were tears in her eyes. "Oh, my dear child," she sniffled, "I don't know what to say . . . ." She trailed off, overcome by her emotions.

Alarmed, Amanda bent over her. "Don't you like it, Aunt Hilda?"

Hilda was shaken, but she was made of stern stuff. She folded Amanda in her arms and held her for a long time. "Yes, dear, I like it very much. I love it. It's the sweetest, most thoughtful gift you could ever have given me. Thank you so much." Then she hugged Amanda again.

We were all pretty much wilted by then. There was an awkward pause while eyes were wiped and noses were blown, then Hilda lifted her tea for a toast. We all followed suit. "To the best Christmas ever, and we still have a week to go!"

CHAPTER 23

....

We awoke Monday morning to fourteen inches of snow. Everything, the trees, the roads, the roofs, the cars, was encased in a thick, puffy blanket of white. Jan and I gazed out the bedroom window, unbelieving.

"I guess they haven't quite perfected the art of weather forecasting yet," she said dryly.

Amanda was up early, running around and squealing with delight. Now that there was actual snow on the ground, she couldn't wait to get out and play in it with her friends. She was gone before breakfast, making snowballs, sledding, generally having a great time, as kids always have. And I had to admit, it *was* a beautiful scene—everything clean and white, the kids playing and laughing, brilliant sunshine highlighting the majesty of our first snowfall in decades.

When Jan came down, she looked outside at the kids playing. "Sure brings back a lot of happy memories," she sighed, smiling.

"It sure does," I agreed. "Kind of makes me wonder why we stopped wintering up here. Maybe it wouldn't be so bad now that we're retired and don't have to go out in it every day."

"Sure," Jan said, grinning, "tell me about it after you shovel out the driveway and the car."

I looked out the window. There was a huge white lump in our driveway, under which was our car. *Oh, yeah,* I thought, *now I remember!* "You know," I ventured, "it'll probably all just melt away before we even finish breakfast. The sun is out and it's warming up nicely."

"Oh, no, you don't!" she shot back. "I remember the last time you tried that. The snow melted, all right, then froze solid and everything was encased in a block of ice. I'll make you a nice hot breakfast right after you finish shoveling." There wasn't the merest hint of humor or compromise in her tone.

Hmm, I mused, *this could be serious.* I truly hated to shovel snow and would go to almost any length to avoid it. My excuses and ploys are the stuff of legend, but I was not feeling good about my chances here. The noose was tightening and Jan was eyeing me suspiciously, well aware of my predilection for squirming out of this onerous chore. Her stance was clear: no shoveling, no breakfast.

"You know," I said, "Amanda's having such a good time out there, I'll bet she'd *love* to make a few bucks—"

She shook her head. "You're pathetic," she said. "She's eleven years old and weighs seventy-five pounds. Have you no shame?"

I didn't see her point, but I did see that she was running out of patience.

"I'll get the shovel for you," she said, going to the broom closet in the front hall. "It shouldn't take you more than an hour or so, then I'll make you anything you want for breakfast." She gave me the shovel and a peck on the cheek as she opened the front door for me.

I stepped outside, out of options. Half-heartedly, I began shoveling the short walkway, which led to the driveway. Once that was done, I could begin the *real* work of shoveling out the driveway, so I could get to the car and shovel *it* out.

The walkway was perhaps fifteen feet long, but I was panting strongly by the time I got to the end. Even though it was a nippy twenty-five degrees, I could feel the sweat inside my jacket. I was slipping and sliding on the icy walkway, my back was aching from the unnatural exertion, and I had just reached the beginning of our drive. It looked like an airport runway. *Maybe I'll just walk to the diner for breakfast,* I thought. *It's only a couple of miles.*

"Hi, Mister Cairns!"

Startled, I turned around. It was Bobby, walking in the freshly plowed street, pulling his sled along with something on top of it.

"Hi, Bobby," I panted. "How're you doing?"

"Great, Mister Cairns. That's a big driveway, huh?"

"Yeah," I gasped between breaths. "What's that?" I asked, pointing at his sled.

He chuckled. "It's a snowblower," he answered, evidently thinking I was pulling his leg.

"A what?"

"A snowblower," he repeated, grinning. He couldn't believe I was serious.

"What do you do with it?"

At that, he laughed out loud. "You blow snow with it; it's how you clear driveways and sidewalks." He was looking at me as if I were an alien being.

"Oh," I said, chagrined. "We don't have many of those in Florida." He laughed again. "Where are you going with it?"

"I clean people's driveways for them; you know, mostly old and sick people who can't shovel their own driveways. The blower works fast and does a good job on the heavy stuff, then I clean up with a shovel. It's how I make money in the winter. I put it into my college fund."

This was a clear sign straight from God. Trying to appear casual, I inquired, "How much do you charge?"

"Ten dollars, unless it's a really big driveway."

"Sold!" I hollered, tossing the shovel off into a snowbank.

"Seriously? But, gee, Mister Cairns, it'll only take you an hour or so to do it yourself."

"Yeah, I know, and I'd love to—great exercise, of course—but my back's been a little tricky lately and I don't want to aggravate it. Besides, it's for a really good cause, so, what the heck, why don't you just go ahead and do it. Okay?"

"Okay, Mister Cairns, but it's a pretty big driveway—"

Perhaps a little too eagerly, I said, "I'll pay you twenty dollars."

His face lit up. "Sure thing, Mister Cairns! I'll get to it right after I do Missus Parsons."

My face fell. "Missus Parsons?" I wondered aloud. "Why can't you just do it now?"

"Gee, Mister Cairns, I always do Missus Parsons first. She's old and can't even get out of her house until I do her front walkway."

"Hmm, makes sense," I said, ashamed of what I was thinking. "But, really Bobby, you're already right here, so if you did ours first, you wouldn't have to come all the way back later. Besides, old folks don't usually get up until noon time. She'll probably never even know. What do you say?"

But Bobby was dubious. "I don't know, Mister Cairns, I always do her first." He paused. "She's so old . . . and so nice to me . . . and she makes me cookies . . ."

"I'll give you twenty-five dollars." I felt like a snake.

"Wow! *Okay,* Mister Cairns!"

"And, Bobby . . ."

"Yes, Mister Cairns?" He was already unloading the blower.

"From now on, could you do our driveway first? Same price?"

"Sure thing, Mister Cairns!"

I walked back inside, whistling. "Breakfast ready?" I yelled up the stairs.

Jan came skipping down, a disbelieving smile on her face. "Are you finished already, honey? That's great! I told you it wouldn't take too long, once you . . . what's that noise?"

We both looked outside. Bobby was going up and down the driveway, blowing all the snow well off the driveway and into the yard. I was enthralled.

"I don't believe it," Jan said. "A little driveway like that and you're *paying* Bobby to do it? You should be ashamed of yourself." She paused, then eyed me. "How much?"

"Not much, and it's going into his college fund." I smiled paternally. "I like that boy; he's a real go-getter."

"How much?" she repeated.

"Not that much, really, considering—"

"How **much**?"

"Only twenty-five dollars," I replied blithely.

"Twenty-five *dollars*?! *I* would have done it for twenty-five dollars! Are you going to pay him twenty-five dollars every time it snows?" She was becoming unreasonable.

"Well, sort of."

"What do you mean, 'sort of'?"

I sighed. "Okay, yes, of course I'm going to pay him every time. But remember, it's a big driveway, *and* he's going to do us first, *and* it's going toward his education. How would you feel if that boy couldn't go to college because you wanted to save twenty-five bucks?"

Jan turned and headed for the kitchen, muttering, "Unbelievable."

It was getting on toward nine o'clock, so I called Angus. I hadn't wanted to call him too early.

"Hi, Jim," he said as he answered the call. "Are you coming over?"

"Sure," I said, "as soon as I finish breakfast. I—"

"You haven't eaten yet?" He sounded surprised.

I should have been used to his crack-of-dawn schedule by now, but I still got caught occasionally. "Well, with the snow and all, I kind of slept in. Besides, I wanted to give you plenty of time to get up and around."

"What snow? That little dusting?" He chuckled. "Heck, I was up early—had to shovel out the driveway and the path to the barn so that . . . what's that noise?"

Bobby was blowing right next to the house. "Oh, nothing, just Jan in the kitchen. Breakfast is almost ready. I'll be over in about an hour, okay?"

"Sure," he chided, "we can have lunch."

"Very funny."

"And be sure to bring Amanda with you when you come. I've got a surprise for her."

My curiosity was piqued, but I just said, "Sure thing. See you then."

I called Amanda in for breakfast and relayed Angus's message.

"Oh, boy," she said. "Uncle Angus told me last night that he had a surprise for me. I wonder what it is." She was beaming. Like all kids at Christmas time, she was strung as tight as a fiddle.

"Maybe he wants you to shovel out his driveway," I teased.

She laughed. "He just told me to dress warm; that's all he would say. I can't wait."

Jan and I exchanged smiles. We were touched to see how Angus and Hilda felt about Amanda, how much they enjoyed her. They doted on her constantly and were incapable of denying her anything. She raced through breakfast, ran upstairs to straighten her room, then helped Jan clean up the kitchen.

"Ready, Grandpa?"

I smiled. "Sure, honey, right after my nap."

"Grandpa!" she protested.

"All right, all right, I guess I'm ready. Coming, Jan?" I called.

But Jan was already flying down the stairs, pulling on her coat. "You bet I'm coming," she said, every bit as excited as Amanda. The way the two of them carried on, you'd never suspect there was four decades between their ages.

We stepped outside to a miraculous sight; the driveway was spotless, the car had been shoveled out, brushed off, and the windshield scraped of ice. Bobby had even cleaned up the sloppy job I had done on the walkway. I could have cried.

He was loading up his snowblower. "All set, Mister Cairns. How does it look?"

I was in awe. "Like heaven, Bobby, like heaven." It had taken him perhaps twenty minutes, slightly less time than it had taken me to shovel the fifteen-foot walkway. I went over to him and put my hand on his shoulder. I resisted a strong urge to embrace him.

"Bobby," I said, "you did a beautiful job." I reached for my wallet, took out thirty dollars, and handed it to him.

He looked apologetic. "But I don't have any change, Mister Cairns," he said.

"Just keep it, son, you earned it."

His eyes got big and he started to say something, but I smiled conspiratorially and put a finger to my lips. "Let's just keep that between us, okay?"

"Sure, Mister Cairns. Thanks, thanks a *lot!*" He finished loading his snowblower on the sled, then glanced over at Jan and Amanda, who were standing by the car. He began fidgeting. After a moment, he said, "Hi, Amanda."

Amanda blushed and smiled. "Hi, Bobby. Nice job."

Bobby was looking at his shoes. "Thanks, Amanda."

I waited eagerly for more witty repartee, but none came. After an agonizing silence, he shuffled once and said, "Well, I gotta go. Bye, Amanda."

"Okay, Bobby, see ya."

He turned quickly around and walked smack into his snowblower. Blushing furiously, he picked up his towrope and said, "Thanks again, Mister Cairns," and fairly ran up the road toward Missus Parsons' house.

I opened the car doors for the girls, Amanda in the back and Jan in front. As she slid in, Jan smiled and said, "Wasn't that cute? What a nice boy."

"He sure is," I said. "I'm glad we can help him."

In a matter of minutes, we pulled into the McTigue driveway and could see Angus and Duncan over by the barn. Strangely, Duncan looked over and barked, but he stayed right there. He knows the car and normally stops everything to run and greet Amanda. When Angus saw us, he waved and motioned for us to come over to join him. As we approached, we could see he was fiddling around with some kind of sled, laying out and untangling long leather straps. Duncan was next to him, prancing around in a frenzy, looking up only briefly to acknowledge our arrival.

We were intrigued. "What's that, Uncle Angus?" Amanda asked.

"It's a sled, honey, and I'm going to harness it to Duncan. As you can see, he's excited to pull it. That's the kind of work he was bred for. He'd rather do that than anything else." Duncan was watching intently, impatient to get going.

"Wow, that's neat, Uncle Angus! Can I ride in it?" Her eyes shone with excitement.

"Sure, you can, honey, but mostly we're going to be walking while Duncan does the hard work." I looked out over the landscape. It was completely blanketed with heavy snow.

"Uh, Angus," I ventured, "that snow is pretty thick. Where are we walking *to*?"

"Into the woods," he said, as if that explained everything. "Here, boy, **come**," he called to Duncan. The huge dog bounded over immediately, taking his place with barely controlled emotion while Angus fitted him to the harness. When Angus was finished, he stood up. "**Stay!**" he said sharply. The dog stopped stamping, but he was quaking with anticipation. It was plain he wouldn't stay still for long.

Amanda couldn't wait. Her attention was riveted on the dog and the sled. "Can I get in now, Uncle Angus?" she asked.

"Uh, not just yet, honey," he replied, and motioned for Jan and me to join him behind the sled. When we were all situated where he wanted us, he grinned broadly and yelled, "**Okay!**"

It was the word Duncan was waiting for. In an instant he was gone, the sled trailing out behind him like a toy. He flew like a dart in a straight line for a while, headed straight for the forest, then veered off, circling widely around the open field. He seemed to be purposely searching for the deepest drifts, then would blast through them with fierce joy. It was an awesome display of brute strength.

We couldn't help laughing at how Duncan was enjoying himself so much. He seemed oblivious to the sled, which was skipping along behind him, flipping over, then righting itself, then on its side; it didn't matter, his pace never changed. Amanda's eyes were wide.

"Still want to go for a ride, honey?" Angus teased. The sled was now upside down and whipping back and forth.

"Wow!" was all she could say.

Angus grinned. "It's his first time this year, so I knew he'd be a little wild. After he runs for ten or fifteen minutes, he'll settle down. In the meantime, we can try out the snowshoes. And Hilda has made a great lunch for us. When Duncan calms down, he'll come back and we can get started."

We were still in the dark. "But where are we *going*?" Amanda asked.

Angus smiled at her. "That's the surprise. We're going into the woods so you can pick out our Christmas tree. After we cut it down, we'll put it in the sled and Duncan can pull it home for us. We'll trim it after dinner."

Amanda listened to all this with wide-eyed wonder. "You mean, you don't just go out and buy a Christmas tree?" She had never thought about where Christmas trees actually came from.

Angus was having fun toying with her. "Nope, this way we'll get the best tree in the forest. And it's a lot more fun, too. Come on, I'll show you how snowshoes work."

We went over to where the large snowshoes were leaning against the side of the barn. This would be a completely new experience for all three of us, and Jan and I were just as excited as Amanda. We donned our snowshoes then watched as Angus demonstrated how to use them. Amanda went first and after a couple of mishaps, was moving along well.

Looks easy enough, I thought and stepped out confidently. I got the two enormous shoes tangled together immediately and went down in a heap. Then, I couldn't get up. The shoes may as well have been cement blocks tied to my feet. Jan was beside herself, laughing at me.

I grinned. "You haven't tried it yet," I reminded her.

"It doesn't look so hard," she said. "Look at Amanda."

Amanda was indeed gliding along effortlessly, grinning with pride at her new skill.

"Come on, Jannie," she urged, "there's nothing to it."

Jan stepped forward tentatively and went down beside me even quicker than I had, her face planting flush into a small snowbank. Now everybody *but* Jan was laughing. She bobbed up out of the bank, shaking her head like a dog, trying to clear the snow from her eyes, her ears, her collar, her mouth. When she finally did open her eyes, I was ready and popped her right in the kisser with a big, loose snowball. She yelped with surprise and lunged at me, but her shoes rendered her utterly helpless. I peppered her with a couple more nice shots before Angus came over to help us up.

"Now, children," he admonished, "no fighting."

He showed us how to get on our feet, then demonstrated again how to walk. We paid much closer attention the second time. And it really was easy enough, once we got accustomed to the size of the shoes. In no time at all, we were moving right along, though we never could keep up with Amanda.

In the meantime, Duncan had wound down and returned to where we were still gathered, beside the barn. His huge chest was heaving from his exertions, every breath spewing enormous clouds of steam. But his pride and joy were unmistakable. He was doing what he was born to do. Angus knelt down beside him and mussed his hair vigorously, telling him what a good boy he was. The dog responded with vigorous tail-wagging, noisy licking, and his usual big, wet grin. Then Angus righted the sled, untangled the harness, and motioned to Amanda. "Okay, honey, you can get in now."

But Amanda hesitated, her enthusiasm no doubt dampened by Duncan's recent display. "Are you sure it's all right, Uncle Angus?" she asked.

Angus laughed lightly. "Sure, honey," he said. "Duncan's calmed down. He just likes to blow off a little steam every now and then, like all young fellas. Besides, he knows you're in the sled now and he'd never do anything to hurt you"—he turned to Duncan and said with a stern voice— "would you, Duncan?" Duncan drooped his ears and looked contrite. The message was clear: fun time was over; now it was time to pay attention.

Amanda was still apprehensive, but she gingerly stepped into the sled and snuggled in. Angus loaded up the sled with everything we would need—a hatchet, an axe, a large saw, a blanket, some rope, and a rifle, wrapped in a large towel. I eyed the rifle, giving Angus a questioning look. He simply shrugged and said, "We're going into the woods. Better safe than sorry." Hilda brought out an enormous lunch basket and we were ready to go.

We crossed the large field fairly quickly, our snowshoes allowing us to move over the deep snow with little difficulty. Amanda was sitting in the sled with the blanket wrapped around her, grinning happily, while Duncan pulled her along with no apparent effort. I estimated the sled to weigh at least two hundred pounds. I was developing a new respect for the big, good-natured boob.

When we got into the woods, the snow was much thinner, so we stopped to remove our snowshoes and stowed them in the sled. Amanda hopped out to join us as we continued, looking at dozens of trees. They all looked pretty much the same to me, but Angus explained the different species and the traits each possessed. It was fun for a while, but after an hour or so, I was getting hungry and Jan was getting cold. The routine was the same with every tree—we would all gather around it, exclaim how nice it was, and Amanda would furrow her brow as she detected some minor flaw. Then, we would move on. She finally seemed to warm up to a lovely small white pine, but Angus pointed out there was no "Christmas tree smell" and the branches wouldn't hold up well to heavy ornaments. Well, we couldn't have that, so we moved deeper yet into the woods.

While Amanda and Angus were so absorbed, I couldn't help noticing that Jan was growing more and more edgy. She walked very gingerly and continuously swept her gaze around, seemingly apprehensive about something.

I grinned. "Honey," I said, "are you all right?"

"No, I'm not," she shot back. "I don't like this one bit. I'm cold and I'm hungry. We're getting deeper into the woods and farther from home. I think we should head back."

I laughed her off. "Don't be silly. Angus knows these woods like the back of his hand. Besides, he'd never do anything to endanger us."

"Then why did he bring the rifle?"

Uh-oh. I didn't think she had seen that. "Oh, the *rifle*," I said with what I hoped was breezy nonchalance. "That's nothing, just a normal precaution. Mainers don't go anywhere without their gun. What do you think could possibly be out here that could harm us?"

"Bears, wolves, coyotes, wildcats, moose, wolverines . . ."

I laughed at her. "Stop, you're being silly. We're not even a mile from town. The most dangerous thing you'll see out here is a chipmunk."

"I don't believe you," she sneered. "ANGUS!"

He turned away from a small spruce he was showing Amanda. "Yes?"

"Are there any bears out here?"

He blinked, as if he wasn't sure he understood the question. "Of course," he replied, "why do you think I brought my rifle?"

Jan turned on me, fists on her hips, in full attack mode. "Chipmunks, huh? Why, you—" she began.

But Angus sought to allay her fears. "It's okay, Jan, I see bears out here all the time. They're really quite shy, unless they're hungry, or—"

Jan interrupted. "You see bears out here all the time? But they only attack when they're hungry? Bears are *always* hungry." She drew her words out slowly, accusingly. "You brought us out here where you see bears *all the time*?"

At least she was focused on Angus now instead of me. He seemed genuinely surprised that Jan would be so upset over the mere possibility of meeting a carnivorous wild animal in the woods. "Well," he began defensively, "we needed a Christmas tree and—"

"We can *buy* a Christmas tree! At a *tree stand*! Normal people do it all the time!" Her voice was rising, like when she found out I had hired Bobby to clear the driveway. Her day wasn't going well.

Now Angus looked like *he* had seen a bear. He was stuttering, trying to sort things out. He loved Jan and couldn't understand what he might have done to upset her. "But Jan," he whined, "there's nothing to worry about. I wouldn't have brought you and Amanda out here if I thought it was dangerous. Besides"—he motioned toward the sled—"we have Duncan to protect us."

We looked over. Duncan, having gotten bored by the slow pace, had lain down in the snow, on his back, feet in the air. His head lolled to one side and his lips hung loosely open, quivering while he snored contentedly—a most reassuring sight.

Jan shook her head in disbelief. "AMANDA!" she barked.

Amanda had been watching all this with increasing unease. "Yes, ma'am?" she answered meekly.

Jan began issuing orders like a demented drill sergeant. "Pick out a tree—any tree. I don't care if it's a palm tree. You've got five minutes." She turned to Angus and me. "Cut it down, load it up. We're getting out of here before some moose eats us." She was in a lather, no question.

Angus was genuinely concerned and sought to put her at ease. In a monumentally misguided effort, he pointed out, "Actually, Jan, you don't have to worry about that. You see, moose are vegetarians and—"

But she was beyond reason. She lasered him a look that cut off any further discussion, then muttered something under her breath as she stomped off to direct Amanda.

Poor Angus. His regard for Jan was so great that any slight from her was crushing. "What did *I* do?" he moaned.

I slapped him on the back. "Don't worry, old friend," I said, "she'll be all right. She's just a little upset. Some women get that way when they think they might get eaten alive. What possessed you to tell her there were bears out here?"

"What could I do, lie to her?"

I grinned. "Maybe just this once."

"Jim, Angus, over here!" Jan and Amanda were standing beside a lovely little balsam fir tree which Amanda had considered and rejected twice before. "This one will do," she said, without any further consultation. "DUNCAN—COME!" The shrill command was like an electric shock to the sleeping dog. He leapt to his feet and dragged the sled to where we stood, looking dazed and disoriented. Jan stared impatiently at Angus and me. "Well?"

We obediently fell to, dropping the small tree with a dozen or so blows of the axe. "There," said Angus. "Now we'll just limb it up a bit and shape it before we—"

"We can do all that back at the house," Jan said curtly. "Load it up and let's get out of here." By now, she was seeing goblins behind every tree.

Angus shrugged meekly, looking like a chastised schoolboy. "Okay, Jan" was all he said. We loaded up the small tree in a few minutes, aligning the branches and tying it securely. "All set," Angus said brightly, hoping to smooth things over. "Now we can relax and have some lunch."

"Great idea," Jan shot back sarcastically. "That'll attract all the hungry bears in the area! No. We're going home—now. We'll have lunch there, inside a house, where there's heat, and chairs, and tables, and hot water, and . . ." She was rambling now, more unhinged than I had ever seen her. I was beginning to doubt her pioneering spirit.

We all gave Jan a wide berth while we gathered everything together for the hike back. Even Duncan seemed to sense the mood had changed and was sitting obediently, awaiting his marching orders.

When all was ready, we set out, retracing our tracks out of the woods. We arrived back at the house in the early afternoon without having encountered even one pack of ravenous carnivores.

When we entered the house, Hilda was working in the kitchen. She looked up, surprised.

"My, you're back early," she said. "I didn't expect you for a while, yet. Did you get a tree?"

"We sure did, Aunt Hilda," Amanda cried. "And it's a beauty. Uncle Angus says it's a balsam fir. I didn't know there were so many different kinds of Christmas trees. It smells great!"

"That's nice, darling," she said. "Did you see any bears?"

Jan, who had dropped exhausted into a chair, started as if she had been slapped. She gaped at Hilda, wide-eyed. "Any WHAT?!" she cried.

Angus and I tried to get Hilda's attention, but her back was to us and she just went on chatting happily while she worked at the sink. "Bears, dear. Angus sees them all the time in the woods. I was hoping you would get to see one."

Jan could only gurgle a weak, gasping sound as she slumped further down in her chair, like a deflating balloon.

Hilda turned to her, alarmed. "What's the matter, dear? You're as white as a ghost."

Jan could only stammer, "See a bear? Why—why would I want to see a bear? Why would anyone want to intentionally see a wild bear in the woods? They're huge, they're mean, they eat people."

Hilda laughed dismissively. "Oh, don't be silly, dear. They almost never attack people—only when they're hungry, or if it's mating season, or if there are any cubs around, or if they're threatened, or . . ." She trailed off, apparently unable to think of any more reasons why we might have been devoured. "Besides, you had Duncan with you."

Jan seemed too drained to argue. "I need a hot shower and some lunch," she muttered softly.

Hilda looked surprised. "But what about the nice lunch I packed for you?"

"Long story," I said. I turned to Jan. "Go take your shower, honey. Angus and I will unpack the sled. After lunch you'll feel better. We'll set up the tree and decorate it then. Okay?"

Hilda watched with concern as Jan nodded dazedly and shuffled off to her shower, then turned on Angus. "Is she all right?" she demanded. "What did you do to her?"

"She's fine," I assured her, "just a little tired and cold. She'll be her old self after a little rest. Come on, Amanda, let's go get the tree."

"YAY!"

CHAPTER 24

....

We went out to the barn and proceeded to unload the sled. While Angus and I unpacked all the gear and stowed it, Amanda made snowballs and tossed them to Duncan. We untied the tree, brought it in, and set it up. As we were doing so, a thought struck me as to what we were going to decorate the tree with. Jan and I had no Christmas decorations; they were all in Florida. And if Angus and Hilda didn't celebrate Christmas, there would be no reason for them to have any decorations, either. I mentioned this to Angus and said, "Maybe after lunch, we can go down to Portland and get some ornaments for the tree."

"No need," he said, "we have plenty," and he pointed to some large dusty cardboard boxes in the corner. "I brought them down from the attic yesterday."

Confused, I said, "But I thought—" only to be cut off by Hilda's calling, "Lunch is ready."

Almost immediately, the back door flew open and in ran Amanda and Duncan, still excited by their play in the snow. Jan had returned from her shower completely refreshed, as if her morning meltdown had never happened. "Boy," she gushed, "I didn't realize how hungry I was. I guess all that walking in the snow really builds an appetite!"

"Right," I agreed, keeping further thoughts to myself.

Angus simply grinned and said, "Great, let's eat."

We tore through lunch. Like all kids, Amanda was of course anxious to get at the tree, but in truth, we were all just as eager as she. Her enthusiasm had infected us all.

Angus beckoned Amanda. "Come over here, sweetie," he said, "and help me unpack these boxes." He cut through the tape that sealed them. Judging from the amount of dust, it had been quite some time since they were last opened. As she opened the boxes, Amanda began removing the contents. There were dozens of ornaments of all sizes and shapes—mostly homemade—things that we don't see much of anymore—varnished gingerbread men, cranberries and seashells strung together, wooden toys, crudely made ceramic figurines, paper cutouts—homely items apparently made by previous generations of McTigue children and evoking visions of Christmases long past. There were a few store-bought items but, true to the McTigue family tradition, most were homemade.

It reminded me of one day when Angus and I were talking in the boathouse and the subject of Christmas came up. We agreed that gift-giving had become overly commercialized of late and he suggested that any presents we give should be made by the giver, and not merely purchased; that it would be more in the true spirit of Christmas. He said that was always the way it was in the McTigue family, and seeing these home-spun decorations made a deep impression on me. I could only imagine the countless stories behind the ornaments and the children who made them.

Amanda was visibly impressed. Expecting the usual array of slick decorations, she seemed touched by the simplicity of a previous age, when people had more time than money, when they had to produce what they needed rather than simply hop down to the mall and buy it.

Angus opened the second box, which contained strings of lights. I stared in amazement. They were the old-fashioned kind, like I hadn't seen since I was a boy. The bulbs were long and pointy and the wires cracked with age, bare copper showing through in many places.

"Uh, Angus," I suggested, "perhaps we should think about buying some new lights, maybe some that were made in this century?"

Angus grinned. "Yes," he agreed, "I suppose so. These are all pretty well shot. I guess we can afford some new ones after a half century or so." He brightened. "Tell you what, there's a sale going on down to the lumber-yard. Why don't I go pick up some new lights while you unpack the rest of the boxes and shape the tree? When I get back, we can decorate it. By then, it should be time for ice cream!"

"Oh, boy," squealed Amanda, "great idea, Uncle Angus!"

When Angus left, Hilda and Amanda retired to the kitchen to start the ice cream while Jan and I unpacked the remaining boxes. It seemed like a simple enough task, but we got bogged down immediately. Instead of simply removing the ornaments from the boxes, we found ourselves admiring them, commenting to each other how unique they were, or cute, or, in some instances, priceless. For, mixed in with the homemade stuff were some delicate crystal pieces that we surmised dated back well into the previous century, and had come over with Hilda from England. It was fascinating. We were having so much fun, in fact, that when Angus returned, we had only unpacked about half the stuff.

I could hear the comforting whir of the ice-cream maker as Hilda and Amanda came back into the room to help with the tree.

"All set," Hilda said. "It'll be ready in a half hour, just about when we finish with the tree."

"What flavor?" I asked.

"Chocolate-blueberry!" Amanda piped.

I wrinkled my nose and looked at Hilda. Laughing, she just shrugged her shoulders. "It's what she wanted."

"Sounds delicious," I said.

We unpacked the rest of the ornaments, then turned our attention to the tree. First, we trimmed off a few errant branches to produce the perfect shape. Then the new lights went on. It seemed Angus had bought enough for a redwood, but somehow they all fit. Next, the strings of shells, cranberries, and paper cutouts were strewn around, from top to bottom. Finally, anything that would hang, bulbs, gingerbread men, baby ceramic animals, etc., were strategically placed. It seemed our little tree would surely collapse under the weight of it all, but it bore up proudly. After we threw on some tinsel and some angel hair, Angus hoisted Amanda up to the peak so she could attach a crystal star. All was set. We closed the curtains, then Angus plugged in the lights, and we stood back to admire our handiwork. The tree was perfect, coming alive with the shimmering of the colored lights and their reflections off all the bulbs and the tinsel.

Amanda was awestruck. "*Byoo*-tiful!" she breathed.

And it was. It surely resembled every other Christmas tree, of course, but the effort we had put forth to locate the tree, then bring it home, then trim it with such homespun decorations had made it uniquely our own. We all agreed it was the finest Christmas tree ever and could only be topped by some fresh chocolate-blueberry ice cream.

Afterward, during the drive home, Jan sat a little closer to me than usual. "What a lovely time," she sighed. "Weren't Angus and Hilda sweet? They seemed as excited about the tree as Amanda was." After a pause, she added, "Sorry I was such a prune this morning. I guess I'm not much of a country girl."

I pulled her closer. "That's okay, honey. It was a whole new experience for you, and you got a little tired and scared, that's all. We'll have to spend more time hiking in the woods so you can get used to it."

She poked me in the ribs. "No chance. Next year we'll be in Florida and we'll *buy* our Christmas tree, like normal people."

We pulled into our driveway and hurried inside. It was twilight and getting cold fast. Temperatures in the mid-teens were forecast for the night and the next couple of days. "Good thing we got the tree today," I said.

"Brrr," Jan shivered as she turned up the heat. "I think I'll make some tea. Want some hot chocolate, Amanda?"

"No thanks, Jannie, gotta run," she answered over her shoulder and flew out the door to join her friends playing in the lamplight.

Jan smiled. "She'll certainly sleep well tonight."

"Yeah," I agreed, "me, too. It's been quite a day."

I poured myself some wine, then we sat down by the window so we could watch the kids play while we enjoyed our drinks. I mused, "You know, I keep thinking about all those beautiful Christmas ornaments. Sometimes I get the feeling there's more to Angus and Hilda than we know."

"What do you mean?" Jan said.

"I can't put my finger on it, but don't they seem a little contradictory at times? They don't celebrate Christmas, yet they have all those ornaments. Angus refuses to work on Sunday, yet they don't go to church. They seem very well thought of everywhere, but they live like hermits right on the edge of town. We're the only ones who ever go see them."

She was dismissive. "You're imagining things. Everyone has idiosyncrasies," she jabbed, "even you. They're a wonderful old couple and we happened to click, that's all. Maybe they're lonely. They didn't have children, so Christmas may not have meant as much. I know it's a lot different for us now that Amanda came into our lives." She smiled reflectively. "Perhaps now, with Amanda, it's more meaningful for them, too. And you said yourself that Mainers tend to be more self-reliant. I'm just glad we've met and become such a big part of their lives. I hope they feel the same about us."

"You're probably right," I agreed, though not thoroughly convinced. We sat for a while and sipped at our drinks as it slowly darkened outside. I felt strongly that Jan was right, that our meeting was merely a most fortunate accident and our friendship bloomed so quickly and firmly simply because we had such a great deal in common. But I couldn't help ruminating over the past six months. I remembered my impression of Angus when we first met and how different my feelings were now; I never quite forgot his brief, strange reaction when he met Amanda in the ice-cream shop; his decision to seek me out with an offer to commit a year of his life to helping me build a boat, no questions asked, just days after turning me down unequivocally. And the two of them living so reclusively at the very edge of such a small town. We had summered there for eight years. I had driven by their place countless times and, despite my many hours spent poking around the boatyard and talking to the old hands, I had no idea they lived practically in our back yard. All these things seemed so inconsequential now, in the light of our closeness, but my mind kept revisiting them, almost subconsciously, trying to piece everything neatly together. Perhaps . . .

But that was the end of my reflections for the time being. "Don't forget," Jan said, "you promised to take Amanda and me Christmas-shopping tomorrow, in Freeport."

"Oh, no," I groaned. "Are you sure? Do you have it in writing?"

Jan smacked me playfully on the arm. "Oh, stop. It won't be that bad. You can drop us off, then go to the bookstore. Have a doughnut and coffee and try not to buy too many books." She snuggled closer. "We'll come find you for lunch and you can take us to The Shack for clams and a lobster roll."

I put my arm around her. "You know, when you put it that way, it doesn't sound so bad."

CHAPTER 25

....

The last few days leading up to Christmas were a blur. First, there were *two* shopping trips to Freeport, not one. Seems Jan and Amanda got so excited about their big day out, they forgot half the stuff they went for in the first place. Plus, Hilda was feeling much better and insisted she was well enough to go shopping, too. So, on Thursday we all piled back into the car for the second hundred-and-fifty-mile round trip in as many days. Hoping for some moral support, I implored Angus to come along. He just grinned smugly, said, "Sorry, old friend," and gave me a gentle pat on the back.

Then, that night came Amanda's school play. It was a joy, a typical middle-school production with muffed lines, collapsing scenery, and exasperated cues from harried teachers in the wings. But what the kids lacked in theatrical polish, they more than made up for in grim determination. Through one debacle after another, they trouped on, sometimes delivering the same lines twice or, becoming confused, simply skipping a scene altogether. But it was great fun for everyone, and the kids were thrilled with the applause they received at the end. To top it off, Mr. Littlefield donated his ice-cream parlor for the post-production party. The kids, their parents, and the teachers all crowded in and noisily celebrated their triumph, slurping gallons of ice cream and soda.

Through all this, of course, no work at all was accomplished on the boat, exactly as Angus had predicted. Between the shopping, the wrapping, the sending, the cooking, and the seemingly endless last-minute holiday emergencies, the days were over before I could get properly started. When I groused good-naturedly to Angus about this, he agreed, but emphasized that certain things were beyond our control.

"Remember Thanksgiving, Jim," he reminded me. "You might as well relax and enjoy it. Besides, the truth is, we've come a long way and we can use a break. It'll recharge our batteries."

He was right, of course, and I knew it. In fact, to be honest, I was having a high old time. We were in Maine, I was realizing a life-long dream, and watching Amanda's mounting excitement had elevated everyone's spirits. The shopping trips, the play, the hustle-bustle of the gift-buying and wrapping, all of it was a lark, especially since I wasn't actually involved to any great degree. I was merely a convenient spectator to be called upon at various intervals to do the girls' bidding. Mostly they wanted me out of the way until some mindless task needed to be done, or an errand had to be run. Fine with me. It was a perfect opportunity to get caught up on my reading, the football season, and my naps. Even Angus seemed to be enjoying the break. Except for Sundays, we had worked on the boat practically nonstop for six months. While every day was new and exciting for me, I had to keep reminding myself that he had done this all his life and the only reason he was putting himself through it again was as a favor to me. He never said anything, but I think he was grateful for the change of pace. We spent a lot of time over coffee, just talking and relaxing.

But, all that acknowledged, the boat was still very much on my mind. I would occasionally wander over to the boathouse just to admire her and plan what we would do next. I'm afraid I pestered Angus almost as much as Amanda did—What was the next step? Did you order the hardware? What about the plumbing? Do you have a buyer yet? Through it all, he displayed a saintly patience, answering all my questions directly and with good humor. I knew I was being a nuisance, but I couldn't help myself. Seeing her propped up in her cradle, with a coat of primer on her, it seemed as if we could slide her down the railway and sail her the next day.

But Angus had to keep cautioning me, as he had from the beginning. "Easy does it, Jim," he would say. "This is where a lot of builders cut corners. It looks like a boat, so there's a strong tendency to rush through the rest of it. But, believe me, there's a lot of work left. It's not hard work, and it doesn't show as dramatically as what we've already done, but it's every bit as important as the rest of it and it needs to be done right." He smiled at my eagerness and patted me on the back. "Patience, Jim, patience."

Then, scarcely before I even realized it, it was Christmas Eve. Somehow, all the last-minute preparations had gotten done and we were gathered around the table, gabbing and feasting. I had been concerned about Hilda, but the week's activity was like a tonic to her. She was once again her radiant self as she bustled about, making sure everything was just right. Amanda was in a state, jabbering on about Christmas, her trip home to Florida on Monday, the boat, who would feed the animals while she was gone, and on and on. I kept expecting her to eventually wind down, but, if anything, she was more frenzied than ever. Even Jan was beyond reason. The three of them, despite the three-generation age gap, were equally overwrought by the mania of the season. It was fun to observe them (from a prudent distance, of course) as they flitted about like water bugs.

All these thoughts and more coursed through my head as we enjoyed our dinner. It was a magical time and I was determined to savor it fully. And, maybe, just maybe, because of all the excitement and activity, and if I got my just deserts, Amanda might sleep later the next morning.

CHAPTER 26

....

"Grandpa, Jannie, wake up—it's Christmas!"

Amanda's shrill voice shattered our peaceful slumber like a grenade. "Oh, no, not again," I groaned as I looked over at Jan.

She smiled, mumbled, "Merry Christmas, honey," and rolled over, chuckling as she pulled the pillow over her head. I glanced at the clock— only three and a half hours until we had to be in church!

I called back through the door, "Amanda, honey, it's kind of early, isn't it?"

"But we don't want to be late, Grandpa." The church was perhaps an eight-minute walk up Shore Road.

"No, no, of course not." I yawned. "Look, Amanda, why don't you make your bed and take your shower and get dressed, then we'll have a nice breakfast before church, okay?"

"I've already *done* all that, Grandpa. C'mon, we're burning daylight!"

Jan began laughing out loud. "You've created a monster," she said. "Call me when breakfast is ready."

"No chance," I said, giving her a sharp smack on her behind. "When I get up, everybody gets up!" She yelped, giggled, and threw her pillow at me.

"Thanks, Amanda, we're wide awake now," I called through the door. "Go downstairs and start the coffee and the hot water. We'll be down shortly."

"Okay, Grandpa. Don't go back to sleep, now."

Jan shook her head. "She must be so excited. Her first Christmas in Maine, and with snow, and all her new experiences . . ." She was smiling reflectively. "It's been over twenty years since we spent Christmas up here. It doesn't seem possible."

"I know," I said. "I watch Amanda and I see us when we were that age. It's like reliving our own childhood."

Jan smiled. "I'm so glad we did this; I mean, building the boat, wintering up here after all these years, becoming so close with Angus and Hilda, all of it. I was afraid how bad the winter might be, but all in all, I wouldn't have missed it for anything."

I hugged her close. "I feel the same. This really has been a life-changer for me, more than I could have hoped for. But, remember," I cautioned, "winter is all of four days old. I hope you feel the same three months from now."

She smiled. "Whatever happens, I have no regrets. It's been an amazing experience, for all of us."

We got dressed and descended the stairs. Amanda had set the table, poured the orange juice, boiled the water for Jan's tea, and plugged in the coffee pot. She had also dressed up everything with Christmas ribbons and bows. She was enjoying her newfound hostessing skills and took every opportunity to display them.

"Merry Christmas," she called happily.

"Merry Christmas," I replied. "And what a beautiful table!"

"Thank you, Grandpa," she said, beaming as she poured my coffee. "Merry Christmas, Jannie."

"Merry Christmas to you, honey, and thanks for getting everything ready." She gave Amanda a kiss. "Sit down and enjoy your hot chocolate. I'll have breakfast ready right away."

In no time at all, we were enveloped by wonderful aromas as Jan worked her magic. We made small talk until Jan served the breakfast, then conversation ceased as we attacked a stack of blueberry pancakes and crisp bacon. Afterward, I gave a contented sigh as I leaned back and poured myself another cup of coffee.

Amanda was bubbling with excitement. "Wait until you see what I made for Aunt Hilda and Uncle Angus!"

"What is it?" I asked, knowing her answer.

"I can't tell you; it's a surprise. I spent all day on it yesterday. Jannie had to help me some, but I did most of it myself."

Jan smiled. "You sure did, honey. They're going to be so proud of you."

Then, more to the point, "I wonder what they made for me. I tried to get Uncle Angus to tell me, but he teased me and said I would have to wait and see. I begged for a hint, but he just laughed and said nope." She was pouting. "It's not fair."

Jan and I smiled. "Did you tell them what you made for them?" I asked.

"No," she admitted, "but that's different."

"Well," I said, "if it's any consolation, he wouldn't tell me, either."

We were interrupted by a shout from outside. "AMANDA! Come out and play!" Her friends were laughing and playing in the snow with their new toys. Amanda looked hopefully to Jan.

"Of course, sweetie, go out and play. I'll clean up. Don't be long, though. We have to get ready for church."

She slid back her chair and raced for the door. As she threw it open, she looked back over her shoulder and cried, "Thanks, Jann . . ."

But she had fallen for the oldest trick in the book. She was immediately pelted by dozens of snowballs from all sides as her friends roared with laughter. Amanda shrieked, then waded in, laughing and returning the fire. Through the window, we watched as the battle raged, snowballs flying every which way, the kids running around stuffing snow in each other's parkas, just like we used to do. We watched as Bobby snuck up behind Amanda and dumped an enormous bucket of snow on her head. She squealed with feigned outrage, then chased after him as he laughed and dodged easily out of her way.

"Some things never change," Jan chuckled. "Good thing she got up early. She's going to have to get ready all over again."

We returned to the table. I had another cup of coffee while Jan poured her tea. Leaning back, we enjoyed a rare quiet moment. We began reminiscing about the events of the past half-year and how we had been affected by them. All of our lives had been profoundly altered by the chance meeting of a complete stranger in an ice-cream shop.

I mused, "If I hadn't taken Amanda for ice cream that day, at that time, we'd be in Florida right now. Amanda would be in her school down there, content, I'm sure, but oblivious to all her new friends and experiences here, and the influence of Angus and Hilda. I certainly would never have had this opportunity to build a boat, especially a boat like that one, and with someone like Angus. I know I wouldn't have missed what I never knew, but I'm so grateful every day for being able to do this. Sometimes I still can hardly believe my luck."

Jan smiled in agreement. "I know. It seems like we've known them all our lives. Hilda and I are so close. She's like the older sister I never had. And, of course, they both adore Amanda." She paused, sipping her tea and gazing out the window. After a moment, she continued her thoughts. "We're doing things we haven't done in years, things I thought we would never do again. And the boat! I get such a kick out of watching you and Angus work on her. You're like a couple of kids doing something you absolutely love. I'm so happy for you."

We sat quietly for a few more minutes, immersed in our thoughts, until Amanda flew through the door. She was panting, soaked to the skin, her hair matted with snow, and her face was glowing red from the cold and the play. But through all that, her eyes sparkled with joy.

"That Bobby!" she cried, trying mightily to appear put out. "He dumped snow on my head! I chased him, but he's too fast. He just laughed at me. But I'll fix him."

Jan laughed and said, "Well, you're going to have to fix him later. You're a mess and we have to get ready for church. Go get cleaned up— again. We'll need to be leaving soon."

"Okay, Jannie," she yelled, running up the stairs, "I'll be back in a jiff." And she was, all decked out and carrying a tote bag with Angus's and Hilda's presents inside.

Despite getting up before dawn, we had to hurry to get to church on time. Bells were already ringing as we strode briskly up Shore Road, crunching the snow under our feet. The day was perfect, a light dusting of new snow, twenty-five degrees, and no wind. Our little village looked like a Currier and Ives Christmas card.

Upon entering the church, Amanda skipped off to visit with her friends. We looked over the crowd and spied Angus and Hilda. Hilda was surrounded by several ladies, excitedly giggling and chattering all at once. From the little bit of conversation I could overhear, it appeared they hadn't seen Hilda for quite some time. I thought that somewhat strange in a town the size of Moosaquit.

Angus was some distance away, conversing with a man whom I didn't recognize. I decided to go over and wish him a Merry Christmas.

As I approached, I could see that the other man, whose back was to me, had cornered Angus and was doing all the talking. Angus was facing him squarely, saying nothing, and sporting a less-than-cordial expression.

"Merry Christmas, Angus," I said. "Who's your friend?"

But Angus just stood there, mute, staring balefully at the man. A few awkward moments passed in silence, then the man stuck out his hand and said, "Morton Dudley's my name, real estate's my game."

I turned. He was a tallish man, with narrow shoulders and a generous paunch. His face had a pasty pallor that indicated he spent most of his time indoors. His close-set, beady eyes hid behind thick glasses, darting about like a cornered rat's, and closing involuntarily when he spoke, thereby avoiding eye contact. He had a pointy, ferret-like face, accentuated with a bristly, mangy-looking mustache. We were in a house of God, on Christmas morning, but my initial impulse was to kick him in the knee. I took his hand reluctantly. It felt like a dead haddock.

"Jim Cairns," I said unenthusiastically.

"I was just telling Angus here about a great opportunity," he said. "I represent a group of developers who are very interested in the McTigue property. They'll offer top dollar." Angus was looking around, assiduously ignoring the bore and growing ever more openly impatient. Oblivious, the man continued. "We, uh, I mean, *they,* have a great plan—condos, swimming pools, an arcade, tennis courts, a mall, the works. We can put together a great deal, Angus." He said all this without looking either of us in the eye. I was liking him less by the second. He tried to ingratiate himself to us with a ghastly attempt at a grin. "You know," he went on, "maybe I'm being a bit of a jerk for bringing this up in church, on Christmas, but Angus here is a difficult man to pin down." He nudged me conspiratorially. "You're a friend of his, right? Maybe you can talk some sense into him." He turned toward Angus. "You're not going to live forever, you know."

At this, Angus stiffened noticeably and gave the man a lethal stare. I leaned back, offering full access to the man's chin should Angus feel the need to deck him. But instead, Angus said, "You know, Dudley, you're right."

Dudley brightened. "Now you're talking—" he began.

But Angus cut him off. "You *are* being a jerk. This is no time or place to be talking business, and I won't sell to you in any case. Now get out of my way." I had never seen him so aggravated. His face was red and his fists were clenched. He appeared on the brink of mayhem.

Insinuating myself between them, I said, "Angus, calm down. We're in church. It's Christmas." But he said nothing, just walked past me and shouldered Dudley out of the way with a determined rudeness.

I was shocked, but Dudley remained unfazed. He just said to me, "He's a strange one, all right; no sense of the dollar. But he'll come around."

That struck a nerve. "I don't think so," I said evenly. "Didn't you hear him? If Angus says he won't sell, he won't sell."

He grunted smugly. "They *all* sell; it's just a matter of how much. I'm really doing him a favor, you know. He has no heirs and, once he dies, that property will get gobbled up, cheap."

What a thoroughly repugnant man. I stepped closer, eager to pursue our discussion further. I was eyeing his soft midsection when I felt a hand on my arm. It was Jan.

"Honey, come along," she said. "The service is starting." Her voice was under control, but she had my arm in a death grip.

I exhaled, weighing my options. She was right, of course. Getting into a brawl in church on Christmas might not look too good in the local paper—no context, so to speak. I stepped back, reluctantly.

Dudley reached into his pocket and proffered his business card. "Call me if I can be of service," he said placidly. I ignored the card and turned away from him. "Merry Christmas," he called after me.

"What was that all about?" Jan asked as we rejoined Angus.

"I'll tell you later," I hissed between my teeth.

Providentially, Amanda came running up to us just then. "Merry Christmas, Uncle Angus!" she cried and flew into his arms. It was exactly what he needed. Angus was incapable of ill feeling while Amanda was around.

"Merry Christmas, sweetie," he replied, folding her in his arms. Then he leaned back and smiled. "Don't you look lovely. Is that a new dress?"

"Yup," she bubbled. "I was going to wear my play costume, but Grandpa insisted on buying me a new dress-up dress for special occasions." It was a simple white dress with a ruffled top and sleeves. She was also sporting a new pair of patent leather shoes and a bonnet with seasonal decorations on it. "Jannie helped me pick it out. Pretty nice, huh?" She twirled theatrically. I told her she looked "*byoo*-tiful" and she collapsed on a pew, giggling. Laughing at her playful antics, we immediately forgot the recent unpleasantness.

We went to fetch Hilda. The service was about to begin and she was still visiting with her friends. When we approached, Angus greeted the ladies gallantly. "Good morning, ladies," he said, making a courtly bow. At once, they all began chattering excitedly.

"Why, hello, Angus." "Merry Christmas, Angus." "Oh, my." "Wonderful to see you, Angus." And so on. It was like a class reunion. Angus introduced us to the ladies, then said to Hilda, "Come on, Hilly, the service is about to begin. We need to take our seats."

"Okay, Angus," she said. The ladies all said their goodbyes, promising to stay in touch (Moosaquit comprised less than four square miles).

We found our way to our pews, nodding and greeting friends as we went, and took our seats just as Reverend Brewster began. The service was timely and short, the Reverend fully aware that everyone was anxious to return home for Christmas. After a couple of hymns and a Christmas carol, it was over, the whole thing lasting less than forty-five minutes.

After church adjourned, we shook hands, wished everyone a Merry Christmas again, and began walking the short distance back to Angus and Hilda's house. The girls lagged behind, discussing how good the sermon was, what all the ladies wore, etc., while Angus and I walked briskly and were soon well ahead of them. Now that we were alone again, I noticed a change in Angus's demeanor. He was quiet, not in itself unusual, but he also seemed deep in thought, perhaps troubled by something.

Thinking it might have something to do with our earlier meeting in church, I asked, "What's up?"

He let out a disgusted sigh. "Oh, just that creep, Dudley," he answered, making a face. "I let him get to me and I shouldn't have."

"Oh, that," I said with a grin. "Well, he got to me, too. I don't know what would have happened if Jan hadn't come along."

"Yeah, I told her to go get you. I could see you were getting close."

"The guy just wouldn't quit, kept saying all the wrong things. He might be the most irritating person I've ever met."

Angus made a snort. "He has that effect on a lot of people."

"What's your connection?"

"He's been after our property for years. Says he represents a syndicate that wants to develop it, but he's the push behind it. He doesn't think I know that, but it's a small town."

"Just tell him to get lost."

"I've told him a dozen times, a dozen ways, but he keeps coming back. You saw him. I'm afraid I'll lose my temper someday. I came real close today. Thanks for being there."

I laughed. "Thank Jan. I wanted to deck him myself."

But Angus wasn't laughing. "The worst part is, he has a point. I'm *not* getting any younger and I want to provide for Hilda. I don't want her to have to deal with people like that when I'm gone."

I saw his dilemma. "You wouldn't actually sell to him, would you?"

"Not in a thousand years," he said, his jaw tightening, "but, realistically, property can be bought a lot of different ways—corporations, trusts . . ." He trailed off, obviously vexed, as we walked on. After a brief silence, he continued. "This property has been in my family for a hundred and fifty years, passed on and taken care of from generation to generation. Now it's my turn and I'm not sure what to do. Heck, I know things change over time. It's just the way it is and I understand that. It's only a third the size now that it was originally. But the thought of that vulture turning my heritage into a tacky seasonal playground galls me." We walked along, his gaze focused on the horizon. "There's an awful lot of history here, Jim . . .."

As we ambled up the walkway, his demeanor improved dramatically when Duncan came running to meet us, barking as joyfully as if we were returning after being gone for a month. Angus bent down and stroked the dog's giant head, talking to him, telling him what a good boy he was. Duncan gazed at him lovingly, absorbing all the praise with relish. We looked back down Shore Road at the girls. They were a good three or four hundred yards back, all three still talking animatedly. After playing with Duncan and watching the girls in such a good mood, Angus seemed rejuvenated.

He smiled, slapped me on the back, and said, "Come on, old friend, I'll buy you a cup of coffee."

CHAPTER 27

Angus and I were on our second cup when the girls finally arrived, bright-eyed and red-faced from the cold, fresh air. Amanda was in a dither. She couldn't wait to give Angus and Hilda their gifts and to find out what they had made for her. But Angus was in a teasing mood. "Well," he drawled, "Jim and I are going to go work on the boat for a few hours. We can exchange presents after lunch. Okay?"

"Noooo, Uncle Angus," Amanda whined comically, "let's do it *now*. It's Christmas!"

Angus feigned disappointment. "Well, all right," he said. "Who wants to go first?"

"Me!" cried Amanda. She reached into her little tote bag and pulled out two packages. They were wrapped loosely in bright Christmas paper covered with little puppies and kittens and tied with large ribbons, one red and one green. She gave them both to Hilda, who took them eagerly, her face betraying girlish pleasure.

"Open the red one first, Aunt Hilda!"

Hilda giggled. "All right, darling." She tore open the wrapping to find a large, round tin. When she opened it, we were enveloped in a sweet, fruity aroma. Hilda looked somewhat perplexed for a moment, as if she were caught off guard, then a look of surprised recognition lit up her face. She looked at Amanda tenderly. "My goodness," she exclaimed, "is this . . .?"

"Yup!" Amanda cried. "Real English plum pudding! Jannie found the recipe and helped me shop for the fixings, but I did all the cooking myself. I made a double recipe." She was bursting with pride.

Hilda's eyes were beginning to get moist. "Oh, thank you, dear, so much," she said, her voice a little unsteady. She lifted the tin to her nose and inhaled deeply. "This smells just like the pudding we used to have on Christmas when I was a little girl. It's one of my fondest memories of childhood." She seemed lost in thought for a few moments as she remembered back all those years ago. "My mother would pour sauce over it and set it aflame; we called it 'hard sauce' because it had brandy in it, and—"

"Open the other present, Aunt Hilda!" Amanda cried. She was hopping up and down with excitement.

Snatched back to reality, Hilda opened the other package to find a one-quart plastic container. She looked at Amanda hesitantly, then slowly opened the lid. The powerful scents of lemon and brandy were unmistakable. "It can't be," Hilda sniffled, her tears now flowing freely.

Amanda was getting concerned. "Are you all right, Aunt Hilda?" she asked anxiously.

Hilda pulled her close. "Yes, I'm all right, darling, I'm fine. I'm just so overwhelmed by your lovely gift, that's all. And to think you made it just for me." She dried her eyes. "I feel like I'm a little girl again, back in England with my parents. Oh, thank you so much." And she hugged Amanda again, for a long time.

After a few moments, Hilda regained her vaunted English composure. Clearing her throat, she said, "Now, darling, I have something for you. I hope you like it." She presented Amanda with a large, loosely wrapped bundle.

Amanda pounced, tearing it open in a heartbeat. Her eyes got big as she held up a lovely pink sweater. While holding it, a couple of items fell away—a matching beret and a pair of mittens. She was thrilled. "Oh, Aunt Hilda, they're gorgeous. You made these for *me*?"

Hilda nodded, smiling sweetly. "I certainly did, darling. It's the finest English wool, warm and soft, but it wears like iron. Someday you can give them to your own little girl."

Amanda ran to Hilda and threw her arms around her. "Oh, thank you so much, Aunt Hilda. I love them. I'm going to wear them every day!" She put on the sweater immediately and ran to the mirror. Posing in front of it, she donned the beret and tilted it a few times until she got it just right, then checked all the angles. She looked at her reflection for several moments, a look of wonder on her face. "You really made this from scratch, Aunt Hilda?"

"Of course, darling. I've been knitting since I was younger than you. Nothing to it."

Amanda seemed amazed. "Do you think I could ever learn how to knit?"

Hilda gave Amanda her sweetest smile. "Of course, you can, darling. I'd love to teach you. Why, as clever as you are, you'll be making things in no time. When you get back from Florida, maybe your grandpa will take us shopping in Freeport so we can buy some yarn to practice with. Would you like that?"

Amanda was thrilled. "Oh, boy, Aunt Hilda, I can't wait!"

Tearing herself away from the mirror, she retrieved her tote bag. "Now you, Uncle Angus." She reached inside and brought out a square, flat package, which she gave to Angus. He was grinning broadly, relishing her excitement.

"Thank you, my lady," he said as he proceeded to unwrap his present. Inside was a cardboard gift box. Again, from the aroma, we could tell Amanda had been busy in the kitchen. Angus smiled slyly and lifted the box to his nose. Drawing out the moment, he mused, "Hmm, now what could this be? Cookies? Pie? Brownies?" He lifted the package higher and made a show of lifting the lid to peek inside. When he did, he smiled with delight. "Shortbread!" he exclaimed. "I love shortbread! How did you know?"

"I asked Aunt Hilda. She said your grandma used to make it for you when you were a boy. I know how you love sweets, so I put frosting on them—some chocolate, some maple, some peanut butter. Try one. I hope they're okay."

As Angus bit into one, he closed his eyes in exaggerated ecstasy and murmured, "Mmmm, delicious! The best I've ever had." Of course, he would have said the same thing if they had tasted like recycled sawdust. Amanda giggled with pride, then began fidgeting in anticipation of her gift from Angus.

He put down the tin and began looking around, as if he had forgotten something. "Let's see, now," he mumbled through his second mouthful of shortbread, "I think I have something here for you . . . now, where is it?" He made an exaggerated show of looking for Amanda's mislaid present. "Hmm," he mused, "can't seem to remember where I put it."

Amanda was squirming. "It's over *there*, Uncle Angus, under the *tree!*" She had discovered the package the day before and had tried every trick in her eleven-year-old book to discern its contents, but to no avail.

Angus acted surprised. "Oh, yes," he teased, "there it is." He retrieved the package and brought it to her. It was a large, flat, heavy object, about four feet long and perhaps a foot wide. I didn't let Amanda know, but I was also intrigued. I had, in fact, picked up the package more than once and employed a few tricks that I remembered from my own childhood, but also came up empty. After all the buildup, I was almost as anxious as Amanda to discover the big surprise. Amanda accepted the present eagerly, dancing with anticipation. Angus's eyes softened as he watched the child's excitement. In a strangely husky voice, he said, "Merry Christmas, sweetie, I hope you like it," and gave her a little kiss.

Ripping off the wrapping, she squealed with surprised delight. It was a nameboard for a boat. It was made of teak, with ribbon carving along the upper and lower edges and rosettes on either end. It glistened brightly with several coats of varnish and, inside the framework of the edge-molding, carved and finished with gold leaf, was the name of the yacht in large script and its hailing port under it in smaller block letters:

AMANDA
MOOSAQUIT, ME

Amanda stared at it, speechless, for a moment, then gushed, "Uncle Angus, it's *byoo*-tiful! I can't believe it. You really named our boat after me?"

"Sure did, honey," Angus replied. "Heck, without you, we never would have built her." Amanda beamed as she held it up for everyone to see. It was indeed a lovely piece of work, perfectly proportioned, crisply carved, and the gorgeous grain of the teak was emphasized stunningly by the flawless varnish. A masterful job. I caught Angus's eye and winked as I gave him a thumbs-up. He smiled bashfully but was justifiably proud of his skills.

Amanda put it down carefully so she could run over and give Angus a hug. While the three girls were making a big fuss over Angus, I picked up the nameboard to admire it more closely and noticed an envelope taped to the back of it, no doubt a Christmas card. "Amanda," I said, "there's a card attached to the back. Come see what it says."

She came back over, still excited about the beautiful gift, and detached the card. She opened it quickly, but her face turned blank with confusion. She looked at one side, then the other. "It doesn't make sense, Grandpa." She handed it to me. "What does it say?"

Expecting a generic greeting card, I glanced at it perfunctorily, but was startled immediately by the format—very formal and not at all Christmasy. As I began reading, its meaning immediately became clear. I got a tingle and read it again, more carefully. When I finished, I looked over at Angus, shaking my head with wonder. We were both grinning like the Cheshire Cat.

"What is it, Grandpa?" Amanda asked. All eyes were on me now, everyone wanting to get in on the secret.

"Go ahead, Jim," Angus said.

Amanda didn't know what to make of all this. I took a deep breath as I pulled her close. "This is a title, honey. Do you know what a title is?"

"No, sir."

"Well, a title is something given by the state of Maine that denotes ownership. People get them for big things like houses and cars . . . and boats. This title is for our boat and it's made out to you." I grinned at her. "So, it's no longer our boat; it's *your* boat!"

She looked at me dumbly, unable to grasp the entirety of the moment. After a brief, stunned silence, all hell broke loose. Jan and Hilda shrieked, congratulating Amanda with hugs and kisses. Jan went to Angus and hugged him, tears in her eyes. "Oh, Angus, that was so sweet!" she sobbed. She could barely talk. Hilda hugged me. Even Duncan got caught up in the frenzy, barking and prancing around like a pup. Everyone was hugging, and talking, and laughing—except Amanda. She seemed in a daze.

"Aren't you excited, honey?" Jan asked her.

But she wasn't sure. She said to Angus. "Is it really mine, Uncle Angus? Really?"

She seemed afraid it was all a joke, that it wasn't real. After all the time and work, it was probably just too much for her little mind to absorb.

Angus told her gently, "It's really yours, honey, honest Injun. No one can ever take it away from you as long as you live."

Finally accepting that the boat was really, truly hers, she flew to Angus and buried her face in his chest, bawling like a baby, her emotions completely out of control. "Oh, thank you, Uncle Angus," she sobbed. "Thank you so much. I can't believe it. Our *byoo*-tiful boat, really, truly mine!"

While she was carrying on, hugging and blubbering, I noticed the camera we had put on the table to preserve the occasion. Impulsively, I grabbed it and snapped a quick shot of the two of them. It was a classic— Amanda overwhelmed with joy, and Angus beaming proudly at the little girl he so obviously adored. Then she went around to the rest of us, hugging, kissing, crying, laughing. She even hugged Duncan. The big dope had no idea what was going on, but he gratefully lapped up any and all attention from Amanda. His huge tail swept back and forth, flinging discarded wrapping paper everywhere.

We were all touched, watching the two of them, but Hilda seemed especially moved. "I had no idea," she said, dabbing at her eyes. She went to Angus and hugged him warmly. "Why didn't you tell me?" she asked, poking him playfully.

Angus chuckled. "Well," he said, "I wanted it to be a surprise and I saw how she was pumping you for clues. I knew you couldn't hold out for long, so I kept it to myself. Besides, it was more fun this way."

They exchanged a long look and hugged again. "Oh, Angus, I'm so happy," she said, almost breaking down.

"So am I, Hilly," he replied, with a slight catch in his voice, "so am I."

Amanda was hopping around, bursting with excitement. "Can I go look at my boat?" she cried.

Hilda smiled. "You go right ahead, darling," she said. "Tell you what, you go admire your new boat and we'll bring lunch over to the boathouse and picnic out there, how's that?"

"Yay! Come on, Duncan!"

I threw my arm around Angus's neck. "Come on, old friend," I joked, "let's get out of the way so the girls can clean up this mess and get lunch ready for us."

Jan shot me a playful rebuke. "Why don't you two do something useful? Go over to the boathouse and clean out a place so we can have lunch. And put some wood in the stove; it must be freezing over there."

I grinned. "Sure, honey. Come on, Angus."

When we got there, we saw that Amanda and Duncan had climbed the steps and were moving about the boat, crawling inside the cabin, playing on the deck, generally having a great time. Duncan had picked up Amanda's mood and was barking with his excitement at sharing her fun.

We chuckled at their antics and set to work. It *was* cold, so the first thing we did was stoke the giant wood stove. It sprang to life quickly and within a few minutes was radiating a soothing warmth. Then we grabbed a couple of brooms and swept a large area close to it so we could set up a table. Next, we cleared the old workbench of tools, plans, shavings, and sawdust, and wiped it down clean. We each took an end and proceeded to move it closer to the stove. It was a bulky old bench with a three-inch-thick maple top and four steel vises. It weighed a ton. By the time we had walked it the twenty feet or so toward the stove, we were panting from the exertion.

"There," I said, "all ready. I'll go get the dishes and tablecloth and our work is done." In just a few minutes, the stove had made everything toasty and the table was set, complete with candlesticks and wine coolers. We had done ourselves proud. As I slumped comfortably in a chair, Angus ambled over to a cabinet, returning with a dusty, familiar-looking bottle. I perked up, smiling in recognition. Without a word, he sat down and poured a small amount into two glasses, handing me one. I could see the bottle was almost empty now, with perhaps enough for just one more celebration. Still silent, we clinked glasses and leaned back. By then, I was quite comfortable with Angus's reticence and simply enjoyed these intimate moments together.

We passed quite some time that way, sipping contentedly and lost in our thoughts. At my first taste, I was brought back sharply to the afternoon we spent overlooking the cemetery on the hill. It seemed so long ago now, though it was barely two months earlier.

I could recall every detail—the valley ablaze with the colors of autumn, the glow of the setting sun at our backs, Angus's poignant story (still the longest I'd ever heard him speak at one time), and the peaceful timelessness of the little cemetery. So much had happened in the short span since then; wonderful times of Thanksgiving and Christmas, informal get-togethers, the sudden cold fear of Hilda's illness, meeting Dame Olivia Hamilton at the opera house, and through it all, the boat. Above all else, the boat seemed the constant that tied us all together. It was the reason we had met in the first place; it was why we were still in Maine in December, something Jan and I would have discounted as impossible only a few months earlier. And now that the boat belonged to Amanda, I could only imagine its influence on her for so many years to come.

"Soup's on!"

I was torn from my thoughts by the clatter of Jan and Hilda struggling through the door under their load of dishes, baskets, servers, and vessels. They had made a huge lobster quiche, home-fried Maine potatoes, fish chowder, and biscuits. Three different pitchers held coffee, tea, and hot chocolate.

"Don't get up, boys, we can handle it," Jan tossed at me. She had a strange way of asking for help. Angus and I grinned as we lightened their load and distributed everything on the table.

"Come on, Amanda, lunch is ready," Jan called.

"Oh, boy. Come on, Duncan!"

Like most kids, she had been so busy playing that she didn't realize how hungry she was. The two of them scampered down the scaffolding and joined us at the bench. We all sat down while Duncan took up his usual post at the middle of the table, ready for whatever might fall or be thrown his way. Angus said a brief but heartfelt grace and we dug in, talking and laughing happily.

CHAPTER 28

....

After the wonderful lunch, Amanda's desserts, more coffee, and a lingering hour or so of delightful conversation, it was beginning to get dark outside. It was only mid-afternoon, but no matter. This far north and just a couple of days past the winter solstice, it was dark for almost twice as long as it was light. I looked over at Amanda to tell her it was time to go. She had been quiet for some time and now I saw why. Her head was propped up on one hand and her unseeing eyes were just barely open. After getting up before dawn, the excitement of Christmas, the big snowball fight, church, the emotional drain of her presents, and a filling lunch, our little dynamo had finally run out of steam. I roused her gently.

"Huh?" she mumbled, sitting up and looking around in a daze. "Did I fall asleep?"

"You sure did, honey," Jan said. "Why don't you relax here with Duncan while we clean up, then we'll go home, okay?"

"Okay, Jannie," she readily agreed, yawning.

We cleaned up quickly, gathered our gifts, and said our goodbyes. Amanda thanked Hilda and Angus again for her presents and gave each a warm hug. Then she hesitated, remembering something. "Wait," she said, "I want to wear my new sweater home." She donned it proudly and twirled in front of the mirror. "All set," she announced, and we set off down the path toward Shore Road and home.

As we walked, I could see she was struggling awkwardly with the nameboard. It was quite heavy and bulky and almost as long as she was. She shifted it first to one side, then to the other side several times, but it was just too big for her.

I reached down to help her. "Here, honey," I said, "let me carry that for you."

"No thanks, Grandpa," she panted, repositioning it yet again. "I can handle it." Jan and I exchanged smiles.

We had a beautiful walk home. Though it was still twilight, the street-lights were on and they cast soft shadows on the new snow. It was cold, but there was no wind and the sky was clear. We took our time.

Upon arriving home, Amanda rushed to the phone to call her parents and tell them all about her Christmas. She seemed rejuvenated by the cold air and exercise, but I knew it would be short-lived. She babbled on excitedly, getting caught up with all the news from home and telling her folks about the boat, her new sweater and how Hilda had promised to teach her how to knit, the snowball fight, and on and on. She even mentioned Bobby, which made Jan and me exchange amused glances. During a brief pause to catch her breath, she listened for a second, then said, "Sure, Daddy, he's right here." She turned to me. "Daddy wants to talk to you." A breathless "Bye, Daddy; bye, Mommy, I love you. See you tomorrow," and she gave me the phone.

I could hear Bill chuckling as I wished him a Merry Christmas.

"Thanks, Jim, same to you," he replied. "Sounds like Amanda had quite a day. I've never heard her so excited. That's wonderful news, about the boat, I mean. I can't get over it."

"I know, we feel the same. No one knew about it, not even Hilda."

"They sure seem like wonderful people," Bill said. "Amanda loves them. She mentions something about them in every letter. We're really looking forward to meeting them when we come to Maine next summer."

"They are special people, no doubt about it. They treat Amanda like their own granddaughter, and we do everything together. I can't say enough about them. I just wish there was more we could do for them."

"That's great. I'm glad she's having such a good time." Then, after a pause, "How's her schoolwork?"

I chuckled. Amanda wasn't renowned for her scholarship. "Still doing great," I assured him, "all As and Bs. And, she's fit right in socially."

"Amazing," Bill said. I could imagine him shaking his head in disbelief. Then he said, "Mary's right here; she wants to say hello. Hang on."

"Hi, Jim, Merry Christmas."

"Hello, Mary, same to you," I replied. Then, a little cautiously, I inquired, "How was your Christmas?"

"It was okay, I guess, but I have to admit that it just wasn't the same without Amanda. The nieces and nephews were over, but . . ." Her voice broke.

Uh oh, I thought. "Well, she misses you both, too," I assured her cheerily, even though Amanda had never actually said so. "She's just so busy with all her new friends and activities, she doesn't have much time for reflection."

There was a brave little laugh, then a small sniffle. "I know, and I'm thrilled she's having such a great time. But still . . ." Sniff.

It didn't sound like she was thrilled. Desperate, I said, "Cheer up, Mary, she'll be home tomorrow, and you'll have a whole week to spoil her.

It'll be like having two Christmases." There was a hesitation while Mary cleared her throat. "I suppose so." Another sniffle.

It wasn't going well. Mary hadn't been wild about the thought of her eleven-year-old daughter going away for an entire year in the first place, and the idea of building a boat must have seemed no less than the rantings of a madman to her. So, I did what any man would do in that situation. "Jannie's right here, Mary. She wants to say hello." I shoved the phone quickly over at Jan before she could catch on, then went into the kitchen to fix a snack. I looked around for Amanda, to see if she wanted anything, but she had disappeared. I went upstairs and called but got no response. When I peeked into her room, I had to smile to myself. The frenzy of the past week had finally caught up with her; she was in bed, fast asleep, still wearing all her clothes. She had managed to kick her shoes off onto the floor, but that was apparently as far as she got. Even her brand-new pink beret was still on her head, though somewhat askew. *This time*, I thought to myself, *she's down for the count!* I removed the beret and placed it on her dresser. Then, I began pulling the blanket up to her chin when I felt something hard under the covers. It was the nameboard. She was hugging her prize closely, dreaming, I felt sure, of voyages to come. I pulled up a chair beside her bed and sat for a few moments, just watching her sleep.

"Great job, honey," Jan said as she entered the room. "Thanks for handing me off to a distraught mother." She was miffed at my momentary lack of spine, but then melted at the sight of Amanda snuggled in bed, clutching her nameboard. "Boy, she's out like a light."

"She sure is," I agreed, "and no wonder. It's been a huge day for her; the whole week, really. Good thing her flight is later in the day tomorrow. She'll sleep until noontime."

"Good," Jan joked, "now maybe *we* can finally get some sleep, too." She got up. "Come on downstairs. I'll fix you some hot cocoa."

"Thanks, honey," I said, "that sounds great. I'll be down shortly."

She smiled and kissed me on the cheek. "Pathetic."

CHAPTER 29

....

Well, Amanda didn't sleep until noon the next day, but she almost did. At ten-thirty, she finally came straggling down the stairs, still dressed in her clothes from the day before and comically disoriented.

"What time is it, Grandpa?" she yawned, looking around, trying to get her bearings.

"Ten-thirty," I replied.

"In the *morning*?"

"Yup, you slept right through. You must have been exhausted."

Slowly regaining her senses, she showed a sudden alarm. "When does the plane leave?" she asked, almost panicky.

"Relax, we don't have to leave for another two hours. Jannie already packed your bags while you were sleeping. You're all set. After you get cleaned up, we'll have a nice early lunch and then we'll leave for the airport. Okay?"

That put a big grin on her face. She was recovering quickly, as kids do. "Thanks, Grandpa. **Thanks, Jannie**," she shouted into the kitchen.

"You're welcome. sweetie," Jan called back. "Now, go take your shower; lunch will be ready shortly."

"Okey-dokey," she said and raced back up the stairs.

The trip to the airport was uneventful except for Amanda's incessant chatter. She really did miss her family and friends, once she had the time to think about them. And now that she was really going home for a week, she was on cloud nine, eager to see everyone and show off her new kitchen skills, the sweater, and, of course, the boat. She had brought a pile of photos, showing every stage of the construction, several times over. She had wanted to bring the nameboard, but I nixed that. I could just imagine her struggling down the aisle of the plane with her suitcase, her two bags of Christmas presents, and the four-foot-long nameboard. She whined briefly, until I tactfully mentioned they might stow it in the cargo hold and it could get damaged down there during the flight.

That cinched it. "Oh, dear," she said, scratching her chin, thoughtfully. "You might be right, Grandpa." But then she brightened. "I know, I'll take a picture instead."

"Great idea," I agreed.

Arriving at the airport, we encountered the usual chaos, plus the added confusion of the holiday traffic. After I dropped off Amanda and Jan, it took fifteen minutes to find a parking space, then I had to find the two of them, get Amanda checked in, and clear her luggage. I noticed some flight attendants standing around, so I introduced Amanda to them, explaining she was traveling alone, and asked if they would please look after her. They surrounded Amanda immediately, chatting with her and giving her little airline trinkets to keep her occupied during the flight.

One of the girls mentioned, "That looks like a homemade sweater. Did you make it?"

"No, ma'am," Amanda gushed, "my Aunt Hilda did. But she's going to teach me how to knit when I get back. I can't wait."

"You're coming *back*?" one of them asked incredulously. "Why would you come back to Maine in the winter if you live in Florida?"

Amanda launched into her spiel, covering virtually every aspect of her life since her arrival the past spring. The girls were captivated by it all, but especially so by her story of the boat. Amanda brought out her photos and began passing them around.

"My goodness," one of them said, "it's so big."

"It's amazing," said another. "You're actually building this *yourself*?"

"Yup," Amanda said, then added modestly. "Of course, Uncle Angus and Grandpa are helping me."

The girls were giggling with such delight that soon other people began crowding around. In moments, there was a huge crowd of people jostling to share in the excitement of the little girl who was building such a beautiful boat, practically all by herself.

By that time, I had been unceremoniously elbowed aside. Jan and I just stood back, shaking our heads. "I guess she'll be all right," I joked.

Jan laughed. "She does draw a crowd, doesn't she? You can't blame them, though. She's so adorable and outgoing, who wouldn't want to dote on her?"

We watched for a few minutes more, then it was time to board the plane. The crowd dispersed rather reluctantly. Amanda ran back over to us for one last hug and a wave, then she was gone.

We drove home in a blessed silence. There was no constant jabber streaming from the back seat, no inquiries as to when the boat would be finished, no whining about getting something to eat; just a blissful calm.

I turned to Jan. "Sure is quiet, huh?"

Jan smiled. "Sure is," she sighed, "and we have a whole week ahead of us. Just think, we can sleep in, eat whenever we want, relax without any interruptions . . ." She stretched lazily. "I think it'll be a nice change for Angus and Hilda, too. I know they love having her around, but she's still a child and that can become difficult for older folks."

"You're probably right. She's over at their house as much as she's at ours. Plus, she'll see all her old friends. It'll be a nice break for everyone."

And indeed, the next couple of days drifted by languidly. We did tend to sleep a little later, what with the late sunrises and quiet mornings. We lounged in our pajamas, drank more coffee and tea as we sat by the window and watched the bird feeder, and generally fell into a lackadaisical routine. It was wonderful.

For three days.

By Wednesday, we were off the rails. I was jittery from all the extra coffee I was drinking. I couldn't sleep because I was so anxious to get back to work on the boat. And, because of all the coffee and the lack of exercise, I began waking at five o'clock instead of eight o'clock. The only thing to do at that hour was drink more coffee. We began bickering.

"Why did you get up so early?" "Nothing else to do."

"Why are you cleaning the house again?" "I wouldn't have to if you would help."

"You're drinking too much coffee." I poured another cup.

And, so it went.

And, while confident that *I* was handling a difficult situation well, I noticed Jan was becoming more unreasonable. The shelter was closed for the holidays, so she wasn't needed there. She began watching more daytime television. And since Amanda wasn't around, she said it was silly to cook large meals for just the two of us, so we ate more snacks and less real food. I mentioned this to her tactfully, but her response was not what I had hoped for. She got out the vacuum cleaner and began cleaning the already spotless house, again, during a very important playoff game. I raised the volume.

"Uh, honey," I screamed over the roar of the vacuum cleaner, "perhaps you could finish that later? I'm trying to watch the game. And could you please bring me a soda and some cheese?"

It got very quiet. *Ahhh.* "Thanks, honey, that's better." I lowered the volume.

"Why don't you go over and work on the boat?" she said, an eerie tension in her voice.

"Angus is busy," I said, raising the volume again.

"Why don't you go work on the boat, anyway?"

I turned. She was holding the vacuum cleaner wand like a weapon, and she had the same expression on her face she had when she thought we were going to get eaten alive in the woods. I sensed that something had upset her. *Maybe she needs a vacation.* Remembering that Angus and I had put a television in the boathouse, I got up. "You know, honey," I said agreeably, "you're right, of course. No reason to sit around here, wasting time, getting in your way. I'll go over and putter around. There's always something I can do."

Silence.

"I should be back around dinner time. If you want to cook, I mean. If not, we can eat out, or have a snack, or leftovers, or anything at all, really. Whatever you feel like." I was eager to get going.

Silence.

"Well, I'm off, then," I said, backing out the door. "Call me if you need me." The only response was the roar of the vacuum cleaner.

CHAPTER 30

....

When I got to the boathouse, I had to shovel away some snow so I could open the door, but once inside, it was quite comfortable. I flipped on the TV, then began cleaning up—sweeping, sorting, stacking—just busy-work, really, with no real purpose. I passed a pleasant hour or two that way, watching the game for a while, puttering for a while, admiring the boat for a while. I even dozed in a chair for a while. It was merely passing time, I knew, but it sure felt good to be back in the pleasant cocoon of the boathouse, gearing up for the new year and my much-anticipated return to the task at hand.

Along about mid-afternoon, the door opened and in walked Angus. "Hi, Angus," I said, pleasantly surprised.

"Hi, Jim, need some help?"

I grinned. "No, not really. I'm actually not doing very much of anything."

"No problem. I'll help you anyway." He glanced at the TV. "How's the game going?"

"Couldn't tell you. I turned down the volume because it was bothering me, then got carried away cleaning up." He nodded knowingly. "I thought you were busy today?"

"I was," he replied, "but everything got taken care of. I had a couple of doctor's appointments, then Hilda wanted to do a little shopping. We were back by two. I took a short nap, then came out here to putter."

"*You* took a *nap*?"

He grinned. "Sure did. Felt good, too!" He paused, taking a quick glance at the plans on the bench, then inquired, "What brings you over here?"

I groaned comically. "I had to get out of the house. Jan and I were getting on each other's nerves, and retreat seemed the better part of valor. I don't know what's gotten into her lately."

Angus laughed out loud. "What's gotten into *her*? Heck, it's the same thing that gets into *everybody* this time of year—cabin fever. Our systems get all confused because the days get shorter and the nights get longer. Winter sets in and it's difficult to get outside and move around, have any kind of schedule."

"Well, I'll be darned," I said. "I always thought 'cabin fever' was just a joke."

"Oh, no," Angus emphasized, "it's real, believe me. Happens all the time."

"Ever happen to you?"

"Why do you think I'm out here?"

We both laughed, but I was concerned nonetheless. "If that's the case," I said, "it's going to be a long winter. It just started and we have three hard months ahead of us. I hope she'll be all right."

Angus shook his head. "She'll be fine. When the holidays are over, things will return to normal. She'll have her work at the clinic, you'll be busy over here out of the way, and Amanda will be back in school." Then, after the briefest pause, "When *is* Amanda coming back?"

I had to chuckle. "Sunday," I replied. It was the third time he had asked me the same question. So much for enjoying the peace and quiet.

"Oh, yeah, that's right, three more days."

We muddled along for a while, accomplishing nothing, making small talk, content to simply pass our time in such a pleasant place.

Then, out of the blue, "Why don't we go to the diner for breakfast tomorrow?"

Angus's invitation caught me off guard momentarily, as he rarely suggested going anywhere. But it was a wonderful idea. Whenever we went there, we always had a great time. The food was terrific, the girls teased us, and it was where all the locals started their workdays—fishermen, carpenters, boat workers. It was always abustle (being the best place in town), but it was particularly raucous in the mornings when the tradesmen came in to start their day. The place was awash with genial energy as the men swapped good-natured barbs, cracked jokes, and flirted with the girls. And it would get me out of the house for a while, no small consideration after my experience that morning. I agreed immediately.

"Good," he said, "we'll get an early start, then come back and try to accomplish something." I concurred and we continued our mindless tasks with renewed enthusiasm.

Next morning, Friday, I picked up Angus at the agreed-upon time and we drove over. It was still dusky, but the lights from the diner shone so brightly that we could see them as we approached from several blocks away. The parking lot was, of course, packed. It was always packed at this time of the morning. We finally found a space about two blocks away.

"Might as well have left the car home," Angus groused as we trudged through the snow.

When we entered the diner, the normal racket got even louder.

"Hey, Angus, how are ya?" "How's the boat comin', Angus?" "How's Hilda?" And so on.

For a guy who seemingly never went anywhere, he apparently enjoyed a universal respect and admiration. Small towns are like that, everyone knows everyone else; they have their whole lives. Angus smiled and waved, answering the banter in his concise manner. He seemed genuinely flattered by the attention and was still smiling broadly as we sat down.

"Good morning, boys," Laverne greeted us. "Coffee?" She was her usual cheerful self, always on the lookout for a friendly joust. She had been pouring coffee and trading barbs at the diner for years and could handle the rowdiest customer or the sharpest wit with equal facility. Most guys who crossed her only tried it once.

"Thanks, LaVerne," I said. "Quite a crowd this morning."

"No, just the usual suspects," she answered dryly. "What can I get for you?"

We ordered, then leisurely sipped our coffee as we waited for our breakfast. As usual, we had ordered too much food. It all looked so good, we couldn't make up our minds. When it arrived, our eyes bulged; there were eggs, bacon, sausage, waffles with slabs of butter and little pitchers of maple syrup, toast, and Indian pudding. We protested that it was far more than we could handle, then plowed in manfully, pacing ourselves like marathon runners. And, boy, was it good; everything cooked perfectly, the coffee, delicious. After a most enjoyable half hour or so, we were surrounded by empty plates.

Laverne came by our table, surveyed the damage, quipped, "Any dessert, boys?" and proceeded to clean up the mess.

I grinned. "No, thanks, Laverne, just a little more coffee, please."

And so, we sat there with the best of intentions, sipping coffee, planning our day, about to get serious. But while we did so, friends of Angus's began to drop by our table on their way out. They would sit down to visit with us, have some coffee, then begin reminiscing about old times. It seemed every time we got ready to leave, another old friend would wander by and it would start all over again. But Angus was thoroughly enjoying himself and I was hearing firsthand about an era long past. In short, we blew the entire morning talking, laughing, and remembering. A change had seemed to gradually come over Angus; he seemed far more at ease than I had ever seen him, outside his house. He laughed easily and often, joking comfortably with his life-long friends. After several such visits, and before we even realized it, it was almost time for lunch. We had gotten a good, early start, only to waste the next three hours sitting around drinking coffee and talking old times. It was wonderful!

Laverne came over, grinning. "We ought to charge you boys rent," she cracked, pouring yet another cup of coffee. "Need a lunch menu?"

We laughed, but in truth, it *had* been more than three hours since we'd eaten breakfast. "What do you think, Angus?" I joked. "We have to eat *some*where." Laverne made a funny face and smacked me on top of my head with her order pad.

But Angus, who was still basking in the good fellowship of the morning, had a different idea. He was gazing out the window with a distant expression. Then he turned to me and said, more than asked, "Feel like taking a ride?"

A ride? That caught me off guard just a tad. It was late December, in Moosaquit, Maine. There was no place to take a ride *to*.

"A ride to where, Angus?"

But he was already up, showing an impatient vigor as he waited for me to join him. "Do you have any plans for the day?" he asked as he strode briskly ahead of me toward the door.

"Not now," I replied, picking up speed. It wasn't like Angus to just take off on the spur of the moment, but I had learned to follow his lead, no questions asked. I was never disappointed.

"I'll drive," he said, and I tossed him the keys.

We turned north onto Main Street and drove toward the outskirts of Moosaquit. Angus had said not a word since we left the diner and I knew better than to try to pry anything out of him. Any small talk or questions would simply be answered with a "yup," a "nope," or one of his grunts. I sat back to enjoy the scenery, and waited.

Just beyond the edge of town, he turned westward onto a two-lane road that began almost immediately to wind through the woods. At that point, I was totally clueless. I had passed that turnoff numerous times, of course, but had never driven on it, nor did I know what or where it led to. All I knew was that there wasn't much west of Moosaquit until Canada.

After a pleasant hour or so of complete silence, we pulled into a long, narrow driveway that led to a small farmhouse. We were right smack in the middle of nowhere. The only signs of life were a plume of gray smoke curling skyward from the single chimney, and a large hound that bounded out to meet us, barking and howling while he circled the car. The front door swung open and a man stepped out to see what the commotion was all about. He was of indeterminate age but looked ancient. He had a full beard, a slouch hat, and wore coveralls with the top unbuttoned and hanging down in front, exposing his bright red woolen underwear. He squinted at us from under his hat brim, surely wondering what kind of fool could possibly have wandered out there, disturbing his peace.

"BRUTUS, QUIET!" he shouted at the dog. The beast stopped barking and sat, but not willingly. His lip continued to curl while he assessed the strangers who had dared to intrude on his turf. *Not at all like Duncan*, I mused.

I decided to sit tight for a while, but Angus got out, smiled, and said, "Hello, Tom."

The old coot stopped abruptly, a disbelieving expression on his face, then broke into a near-toothless grin. "ANGUS!" he shouted. "ANGUS MCTIGUE! Why, you old horse thief! How the devil are you?"

The two men shook hands warmly and embraced, the codger peppering Angus with nonstop questions while Angus just smiled and nodded yes or no. The dog, following his master's lead, joined in, leaping around like a dervish, almost knocking Angus over in the process. When things calmed down a bit, Tom looked over at me. "Who's your friend?"

Angus waved to me to join them. I got out of the car and, seeing the dog's playfulness, called to him, "Hey, Brutus, c'mon, boy." But I had apparently not passed muster. He stopped jumping around immediately and lowered a gaze at me, the fur rising on his back. A low rumble began deep in his chest. It seemed prudent to take a step back toward the car.

"Brutus, NO!" scolded Tom. The growling stopped, but it was plain from the dog's demeanor that I was definitely on probation.

I walked over. "Jim," Angus said, "this is Tom Carmody. He's my oldest and dearest friend. Tom, this is Jim Cairns."

We shook hands. "Nice to meet you, Tom," I said.

Tom held the handshake for a moment and peered at me warmly. "So, this is Jim," he said. "Nice to meet you, young fella, I've heard all about you."

I puzzled over that remark briefly, then decided the old guy was just being polite, or perhaps even dotty. They continued their chitchat, with Tom doing most of the talking, of course, while we gratefully adjourned to the cabin. I was wearing several layers of clothing and a parka, but I was numb from the cold. Tom might just as well have been on a beach in Florida. His only concession to the frigid temperature was a single layer of woolen underwear and the cotton overalls, and even the underwear was unbuttoned at the neck. It made me cold just to look at him.

We went inside and sat down. The decor was that of a longtime bachelor. There was a kitchen table with two chairs, a small couch (upon which Brutus immediately settled, daring me to sit next to him), a writing desk, and a small cot in the corner. Despite the scarcity of furnishings, everything was shipshape and relatively clean. A comforting fire was crackling away in the fireplace, and I inhaled a powerful aroma of coffee. I went immediately to the fireplace to warm my hands.

"How 'bout some coffee, boys?" Tom offered.

I brightened. "Sounds good," I replied through chattering teeth.

Tom went to the stove, an old wood-burner, and filled three large mugs. He handed me one of them, told me to make myself comfortable, and offered to take my parka and hang it up. "No, thanks," I said. "I think I'll just keep it on for a while."

"Suit yourself, son," he cackled, "but it's not good to get overheated, you know." With the two fires from the fireplace and the wood stove going full tilt, it might have been as much as forty-five degrees inside.

"I'll be careful," I assured him and took a long draught of the steaming coffee. My mouth went numb. Not only was it scalding hot but it was also the worst coffee in history—overboiled and tasting like pine pitch. Fortunately, he had turned away from me to return to the table, because it immediately went back into the cup or I would have gagged. My God, it was awful! I glanced over at Angus. He was serenely sipping away, albeit without his usual gusto. I was in a pickle, all right. I certainly didn't want to offend Angus's friend, but the stuff was undrinkable. It was in dire need of a civilizing influence.

"Uh, Tom," I ventured casually, "would you perhaps have a bit of cream and sugar around?"

"Sure thing, son" he said. "Be right back." He got up and went out to the barn.

I said to Angus, "He keeps his refrigerator in the barn?"

"No," Angus responded with a grin, "he keeps his cow in the barn."

"Oh."

Tom returned with a small tin cup full of rich whole milk, still warm from the udder. "There ya go, son," he said cheerfully. "Sugar's in the cupboard." And he returned to the table to resume his conversation with Angus.

I added a good half-cup of the milk and a couple of tablespoons of sugar to the malevolent brew and stirred briskly. When I was certain all the sugar had dissolved, I closed my eyes and took a cautious sip. It still tasted like dirt, but a sweeter and more diluted dirt. I decided it probably wouldn't kill me before I could get to a doctor, so I left the comfort of the fire and joined the two old friends, who were having a grand time regaling each other with their past exploits.

For the next two hours, I was witness to an enlightening and fascinating afternoon. I found out that Angus and Tom had known each other since the first grade, receiving their entire education together in the same one-room schoolhouse (that was my first surprise—Tom looked easily fifteen years older than Angus). They were inseparable best friends and had spent their youth hunting, fishing, and trapping in the woods in and around Moosaquit. The Great Depression was something they learned about in school, but which never affected them directly. Everything they needed was right there on their farms or in the woods they loved. It appeared they enjoyed every aspect of an ideal boyhood.

Angus, of course, worked in the family boat-building business since before he could remember, but there was plenty of spare time in those days and most of it was spent outdoors, in all seasons. He finagled a job in the boathouse for his friend and Tom showed considerable promise, but the war came along and changed everything. Tom went into the Marines and spent three and a half years in the Pacific, getting wounded twice and becoming highly decorated. He came back a major and a local hero. He also came back, like so many returning veterans, a changed man. He didn't seem to fit in anymore, and when he decided, in 1948, that Moosaquit had become too "crowded" for him (Moosaquit has one traffic light at the juncture of Main Street and Shore Road), he squatted on this property in the middle of the woods and built the cabin we were now in. He acquired enough livestock and goods to support himself and has lived off the land ever since, never again leaving the state of Maine. Angus had tried several times to entice Tom to come back to the boat shop, but his course was set and after a few years, the two old friends drifted slowly apart.

This set up my second jolt. As I listened to all this, I casually asked, "So, how long has it been since you two have seen one another?"

They looked at each other frankly. "Oh, I dunno," said Tom, "thirty years, maybe, Angus?"

"More like forty," Angus corrected.

I was stunned. "FORTY YEARS?!" I blurted. "How is that possible? You're best friends!"

Upon consideration, they both looked a little sheepish. "Well, gosh," said Angus, "we did kind of keep tabs on each other, but, you know, with work and all . . . I guess time just passed by."

"For *forty years*?" I exclaimed again.

"Heck," said Tom, "we both knew where the other one was if anything important came up. Don't like to impose, you know."

I thought back forty years in my own life; I was still in high school! "Forty years!" I murmured again, shaking my head.

But neither of them appeared to find anything unusual about not seeing one's best friend for four decades. What's more, they found *my* reaction amusing. "Jim's from the big city, Tom," Angus explained with a grin. "He doesn't understand how we do things here."

Tom gave me a patronizing pat on the back. "That's okay, son, city folks are a little slower, but you'll catch on eventually." He walked back to the stove. "More coffee, boys? Got plenty of it."

"No, thanks, Tom," I answered, maybe a tad too quickly. "The wife says I need to cut back on my caffeine." As sincerely as I could, I added, "Good coffee, though."

He grinned proudly. "It sure is, ain't it? I got my own way of makin' it. I use twice as much coffee as it says to use, then I boil it longer—brings out the flavor. I also throw in a good dose of chicory. I hate a weak cup of coffee."

"Yeah," I agreed, "me, too." I glanced over and noticed Angus had also decided to cut back on his caffeine.

As the two old friends reminisced a while longer, it began to darken outside. The mountains to the west shielded the setting sun, making the days even shorter in the woods than they were in town. The conversation began to wane and I sensed our visit was coming to an end when I received my third startling insight into small-town life.

We had stood up and were preparing to leave, saying our goodbyes, wishing Happy New Years, hoping it wouldn't be another forty years before the next visit, etc., when Tom asked Angus casually, "How's the *Amanda* coming along?"

"Oh, fine, Tom, just fine. Jim here's got a natural talent. We should be launching her around May or so."

"Glad to hear it," Tom said sincerely. "I bet she's a beaut. I'd sure love to see her. Maybe I'll mosey over, come springtime."

"I wish you would, old friend."

The two shook hands warmly and we all walked toward the car. As we did so, my mind was reeling. How on Earth did Tom know about the boat? He even knew the name, something I hadn't known until six days earlier. We were an hour away from Moosaquit, and Moosaquit was an hour away from anything else. Was there some kind of small-town telepathy I wasn't privy to? And Tom said he'd heard all about me! How? Why?

I was still going over these things when Tom shook my hand and said, "Nice to meet you, young feller. Feel free to drop by anytime. Any friend of Angus is welcome here."

It was the ultimate compliment because I knew he meant it. Mainers never say anything they don't mean. "Thanks, Tom, maybe I will. So long." I glanced over at Brutus, but he was still eyeing me warily. I got into the car.

After we had driven for a while in the usual silence, my curiosity was getting to me, so I ventured, "Quite a character."

Angus was looking out the window at the deepening shadows. "Hmmpf."

Now, I had known Angus long enough at that point to understand the nuances of his abbreviated form of communication. Knowing that to be his positive grunt, which allowed further inquiries, I continued cautiously. "Is he, uh, all right?"

"How do you mean?"

"I mean, he's been living out there, alone, for forty years. That's not exactly normal. Is he, uh, you know . . .?"

"Crazy?" Angus offered helpfully.

"No, no, I didn't mean that, exactly. I mean, is he all right mentally, emotionally?"

Angus took his time answering. I got the impression he was gathering his thoughts and choosing his words most carefully.

After some moments, he finally said, "Tom's fine. He lives that way because he couldn't live any other way." A long pause. "The war changed a lot of people, Jim, and not all of them could return to a normal life. Tom spent three and a half years killing people, seeing his friends get killed, and knowing in his gut that it was just a matter of time before he got killed. It was mere luck that he got wounded instead, twice. He was recuperating the second time when the war ended. When he came home, we spent a lot of time together, just like before the war. But something was different. With me, in the woods, he was pretty much the same as always; a little quieter, maybe. But he couldn't mingle with people, even in such a small place as Moosaquit. He couldn't hold a job, began drinking. I guess he had just seen more than he could bear. His solution was to withdraw into himself, move off away from everybody, and try to sort things out." This time he paused so long that I almost spoke before he finally said, "I didn't understand that for a long time, but I do now."

We passed a while in silence. I could see that the visit had struck a chord which had affected him deeply, and I think he was slightly embarrassed. Angus was not one to wear his heart on his sleeve. Hoping to break the silence and continue our conversation, I said, "You're a good friend, Angus."

He was still looking out the window.

"Hmmpf."

It was not his positive grunt.

CHAPTER 31

....

It was totally dark by the time we got home and pulled into Angus's driveway. Lights flashed on, Duncan rushed out, barking, to greet us, and Hilda flew out the back door like a shot.

"Angus McTigue," she scolded, "where in the world have you been? I've been worried sick. You left here at seven this morning and I've not heard a word from you since. What's the matter with you?" Then she turned on me. "And you, James, should be ashamed of yourself. Your dear wife was here all day and she's frantic."

"But . . ."

"No buts about it," she interrupted angrily. "There's no excuse for behavior like that. Imagine, two grown men acting like schoolboys." She caught her breath, then continued her diatribe. "And what, pray tell, was so important that you couldn't just pick up a phone and let me know where you were?"

Angus smiled and gave her a hug "Hilly, calm down," he said gently. "We went to see Tom."

Hilda reeled backward immediately, seemingly in shock.

"TOM?!" she exclaimed, eyes wide. It was all she could say for several moments. "Oh, Angus, you went to see TOM? Really?"

Angus was grinning broadly as he assured her it was true.

"That's *won*derful! How *is* the dear boy?"

She was in a dither, all right. She was so excited that she seemed to forget all about her recent harangue. "Oh, come inside, darling, right away. I'll make you a nice dinner while you tell me all about it. Is he all right? How does he look? Oh, this is such good news. I'm so sorry I was upset with you, dear. I don't know what to say."

Angus waved a quick "bye" and just like that, apparently, all was forgiven. *Well, that sure seemed easy enough,* I mused. But I doubted it would work with Jan. *Maybe I should bring Angus home with me.*

Duncan nudged me. I kneeled down, ruffled his ears, and said, "What do *you* think, boy?" He responded by playfully bowling me over backward into a snowbank, then piling on while we wrestled around in the snow. It was great fun for both of us, but in just a few minutes, I was cold, wet, and disheveled. "Okay, Duncan, time to go home and face the music." Reluctantly, he let me up so I could brush off the snow. "See you tomorrow, boy," I said, giving him a few more pats before finally getting in the car and driving home.

At the front door, I hesitated briefly to gather my courage, then poked my head inside and called out a cheery, "Honey, I'm home."

Jan swept out of the kitchen. "Well, well, well," she chided, "look who found his way home. Did you finally get hungry?"

She was wearing a pretty yellow dress, a pink sweater, and a green-and-white apron, and her hair was done perfectly. She looked radiant, like she does when we go out somewhere . . .. *Uh, oh.* Suppressing a sudden rise of panic, I glanced into the dining room. The table was set, so we weren't going out; and there were only two place settings, so we weren't having company. I exhaled. There was an awkward silence as I tried to think of something witty to say. She was studying me with a mockingly superior air, apparently enjoying my unease.

"Something smells great," I said.

"It's the apple crisp."

"You look great," I said, obviously floundering.

"Thank you."

"Is that a new dress?"

"No, you bought it for me two years ago."

"Oh." *Perhaps I should try a different tack.* "Table looks nice. What's the occasion?"

"Oh, no 'occasion,'" she answered airily. "I just thought you might be hungry once you remembered where you lived."

I grinned. "So, you were worried about me?"

"Oh, don't flatter yourself." She was smiling in spite of herself. "I knew you were with someone responsible. I was more worried about Angus than you."

I laughed, relieved at the thought of being back in her good graces. I made a move to hug her, but she gave me a stiff-arm that would have made Larry Csonka proud.

"Oh, no, you don't," she said. "Look at you—you're a mess. You've been wrestling with Duncan again, haven't you?"

"Sure," I said, grinning, "*he* was glad to see me."

"Well, maybe *he* should have made your dinner," she retorted.

Feeling safely out of the woods, I got to the point. "So, when *is* dinner?"

"Right after you shower and put on some decent clothes."

"But I'm hungry now," I whined.

"Then you should have come home earlier," she said without a trace of compassion. "I'll put the steaks on *after* you've cleaned up; and put those clothes in the hamper," she added.

"Okay, okay," I grumbled as I walked toward the stairs.

I was halfway up when she asked casually, "By the way, you never did tell me where you were all day."

"Oh, yeah," I yelled over my shoulder, "what an amazing day. You won't *believe* what happened."

Just as I suspected, by the time I reached the top of the stairs, she was right behind me. "Really?" she said, her eyes wide with curiosity. "What happened? Where did you go? What did you do?"

"Sorry, honey, I can't tell you right now. I've got to take a shower. If I'm not too tired later, I'll tell you then."

"Very funny!"

I couldn't help laughing at her look of frustration. "Look," I said, "you go downstairs and put on the steaks. I'll take a quick shower and be down before you know it. I'll tell you all about it over dinner. Deal?"

She pouted, gave me a grudging "okay," and flounced downstairs.

I was barely out of the shower and I could already smell the enticing aroma of the sizzling steaks as it wafted up the stairs. I hadn't had anything but that toxic cup of coffee since breakfast and I was famished. As I came down the stairs, Jan was just setting everything on the table.

She looked up and smiled. "Don't you look nice," she said. Making sure everything was in order, she said, "Dinner's all ready. Now, sit down and tell me all about your day."

I sat down to a rib-eye steak, sweet potatoes, and fresh green beans— just what the doctor ordered. "This looks great, hon. I can't tell you how hungry I am."

"Good," she said. "Now, start at the beginning. I want to hear everything."

Tickled by her eagerness, I took a sip of my wine and launched into my tale. At first, she was all ears as I described our marathon breakfast—what we had to eat, our verbal sparring with Laverne, etc.—then how Angus's friends began dropping by, one by one, until we discovered we had blown the entire morning eating breakfast and drinking coffee and chatting, and how it seemed we might do the same for the afternoon.

She slumped. "You spent all morning flirting with Laverne, stuffing your faces, and gabbing like a couple of washerwomen?" she wailed. "That's it?"

"No, that's not 'it.' You told me not to leave anything out—can I have some more wine, please?—so I started at the beginning, like you said to." I took a sip. "Besides, I think all this had a lot to do with what happened next." Another sip and I continued.

"Now, as I was saying, as more and more friends stopped by our table, Angus's mood seemed to change. It's hard to describe exactly, but he seemed flattered, even touched, by the attention of his old friends. He began to open up, joking and bantering with the guys, reminiscing about old times. I thought that rather odd, having lived his entire life in a town of this size, but, as I was soon to find out, there's a lot I don't understand about small towns."

"How do you mean?" Jan asked, intrigued.

"Here's where it gets interesting," I said, and proceeded to relate the rest of my day.

Jan has always been my best audience, and this time was no exception. She looked surprised when I told her about Angus's sudden urge to go for a ride in the middle of winter in Moosaquit. She laughed when I described Brutus and the noxious cup of coffee; she was enthralled as I related our afternoon visit with Tom. And, toward the end, she expressed disbelief when I told her they hadn't seen each other for forty years.

"Oh, stop it," she said, leaning back. "That's not possible. You're just teasing me."

"No, it's true," I insisted. "I didn't believe it either, but they were quite matter-of-fact about it, like it happens all the time. And maybe it does, I don't know. But I do know they were serious."

"So, he's been living out there, in the middle of the woods, alone, for *forty years?*"

"That's right."

She was having difficulty grasping the entirety of the situation. "But, why?"

"That's what I asked Angus," I said, and as I related Angus's explanation, her tears began to well. "Oh, that poor man," she said softly. "What he must have gone through, to stay out there, by himself, all that time. It's so sad."

"I know. At first, I thought he was just some old crank that Angus happened to know, and I wondered why we had driven all that way to see him. I mean, he looked like a bum. But as the day went on and the two of them talked, the conversation was so interesting that I forgot about his appearance and realized that he was an intelligent, interesting man, if a tad eccentric. He had shelves of good books and he was well-spoken for a man who lived like a hermit."

"I feel so bad for him," Jan said pensively. "Why do you suppose they stayed apart for so long?"

"I don't know for sure, Angus was vague about that. But it seemed to be by mutual agreement and without any apparent ill feeling."

"Strange," Jan said.

"It sure is," I agreed, then suddenly remembered. "Oh! And here's the strangest part: he seemed to know all about *me*. I thought he was just being polite, but he really did know things about me. And, get this, he knew about the boat. He even knew its name."

"But, how . . .?"

"I don't know. I was trying to get Angus to talk about it, but after he told me what happened to Tom during and after the war, he just clammed up, wouldn't say another word. We rode the rest of the way home in complete silence." Another sip and I continued. "And you should have seen Hilda when Angus told her we had been to see Tom! She was beside herself with joy, forgot all about chewing out Angus and me for being gone all day. She was actually crying, she was so happy. I still don't know what to think. All I know is, it was quite a day."

"That *was* quite a day," Jan agreed. "I can see why you were so self-absorbed."

I chuckled at the dig. "So, I'm out of the doghouse?" I ventured.

She smiled. "Oh, I was never really that upset, except for Hilda. She was quite concerned about Angus, but I knew you'd call if there was a problem." She reflected for a moment, then continued, "You know, as close as we have become to Angus and Hilda, things like this happen and I'm reminded that there is so much we don't know about them. We've only known them for a little over six months, after all. Imagine all they must have seen and done over the past fifty years."

"Same with us," I reminded her, then changed the subject. "Now, tell me about *your* day. How long were you there? What did you talk about?"

She leaned back and sipped her tea. "Well, after I *walked* up there because someone took the car all day, I guess I was there a couple hours or so," she mused. "We had a nice lunch and chatted about lots of different things; just a good visit. It was so touching to see how excited she is about Amanda's coming back."

"So is Angus," I said. "He's asked me three times when she's returning."

"They're so sweet," Jan smiled, "like doting grandparents."

"Just what Amanda needs," I grinned, "more grandparents. Now, where's that apple crisp?"

CHAPTER 32

....

The next day being New Year's Eve, we had agreed to celebrate, how-ever sedately, by having dinner with Angus and Hilda. We had asked them to come to our house to spare Hilda any trouble, but they both had insisted we go there instead. Angus was particularly adamant, saying he had some-thing special he wanted to share with us. He also was adamant about its being an early celebration ("I haven't been up 'til midnight in fifty years and I'm not about to start now!"). I teased him about that but, in truth, it suited me just fine. When it gets dark at four o'clock, staying up another eight hours just to watch the clock tick down to midnight holds no fascination for me.

We arrived around five-thirty to Duncan's usual raucous welcome. Upon entering the house, Angus and Hilda greeted us warmly. A cozy fire was crackling away and the silver tea set was perched on the low table, surrounded by a few simple hors d'oeuvres. I could smell dinner cooking in the kitchen. Once again, I was touched by how easily they made us feel so welcome in their home. Hilda poured tea and coffee, passed out some finger food, and we settled in.

"So, Angus," I inquired, "what's this big surprise you have for us?"

He smiled. "Oh, it's not that big a deal," he said modestly as he rose. "But I was poking around in the attic the other day and I came across something I hadn't seen in years, had completely forgotten about. I thought you might enjoy sharing it with us tonight." He was walking across the living room when I saw it—an old-time record player like I hadn't seen since I was a child. We used to call it a Victrola. It was a beautiful old piece, in perfect condition. The record player and a radio were combined in a handsome blond wooden cabinet. Underneath, two doors enclosed the storage area for the records, brittle old 78 rpm disks the size of dinner plates. I remembered one very much like it that my parents had when I was a boy. Grinning broadly, Angus opened the doors to reveal what must have been a hundred or more records in their individual jackets. "Pretty neat, huh?" he beamed.

Like curious children, Jan and I were drawn over to admire it. It looked brand new, as if it had just come out of the box. "This is beautiful!" I gushed. "How old is it?"

"Oh gosh, I don't know for sure," Angus replied, "but at least fifty or sixty years. My father had it before me. He gave it to us before he died."

"Does it still work?" I wondered hopefully.

"Of course, it does," he said, "that's why I brought it down." Hilda was looking on sweetly, sharing Angus's excitement. "Now, we haven't played anything in years, so I can't promise how good it will sound, but just looking at all those labels brought back a flood of memories. I was up there in the attic for hours, going through them all." He was as eager as a child. "We were hoping you two wouldn't mind listening to some of these with us for old times' sake, its being New Year's Eve and all."

Jan and I exchanged excited glances. "Of course," we both said at once. "We'd love to!"

And, we did. While Hilda and Jan set out dinner, Angus carefully unsheathed a few of his favorites and stacked them on the post. He could only put on five at a time, which meant he would have to change the stack every fifteen minutes or so, but there was no rush. While we ate, we listened to songs I hadn't heard since my parents had played them when I was young, pieces by Benny Goodman, Count Basie, the Dorseys, Duke Ellington, early stuff by Bing Crosby and Ella Fitzgerald—wonderful old songs that evoked a time I knew only from history books. Their sound was scratchy, but that only added to our feeling of nostalgia.

As the songs played, Angus and Hilda would eye each other and smile, no doubt reliving private moments of long ago, sharing with us what they might have been doing or where they were when that particular song was popular. Sometimes, when certain wartime songs came on, perhaps by Vera Lynn, or the Andrews Sisters, eyes would mist over and very little was said. Even though Jan and I were too young to have lived through that desperate time, we could see by Angus and Hilda's emotion that they still were deeply touched by the sacrifices made by so many, so long ago. We listened through dinner, then dessert, then coffee and tea. We must have heard fifty or more songs and there were still dozens more left unplayed.

It was, as it always was in their company, a wonderful, heartwarming evening, but it was getting late (almost nine!) and Angus had begun stifling yawns. I grinned and stood, indicating we should be leaving. Jan followed my lead, but Angus protested. "One more song," he pleaded, suddenly rejuvenated. "I've been saving this for last." I smiled, guessing immediately what it would be, but when he rose, he went to the kitchen first. When he returned, he was carrying a silver tray with two bottles and four aperitif glasses. He poured sherry into two of them and handed them to the ladies. He then emptied the other bottle, the long-ago wedding gift from his father, into the other two. There was barely enough left to fill the tiny glasses half full. He handed me one, then went to the record player to start the record. Lifting his glass, Angus said simply, "For auld lang syne." We clinked our little glasses and sipped slowly while we listened to the strains of that haunting melody that over the years had become symbolic of reflection upon the old year and anticipation of the new.

CHAPTER 33

....

The next afternoon, Sunday, we all rode down to Portland to pick up Amanda at the airport, having lunch on the way. We were, of course, all eager to see her again and have her back, but we had become just a little concerned that perhaps Amanda may not want to come back to Maine in midwinter after being in Florida for a week, especially after spending time with her old friends and family. We needn't have worried. From the moment she saw us, she was bubbling over with news of her trip, what was happening in Florida, the presents she got, what her friends said about the boat, and on and on. She would occasionally slip in a query about our well-being, but she was so excited, she couldn't wait for any answers. She would just blurt on to the next thing that popped into her mind. Initially, we attempted having a dialogue with her, but her fever was such that finally we simply let her ramble on, occasionally interjecting an "uh huh" or a "that's nice" while she babbled on, oblivious.

Amanda was especially anxious to go to the farm first, to see Duncan and the other animals and the boat (and maybe discover something in Hilda's kitchen), before going home. It was almost dark as we made our way up the driveway. When Duncan heard the car, he trotted out to meet us as usual but, upon seeing Amanda, he went absolutely berserk, dwarfing his usual welcome by dancing around, barking, and then, unable to expend enough energy that way, tearing off into the field, running around in circles, and yowling before racing back to her side, a wildly rapturous expression on his huge face. He acted as if he hadn't seen her for a year. After finally calming down somewhat, he refused to leave her side for an instant. He followed her closely out to the barn as she checked on the other animals, where followed yet another outburst as the geese, the chickens, the turkeys, and the ducks all swarmed around their familiar friend. Finally, secure in the knowledge that her animals hadn't perished in the week that she was gone, she went with us to the boathouse. When we entered, she simply gazed up at the boat in awe. Angus and I hadn't touched it in the entire week she was gone, but it was as if she were seeing it for the first time. She was almost speechless. "It's so *byoo*-tiful!" was all she could utter.

Just then, Hilda came out and announced that pie and cocoa were ready, if anyone was interested. Of course, everyone *was* interested, so we all adjourned to the kitchen, Amanda casting a longing glance over her shoulder as we left the boathouse.

The next day, as Angus had predicted, things did seem to return somewhat to normal. The holidays were over, Amanda started school, Jan resumed her work at the clinic, and Hilda's frightful illness was a thing of the past. Angus and I returned to our work on the boat with renewed spirit. And it happened just like he said it would. We all fell back into our routines comfortably, picking up right where we had left off.

The next several weeks drifted by as if in a pleasant dream, everyone happily immersed in their respective projects, getting things accomplished and looking forward to spring, then summer. Even the weather gods were cooperating. Weeks went by with clear, calm days and little or no snow. The temperatures remained moderate, with some days climbing into the forties. It was pure delight.

As we were finishing up one day in early March, I remarked idly to Angus, "You know, this really has been an easy winter. Jan was nervous about it back when we decided to do this, but, except for that little storm before Christmas, it's been a piece of cake. In another couple of weeks, it'll be springtime. I guess we dodged a bullet."

Angus gave me a comically terrified look, glanced skyward, and said quietly, "Shh . . ."

I laughed. "Oh, come on," I said, "we're over two-thirds of the way through winter already and it's been a breeze. How bad could it get now? In a couple of weeks, winter will be over and the robins will be singing. I think you're getting old and cranky."

Angus grinned amiably. "That may be," he allowed, "and I can't say how bad it *will* get, but I know how bad it *can* get, and that's very bad. I've lived up Maine my whole life and I've seen it all. You're right, the calendar says we have three months of winter and that's fine in Virginia. Up here, you can pretty much tack another month on to each end, making it five months. That means we have another couple of months of very unpredictable weather. Believe me, anything is possible." He paused, then added cryptically, "I always feel a lot better when May rolls around."

Poor Angus, I thought, always the crepehanger. Nationwide, it had been the mildest winter in memory. The ski resorts were devastated, people had golfed virtually the entire winter, and the biggest concern seemed to be that the tulips and crocuses would come up too early and then get hit with a spring frost. I considered teasing him about being an old poop, but I saw something in his eyes that gave me pause. Remembering his track record, I wisely held my tongue.

We carried on uneventfully, in spite of Angus's dire forebodings. The work seemed to flow more quickly now as the *Amanda* neared completion.

The bulk of the heavy work was done and, as she sat there with her primer coat on, she looked like she could launch the next day. There was much left to do, but the overall feeling was that we were buttoning things up. When we installed, say, the engine, or the plumbing, it would take a day or so instead of weeks, and it would be done, checked off the list. Another month or so and we'd be painting, then launching her. It was an exhilarating time for me and I was certain I detected a new sense of urgency in Angus also as we raced to the finish line.

It was about this time, the beginning of April, as the weather was getting even better, that Amanda was sent home from school with a cold—a common occurrence in northern schools, what with thirty or forty kids cooped up together in a classroom all winter. The next morning, as we were taking a break, I mentioned in passing to Angus and Hilda that Amanda wasn't feeling well, had some minor thing, probably a cold. Their response took me completely by surprise.

"What do you mean," Angus asked, eyes wide, "not feeling well? What's wrong with her?" Hilda also seemed suddenly alarmed.

I knew how they felt about Amanda and was touched by their concern, but I was taken aback somewhat by the abrupt change in the tenor of the conversation. "Oh, she's fine," I assured them, "just a cold and a sore throat."

"How do you know that?" Hilda demanded. "Has she seen a doctor? It could be anything."

I began backpedaling. "I'm sure she's okay," I said defensively, "it's just a cold. Kids get these things all the time."

"You don't know that," Hilda said sternly. "She should see a doctor immediately."

I almost smiled at their overreaction, but their feelings were so obviously genuine that, to calm them down, I said, "Maybe you're right. When I get home, I'll talk to Jan and see if she can make an appointment to see Doc Perkins sometime this week."

Angus and Hilda exchanged scowls, then Hilda immediately picked up the dishes and the rest of the pie and went back into the house. It was an odd situation. Anxious to put it behind me, I poured another cup of coffee and prepared to go back to work.

But we had no sooner gotten started again when Hilda reappeared in the boathouse and said, "I just called Doc Perkins and he said to bring in Amanda. He can see her right away."

I sighed. "Hilda," I said, "do you really think that's necessary? It's just a cold." But they were adamant. "All right," I said, "I'll call Jan and—"

"I've already called her," Hilda said. "She pooh-poohed me too, but I told her I'd already made the appointment and the doctor is waiting. Told her we'd meet them there in fifteen minutes."

"Meet them there?" I said, "for a *cold*?"

I was astounded, but they acted like I wasn't even there. "Ready, Angus?" Hilda asked.

"Yup."

Having seen firsthand how determined Hilda could be, I shrugged, dropped my tool belt, and went with them to their car for the half-mile ride to the doctor's office. Just as we arrived there, we saw Jan and Amanda getting out of our car. Amanda brightened upon seeing us.

"Hi, Aunt Hilda; hi, Uncle Angus!" she cried and ran to give them a hug. Her little nose was red and her voice was stuffy, but otherwise, she looked perfectly normal.

"Ooh," Hilda cooed, "how *are* you, darling?" She hugged Amanda tightly, then held her at arm's length and looked her all over for any life-threatening signs. Angus looked on, his concern also apparent.

"I'm fine, Aunt Hilda," Amanda said brightly. "I wanted to stay in school, but the nurse said I had to go home so I didn't make anyone else sick. Ruined my perfect attendance record, though. Did you bring me any cookies?"

Hilda laughed lightly. "No, darling, but after we see the doctor, we'll go back to the house and have some rhubarb pie. How does that sound?"

Amanda made a happy face. "Oh, boy, Aunt Hilda, that sounds great!"

We entered the office and checked in with Doc's wife, Trudy, who was also his receptionist. She looked us all over with a fair bit of skepticism and said, "So, who's the sick one?"

Amanda piped up. "I am, Missus Perkins!"

Trudy gave her a doubtful smile. "You don't look very sick," she said. "Are you sure you're not just playing hooky?"

"Oh, no, ma'am," Amanda said, laughing, "I wouldn't do that. I like school."

Doc Perkins appeared then and ushered us into his office. "So," he began, looking at Amanda critically, "what seems to be the problem?"

"I think I have a cold, sir," she replied timidly.

"Well, let's see," said the doc, and proceeded to make a big show of checking Amanda's blood pressure and her temperature, looking into her ears, peering down her throat while she said "aah," and listening to her heartbeat and breathing. He tapped her on her knee with a little hammer, then shined a light into her eyes. During all this, he would occasionally make a noncommittal grunting sound, signifying nothing. Angus and Hilda hung on every gesture.

Finally satisfied, the doc finished and stood up.

Hilda was breathless. "What is it, Doctor?" she whispered.

The doctor smiled. "She has a cold, Hilda."

"Are you sure? Is there anything you can prescribe that would help her?"

"Yes," he answered kindly, "I'm prescribing some pie and ice cream. That, and a couple days' rest and she'll be fine."

Hilda heaved a huge sigh of relief and gave Amanda another hug. "That's wonderful news, sweetheart," Hilda said.

"It sure is," echoed Angus. "Now, let's go have that pie and ice cream. Doctor's orders, you know!"

Amanda was grinning happily as she, Angus, Hilda, and Jan left the office, but I hung back for a minute, curious. "Doc," I said, "is there something going around?"

"No," he answered, "nothing unusual. Why?"

"Oh, I don't know, it just seemed you were very thorough in your examination. You must have known it was only a cold, but you checked everything as if you thought she might have the plague."

He smiled. "Sometimes people feel more secure if you go through more motions. Sure, it was just a cold. But Angus and Hilda are getting older and they love Amanda and were worried about her. Now they feel better." He paused, then added, "I guess you can't blame them after what they went through."

Remembering Hilda's recent scare with pneumonia, I agreed. "Yeah, I suppose so." I shook his hand. "Thanks, Doc."

"Anytime."

Two days later, Amanda was back in school, rejuvenated by the restorative powers of Hilda's baked goods. And that should have been the end of a very minor episode in our lives that winter, except that, in the process of taking care of Amanda, Jan had caught her cold. Now, when most people catch a cold, they're down for a couple of days, they rest, they drink fluids, they eat pie, and that's it.

But not Jan.

Whenever Jan gets a cold, it's an epic battle, a long, drawn-out siege—her immune system versus the common cold virus. Knowing this, at the first sign she immediately began infusing massive doses of Vitamin C, herbal tea, broth, cold medicines, and aspirin, all to no avail. The viruses loved it all and settled in for an extended stay. On the first day, she got the sniffles and began to sneeze. The second day, her sinuses ceased functioning and she ached. By the third day, her face was a grotesquely puffy caricature, accentuated right in the middle by a bright red, crusty nose. She could barely talk, her voice a thick, stuffy rasp that turned her m's into b's, and her n's into d's. I knew from sad experience that she wasn't even halfway through her ordeal yet and, try as I might, there was nothing I, or anyone else, could do to assuage her misery. It simply had to run its wretched course.

As one might expect, Jan's mood deteriorated along with her condition. Through it all, she railed against the cold, the snow, the sleet, the abbreviated days, and every other possible facet of the dreaded Maine winter. "I don't know what I was thinking," she began one morning, "letting you talk me into staying up here all winter. This is exactly why we began going to Florida years ago. No sane person would live here year-round. I must have been out of my mind. Never again." And on and on.

I considered reminding her that she got colds in Florida also, that it had been an extremely mild winter, and that, up until three days earlier, she had been having a grand old time. But I didn't. Instead, it seemed like the perfect time to go to work.

"At least there's no more snow," I said cheerily as I left her room to go to the boathouse. She just peered back at me through the slits where her eyes once were and said nothing.

Poor Jannie, I thought as I left the house and began the walk up Shore Road. The sky had a low, thick overcast and there was a sharp nip in the air. *Brr.* I considered going back for my jacket, but convinced myself the walk would warm me up. I also didn't relish the thought of confronting Jan again. "Just a nice little spring cool snap," I told myself hopefully. Along the way, I waved and smiled at everyone, as I always do, but that morning all were bustling around, seemingly preoccupied. It was a quiet walk indeed as I ambled along—no jocular greetings, the air dead still, even the birds apparently not awakened yet. And the cold, instead of waning, seemed even more biting than when I left the house. I pulled my collar closer and picked up the pace, eagerly looking forward to warming myself beside the wood stove with a cup of coffee.

"Morning, Angus," I hollered as I came up the walkway.

He was puttering in the yard and looked up as I came through the gate. There was an expression of mild surprise on his face. "What are you doing here?" he asked.

Thinking he was referring to Jan, I replied, "Oh, Jan's fine. She'll just spend the day in bed and—"

"Don't you listen to the weather reports?"

"Huh?" In fact, I had stopped watching the weather weeks ago. It had been so nice for so long, I had lost interest. "No, why? What's up?"

He gave me his best I-told-you-so smirk and said, "You better get home and button things up. We're in for a doozie. A big system is moving in from Canada, should be here by this afternoon. Kinda caught everybody by surprise."

I looked around. It was like any other spring day in Maine—overcast, cool, maybe a little rain later on. But we were three weeks into spring; it couldn't possibly snow now, certainly not to the extent that Angus was saying. "I can't believe it," I said.

"You better believe it," Angus retorted.

"How much snow, two, three inches?"

He grinned again. "More like two or three *feet*. It's a big one."

"Are you sure?"

Now the grin was gone. "Jim," he began, slowly and deliberately, "this happens up here all the time. The eastern half of Canada is paralyzed and the storm is gaining strength. It's very serious and you need to get ready. Now go home and get everything inside, make sure your oil tank is full, and do some shopping if you have to. This could last a few days."

I was in a state of disbelief, but Angus's demeanor left no room for doubt. A few days! Jan *really* wasn't going to like that. *Perhaps I'll let Amanda tell her,* I thought.

At the thought of her name, I perked up. "Amanda's in school," I said suddenly. "I'd better go get her before it starts."

"School's been cancelled," Angus said. "She's probably already home. Now go on and get ready. Don't forget to buy candles, and sterno, and matches . . ."—I was already down the path on the way home—". . . and stay inside until it's over!"

I half-ran all the way back, my mind racing with everything I had to do, and with my concern for Amanda. When I got there, I was relieved to see that she was indeed home and playing in the yard. I gave her strict orders to stay inside and take care of Jan while I went shopping. I called the oil man and he assured me he would be over to our neighborhood within the hour to make sure our tank was full. By noon, I had done everything I could think of. I finally turned on the television then and saw for the first time the magnitude of the impending storm. They showed a map of Canada with nothing but a huge white blob covering the entire eastern part of the country. It was the only thing on all the local stations, reminding me of the hurricane broadcasts we have in Florida. I stepped outside and looked around. Everything seemed normal, except that there were no garbage cans, or lawn furniture, or children's toys, or children, for that matter, that could get blown away. It was still and silent as death.

The temperature continued to drop as the afternoon wore on, dipping down into the thirties, then into the twenties. In mid-afternoon, the wind began to rustle a bit, then freshened, then grew into a full gale, all within a half hour. Around three, we began seeing the occasional snowflake racing across the window. In less than fifteen minutes, the storm was at full force, the wind howling and the snow so thick we couldn't see across the street. I was stunned by the suddenness of the fury. In less than an hour, it had gone from a typical Maine spring day to a raging blizzard. It was easy to imagine the terrors such a calamity would hold for people in earlier times. I could also understand why Angus told me to stay inside. It seemed impossible to even go to the mailbox and back. We all simply sat there and stared out the window at the maelstrom. Jan leveled a gaze at me, eyes bloodshot, her nose completely stuffed up.

"Doe bore sdow, huh?"

CHAPTER 34

·····································

For three days and three nights, the wind howled nonstop as the storm pummeled us, the house creaking and shuddering the whole time. It seemed at times that our little home must surely buckle under the onslaught, but, through it all, we were safe and warm. For the entire three days, though, we were housebound. I wanted to go outside and assess the storm's effects, but that would have been foolhardy. After the first day, the first-floor windows were completely covered by drifts. I doubt if I could have gotten out if I had tried. The power kept going off and on periodically, making it difficult for us to track the storm's progress. We simply had to hunker down, completely at its mercy, and ride it out as best we could. Between Jan's cold and Amanda's pent-up energy, it was a long three days.

Then, one morning, it was over, the storm barreling out to sea as suddenly as it had arrived. We awoke, not to howling and creaking, but to the sweet scraping sound of the snowplows as they cleared our road. Excitedly, we threw on our clothes so we could rush outside and see the effects of the storm. Even Jan seemed more her old self now that it was over. I threw open the door and saw . . . nothing. The snow had drifted so high that it had completely covered the front door. I shut it immediately before the snow could tumble into the living room. We tried the back door and had better luck. It was only about two feet deep there. We climbed out of the house, sinking deeply into the loose drift, and managed to work our way around to the front. What we saw there was stunning. Trees were down, houses were heavily damaged, and the snow in some places was over eight feet deep. The neighborhood was unrecognizable. Already, though, power crews were out and working, right behind the plows, reattaching downed lines and removing threatening limbs to avoid further damage. The plows had already finished our street, as well as they could (there being no place to put all the snow), and had moved on. We could hear them in the distance, methodically pushing snow around, trying to at least get the main streets cleared, in case of emergencies. I couldn't imagine that so much snow could possibly melt before July. I waved to my stunned neighbors who, like me, had to be wondering what to do next. The answer, of course, was that nothing *could* be done. We simply had to wait until nature took care of things with warmer weather, or rain, and melted the snow.

But everything makes somebody happy. The kids, at least those who could get out of their houses, were already sliding down the mountains of snow, making snowballs, and generally having a ball. There being no chance of the school opening in the foreseeable future, this was to them no more than an unscheduled vacation.

"Come on, Amanda!" they yelled. She looked up at me expectantly. "Go ahead, sweetheart"—she was off like a shot—"and be careful!" I hollered after her, to deaf ears.

Behind me, I heard Jan say, almost in a whisper, "I can't believe this. It's the middle of April. This can't be happening." She seemed in a daze.

Putting forth what I hoped was my bravest manner, I said confidently, "Oh, it's not so bad, honey. Heck, in a week or so, it'll be like this never happened." I added as cheerfully as I could, "It's springtime!" We looked around. Kids were jumping out of their second-story windows into the enormous drifts. Most front doors were hidden by the huge mounds of snow that either drifted or were pushed up against them by the snowplows. And, any thought of driving anywhere was out of the question—all the cars were completely buried or imprisoned in their garages. "It'll take months for all of this to go away," she said, a look of stunned depression clouding her face.

I put my arm around her. "Oh, come on, honey," I said, "you're just feeling down because of your cold. Sure, it was a big storm, but this will all be gone soon. It's already up into the forties and it's just going to get warmer. A little rain and all this snow will all melt away. You'll see." I hoped I sounded more convincing than I felt. I turned her gently around and guided her back inside the house for a soothing cup of cocoa.

Over the next two days, an amazing transformation took place. Heavy machinery was dispatched immediately, working around the clock. Loaders would fill dump trucks with snow, which would then haul it to a ravine that sloped down to the river. There, the trucks would dump the snow so that it fell down the embankment. The trucks didn't seem large enough to make a dent in such a huge amount of snow, but there were five of them and they never stopped. As soon as one truck left with its load, the next one would be right there to take another, like clockwork. There was no sense of urgency, just a smooth-running system that the town had apparently perfected through countless blizzards.

On the second day, because of the warmer weather, it began to drizzle. The snow was melting steadily now, making little rivulets as it ran down the streets, then becoming stronger before it emptied into the storm sewers. The sewers directed it to the river, where it combined with all the rest of the drainage from a hundred miles upstream, turning the river into a boiling torrent. It was most impressive, and a bit frightening, to see and hear the river's angry wrath as it flung headlong on its barely controlled rush to the sea. The roar was constant and could be heard for miles.

On the morning of the third day after the storm, I awoke to the dulcet tones of Bobby's snowblower. It was only six o'clock, but I didn't mind a bit. I just smiled and lay back contentedly.

"What's that racket?" cried Jan suddenly, as she sprang upright in bed.

"That's just Bobby, honey. He's clearing our drive."

"But it's six o'clock!"

"Yeah, I know. We're first on his list, remember?"

"Oh, great," she groaned and flopped back down on her pillow.

I smiled. "Tell you what, let's give Angus and Hilda a call and meet them at the diner. We'll have a nice visit and get caught up with all the news. We haven't seen them since before the storm. And, you won't have to cook breakfast!"

As I hoped, she brightened considerably at that idea. She was pretty much over her cold now and needed to get out of the house. We all did. "That does sound like fun," she said. "Go wake Amanda and I'll get ready."

I called Angus, knowing he'd be up early, and he agreed it was a wonderful idea. "I'll wake Hilly and we'll meet you there at seven-thirty."

"Great."

By the time everyone was up and ready, Bobby had finished our driveway and had moved next door. *He must be making a fortune!* I thought. "Hi, Bobby," I yelled and waved. He pointed to his ear, indicating he couldn't hear me over the snowblower, and gave me a perfunctory smile and wave. When he saw Amanda, though, he shut off the machine.

"Hi, Amanda!" he called.

"Hi, Bobby," she waved back, all grins. "Some storm, huh?"

"Yeah, that was a big one, all right."

"Sure was."

I glanced at Jan, grinning. She smiled back at me, then called over to Bobby, "The driveway looks great, Bobby. Thanks."

His face lit up. "Thank *you*, Missus Cairns. I'm glad you like it." Then, again addressing Amanda, "Gotta get back to work, Amanda; see you later," and started up the blower. Amanda waved as we got into the car for the drive to the diner.

Upon arriving, we could see it was even busier than usual. It was the first day since the storm that the roads were cleared, and everybody, it seemed, had the same idea. Angus and Hilda arrived shortly after we got there and we all exchanged hugs and pleasantries. It was good to see them again and to know they had weathered the storm with no ill effects.

"My, you look *won*derful," Hilda said to Jan.

"Thank you, Hilda," Jan replied. "Between the storm and the cold, I might have let myself get down just a bit, but I feel much better now."

Laverne seated us immediately and already had the coffee pot ready to pour. "Everybody get through the storm okay?" she asked. We assured her we were fine and inquired about her. She had minor damage, she said, but nothing serious. Then we exchanged the usual banter while she took our orders. "Be right back with your tea and cocoa, girls," she said and hurried off.

The restaurant was abuzz with talk of the storm—whose property got damaged, who lost trees, how long it might take to get back to normal, etc. But, as bad as it seemed, there didn't appear to be a lot of serious damage and nobody got hurt or lost any animals. It seemed a miracle for a storm of such severity. Everyone was relieved and glad it was over.

But Jan was still shaken by the events of the last few days and all the talk wasn't helping. "I can't imagine ever living up here year-round again," she said. "That storm terrified me. Isn't it unusual to have one of that intensity so late in the season?"

Angus sipped his coffee for a moment before answering. "It is unusual," he admitted, "but not greatly so. We've had snow up here every month of the year. When I was a boy, we had a nor'easter blow through in late May. Tore up trees, killed a lot of farm animals, dumped three feet of snow on us. We didn't have weather forecasting back then like we do now and it took us completely by surprise. It was terrific, but in a week, except for some downed trees, there was not a trace left. From then on, it was a normal spring," he added with a grin, "whatever that is."

But Jan was still unnerved. "How do you deal with all that, the uncertainty, the miserable weather, the short days . . .?"

Angus glanced at Hilda, who was quietly sipping her tea. She smiled at him. "Heck, Jan," he said, "every place has uncertain weather. Florida has hurricanes, the Midwest has tornadoes. But except for the war I've lived here all of my life. Hilly and I never give it much thought. I know it's not for everyone, but we've spent our whole life together right here. We wouldn't even consider living anywhere else. It's our home." Hilda reached over and put her hand on top of Angus's.

Jan was touched by Angus's sincerity. "That's sweet, it really is," she said, "and we love Maine, too. I just can't imagine going through that every year. Maybe I'm getting too old."

At that, we all burst out laughing, even Amanda, who up to then had been a silent bystander. Jan flushed, a bit embarrassed by the commotion she had caused.

We were still kidding Jan when Laverne returned with our breakfast, two full trays of it. We plowed in, and Amanda steered the conversation to a subject more dear to her heart. "When will the boat be finished, Uncle Angus?" she asked between bites of blueberry pancakes.

Angus smiled mischievously at her, seemingly giving the query a great deal of consideration. "Well . . .," he said, drawing out his response, then taking a sip of coffee for effect, "I figure if we work reeeal hard and don't get any more interruptions, we should pretty much have her wrapped up by October. That means we could launch her next spring. How's that?"

It was a game they played often. Angus would make a preposterous claim, then Amanda would respond with a perfectly pitched whine. "Nooo, Uncle Angus," she cried, her face all pouty, "seriously, when?" It was a performance I never tired of watching.

"Seriously, huh? Well, let me see . . ." Angus was deep in thought now, his face a mask of exaggerated concern. "The carpentry is done, the rudder is ready to put in, all the rigging was delivered weeks ago . . ." He suddenly lit up. "Gosh, we're almost finished!"

"Yay!"

Angus was at the top of his form, enjoying himself immensely. "Tell you what," he said, "we'll be painting her soon and we can't get to the boathouse yet anyway, so let's do something fun today. Come over this afternoon and we'll look at paint samples. You can pick out the colors you want and we'll order it. Then, it'll be here when we need it. And," he added, glancing at Hilda, "maybe Aunt Hilda can make us a pie. What do you say?"

"Oh, boy," Amanda squealed, "that sounds like fun. I can't wait!"

She gobbled the rest of her breakfast in record time, then sat and fidgeted while we old folks enjoyed the rest of our morning. When we finally finished, she popped up like a springboard.

"Whoa," Angus chuckled, "slow down. I've got some things to do this morning. Come over sometime after lunch. That'll give us some time to relax. In the meantime, you can look at some of your grandpa's boat books to get some ideas, if that's okay with Jim."

The idea of spending a lazy couple of hours in my study, looking over boat books with Amanda was always appealing. "It sure is," I said. "That is," I added, "if she really wants to."

Amanda laughed and said, "I sure do!" and hugged me around my waist. I felt ten feet tall.

We left the diner, said our goodbyes, and went our respective ways. Upon arriving home, Jan got busy in the kitchen while Amanda and I retired to the study. I got out a dozen or so of my favorite books and we started poring over them. I was reminded immediately of the day, almost a year earlier, when we had done the same thing, and what it had led to. I watched her as she scanned the books, a purposeful frown of concentration on her face. We looked through all the books a couple of times while she dissected the pros and cons of dozens of different colors. It was becoming a lot more tedious than I had assumed.

She suddenly looked up from one of the books. "What do you think, Grandpa?" she said, pointing to a large schooner with a dark green hull, black trim, and lots of varnish.

"I don't think so, honey," I said gently. "Too much color and too much maintenance. Your little ship wants to be more dignified and easier to take care of. Remember, you're going to be responsible for maintaining her. Do you want to spend more time having fun sailing her or working on her?"

She liked the sound of that. "That's true," she said thoughtfully. "What do you think?"

"Well," I replied, "let's start with the biggest part, the hull. A much wiser man than I once said that there are only two colors to paint a hull: black or white. And only a fool would paint it black." She giggled. "So," I continued, "I would suggest a bright, shiny white. It looks great and requires the least maintenance. Then, you can add any color you want for accent."

"Great idea, Grandpa!"

I beamed. *Now we're getting somewhere.* "The bottom paint can be almost any color, because you don't often see it, but I've always liked blue."

"Me, too!" she chimed. She was getting into it now.

I leafed through some more pictures until I found what I was looking for. "You'll need a water line accent stripe. Makes it easier to clean and it looks nice, too. Look at this," I said, and pointed to a beautiful little double-ender with a bright red boot stripe. She loved it immediately. Three down.

Jan came in just then to announce that lunch was ready. But Amanda frowned. She was on a mission and anxious to push on. "Come on, honey," I said, "Jan went to a lot of trouble. We don't have much left to do and we can finish after lunch."

"But—"

I gave her a stern look.

"Okay," she moped.

Jan smiled. "I made BLTs."

"Okay!"

After lunch, we finished up pretty quickly. Since she liked blue, she settled on a light powder shade for the cabin top and varnish for the rails. She wanted more varnish, but when I explained how much work it was to maintain, her enthusiasm waned. But, all in all, she was quite satisfied with her choices and I must say, so was I. All that remained was to go see Angus and match her choices to his color samples. We were in high spirits to finally be so close to actually finishing the boat.

"Come on, Jannie," Amanda cried up the stairs, "we're ready!"

Jan came to the landing and smiled down at our eagerness. "Okay, okay," she said, "I'll be right down. I wouldn't want you two to eat all the pie."

CHAPTER 35

··

In our excitement, we covered the short distance quickly. The streets had completely cleared and the temperature was a comfortable fifty-five degrees. Except for some huge piles of snow that were pushed off to the side, things looked pretty normal. Even the trees were budding out. It had only been three days since the end of the storm but, amazingly, all utilities were back up and running and the houses were dug out.

As we turned into the pathway, I noticed a car parked out front, one I didn't recognize. I was mildly curious, because they so seldom had visitors, but gave it little thought.

Duncan charged out to greet us, always eager to see Amanda. "Hi, boy!" she cried, mussing his hair and hugging him. We saw Hilda over at the barn and waved to her. She was running around in circles, chasing after a gaggle of geese as they darted off in all directions. We couldn't help laughing as we watched.

"Aunt Hilda must be feeding the animals," Amanda cried. "Let's go help her, Jannie." She turned to me. "We'll be right back, Grandpa. Come on, Duncan." They headed off toward Hilda, but the dog held back, as if uncertain. Normally, he would follow Amanda without question, but he seemed unsettled, looking from me to the house to Amanda and back. "Duncan, COME!" she repeated, more forcefully. He turned and trudged toward Amanda, but reluctantly, and continually looked back toward the house.

As I turned and went in the back way, through the kitchen, I was greeted by the unmistakable aroma of a rhubarb pie. Mmm. I could hear voices coming from the living room, but I stopped for a moment to savor the delicious smell before I continued. When I did reach the living room, I was stopped cold by what greeted me. It was Dudley and two other men, all standing and talking to Angus at the same time in a blatantly intimidating manner. He seemed very ill at ease. Alarmed, I entered the room and immediately insinuated myself between them and Angus.

Dudley was momentarily taken aback by my sudden appearance but tried to cover up. He made an attempt at a smile and said, "Well, hello, John. Good to see you again." He put out his hand.

"It's Jim," I corrected curtly, ignoring his hand. "What are you doing here?"

The other two men stiffened noticeably and moved slightly toward me. Dudley began fidgeting, no doubt at the prospect of having suddenly to deal with two of us instead of just Angus. "Now, now," he stammered, trying to sound diplomatic, "no need for any trouble here. We just stopped by to try to talk some sense into Angus and the missus. My group has increased their offer and I know that if Angus will just hear us out—"

I turned away from Dudley toward Angus. "Did you invite them in?"

"No."

"Do you want to talk to them?"

"No." Angus was standing next to me now, more confident and defiant.

I tried to assess the situation. Dudley was soft and posed no serious threat, but the other two men were in their thirties, and stocky. It was clear why they had come. Even discounting Dudley, though, we would still be going up against men half our ages. It was a tense situation and promised to get ugly, but I didn't see many options. Besides, I was boiling.

As all this was racing through my mind, I heard the back door open and close. *Oh, great,* I thought, *that would be the girls—just what we need!* Hoping to put a quick end to the standoff, I looked hard at Dudley. "Get out," I said, "and take your goons with you. Angus has nothing to say to you."

An immediate and profound change came over Dudley. His eyes turned flinty and mean, his face twisted with hate. "Now see here," he said to me, "you can't tell me what to do. I came here to talk to Angus and I'm not leaving until he hears me out." The two men stepped forward, feet apart, ready. At that point, Dudley looked at Angus and snarled, "I know your secret, Angus."

The shocking statement stunned Angus. He recoiled as if slapped in the face, but his expression changed immediately to one of angry loathing. He leaned forward, apparently resolved to settle things physically, regardless of the consequences.

It was at this moment, when things were at the flash point, that I discerned a movement and a sound behind me. I paid little attention to it at first, being focused on the imminent threat before us, but it grew louder as it imposed more on my consciousness. What began as a mild distraction quickly grew into a deep, ominous rumble. I glanced quickly behind me to see that Duncan had entered the room from the kitchen and was advancing slowly and deliberately toward the three men. His eyes blazed with fury and his normally happy face was twisted into a raging snarl. His lips twitched back, revealing enormous white teeth. Because of his anger, his fur was standing on end, making him appear as big as a bear. It was a terrifying sight.

He continued his unwavering stalking, moving closer by the second, his entire being one of unbridled menace. The men were aghast, each one trying to hide behind the other two, their faces white with terror. When Dudley could finally speak, he whined, "Call him off, Angus, please. He'll kill us . . . nice doggy."

But Angus did nothing. He merely stood by as Duncan focused on his prey like a mountain lion, moving ever closer, sealing off any avenue of escape. His growl by then was deep, dark, and continuous, his lips dripping saliva. He had backed the men into a corner and appeared ready at any instant to pounce on them as a cat would on mice.

I could never have imagined Duncan in such a state. This was not the big, good-natured pup I had known. This was a focused, fearless, enraged beast that promised serious harm unless something stopped him. I stumbled out of the way and heard myself say, "My God, Angus, you've got to stop him. They don't have a chance!"

But still he did nothing, just watched as the three men cowered in the corner, paralyzed with fear. As Duncan kept advancing, I began to think that even Angus would be powerless to stop him.

Duncan was mere inches away now, and the men were crouched down, whimpering, their eyes closed from sheer horror. I was trembling from the unbearable tension, but Angus remained unmoved.

At the last possible second, when mayhem seemed certain, Angus said just one word: "Sit!" Duncan stopped his advance, turned to Angus as if to make sure, then did as he was told, though he remained fixated on the men. Angus approached them and in an icy, deliberate voice, said, "Dudley, I'm not sure how long I can control this dog. I want you out of my house, right now, and don't *ever* come back. Understand?"

Dudley wheezed a barely audible "Yes," and they backed away toward the door, still on their hands and knees. They never took their eyes off Duncan, who remained sitting, but was still trembling with ferocity. When they reached the door, there was a mad scramble as the three of them clamored over each other in their desperation to escape.

I watched as they ran to the car and sped out the driveway, then lowered myself shakily into a chair. My heart was pounding like a jackhammer. I looked over at Duncan, who remained where he was told to sit, and wondered how Angus could possibly handle the brute. I was still dazed by the specter of strength and aggression he had displayed. As Angus approached the dog, I cringed involuntarily, not knowing what to expect. But he merely said, "Come," and Duncan obediently followed him to the kitchen, where Angus cut the freshly baked pie into fourths, then gave him one of the pieces. "Good boy!" was all he said. Duncan gratefully gulped the entire quarter of a pie in one swallow and was once again his old self, looking around happily and sporting a goofy grin on his enormous mug. He licked the last of the crumbs from his face just as the girls came in the back door, laughing and chatting.

"Well, that sure was a workout!" Jan exclaimed, still giggling.

"What were you girls doing out there?" Angus asked.

"I went out to feed the birds and I guess they were all hoopy from being inside during the storm," Hilda answered. "As soon as I opened the door, they were out like a shot, in all directions. We'd get a couple of them corralled, then the others would take off. It was like trying to round up eels."

"We tried to get Duncan to help us," Amanda chimed in, "but he kept insisting on going back to the house. He wouldn't listen. I finally had to let him in." She giggled. "Guess he smelled the pie." Duncan heard Amanda say his name and immediately began wagging his tail.

Jan eyed the remainder of the pie on the stove. "Yeah," she cracked, "just when we need him most, he's in here looking for food. Typical male!" I was still slumped in the chair, breathing heavily, as she arched her eyebrow at me. "And look at you," she said, "you're all sweaty." She went around the room, opening the windows and muttering, "Honestly, I don't know what you two would do without us."

CHAPTER 36

·····································

For the next couple of weeks, our work progressed smoothly as the boat neared completion. Almost all the structural and mechanical work was complete and most of what remained was painting, a little rigging, and some touch-up work, which was moving along uneventfully. Amanda was euphoric at the prospect of sailing her boat all summer, I was wrapping up a once-in-a-lifetime experience, and spring had burst upon us with a dramatic suddenness. The gloomy mounds of old snow were gone, replaced by endless expanses of lush grass and dazzling wildflowers. The days were growing longer and the weather remained gorgeous, day after day. It was how spring in Maine should be, but so seldom is.

In short, my life was perfect. I should have been savoring every moment, but the unpleasant memory of the near-disaster with Dudley and his henchmen haunted me like a bad dream. Images of the encounter were constantly interrupting my thoughts and playing havoc with my concentration. The threat of the thugs inside Angus's house; the imminence of physical violence; Duncan's terrifying metamorphosis into a snarling monster—all these incidents kept recurring in my mind. But overriding all else were Dudley's threatening words, "I know your secret, Angus." What could he have possibly meant? And just as disturbing was Angus's reaction. He was galvanized into a cold rage, apparently willing to risk serious harm in his hatred for Dudley. What could cause a man like Angus, perhaps the most self-possessed man I've ever met, to change so completely and profoundly? I knew how reticent Angus was and respected him far too much to broach the subject, but it was eating me up. I couldn't discuss it with Jan, either; it was obviously something no one else knew about, and I could never betray Angus's trust. I took to watching him more closely in the ensuing days for any sign, any clue, but got nothing. He moved along at the same pace, unhurried and deliberate. I thought I could detect a subtle change in attitude, perhaps a little more reclusiveness, but it was hard to tell with Angus. It could simply have been my overheated imagination. I was in a state, all right.

"GRANDPA! UNCLE ANGUS! COME QUICK!"

Angus and I were in the middle of a delicate varnish application, but Amanda's shrill cry chilled our blood. We immediately tossed down our brushes and rushed out the door, alarmed by the urgency in her voice. There stood Amanda and Duncan, staring at what looked like a crumpled-up glove on the ground. As we approached, it moved slightly. I knelt down for a closer look and heard a faint "meow." It was a kitten, quite young, and in a pathetic condition. Its eyes were barely open, it couldn't lift itself to walk, and it was covered with filth. It was utterly helpless.

"Duncan brought him to me," Amanda said pityingly. "The poor thing. Where do you suppose his mother is?"

Angus put a hand on her shoulder. "It's that time of year, honey," he said. "There are lots of stray cats around here and they mate in the springtime. This one looks too young to have wandered off. His mother might have been killed somehow, maybe hit by a car, or killed by a coyote. Happens all the time."

Amanda's compassion was aroused. "You mean, there might be more babies without their mother?" She was close to tears.

Angus tried to be gentle. "Well, there might be, honey," he said, "but it's probably too late. Young kittens like this can't survive long without their mother. They have no protection, no food. There's not much anybody can do."

But Amanda wasn't listening. "We've got to find the other babies," she said, suddenly very much in charge. "Come on, Uncle Angus, I'll bet Duncan could take us to where he found this one. Maybe the others will be there, too."

Angus and I exchanged glances. "Honey," I began, "there's no chance. They're too far gone. Even this little guy is almost dead. It looks like he hasn't eaten in days. Besides, we just started varnishing. If we stop now, the job will be ruined and we'll have to start all over again when we get back, and . . . where are you going?"

"Be right back," she hollered over her shoulder. And, in less than a minute, she *was* right back, with Hilda, and carrying a cardboard box. "Here he is, Aunt Hilda," she said, pointing at the little wretch.

"Oh, the poor thing," Hilda cooed. "Here, let's put him in the box." She removed her apron and folded it to fit in the little box, then picked up the kitten and laid it gently inside. It was as limp as a noodle.

"Can we try to find the rest of the litter, Aunt Hilda?" she asked. "Uncle Angus thinks they're already dead."

Hilda threw Angus a withering glare and replied, "Why, of course we will dear. We can't just abandon them, now, can we?"

Angus sighed and turned to me. "You go ahead, Jim. I'll clean the brushes and wipe off the varnish. I'll catch up to you later." He ambled off, shaking his head and mumbling.

Amanda turned to Duncan. "Come on, boy," she coaxed, "go find the kitties." He looked lovingly into her eyes and wagged his tail as he always did, oblivious to any meaningful concept. "Duncan!" she repeated louder, assuming the problem was with his hearing instead of his cognition. "Find the kitties!" The dog looked around, happily aware that he was the center of attention, but comprehending nothing. Amanda was clearly getting impatient. "DUNCAN!" she screamed in frustration. "You're a bad boy!" *That* he understood. He drooped his head, crushed that Amanda would yell at him, and totally clueless as to what he had done to arouse her ire.

"Amanda," I said, "try showing him the kitten. Maybe he'll get the message."

"Good idea, Grandpa," she said. "Look, boy," she soothed, putting the box up under his snoot, "let's go find the kitties." His expression began slowly to transform, as if a very dim bulb were being turned on inside his massive cranium and, after a few more seconds, his face brightened. He wheeled about and charged off around the boathouse toward the barn. When we got there, he was standing by a large oak tree which had a hollow at its base. On the ground next to him were six more kittens, strewn about like so many used socks. "Ooh, look, Aunt Hilda," Amanda cried, "they're so tiny." She turned to me. "Are they all right, Grandpa?"

I approached them cautiously, trying not to startle them, but it didn't matter. They were all in a desperate state—dirty, emaciated, and barely breathing. Some were not moving at all. It was impossible not to feel sorry for them, but it was just as Angus had said—without their mother, they didn't stand a chance. "I'm sorry, honey," I said to Amanda, "but we're too late. I'm afraid they're just too far gone."

Tears were forming in her eyes as she looked down at the helpless kittens. "But we've got to do *something*, Grandpa." She was casting about, desperately trying to think of something, when her face lit up. "I know!" she cried "We can take them to see Doc Thompson, where Jannie works. They'll know what to do!"

I felt terrible. The kittens were truly in a hopeless situation. Some of them were probably already dead. But I couldn't hurt her feelings any further. I wanted to stop her and comfort her, but she was already gently scooping up the still little bodies and positioning them inside the box. I looked at Hilda, shrugged my shoulders, and carried the box back to the boathouse, where Angus was just finishing the varnish cleanup. "We're off to see Doc Thompson, Angus," I told him. "Would you call ahead and tell them we're coming?"

"Sure," Angus replied, giving Amanda a warm look. "Good luck, honey."

"Thanks, Uncle Angus. Come on, Grandpa."

Jan was waiting for us in the parking lot when we got there, anxious to see the baby kittens. "Oh, the poor things," she moaned, picking up one of the near-lifeless little bodies. "Bring them inside, honey. The doctor is with someone right now, but he'll be available soon."

We went into the waiting room, where a few other people were sitting with their pets. Few things stir people's emotions like sick baby animals, and we were immediately surrounded by everyone in the room, all talking at once. "Oh, they're so tiny." "Are they alive?" "Where's the mother?" "Can I pet them?" The cats, all the while, remained unresponsive.

Doc Thompson came into the waiting room, took a quick glance into the box, and shook his head, frowning. He reached in, took out each kitten, and set them on the countertop, where they simply lay where they were put, all but motionless. He looked at Amanda for a long moment before telling her, "Amanda, I'm sorry. They're in very bad shape. It looks like they've been without their mother for a couple of days. They're dehydrated and nearly starving." Then he turned to me. "I'll put them down for you, Jim. The poor things are suffering and there's nothing I can do. I'm sorry."

Amanda was devastated. In the thirty minutes she had known the kittens, she had become their sole protector and was convinced that she could save them. I think it occurred to her at that moment that their only hope for salvation lay with her. She became desperate. "Doctor Thompson," she begged, "please don't kill them. They're only babies." She turned to me. "Grandpa, please can I take them home? Please? I'll take care of them, I promise." She was openly bawling by then. The people in the waiting room were looking at me like I were an axe murderer.

I put my arm around Amanda's shoulder. "Honey," I began, as gently as possible, "the doctor doesn't think there's any—"

"Doc," Jan interrupted, "I agree with Amanda. There must be something we can do, or at least try. We certainly don't have anything to lose." She gazed at the kittens for a moment, then turned her misty eyes toward him. He looked around uneasily. All his customers were staring at him, Jan was weepy-eyed, Amanda was blubbering. He never had a chance.

"Okay, okay," he relented, "take some formula, keep them warm, and try to clean them up. The problem is to get them to eat something without eating too much. Their systems won't be able to handle it in their condition." Amanda immediately ceased crying and sprang into action, putting the kittens back in the box. But when she picked up the last one, an emaciated, pathetic patch of orange, half the size of the others, the doctor interrupted her. "This is the runt," he said, "he's barely breathing. Best to put him down now. I'll just—"

Amanda gasped. She had been small all her life and was sensitive about it. The thought of killing something just because it wasn't as big as the others didn't make any sense to her. She threw a pleading look at Jan.

Jan simply said, "We'll take them all," with an air of finality. The people in the waiting room, who had been silently watching the drama unfold, erupted with applause. Jan blushed from the outburst but took the runt and placed him in the box with his litter mates, then went into the back to get some formula.

I took the vet aside. "Well, Doc," I said, "any chance they'll survive?"

"Not much," he answered. "Cats are tough, but they're in real bad shape. They might not even make it home. And if they do live, there is always the possibility of brain damage." He paused, looking down into the box. "One or two might possibly make it, but I doubt it. You never really know for sure, though, especially with cats." Then he grinned. "One thing I do know for sure," he added, "they're in good hands. Those are two determined gals."

"You got that right."

On the drive home, Amanda talked to the kittens constantly, encouraging them, telling them everything would be all right. Her compassion was heartrending, but I knew the odds. Immediately when we arrived, she raced upstairs to her room and lay the kittens on her bed, where she proceeded to try to feed them. She filled the little bottle that the vet had given her with formula, but the kittens were too weak to take the nipple. She put some in a shallow saucer, but when Amanda put them near it, they just upset the saucer, slopping formula all over the bedspread. She was openly frustrated, but she kept at it and her persistence was rewarded when she lay one of the kittens down next to the spilled formula, accidentally dipping his little nose in it. The kitten snorted at the unpleasant sensation and began licking it off. Amanda's eyes filled with triumph and she began dabbing tiny drops of the formula onto each cat's nose, with the same result. It seemed impossible such a minuscule amount of food could make any difference, but at least they were taking *some* nourishment. Amanda was ecstatic, moving from one kitten to the next, petting them, dabbing their noses, cooing like a little mother as she encouraged them along their seemingly hopeless journey.

Jan poked her head inside the room. "Dinner's ready."

Without looking up, Amanda asked, "Can I eat up here, Jannie? I want to stay with the kittens."

"Of course, sweetheart," Jannie smiled, "You stay right here. I'll bring your dinner up for you."

"Thanks, Jannie."

"I'm going downstairs, honey," I said. "If you need me, just call, okay?"

"Okay, Grandpa," she muttered absently. I doubt if she even heard me.

I went downstairs, feeling a warmth because of Amanda's obvious compassion for the kittens, but at the same time, dreading the massive disappointment that surely lay shortly ahead. Over dinner, Jan and I discussed our quandary. "I think this was a mistake," I said. "She's just going to be that much more heartbroken when the kittens don't make it. I hate to see her go through that."

"I know," Jan said. "Me, too. But I know exactly what Amanda was feeling. I couldn't bear to let them be put down without at least trying to do something. They looked so helpless. Besides, if they don't make it, at least she'll know she tried. And kids are resilient; she'll get over it. It's all part of growing up."

I wasn't so sure. The thought of finding seven dead kittens in Amanda's bed in the morning was sobering, to say the least. At bedtime, I went into Amanda's room to check on her. Her dinner lay on the nightstand, untouched, and she was still at it, coaxing the poor little wretches to keep trying, keep trying. But they looked as if they were wrung out and just wanted to be left alone. "Grandpa," she said, "would you please get me a small container of warm water and a facecloth? I want to clean them up a little. Maybe they'll feel better when they're clean."

I smiled. "Sure, sweetheart." I went downstairs and fetched a small bowl, half filled it with warm water, put in a tiny amount of liquid soap, stirred it, went back upstairs, got a facecloth from the closet, and brought it to Amanda. She had gotten into bed and was snuggled under the covers, her little brood gathered close by. I put the bowl down beside her, whereupon one of the kittens immediately knocked it over, drenching itself and the bedcovers. The poor thing yowled with surprise and shook itself vigorously, suddenly very much alert and put out. Amanda tossed me a beseeching look and I proceeded downstairs to repeat my assignment. Jan was at the sink, smiling.

"What's so funny?" I said. "That bed is soaked with water and formula already. By morning, it's going to be a real mess."

"Do you do the laundry?"

I had to smile. "Good point."

"How are they doing?" she asked.

I shrugged. "The same. The one who knocked over the bowl perked up momentarily, but it didn't last. They're just worn out, exhausted, the poor things. Amanda keeps pushing them, though, she just won't quit."

"She's so sweet," Jan said, but her expression turned sad. "I hope at least one or two make it. It would mean a lot to her." She paused for a moment, afraid to bring up what was on both our minds. "What are we going to do, you know, when . . ."

I exhaled deeply. "I don't know," I said. "There's no good solution. I think I'll go to her room real early tomorrow and get them before she wakes up. I don't know what else to do."

Jan nodded and said nothing, her eyes misting over.

I went back upstairs, this time putting the bowl on the nightstand, where she could easily reach it. "It's getting late, honey," I said, "time to go to sleep."

"Okay, Grandpa," she replied, "I'll feed them for just a few more minutes, then I want to clean them up some more. We'll all go to sleep after that, okay?"

"Of course, sweetheart. Just don't stay up too late. Remember, you've got school tomorrow." I gave her a kiss and tucked her in. "And eat your dinner."

"Okay. Goodnight, Grandpa."

"Goodnight, honey." I turned out the light when I left, leaving just her bedside lamp on. She was in her own little world as I shut the door, still encouraging the pathetic little creatures, softly but firmly.

CHAPTER 37

....

It was well before daylight the next morning when I crept silently into Amanda's room. She was sound asleep, surrounded by the seven little bodies strewn about the bedspread. It was heartbreaking. Feeling miserable, I took a deep breath and reached for the first kitten.

"Meow."

The poor thing was so weak that I could barely hear it, but Amanda bolted awake, instantly alert to the pitiful cry. She picked him up gently. "Ooh, I'm sorry," she cooed, "I must have dozed off." She cuddled it for a moment, talking soothingly until it began to respond. The sudden activity roused the others and in short order all were vying for attention from their new mother. They were still bedraggled and unable to walk, but there was nothing wrong with their lungs. The room was filled with the tiny yowls of hungry kittens, begging for the life-giving nourishment they so desperately needed. Only the runt lay still, not making a sound.

I was flabbergasted. While they didn't look any healthier, they had survived the night—a major accomplishment. I watched Amanda as she busily dabbed formula on their little noses and talked constantly in low tones, always encouraging, as if they were children. Her eyes were heavy with fatigue and I noticed her uneaten dinner on the nightstand. "Amanda," I asked, "how late did you stay up last night?"

"I couldn't help it, Grandpa," she said, "they needed to eat and I can only give them tiny little amounts. They kept me up all night. I didn't even get the chance to wash them. It was four o'clock the last time I looked. I must have fallen asleep right after that." She said all this without looking up from her feeding ritual.

As happy as I truly was that the kittens had survived the night, I could see a problem looming. They had beaten the odds temporarily, but they were still very much in dire straits and Amanda had to get ready for school, leaving no one to take care of them. "Amanda, honey," I said gently, "it's time to get up and get ready for school."

She looked at me in genuine alarm. "But, Grandpa," she wailed, "what about the kittens? They need me. Can't I stay home just this once and take care of them?" She made her eyes big like she always did when she wanted something from me.

But school is school and she had to learn responsibility. "Amanda," I began, "I don't think that's a very good—"

"Of course, you can, honey, take all the time you want." I turned around. Jan had come into the room and overheard the request.

"Shouldn't we talk about this?" I said, a bit miffed that I had been so summarily overridden.

"Nope."

"But—"

"Look," Jan said, "Amanda's doing well in school—better than she's ever done—and missing one day isn't going to hurt. This is important to her." She grinned. "Besides, do *you* want to take care of the kittens?"

"Well, . . ."

"I didn't think so."

"But—"

Jan brushed past me, sitting down on the bed. The two of them stroked the kittens, talking baby talk. And I have to say, with all the attention, they did seem to perk up a tiny bit.

I was already feeling a bit irrelevant when Jan, without looking up, said to me, "Jim, why don't you make some breakfast for Amanda and me and call the school to let them know she won't be in? Thanks, honey."

After making breakfast, cleaning up, washing the dishes, taking out the garbage, and refilling Amanda's cat bath, I was looking forward to the sanity of the boathouse. Despite the late start, when I got there, Angus was not around. I was mildly surprised, expecting a little razzing for being so late myself, but began getting everything out that we would need for the day's work. I say "work," but in truth, we had got to a point where we were spending more and more time drinking coffee and chatting. The boat looked finished. All the hardware was installed, ready for the rigging, and all that remained was to finish the paint and varnish and install the electronics. Paint and varnish work always goes slowly because of the necessary drying time between coats, leaving plenty of time for reflection between friends.

Angus came in shortly, looking a bit haggard, nodded a "good morning," and asked, "How are the cats?" expecting the worst, no doubt.

"Well," I answered, "they survived the night, amazingly. Amanda was up until four, feeding them. She's thrilled, of course, but they still don't look good. She's staying home from school to take care of them and we'll see what happens over the weekend." I grinned. "One thing I'm sure of: if anyone can save those kittens, Amanda can."

"Amen to that."

I eyed him closely. "You okay?" I asked. "You look like you slept in the barn."

He grinned, but without his usual gusto. "Just tired, didn't sleep very well last night." He yawned. "By the way, I've got a doctor's appointment tomorrow. Can you finish the varnish yourself? I'm taking the day off, in case I'm coming down with something. That should be the last coat, then we'll rub it out Monday, okay?"

"You've got a doctor's appointment on Saturday?"

"Yeah, Doc's an old friend. He told me to come in tomorrow. I'll be his only appointment."

"Sure, no problem," I said easily, but I eyed him again, more closely. He looked older, not at all well. "You sure you're all right?"

He grunted. "Don't be a nag; that's Hilda's job," he joked. "Come on. If we don't get to work, we'll never get this boat launched."

We fell into an easy pace, rubbing the varnish Angus had brushed on the day before while I was at the vet's office. Because we began so late, it was lunchtime by the time we had finished. I took the opportunity to call home to check on Amanda and the cats. Amanda answered the phone, yawning, and told me they were doing well. I could hear the constant meowing in the background. "I'm worried about the little guy, though," she said (that's what she had taken to calling the runt). "I can't rouse him long enough to make him eat. Every time I try to feed him, he takes a couple of licks, then just falls back asleep. I keep waking him, but it doesn't do any good." Her concern was obvious.

"Remember what the vet said, honey," I reminded her. "They can't take too much food at one time or they'll get sick. Maybe he just has to go slower."

"I hope so," she said. I could hear the yowling getting louder. "Gotta go, Grandpa."

"Okay, honey, see you this afternoon."

When I got home that afternoon, I raced upstairs immediately to see how the kittens were doing. Against all judgment and logic, I was becoming emotionally attached to them. Amanda was so committed, and they were struggling so hard to survive, that I couldn't help rooting for the poor little things. Their sole chance for life lay with us.

"How are they doing, honey?" I asked when I entered her room.

Amanda looked up, her face glowing with pride. "They're doing much better, Grandpa. They're sleeping now, but they've been eating and moving around a little. I spent most of the day cleaning them." She paused, a little sadness creeping into her voice. "But I still can't get the little guy to eat, Grandpa," she said, indicating the runt, who was lying in the crook of her arm. "He just lays around and sleeps. I had to put him up here because the other kitties stomp all over him when they eat." She stroked him gently. "I don't know if he's going to make it."

I looked them over. Six of them were all curled up next to Amanda, snuggled in for warmth and purring contentedly. They still looked emaciated, but there was a sheen to their coats and, for the first time, I began to think that, maybe, they just might make it. I couldn't help smiling, feeling ridiculously proud and happy over the plight of seven orphaned kittens.

But the runt was indeed looking poorly. Aside from being by far the smallest, he was scrawnier, his coat dingier. And as he slept, his breathing wasn't the soft, easy rhythm of his mates, but a shallow, ragged gasp, as if he were struggling with every breath to stay alive. I reached over and patted the tiny body, but he didn't stir. "Keep at it, honey," I said.

"I will, Grandpa."

Dinnertime was a repeat of the previous night. I took her supper up, she asked me to put it on the nightstand, and she assured me she would eat it "as soon as I can." She was dabbing the kittens with a damp cloth, trying to remove all the dirt they had accumulated. Each kitten would respond by stretching and preening, probably just as it would if their mother were grooming them.

"You need to eat, honey," I gently coaxed her.

"I will, Grandpa," she answered distractedly, and continued moving from kitten to kitten.

I bent over and kissed her forehead. "I'll be downstairs if you need me."

"Thanks, Grandpa."

Jan was doing the dishes as I entered the kitchen. "I'm getting a little concerned about Amanda," I said.

She looked up. "How so?"

"Jannie, she's been in that bed virtually nonstop for almost a day and a half. She's not eating, she's getting very little sleep, she hasn't even showered since the kittens arrived. This can't go on."

Jan smiled and looked at me as she might a rather simple child. "Oh, stop worrying," she chided, shaking her head a little. "So what if she misses some sleep or food? She's doing something that's very important to her. I know exactly how she feels. She *needs* to take care of those kittens. And don't worry," she added, "when she gets tired enough, she'll sleep; when she gets hungry enough, she'll eat." She gave me a light kiss. "You're still thinking of her as a child. We girls are a lot tougher than you give us credit for. Don't you worry about her; she'll be just fine, trust me."

And it did seem logical. In a day or so, surely before the weekend was out, we would know the fate of the kittens, one way or the other, and things would return to what passes for normal in our household. I slept blissfully that night, comforted by Jan's wisdom.

In the morning, I decided to look in on Amanda before I went to the boathouse. What I encountered was utter chaos. The kittens were crawling all over while Amanda frantically tried to keep them from falling off the bed. She would retrieve one and bring it back, only to have others sprint off in all different directions. The bedspread was soaked with the water they had turned over during the night and the youngsters were screaming for their breakfast. Amanda was a mess. Her hair was unkempt, her face was unwashed, and her haggard expression showed the effects of almost two days without sleep.

"How's it going?" I asked brightly.

"Oh, Grandpa," she moaned, "I didn't get any sleep at all last night. They either wanted to play or get fed. When one or two slept, the others wanted to play. Why can't they all play and all sleep at the same time?" She was whining. "I don't know what to do."

In spite of her obvious distress, I couldn't help chuckling. "Yeah," I agreed, "kids sure can be a nuisance."

"I need help, Grandpa," she pleaded shamelessly, making her eyes big. "Can you watch them so I can get cleaned up? Please?"

In a flash of inspiration, I answered, "Of course, I'll help you, sweetheart. Wait here, I'll be right back."

"Oh, thanks, Grandpa," she gushed, "you're the best."

I went back to the bedroom, where Jan was still sleeping peacefully, as she always did on Saturday mornings. I sat down on the bed and nudged her gently. "Honey, wake up."

Nothing.

"Honey," I said more forcefully, "wake up," and shook her harder.

She began mumbling. "Huh? What? Whatsa matter?"

It takes Jan a few minutes to get up to speed in the morning. "Wake up, honey, Amanda wants you."

"Huh? Why? What time is it?"

She was coming around. "It's seven o'clock." She groaned. "Amanda wants to see you."

"What about?" She was rubbing her eyes.

"I don't know, but I think it's important. Are you awake?"

"Yes, yes, I'm awake," she said, yawning; then suddenly wide awake, "Is she all right?"

"Sure, she's fine, just like you said she'd be." I got up. "I have to run. Be home by lunchtime. See you then."

"Okay, honey, have fun." She was rubbing her eyes and padding down the hall in her slippers just as I ducked out the door.

CHAPTER 38

....

Once free of the domestic chaos, my focus switched quickly back to the boat and the dwindling number of steps now needed to finish her up. The morning promised to be a few stress-free hours of easy, pleasant work, making my short walk all the more enjoyable. When I entered the boathouse, I couldn't help gazing up at the *Amanda* and smiling once again. It still gave me goosebumps to know I had a part in creating a thing of such timeless beauty. Within weeks, we would be launching her and Amanda would be spending the entire summer sailing her new boat and eating ice cream.

The morning couldn't have been nicer, so I opened all the windows and got right to work. It seemed a bit strange working there without Angus to chat with, but the quiet allowed my mind to wander while I varnished away. Almost before I realized it, most of the morning had passed and I was finishing up. I stood back to admire my work, made a few minor corrections, and cleaned the brush. There being no need to hurry home, I began finishing up odds and ends—sweeping, organizing, sorting, etc. When that was done, I began poking around, admiring the wood in the storage room, opening up old tool chests, examining tools I had never seen before, and trying to figure out their purpose. Some of them must have been well over a hundred years old, from the looks of them. A few were obviously homemade and probably served a unique purpose long since forgotten. I was fascinated. The more I found, the more I looked. I had worked there for almost a year but had been so engrossed in the building process that I hadn't spent much time just nosing around and appreciating the history that surrounded me.

I wandered up to the loft. I had asked Angus some time back what was up there, but he just shook his head. "There's nothing up there," he said. "Just some old patterns and junk that we used to use for lofting, and some sketches that don't amount to anything."

And when I got to the top of the stairs, that certainly appeared to be the case. The floor was bare, except for some trash and scrap wood. It was coated with an old layer of peeling white paint, and there were several sets of barely discernible lines which appeared to have been laid down many decades past. I wanted to believe that the loft had been abandoned for many years, but that everything had been left in place, ready to serve its purpose again at a moment's notice.

The loft was quite large, of course, and I moseyed around, admiring the shapes of the boats on the floor and trying to imagine what it was like in the glory days, a hundred or so years earlier, when the entire boathouse bustled with the activity of the many men working there, several boats under construction at once. My imagination was taking hold of me, transporting me back to a simpler and, to my impractical mind, a pleasanter time. I could almost hear the voices, smell the tar and the oakum.

Off in a far corner, well out of the way, was a simple high desk where the architect's plans would have been spread out to assist in the lofting process. Now, instead of plans, the top was covered with a thick layer of dust and some trash, emphasizing the sad decline of the once-vital industry. I had become maudlin by then and almost didn't bother opening the drawer beneath the top of the desk. But I tugged on its handle, gently at first, then more firmly, as the drawer resisted. It appeared to be stuffed full, making it difficult to open. I reached my fingers up under the desktop and pushed down inside the drawer on the contents so I could open it fully. The drawer was shallow, perhaps only four or five inches high, but quite wide and deep, making it awkward to handle. Once I got the thing out and set it on top of the desk, I was thrilled to see that it was crammed full of boat plans and sketches. Instantly mesmerized, I pulled over an old nail keg and sat down to examine my treasure. There were dozens of sets of plans and many more working sketches. Some were dated, some not, but it didn't matter; they were clearly of another time. I began carefully lifting out the plans, impressed by their condition. The oldest dated plan was from 1862, a small coastal cutter for the Union army. It was drawn and signed by Tom McTigue, Angus's great-great-grandfather, and, except for some minor smudges, it looked almost pristine. All the plans had been stashed away in the drawer, away from light and abuse, and were in perfect condition.

The next couple of hours drifted by languidly while I pored over the plans, riveted by the attention to detail, the careful pride that shone so clearly across so many years. The sketches were especially fascinating for me—freehand drawings of sloops, ketches, schooners, various sail plans— and I spent a great deal of time admiring them. About halfway through the pile, my eye was caught by one of the sketches. It possessed an immediate familiarity, a look, that was unmistakable. Upon closer examination, I came to the realization that it was our boat! There were some discrepancies, minor changes that were made during the design stage, but it was, without question, our boat. There were several different drawings on the large sheet, along with notes jotted off to the sides or next to the relevant drawings, some erasures, and a few half-finished sketches simply crossed out. I scanned the entire sheet carefully, reading all the notes, mesmerized by the thought that I was seeing the very birth of the ideas that led to the development of what was such a milestone for me. I couldn't wait to show Jan! As I excitedly turned it over to fold it so I could take it home and show her, I noticed some printing on the bottom of the page. My eyes dropped down and I froze. There, neatly hand-lettered in capital letters were two words that leaped at me like a snake:

THE AMANDA

I stared at them for what must have been several minutes, my mind racing, unable to sort my thoughts, trying to reason out what this could possibly mean. The drawings were clearly originals; how could they be otherwise? But how did the name get on the original sketches from forty years ago? Maybe Angus penciled it in after he decided to give it to Amanda. But why? He would have no need to; the boat was practically finished by that time. It didn't make any sense. As I thought more about it, I became even more perplexed at the realization that I had stumbled upon this discovery surreptitiously. What began as a lark had become an invasion of Angus's privacy. My initial elation gave way to feelings of embarrassment as well as confusion. Unable to make any sense of it, and feeling rattled, I put all the plans back and carefully replaced the drawer, guiltily trying to make it appear as if I had never been there. I went downstairs and made sure everything was in order before leaving the boathouse to return home. I noticed Angus had still not returned from the doctor and, relieved at not having to face him, I slunk away like a thief in the night.

Jan was in the kitchen when I got home. "Where have you been?" she asked. "I thought you only had a little varnishing to do."

"I did," I replied, "but I did some cleaning up and then puttered around some." I looked around. "Lunch ready?"

She gave me a sly look. "It's been ready for two hours," she retorted. "Not that you deserve any lunch after your little joke this morning."

Oh, yeah, I thought. I had forgotten all about that. "Sorry, honey," I grinned, "but it seemed pretty funny at the time." I gave her a hug. "How's she doing?"

She backed off, crooked her finger at me to follow her, and headed up the stairs. When we got to Amanda's room, she put her finger to her lips and slowly opened the door. There, on the floor, was a makeshift kennel constructed out of books and cardboard boxes, and a card table stood on its side. Inside, six of the kittens were playing, fighting, meowing, and generally tossing everything about, making an ungodly racket at their being trapped inside the enclosure. Next to them, secure in her knowledge that the kittens could cavort to their hearts' content and not get away, lay Amanda, stretched out on the floor in a deep sleep. She had a blanket pulled up over her head, and on top of her lay the little guy, curled up in a tiny orange ball, safe from trampling by his mates and also fast asleep.

I couldn't help chuckling. "Was this your idea?" I asked.

"Nope. She came up with this all by herself. Pretty clever, huh?"

"It sure is," I had to admit. "I can't believe those kittens. Two days ago, they were at death's door, and now look at them; they're hellions." They were bouncing off the walls of their prison, rolling around, slopping their food and water all over the carpet. They were cute, of course, but making an awful mess. Which brought me to the next subject. As we quietly slipped out the door and descended the stairs, I mentioned casually, "Have you given any thought to what we're going to do with them, now that they're on the mend?"

Jan gave a pause. "I hadn't really planned that far ahead, to be honest," she answered. "It's obvious we can't keep all of them."

"It's obvious we can't keep *any* of them," I corrected. "We don't need any more complications. They're destroying that room, the carpet will never be the same, and (I sniffed the air for emphasis) have you noticed Amanda's room doesn't smell quite as fresh as it used to?"

"Ooh, I know," Jan whined, "but Amanda will be heartbroken. They're like her own little babies now."

I grimaced. "Now, don't start tugging at my heartstrings. We rescued them and I'm happy we could do it, but we can't keep everything we rescue. You know that from working with Doc Thompson." I brightened. "I know—I'll bet you could find homes for them at the clinic. That's what you do, right?"

"I doubt it," Jan moped. "We have more kittens now than we can find homes for." She sighed. "It's a constant problem."

"Regardless," I reiterated, "we're not keeping any kittens, and that's final. It's time for them to move on and the longer we postpone it, the more difficult it will be. Now, how about some lunch?"

She was pouting. "It's in the refrigerator."

CHAPTER 39

....

Later in the evening, Amanda finally stumbled downstairs to have some dinner with us. Her eyes were half-closed and she couldn't stop yawning. "Hi, sweetheart," I said. "How are the kittens?"

"Hmm?" she mumbled.

I grinned. "I said, how are the kittens?"

"Oh, sorry"—she yawned—"they're fine, finally asleep." It was apparent she was only partially awake and offering no more than was necessary to make basic conversation—perhaps a good time to broach a delicate subject.

"The kittens sure seem to be doing well. That was a wonderful thing you did, honey; without you, they wouldn't have made it."

That cheered her up a little. "Thanks, Grandpa." She took a sip of milk. "It *was* a lot of work, but they seem to be fine, now, except maybe for the little guy. He's better, but he isn't as strong as the others. He's finally eating a little, but all he wants to do is lay around and sleep."

"I wouldn't worry too much about him," I said. "He'll be fine. He's been through a lot, and he was the sickest and weakest of the bunch. What he needs now, more than anything else, is plenty of rest." I paused. "Just like you." She gave me a tired smile.

"Soup's on!" Jan brought in BLTs and salad and gave Amanda a big hug. "How are you doing, sweetheart? Did you have a good nap?"

"I sure did, Jannie," she answered, then waded into her dinner. It had been a long two days for her, with very little to eat. She made short work of two sandwiches and a large salad, then polished off a big dish of ice cream.

The time had come. "Amanda," I began, "you understand that we have to find homes for the kittens, don't you?"

She looked at me with her big eyes. "All of them?"

"I'm afraid so, honey. You see, we can't keep them, and the sooner we find new homes for them, the sooner they can adapt to their new families. I talked to Doc Thompson. He said they're old enough and, as long as they're healthy and active, they're ready for adoption." She was looking down. "He also told me what a good job you did. He was very impressed and proud of you."

She smiled bravely at the praise, but still was not accepting it well. "I suppose you're right, Grandpa, but the little guy is still not doing well. Can I at least keep him until he's all better?"

I was ecstatic. She had taken the news better than I had dared to hope, showing a maturity far beyond her tender years. In that light, keeping the little guy a while longer seemed both reasonable and compassionate. I congratulated myself. "Why, of course you can, sweetheart," I beamed. "Heck, I'm sure he'll be up to snuff in no time, with you taking care of him." I looked over at Jan. She was at the sink smiling, I was certain, at how masterfully I had handled things.

Amanda jumped up from the table. "Thanks, Grandpa," she said and ran back upstairs.

Feeling pretty smug, I sidled up behind Jan and put my arms around her waist. "Well," I gloated, "I guess I handled that pretty well, if I do say so myself."

She turned around, grinning, and said, "Yeah, terrific job, honey." She was shaking her head, like she knew something that I didn't.

"What's that supposed to mean?" I asked, instantly on guard.

She sat me down. "Now," she said, "let me get this straight. You told her, an eleven-year-old girl, that she had to get rid of all the kittens, she suckered you into keeping one of them, and now you think you're Henry Kissinger. Have I got that right?"

She made it sound a lot different than how I remembered it. "How can you be so cynical?" I said, a shade more defensively than I meant to. "It's only for another week or so, until he's stronger."

She was giggling. "Sure."

Jan could be quite exasperating. "She's *eleven*," I said. "Do you really think she tried to outsmart me?"

"She didn't have to try."

"Very funny."

"And by the way," she asked between giggles, "how do you plan to get rid of the other ones?"

"Ahh, I've been thinking about that and I've come up with a brilliant idea. The last PTA meeting is this Monday night, right? Well, tomorrow, I'll go get some boxes and some cat litter. After the meeting, we'll be waiting outside with the kittens and a 'free kittens' sign. When the kids see them, they'll start whining to their parents and it'll be all over. Who can resist a kitten?"

"You're resisting seven of them."

"That's different."

"Right."

Later on, we were discussing what we would be doing the next day, Sunday. Amanda was on the floor with the little guy, teasing him with a piece of yarn. "Have you talked to Hilda today?" I asked Jan.

"No, I thought I'd call after dinner and get caught up. Why?"

"Nothing, really, I just hadn't talked to Angus and I was wondering how he did at the doctor. Maybe I'll just call him now."

I dialed their number, and when Angus answered the phone, he sounded tired. "How are you, old friend?" I asked.

"Oh, hi, Jim," he said. "I'm fine, just had kind of a long day, that's all. After the doctor, Hilda wanted to go shopping. That pretty much killed the day."

"Everything go all right at the doctor?"

"Yeah, probably coming down with a cold, nothing serious. I'm sure I'll be fine in a day or two."

"Well, I'm glad of that. Are we going to see you in church tomorrow?"

"Sure," he half-chuckled, half-grunted, "why wouldn't you?" He paused briefly. "Did you finish up the varnish today."

"Sure did," I said. That reminded me of the sketch I found and made me bite my tongue.

"Good. Sorry I wasn't there to help. Maybe we'll rub it out on Tuesday if I'm not up to it on Monday. Would that be okay?"

"Of course. In fact, let's just plan on doing it Tuesday. Take it easy and shake the cold. There's no rush now; we're almost finished."

"Yup," he agreed, "I think we'll launch her next Saturday." He lowered his voice. "Don't tell Amanda, though. I want to surprise her."

"No problem," I assured him, saying no more on the subject. "Now, get plenty of rest and we'll see you tomorrow in church."

"Okay, old friend; thanks for calling."

Jan and Amanda had been listening to the conversation, and when I hung up, Jan seemed concerned. "Angus has a cold?" she asked.

"Yeah," I replied, "but it's nothing serious. Said they'd see us tomorrow. Maybe after, we can go to the diner for lunch. Would you like that?"

They both liked that. "That's a great idea, honey," Jan said. "With all the excitement and confusion with the kittens, we haven't spent much time with them lately. It'll be fun, and a nice break for Hilda."

When we got to the church the next morning, Angus and Hilda were already there, chatting with friends. We spotted them, waved, and headed in their direction. We greeted them enthusiastically, but I was more than a little shaken by Angus's appearance. He looked terrible. His eyes were sunken and his skin was a pasty gray, not at all like his old self.

"Hi, folks," he croaked, then gave a little cough.

"Angus," I said, suddenly concerned, "are you sure you should be here? You look like you should be home in bed."

"That's what I told him," Hilda seconded. "But what do I know. Honestly, he's the most stubborn man I've ever known."

Angus grinned at that. "Seems I remember someone who had pneumonia a while back and wouldn't stay put, either."

"That was different," Hilda huffed.

Their antics were cute, but Angus did indeed look ill. I took him aside. "Angus," I said, "I was going to suggest we go to the diner after church, but we probably should do it another time, when you're feeling better."

He looked at me as if there was something wrong with me. "Why? Because of a little cold?" He shook his head. "Wouldn't hear of it. In fact, I was going to suggest the same thing." Then, he pulled me even further aside. "Look, I'm planning on telling Amanda that we're launching. She's been pestering me for a month, wondering aloud about it, hinting that it sure looks to her like it's finished. And it is, really, but I wanted to clean up that last little bit of varnishing. You know how it is; once the boat's in the water, you don't want to work on her, you want to sail her." He was talking low, conspiratorially, and enjoying himself immensely. "Friday is the last day of school, then she can look forward to sailing all summer long. I think I'm as excited about it as she is, to be honest." He paused and sighed. "It's been a long road."

I grinned at his fervor. I didn't understand what he meant about its being a long road, but in his excitement, he could have meant anything. "Okay," I said, "but you go home and take it easy the rest of the day, *and* tomorrow. We've got all week to prep her for the big day." I put out my hand. "Deal?"

He grabbed it enthusiastically. "Deal!"

We wandered back to the girls. "So, what's so top-secret, boys?" Jan asked, an inquisitive smile on her face.

"Oh, nothing," I replied, "just discussing lunch. We decided to go to the diner after church, that's all."

Jan and I were a little removed from the other three, who were chatting with a neighbor. "You decided that last night," she accused, her voice low, "what's up?" Honestly, she's the most suspicious woman I've ever known.

"Whatever happened to trust?" I said, trying to appear hurt. I laughed lightly and patted her arm. "Sorry, honey, you're just going to have to wait like everyone else." I knew that would eat at her, but just to make sure, I whispered, "It's *big*, though," and walked away toward our pew.

Afterward, as we were milling around outside, Angus offered to drive us to the diner. Before thinking, I blurted, "You drove?" Ever since my embarrassment the first day at the boathouse, none of us drove anywhere unless the weather threatened. The whole town was only two miles wide.

"Yes, I drove," Angus replied, smiling sheepishly. "I wasn't feeling too chipper and decided it would be easier, you know, in case it rained or something." We were squinting against the bright sunlight.

"Of course," I said, angry at myself, "let's go."

In three minutes, we arrived at the diner. Laverne told us to take any booth and she'd be right with us. As we slid into our seats, Angus and I were mugging and grinning like baboons. By then, Jan was beyond curious; she was approaching testy.

"All right, boys, enough is enough," she said. "What's going on?"

"Yeah, Grandpa, you're acting funny."

"Go ahead and tell them, Jim," Angus said.

"No, I think you should tell them," I replied.

"No, really, you—"

"Will *someone* please tell us *something*?" Jan blurted, causing everyone around us to stop eating and look up. She embarrassed easily and slunk down in her seat, her cheeks turning a bright crimson.

"Okay, okay," I said, calming her down. "We're just having a little fun with you. "Go ahead and tell them, Angus."

"No, you go."

Amanda slapped her forehead comically and all three girls began laughing.

It was really Angus's party, so I made a sweeping gesture toward him. "Okay," he said, "here goes. We're launching the boat Saturday!"

"I knew it!" Amanda cried, clapping her hands.

Jan whooped, cried, "That's great, honey, all is forgiven!" and leaned over to give me a kiss. The people in the diner were again staring at us, but this time Jan stood up and shouted, "We're launching the *Amanda* Saturday!" to raucous applause and congratulations. Apparently, the entire town had followed our progress and they were also awaiting the big day.

Amanda was beside herself, her eyes sparkling. "I'm so excited, Uncle Angus. I can't wait!"

"Me, too, hon," he said, sharing her excitement. "If we do it in the morning, maybe we can get her all rigged so we can take her for a short sail before dark. No promises, though. These things always seem to take longer than you think they will."

Laverne came to our table sporting the biggest smile I'd ever seen on her. "Did you hear the news, Laverne?" I asked.

"I think they heard it in Augusta!" she laughed. "That's great news, folks; congratulations." She was gazing fondly at Amanda. "I hope you enjoy it for a long time, sweetheart."

"Thank you, Miss Laverne, I know I will." She paused to catch her breath. "I hope you'll go sailing with me sometime."

"I sure will, honey, I promise."

"Oh, boy!"

Laverne took our orders, then left to put them in and get us some coffee. As she walked around the booth behind Angus, she reached over and tussled his hair in a sweetly affectionate way. We were both used to trading barbs with Laverne, but that simple gesture of genuine affection showed a side of her we hadn't seen before. It also caused Angus to blush like a beet.

After we ate and were lingering over our coffee, people began dropping by our table, offering comments on their way out. "Congratulations, Angus!" "Can't wait to see her, Angus." "What time is the launch, Angus?" "I wouldn't miss it for the world." "You're a lucky little girl, Amanda" and so on. Angus was beaming, obviously touched by the good wishes of his friends. He thanked them all and reminded them what a big help Amanda had been.

Outside the diner, Angus again offered to drive us home, but it was such a nice day that we decided to walk. We said our goodbyes and waved as they drove away. On our way home, we were all seemingly engrossed in our own thoughts. Amanda said nothing, merely floated along silently, immersed in dreams of exploration in her new sailboat after all these months of anticipation. I shared her optimism, but also was aware of a tinge of pathos. After an entire year of being totally consumed with the project of a lifetime, I couldn't help wondering, *What next?* Do I merely throw myself back into golf? Perhaps write about my experiences with Angus? Dare I hope to build another boat? I tentatively decided to make no long-term commitments and just enjoy myself for a while, let things work themselves out. The whole summer lay ahead—puttering around the boathouse, sailing with Amanda, golf, reading, relaxing. I was feeling better already.

Jan alone felt talkative. "What a wonderful time!" she effused. "Everyone was so friendly and warm. Do you think that's because of living in a small town?"

"Hmm? Oh, I'm sorry, hon, I was just thinking about something. What were you saying?"

She was hugging my arm as we walked. "The people in the diner, all of them, they seemed so warm and sincere, so honest. I almost cried."

I grinned and put my arm around her, pulling her close. "I know," I agreed. "It *was* nice to see Angus enjoying himself so much with his friends. They seem to hold him and Hilda in very high regard." I paused and chuckled. "They're even accepting us, almost like we're natives."

"It *is* a nice little town," she said. "Too bad it's so far north."

CHAPTER 40

....

After two more days of yowling, mass confusion, and the unsavory aroma, any qualms I may have had about evicting the kittens had been put to the torch. Monday evening, promptly at seven o'clock, I crated up the six little demons and headed for the school.

"Bye-bye, babies," Amanda sniffed, looking down into the box as if they were headed to the guillotine. I looked to Jan for support but got only a stony stare.

"You know, honey," I said to Amanda, "it's not like you're never going to see them again. They'll all be adopted by your friends. You can go see them any time you want to." She was looking down, making low sighing noises. "In fact," I added, "you can even invite them over for playtime. You know, for short visits." I was very much alone and in trouble, but I was also very much determined. "Look," I said, "why don't you come with me, then you can see who adopts them. You'll know they're getting a good home. Okay?"

Another sigh, louder this time.

"We could stop at Littlefield's on the way home . . ."

The sighing ceased. "Okay, Grandpa, I'll get my coat," she said, and raced up the stairs.

In a little over an hour, we were back, still licking our ice-cream cones. "How did it go?" Jan inquired.

"Smooth as silk," I gloated. "We were out of there in twenty minutes, tops. The kids all knew about it and were waiting, almost as if someone had tipped them off."

I glanced at Amanda, who was very busy finishing up her cone and acting like she hadn't heard me. "And I only got a few threatening glares from parents," I joked, "nothing serious."

"Perfect," Jan deadpanned, "just as we were being accepted." I chuckled. "Who took the cats," she asked, "anybody I know?"

"Most of them were classmates of Amanda's, but Bobby and his mom took one. He was thrilled."

"I'm sure he was, but that's probably the last thing they need—another mouth to feed."

"Actually," I said, "they took the first one. The parents were avoiding us like lepers at first, but after Bobby got one, the other parents couldn't say no. It was over in minutes."

"Well, I'm glad they all got good homes," Jan said, kissing Amanda on the cheek. "Congratulations again, sweetheart; you did a wonderful thing."

"Thanks, Jannie," she said. "I think I'll go upstairs and play with Marmalade for a while."

I wasn't sure I heard correctly. "Play with *what*?"

"*Marmalade*, Grandpa, you know, the little guy."

"You *named* him?"

"Of course." She shrugged. "He has to have a name. I thought Marmalade was cute because he's orange, you know, like orange marmalade."

"Yes, I get it," I said drolly. "However, I don't think . . ." She was looking at me with her big eyes again. I decided it was not the right time. "Never mind, honey, go play with Marmalade. Come down later and we'll have some cocoa before bedtime. Okay?"

"Okay, Grandpa, thanks," she said, then kissed me and raced up the stairs. Jan, to her everlasting credit, said nothing.

I was up early the next day, eager to finish up the little bit of work left before launching. A quick breakfast, a brisk walk, and I was at the boathouse. Angus hadn't arrived yet, so I began working by myself, peeling off masking tape, cleaning up the residue, and then the monotonous task of actually rubbing down the varnish. It was mindless work, allowing me to coast along at an easy pace, my mind wandering as I worked.

Around nine, Angus straggled in looking no better than he had two days earlier. "Sorry I'm late," he rasped. "Guess I overslept."

"Angus," I kidded, "you *never* oversleep. Are you sure you're all right?" He was harried and unkempt, and his gait was unsteady. "Why don't you go back to bed and rest. I can finish this little bit by myself in a couple of hours."

He gave me a look of exaggerated bravado that didn't quite come off. "Wouldn't think of it," he said. "Heck, the best thing for me is to get off my duff and get some work done. Besides," he added with grim determination, "we have to get the boat ready for Saturday. The cat's out of the bag, now." He scurried off, his features marked by a pronounced scowl.

We continued through most of the morning, but it was obvious Angus was off his game. He was unfocused, moving from task to task to task, leaving previous things unfinished. He seemed under enormous pressure to complete this piddling amount of work that would take us a couple of hours, at most. And he was talkative, as he had never been before. He rambled on about a variety of things, none of them pertinent to what we were doing, never pausing long enough to let me get a word in.

At eleven-thirty, Hilda came over to tell us she had prepared lunch. "Oh, thanks, Hilda," I said, "but Jan's expecting me back home."

But she was insistent. "Please do stay, James," she said, her eyes pleading. "I've fixed a wonderful meal." She was clearly bothered by something.

"Well, sure, of course," I said, "I'd love to stay. We can finish this after lunch. I'll just call Jan and tell her not to wait for me."

When we got to the house, I called Jan to tell her I wouldn't be home for lunch, then took Hilda aside. "Is anything wrong, Hilda? You seem upset about something."

"Oh, I'm probably just being silly," she said, "but Angus has been acting so strangely all morning."

"Yeah," I agreed, "I noticed the same thing. Is he all right? Is the cold still bothering him?"

"I don't know, he just seems so unlike himself. I wonder if he has a fever. I mentioned going to the doctor, but he would have none of it. You know how he is." She paused. "I was hoping you might talk to him."

I smiled and gave her a hug. "Of course. I'm sure it's nothing serious, Hilda, but I'll tell him Jan has something for me to do at home and we'll finish this tomorrow. Between the two of us, we'll have him all better in no time."

"Thank you, James. I feel so much better that you're here."

I put on a brave face for Hilda, but in fact I was having my own concerns—concerns I kept to myself but which became more pronounced as we ate lunch. Angus continued his erratic behavior for most of the meal, then abruptly switched gears, becoming more withdrawn. It was while we were having dessert that it happened. I was on the verge of suggesting we take the afternoon off when I noticed that he wasn't responding to my conversation. I saw immediately that something was terribly wrong. His eyes were staring straight ahead, unfocused, and he appeared to be trying to speak, but nothing was coming out. His left arm was hanging limp at his side and he began sagging backward. I jumped up and grabbed him before he could fall to the floor. "ANGUS!" I shouted. "Are you all right?" But there was no response. Hilda was beside herself, sobbing and calling his name.

"Hilda!" I yelled, trying desperately to shock her into action. "You've got to call the doctor, quickly! I'll lay him down on the sofa."

Hilda somehow gathered her wits and managed to make the call as I laid Angus on the couch. Within minutes, there was an ambulance in the driveway and the men were hovering over Angus, performing preliminary tests before transferring him to a stretcher. As they were loading him in the ambulance, Hilda begged them to let her ride with them to the hospital. The young man in charge never hesitated. "Sure, ma'am," he said. "But please hurry. We have to go *now*."

She turned to me, completely unraveled. "Oh, James," she sobbed, "what should I do?"

"Go with him," I said immediately. "I'll clean up here and follow right away. I'll bring some things for you and Angus. Don't worry about a thing, just go."

She couldn't speak, just shook her head and climbed into the ambulance beside Angus. Immediately, the ambulance sped out the driveway, siren blaring. I watched them go, stunned to my core. Stumbling inside, I glanced at the clock on the wall. It was just past twelve-thirty. A little over an hour earlier, Angus and I had been working along as we had for a year, our biggest concern being the completion of perhaps six hours' work in the next three days so we could launch the *Amanda*. Now I was in a fog, trying to come to grips with what just happened, groping for balance. My first coherent thought was to call Jan. She needed to know, of course, and would surely want to come to the hospital with me. I sat by the phone, took a deep breath, and dialed our number.

"Honey," I said as soon as she answered, "something terrible has happened. Angus has had an attack of some kind. We called an ambulance and he's on the way to the hospital. Hilda is with him."

She was numb with shock, asking several questions at once—"What kind of attack?" "Do you know anything?" "How serious is it?" "How is Hilda?"—none of which I could answer with any certainty.

After she began to settle down a bit, she asked, "Amanda is due home from school in an hour. When do you want me to come over?"

"Now. Go take Amanda out of school and get here as soon as you can. Hilda is all by herself and this could be serious. I'll be ready when you get here."

"Okay" was all she said. I could hear her choke back a sob.

In ten minutes, I had made a perfunctory cleanup, gathered some things for Hilda, and stepped outside to wait for Jan in the driveway. Duncan was there so I stopped briefly to pat him and talk to him. He wasn't his usual boisterous self; he seemed to know something was afoot but was unable to grasp the full enormity of the situation.

Jan arrived almost immediately. I got in and started driving.

"How far is the hospital?" she asked.

"About an hour," I answered tersely, trying to keep my mind clear.

From the back seat came a small, scared voice. "Is Uncle Angus going to be all right?"

Amanda's childish fear gripped my vitals. Angus was every bit as dear to her as he was to me. "I don't know, sweetie," I answered softly, "I certainly hope so." Then I added, "But remember, as bad as we feel, it's much worse for Aunt Hilda. We have to be there and do everything we can for her. Okay?"

"Okay, Grandpa." Her voice sounded far away.

When we got to the hospital, we found Hilda in the waiting room. Jan and Amanda rushed to embrace her, trying to console her while themselves crying uncontrollably. I began asking questions immediately.

"Do they know what happened?"

"Yes," Hilda said, wiping her eyes, "he's had a stroke. He's in surgery now." She was trying hard to be brave, but her fear was palpable.

I didn't know much about strokes, but it sounded ominous. "Is there any prognosis?"

"No," she said, "just that it was very serious and they would do all they could." She was calming slightly, struggling to get her emotions under control.

"How soon before they'll know something?"

"They didn't know for sure, but they did say it could be as much as several hours." Then she broke down again and clutched at Jan. "I'm so afraid," she sobbed. "He needs me so much and there's nothing I can do for him." She moaned and lay back on the sofa in Jan's arms.

Through all this, Amanda had been at Hilda's side. Now, she snuggled close, fighting back tears. Hilda put her arm around the child and drew her in, rocking back and forth. Nothing more was said, all of us alone with our thoughts and our fears. After what seemed like ages, the doors swung open and the doctor entered the waiting room with Reverend Brewster at his side.

OH GOD, NO!

Hilda immediately grasped the significance and swooned, emitting a piteous wail. She began sobbing, holding on tight to Jan and Amanda. I had risen reflexively when the two men had entered, but the cruel suddenness caused me to slump down on the sofa beside Hilda. I wanted to console her, but I knew there was nothing anyone could have said or done to ease her pain at that terrible moment.

Reverend Brewster pulled a chair close and took her hand but said nothing.

After a few moments, the doctor spoke briefly. "I'm very sorry, Missus McTigue. We truly did everything we could, but the stroke was severe. I don't believe he could have been saved under any circumstances." He paused, then added, "I know it's no consolation, but he didn't suffer. I'm terribly sorry."

Hilda looked up at the doctor, then reached to take his hand. "Thank you," she whispered softly. It was all she could say.

The doctor patted her hand somberly, then sadly turned and left the room. It was some time before Reverend Brewster spoke. In a calming voice, he asked if he could do anything.

"No, thank you, Reverend," she answered softly.

"I understand, Hilda." He got up. "But please call me at any time if I can be of assistance."

She nodded.

After the Reverend left, we sat there for a long time in complete silence. I'm sure we all felt the same—dazed and lost—and there seemed no reason to try to say anything. The day before, everything had been perfect; now it seemed unimaginable that our lives could ever be the same again, that we could even go on.

But we did, of course. We somehow made the drive back home, though I don't remember it. When we pulled into the driveway, Duncan came running out to greet us, as he always did, but immediately sensed something was wrong. Hilda knelt down beside him and gently hugged his huge head, barely containing her emotions. The poor dog lowered his ears and began to whimper, perplexed by Hilda's pain.

We escorted Hilda inside, emotionally exhausted. Then Jan, God bless her, summoned her strength and took charge. She put a kettle of water on the stove to make tea and set out a little something to eat. Then, to preclude any discussion, simply said, "You shouldn't be alone tonight, Hilda, I'll stay with you. Jim and Amanda can come by in the morning and we'll all have breakfast. Is that all right?"

Hilda looked gratefully at her. "That would be nice, Jan," she said. "Thank you."

As it got dark, we had tea and nibbled at whatever it was that Jan had prepared. After, Amanda and I rode back to our house in silence, except for poor Amanda's occasional sob. She had lost a remarkable and dear friend and simply couldn't comprehend the totality. She sat very close to me.

The next morning, I called the school and told them Amanda would not be back for the rest of the week. She would miss only the last three meaningless days of school before summer vacation, and I saw no reason to put her through that. Mrs. Taylor, the principal, had heard the news and concurred fully. "I understand they were very close," she said. "Tell her we shall pray for her and for Mister McTigue." She paused and I could tell she was wiping her eyes. "He was a fine, fine man. He'll be missed."

"Indeed, he will," I said. "I'll be sure to tell her, Missus Taylor. Thank you."

"Goodbye."

I woke Amanda. While she was getting ready, I called Reverend Brewster. My senses had been deadened by grief, but I was beginning to realize there were many difficult things that needed to be done. I had decided to take care of as much as possible, thereby easing Hilda's burden, but my own experience in this area was woefully inadequate. I knew I needed help, and my immediate reaction was to contact the Reverend. I had been deeply impressed by his sympathetic manner and his sincere offer of assistance. As soon as he answered the phone, I knew I had done the right thing.

"Hello, Jim," he said, "what can I do for you?" His calming voice inspired a much-needed faith.

I took a deep breath. "Reverend, Hilda is devastated and I'm trying to help as much as I can, but I'm at a loss. I have no idea what has to be done. Can you help me?"

"Of course, Jim, of course," he answered immediately. "I'll make up a list and do whatever I can, then you can drop by and we'll discuss the rest of it. Before I do anything, I'll contact you and you can advise me or consult with Hilda, at your discretion. For now, though, just spend time with her and be there if she needs you." He added, "Don't worry about a thing."

"Thank you, Reverend, you've taken a great weight off my shoulders." I have never voiced a truer emotion.

My spirit rekindled somewhat, I turned my attention to Amanda. The poor thing was still in a fog, unable to function normally. Her eyes were bloodshot from crying, her movements wooden. I helped her get ready, then we got in the car and drove over to have breakfast with Hilda and Jan. Not a word was spoken during the short drive.

Upon seeing Hilda, Amanda flew into her arms and started crying again. Hilda held her closely, murmuring words of comfort. She seemed bolstered by the child's presence, as if consoling Amanda helped assuage her own grief.

Presently, we sat down and had breakfast. I mentioned that I had contacted the Reverend and relayed his assurance of help. Since I had done so without consulting Hilda, I wanted to make sure she approved.

She looked weak and frail, but she gave me a little smile. "Of course, I approve, James, thank you," she said. "I'm not thinking very clearly right now and that will help a great deal. The Reverend is a fine man and a long-time friend. You couldn't have made a better choice." I felt much better upon hearing that.

After breakfast, Amanda began clearing the table, but Hilda insisted on helping—said it would do her good to be busy. "Okay, Aunt Hilda," Amanda said, smiling faintly for the first time. "I'll wash and you dry."

While they cleaned up, Jan and I retired to the living room. "How is she doing?" I asked immediately.

"Last night was tough," Jan said. "We were both so distraught that neither of us wanted to go to bed. We were up until well past midnight, crying and talking. I think we finally were simply overcome with fatigue." Her voice caught. "What a terrible, terrible thing," she murmured. "I still can't believe he's gone." There were tears in her eyes. "Oh, Jim . . .," she sobbed, burying her face in my chest. I tried to comfort her, but I was wrestling with my own emotions of anger, fear, remorse, the unbearable sadness at such a sudden and profound loss.

"Now, now," I soothed, "we have to get through this somehow. Amanda and, especially, Hilda need all the support they can get. That means us." I held her close for several minutes. "I don't think Hilda should be alone. One of us—and it's going to be you, mostly—needs to be here constantly. I've already called the school and Amanda is excused for the rest of the week. She can be a big help, feeding the animals, cleaning up, just being with Hilda. I'll do what I can with Reverend Brewster and be here as much as possible." I turned her face up and kissed her forehead. "Okay?"

"Okay," she said softly. "You're right, of course. Poor Hilda. Imagine, more than fifty years together. God bless them."

We sleepwalked through the rest of the day, trying to stay busy, trying to get through. Our overriding concern was for Hilda, but we soon learned once again what she was made of.

During lunch on Thursday, the Reverend called, saying he had completed the list and inviting me to stop by at my convenience to discuss it. "Thank you, Reverend," I said, "I'll come by immediately after lunch."

I relayed the message to Hilda, asking her if she had any particular requests. Her response surprised me completely. In spite of the massive blow she had suffered, she insisted on coming with me. When I demurred, she was firm. "No, James," she said, "I need to do this. I should be busy, and it's my responsibility, no one else's."

"But Hilda," I pleaded, "it's only been two days. Are you sure?"

She gave me her sweet smile and patted my hand. "I'm sure," she said simply. "I *have* to do it. It's the last thing I can do for my dear Angus."

I put my arm around her gently. "Okay," I conceded, "whatever you say. I'll drive you."

"I'd like that, James, thank you," she said, then hesitated, her emotions not yet under complete control. After a moment, she continued, looking around the table at Jan and Amanda. "I can't express how much it has meant to have all of you with me through this. It would have been unbearable on my own."

And so, Hilda and I began the afternoon by visiting Reverend Brewster. He greeted her warmly, embracing and reminiscing for an hour or so. Then, when he felt it was prudent, he brought up some of the things that needed to be done, things I would never have thought of—the hospital, the newspaper, her lawyer, the funeral parlor, etc. He assured her the church service was taken care of, but he hadn't set a date yet because of all the other considerations. The list was long, so we thanked him sincerely for his help and left. There was much to do.

We spent the rest of the day checking off the mundane tasks from our list. As we did so, Hilda seemed to become more emotionally secure, holding up well under what had to be a grueling ordeal, never betraying her grievous burden. Also, as we drove, we began to chat more. At first, it was small talk, but as we continued, we delved deeper. This was a welcome diversion for a couple of reasons. First, of course, it helped in dealing with the awkward tension and pain of the situation, but it also allowed us to enjoy an intimacy we'd had little opportunity to share previously. Over the past year, she had naturally spent the bulk of her time with Jan and Amanda, while I, necessarily, had spent most of my time working and conversing with Angus. As we drove, we talked of many things. She asked me about things in my and Jan's past, told me about her childhood in England with her family before the war, things like that; nothing profound, but warm, sincere conversation that flowed naturally and brought us closer together. She seemed to be probing, not in a snoopy way at all but in a genuine effort to better understand us. It made our sorrowful mission more bearable and, though we hadn't completed our list, a mere few hours on Friday morning would close out a painful chapter.

We all had dinner together that night at our house, and then, since Hilda and I had taken her car, Jan drove Hilda home and stayed the night. I would drive back in the morning with Amanda for breakfast, as I had before, then chauffeur Hilda around to complete the unfinished business. Everything was done except for a couple of minor stops and an appointment with her attorney. The church service and the funeral had been scheduled for Saturday.

At breakfast the next morning, I marveled anew at Hilda's poise; through her natural dignity, she exuded an aura of unshakable strength. She seemed to be conquering her adversity by sheer force of will. When Amanda and I arrived, she was already dressed immaculately in a black dress, perfectly groomed and ready to take on the day.

After breakfast, she was all business, probably eager to put the unpleasantness of our chores behind her. "Ready, James?" she asked, gathering her purse and gloves.

"Yes, ma'am," I teased, attempting to lighten the moment.

"When will you be back?" Jan asked.

"Gosh, I don't know," I said, "probably around noontime. We don't have much left to do, just a couple of stops."

"Amanda and I are going back to the house," she said. "We'll come back around noon and have lunch. How's that?"

Hilda spoke up. "Actually, we don't know how long we'll be. Why don't we just call you when we get back." She was putting on her gloves, looking very business-like.

Jan glanced at me and gave a little smile. "Sure, Hilda, whatever you say." She and Amanda kissed Hilda goodbye and we were on our way.

The morning went easily enough, much like the previous day, but Hilda was not nearly as chatty as she had been then. She seemed more focused, more determined. I felt sure that, in spite of her outward demeanor, the stress was getting to her. I tried engaging her in small talk to set her at ease, but she seemed preoccupied, answering my queries with distracted replies. After a few attempts, I gave up and we continued mostly in silence.

By late morning, we were at her lawyer's office, the last stop. As she took care of this final piece of business, I waited in the car, alone with my thoughts. Up until then, I had successfully kept my feelings under control by staying busy and by my overriding concern for the three girls. But whenever I was alone, gloom descended upon me like a storm cloud. I needed to get out of the car and take a walk, push back against my suffocating emotions.

Just as I returned to the car, Hilda was exiting the lawyer's office, stuffing a large brown envelope into her purse. "James," she exclaimed, "are you all right?"

I didn't feel all right, but I answered as upbeat as I could. "Sure, Hilda. Why?"

"You're as pale as paste," she scolded. "Come, let's go home. What you need is a nice cup of hot tea."

I was quite certain that tea was the last thing I needed, but to Hilda, tea was a timeless ritual and a sure cure for any and all ailments, illnesses, maladies, and disorders. Besides, I knew *she* wanted to have tea, and I hadn't yet devised a method of denying Hilda anything.

When we got back to her house, she immediately set about preparing the tea. Now, to an Englishman, one doesn't just slug down a cup of tea— one *has* tea. Tea is not a beverage, but a highly civilized social ritual, to be carried out with style and grace. It is always served with food, perhaps the infamous scones, but more likely in this case, pie or cake. Tea is a meal.

Knowing this, I mentioned to Hilda that perhaps I should call Jan to bring Amanda over and join us.

She stopped her puttering and turned to face me, then walked over, motioning for me to sit on the couch. Sitting down beside me, she said, "James, I need to talk to you, alone."

Caught completely off guard, I blurted, "Hilda, what's wrong? Is there anything I can do for you? Are you all right?"

"I'm fine, James," she said, taking my hand in hers. "But I need to discuss something with you, something Angus and I wanted to tell you earlier, but, sadly, never got the chance to."

What the heck? "Hilda," I cried, "what is it?"

She got up. "I'll have tea ready in a trice," she said, "then we can talk."

Oh, yeah, of course, I thought, *gotta have the tea!* I sat squirming for the next fifteen minutes, wondering what could possibly be so important that it had to be imparted to me alone. And, if it *was* so important, why did we have to wait for tea? I've spent more tranquil moments in a dentist's chair.

Hilda finally brought the silver tea set over and set it on the low table, then went back for the cake and cookies to go with the tea. Then, she poured the tea very carefully into the two cups, offered me first the milk, then the sugar, and finally passed the cookies. Then she sat down and precisely mixed just the right amount of milk and sugar into her own tea. I was beginning to twitch, but she absolutely would not be rushed.

At last, she was ready. "James," she began, "first off, we have not been altogether honest with you." She took a sip of tea. "It was never our intent to delude you, please understand, but our friendship grew so quickly and so profoundly that it soon became very awkward to correct the record, so to speak." She took another sip, then a bite from her cookie.

Attempting to put her at ease, I said, "Hilda, I'm sure there's nothing you could possibly say that would—"

"James," she said, "we had a child, a daughter."

My first reaction, as I can best remember, was that I was sure I had heard wrong, but immediately knew that of course I had not. I was struck dumb, utterly unable to think of one single thing to say or do.

After a brief moment to let me recover, Hilda continued. "She was the sweetest little girl, the light of our lives. Angus had always wanted a son, but she soon became the center of his universe. He taught her to swim, to sail, even how to shoot a gun. She worshipped Angus and spent endless hours with him, in the boathouse, in the woods, on the water. They were inseparable."

While she was saying all this, my mind raced back over the past year, remembering various incidents that began to link together, that baffled me at the time, but which now began to point in an eerie direction. I felt the hair on the back of my neck tingle as I asked, "What was her name, Hilda?"

"Amanda."

I was aware of a rush of emotional release, almost physical in its intensity—for Hilda, for Angus, for the little girl I never knew. Not knowing what else to do, I embraced Hilda and held her close, my emotional state in tatters.

After a long time, I sat back. By then, I realized there was going to be much more to the story and that it was going to be painful. I wiped my eyes and braced myself. "What happened to your daughter, Hilda?"

I was a mess, but Hilda was serenely composed. Her eyes were dry and she was sitting erect. "She contracted polio. The summer she turned eleven, she came home one day after playing down at the river and said she wasn't feeling well. We assumed it was a cold and put her to bed early, but the next morning she was running a high fever, so we took her to the doctor." She paused and had another sip of tea. In spite of her outward calm, she was having difficulty talking. She took a couple of deep breaths and continued. "They did everything possible, but it was an extreme case. She lingered for a few months in an iron lung, but only got worse." She paused again. "We lost her two days before Christmas." Now, a tear was tracing its way down Hilda's cheek.

I took her hand. "Hilda," I said softly, "you don't have to go on."

"It's all right, James," she answered. "It's important that you know this. Please bear with me."

I felt weak from the emotional strain, but discovering this completely new facet of my dear friends' lives, as painful as it certainly was, was mesmerizing. She poured another cup of tea for both of us and continued.

"Everything changed for us the day Amanda died. One never fully recovers from the death of a child, but after a long time, I felt I was making progress in dealing with our loss." A sip of tea. "Angus never did. He is a good and decent man, a strong man spiritually, but his faith was shaken to its roots. When the polio vaccine came out just months after Amanda died, it was the final crushing blow for him (I did a quick mental calculation—about forty years ago!). We stopped going to church. We never celebrated Christmas again, nor Thanksgiving, anything. It wasn't long before we ceased having any meaningful contact with our friends. We still knew everyone here, of course, and saw them regularly in town, but I think people felt our pain and began to leave us alone out of respect. We became more withdrawn, finally closing ourselves off almost entirely. It didn't happen overnight, but gradually we became virtual hermits right here in the middle of town."

It was true. I had summered there for eight years and driven by their place hundreds of times, never suspecting there was such a beautiful homestead there. And even though my friends at the boatyard had mentioned Angus's name, they talked as though he was of another age.

At this point, Hilda rose and carried the silver pitcher into the kitchen, where she filled it again with more tea, then brought it back into the living room. I was feeling weak, trying to imagine the pain and the guilt and the remorse they must have endured for almost forty years. "Hilda,"

I said, "I'm so sorry." I was groping. What can one possibly say at a time like that?

She poured me another cup of tea, my third. "Angus is a strong, responsible man," Hilda went on. "He got up every morning and went to work, maintained the property, fed the animals, did whatever needed to be done, but he never again was the man I married." She cast me an almost saintly expression. "Until last year."

I squirmed in my seat under her steady gaze and asked for my fourth cup of tea.

After pouring, she continued. "Do you remember when you came to our house the first time?"

I nodded.

"Just days before, Angus had been diagnosed with a rare nerve disorder that neither of us had ever heard of. It was a terrible shock, naturally. The doctor told him that there was no cure, but that he could participate in an experimental treatment." She hesitated again, obviously affected by the memory of such a traumatic event. "Because it was caught so early," she continued, "the doctor told us that Angus might expect several years of relatively normal activity if nothing was done. If he took the experimental treatments, he might live longer, but the side effects could be quite severe. We were struggling with those choices when you showed up."

I remembered back, how I had simply dropped in on them, upsetting everything, invading their privacy at what was surely the most intimate and frightening moment in their lives. "Oh, God, Hilda," I moaned, "I feel awful."

But she wasn't upset. In fact, she did something completely unexpected—she smiled.

"Everything happens for a reason, James," she said gently. "After you left, Angus began to feel bad. You had been so enthusiastic about building a boat that you got him excited, too. But it was out of the question, so he tried to forget about it." She sipped again at her tea as I reached for a cookie. "And that would have been the end of it, if not for running into you and Amanda the next day at Littlefield's." Here she stopped for a moment and smiled wistfully. "I wish you could have seen him when he came home that day," she sighed. "He was like a little boy; he was so excited. He told me all about meeting you there and, of course, Amanda. He was a different man. He must have talked for more than an hour about you two and how cute Amanda was, and on and on. Then he went into his study and stayed there the rest of the afternoon. When he came out for dinner, his mind was made up. He decided against the treatments and would help you build the boat. He would use the plans and the keel that he already had from forty years ago. Just what he needed, he said, to focus his energy. When he asked me what I thought, I was truly afraid, but I didn't have the heart to say anything. I hadn't seen him so animated about anything in years. After the previous several days, it was like a miracle."

Things were coming into focus: the completed keel, the old plan that I found in the loft. "So, the boat was—"

Hilda nodded. "It was to be Amanda's. Angus designed it the summer she got sick, planning to build it for her over the winter. He ordered the keel and carved the nameboard, but she got sick before the keel was even delivered. I thought he had destroyed the nameboard. I hadn't seen it in more than forty years until he gave it to Amanda."

I sat in a daze, struggling to come to grips with these incredible revelations, when Hilda put her hand on my arm. "James," she said gently, "there's something else."

By then I had been rendered pretty much speechless, unable and unwilling to even venture a guess as to what lay next.

Hilda reached inside her purse and removed a large envelope. I recognized it as the one she had carried out of the lawyer's office. Without a word, she passed it to me.

Feeling gun-shy, I asked, "What's this?"

"It's the deed to our property," she answered. "It's made out to you." She said this as matter-of-factly as if she were discussing the weather.

I must have spent several moments straining to ascertain exactly what she had meant. Finally, unable to fully absorb this latest nugget, I just blurted, "But, Hilda, I don't understand."

She explained. "James, when you came along, our lives were falling apart. We were suddenly faced with Angus's frightening illness and the very real prospect of his mortality. We vacillated back and forth over which path to pursue, medically. We had no family to help us deal with it. We were very alone, James, alone and afraid." She paused for a moment and sipped at her tea. I didn't trust myself to try to say anything, but Hilda, despite the gravity of her narrative, continued in a clear, strong voice. "And Angus was worried, about me, about the property, about his family's heritage. After days of discussion, we were more bereft than ever. The one thing we had absolutely settled on was to keep it to ourselves. Only our doctor and our lawyer knew, with strict instructions to not tell anyone. Angus was deeply concerned someone would try to steal the property if something happened to him."

"With good reason," I muttered.

"Pardon?"

"Sorry, Hilda," I said, "it's nothing. Please go on."

She began reflecting on the early days of our friendship. "James," she said, "when you folks entered our lives, everything changed immediately. Angus was revitalized, up early every day, eager to begin working at what he so loved to do, enjoying life. And having a little girl around again brought so much joy to both of us." She had a far-off look in her eyes. "Almost before we realized it, you had become our family. We got our little girl back, Janet is as close as any daughter could be, and you became the son we never had. For you to have come along at that exact time was more than a coincidence; it seemed nothing less than a miracle." She was gazing far off, a serene smile on her face.

I sat in silence for a while, thinking back over the past year, how Jan and I had voiced the same feelings, the sheer improbability of such an intricate and profound relationship developing so quickly and easily. We loved them unequivocally, but this . . .

"Hilda," I began, "you're very upset now. I wouldn't want you to do anything that you might regret later—"

She interrupted me. "James, we have no family except you folks. Angus's illness forced us to consider the future of the property, to make some decisions. And because of everything that has developed between us, we decided on this course some time ago. Angus and I both have complete confidence in you and Janet. But, like everyone, we kept putting off actually doing anything. Then, a few weeks back, something happened— Angus never told me what it was—that spurred him to get this drawn up immediately." She paused for a sip of tea. "For some reason, he insisted on hiring a new lawyer who was out of town, to keep it under wraps. I didn't understand, but he was adamant."

I remembered the incident with Dudley and his goons. *I know your secret, Angus!*

I looked at the deed, my emotions very much in turmoil. "Hilda," I said, "I can't tell you how honored and flattered I am, but I feel awkward. I'm not sure I'm right for this. Why didn't you tell me earlier? Why didn't Angus say something?"

Again, Hilda smiled gently. "We wanted to, but the lawyer just finished it last week and we wanted to make sure everything was in order before bringing it up." She paused and cast her eyes down to her lap. "We wanted to give you plenty of time to think about it, so we were going to surprise you after the boat was launched."

Oh, God, I suddenly remembered, *that was to be tomorrow!* It seemed ages ago that we had all celebrated Angus's announcement, but it had been less than a week. Now, instead, it was to be the day of his funeral. My eyes began to mist over and I was having difficulty focusing. "Hilda, I'm sorry," I mumbled. "I just don't know what to say."

"You don't have to say anything, James," she said. "It's all right." I was still struggling to get myself under control as she continued. "If you decide you don't want to do this, James, I'll understand completely. I know how Jan feels about the winters up here; they're certainly not for everybody. And I know there are many other considerations, too. But if you do want to go ahead, you merely have to sign the contract. Our part is all completed. We knew this would be a big decision and we didn't want you to feel obligated or rushed. So, go home and talk it over. Take all the time you need. I hope with all my heart that this is something you and she want, but most of all, I want you to do what's right for you two."

We both rose. I embraced her warmly, then turned toward the door. I wanted to say something, say how much they both meant to us, how the past year had changed our lives forever, how I could never repay all they had done for us. But I was unable to form any words. I hugged her again and left.

On the way down the path, I encountered Duncan. He greeted me with a wave of his huge tail, but his spirit wasn't in it. It was plain by his actions that he knew something was terribly wrong. I squatted down and tousled his ears and talked to him. He continued wagging his tail but seemed to be looking around for someone else. I stood up to continue down the path to Shore Road and began my walk home. It was getting late. Hilda and I had talked the entire afternoon.

All the way home, my muddled mind churned with conflicting emotions. I was flattered beyond words and the opportunity was obvious, of course, but there were daunting drawbacks. The responsibility was enormous. Hilda was putting her entire life, and Angus's legacy, in my hands. I was intimidated, my mind paralyzed with doubt. What would Hilda do? What about the house in Florida? Would Jan even consider living in Maine year-round after her recent tirade against winter (which consumed over a third of the year)? Heck, I was no big fan of winter, either. The property is enormous; could I even maintain it? Would I have to hire help? How much would that cost? What, ultimately, would I even do with the property? Whatever I *did* do, would it be what Angus would have wanted? If I didn't take it over, what would Hilda do? Sell it to Dudley's group? I could imagine Angus rolling over in his grave if that happened.

And I kept returning to the little girl who had died so long ago. She would be about Jan's age now, and likely have children of her own. I tried to imagine the pain, the heartache, the emptiness they must have suffered all those years, and it chilled me to think of something similar happening to Amanda. It ate at me all the way home.

I was still mulling all these quandaries when, after what seemed like mere minutes, I found myself on our front porch. Not only had I not come up with any answers, I was more confused and depressed than ever. I paused on the porch for a moment, tried to compose myself, and opened the door. Jan was in the kitchen.

"Is that you, honey?"

I didn't answer.

She came into the living room to greet me. "Where have you been all this ti—" She stopped, a startled look of concern on her face. "What's the matter, honey? Are you all right?"

I must have looked as forlorn as I felt. I took her in my arms and held her tight for several long moments until I could speak. "Come sit down, honey," I said finally. "We have to talk."

END